The Wind Merchant

Ryan Dunlap

First Printing, August 2012
Copyright © 2012 by Ryan Dunlap
All rights reserved.
ISBN-10: 0985997605
ISBN-13: 978-0-9859976-0-1

Printed in the United States of America

Cover art, "The Getaway" by Grant Cooley (www.GrantCooley.com)
Illustration by Marisa Draeger
Cover design by Phil Earnest (www.PhilEarnest.com)

www.TheWindMerchant.com

The text type was set in Adobe Caslon Pro

For Sarah, because you told me to never give up.

ACKNOWLEDGMENTS

There is something that creatives need in order to affirm they aren't merely broadcasting into the ether: support. Whether that support came in the form of being an early draft reader, financial supporter, or cheerleader, I will risk the cliche and dare to say that this book wouldn't have become a reality if not for the following people.

Steve Arensberg, Dustin & Gloria Ballard, Andrew Blankenship, Jason Carter, Donna Coker, David & K Cole, Grant Cooley, Jessica Cox, Laurie Cummings, Shirley Darch, Marisa Draeger, David & Lory Dunlap, Sarah Dunlap, Phil Earnest, Scott Fujan, Zach Garrett, Matt Giesler, Mark Gullickson, Tammy Haxton, Joanne Heck, Bill & Ola Jordan, Timothy Kane, Lee Kebler, Michael Kennedy, Ellen Knight, Jason Knight, Michael Lewis, Thomas Loyd, Stan Meador, Elisha McCulloh, Josh McKamie, Lindsay Morris, Nathan Nasby, Heather O'Daniel, Gloria Olman, Dan Pavlik, Nic Peaks, Adria Pendergrass, Austin Penick, Patrick Riffe, Tiffani Sahara, Clara Seaman, Logan Sekulow, Adam & Andrew Smith, Kawana Smith, Greg Thorne, Josh Toquothty, Kevin & Becky Tucker, Stuart Turner, Will & Carol Underwood, Tiffany Unruh, George Vuckovic, Nicki Waldorf, Nick Whiley, & Erik Yeager

At risk of further sounding cliche, I also must chiefly give thanks to the Originator of Creativity and Story, who I am daily inspired by. Without Christ, I am nothing. I offer my utmost and sincerest thanks for your contribution to *The Wind Merchant*, and can only hope that I told the best story I had in me.

Sincerely,
Ryan Dunlap

The Wind Merchant

Prologue

As any pilot with a few years under his belt knew, turbulence alone never downed an airship. However, cannonballs were a different matter.

Elias Veir madly spun the large, spoked wheel in a desperate attempt to avoid the next barrage as an explosion of splinters, glass shards, and twisted brass melded cacophonously with a scream of pain. Under more favorable circumstances, Elias would have considered world above the field of amber clouds truly beautiful, but the air tasted oddly of cinnamon and blood, marring the effect.

"Morris?" Elias called, still devoting the greater part of his attention to the second enemy airship joining the fray.

"I can't feel my legs," came the reply.

Elias looked back to see the young man slumped against the railing near the Captain's quarters with a large scrap of fuselage protruding from his midsection. "We'll get you to a doctor," Elias said, hoping his hollow words at least sounded comforting.

With the only other surviving member of the crew out of commission, Elias' options were dwindling. The engines no longer responded to climbing maneuvers. Desperation crept into his growl as he shoved the wheel forward, and his stomach leapt into his throat.

The airship dove into the clouds, then shot through to the blood-red world below. Elias leveled off the ship and looked back. Superstitious or no, their pursuers wouldn't take long to decide it worthwhile to risk dropping beneath the clouds.

"What have you done?" Morris said, eyes glassing over as he stared up. "I can't be down here."

"It's only for a little bit," Elias said.

Three airships descended from cloud cover in attack formation. Elias spun the wheel hard to starboard hoping to buy enough time to enact his plan. He stabilized the rudder and dashed across the deck to fling open the Captain's quarters door.

Faint pops of cannon fire encouraged him to work quickly.

Elias was scrambling to open the desk drawer containing his flare gun and parchment when an unholy shriek assailed his eardrums. An instant later, a concussive force blasted through the back wall, showering the quarters with wood splinters and rocking the ship side to side.

A streak of red hot pain shot through his left leg. Elias looked down to see a scrap of wood paneling jutting from his thigh, but he had no time to address it. Grabbing a scrap of parchment, he scrawled a note and stuffed it into the message tube that he had already loaded in the flare gun. Too much rode on the success of this mission for him to fail here.

As he hobbled back to the outside deck, another volley rocked the ship, severing the bow ropes connecting the balloon to the deck. The horizon climbed and Elias braced himself against the console. He grabbed the transmitter. "Mayday, Mayday! This is Elias Veir, I—"

Another lurch threw Elias to the floor, yanking out the transmitter cabling with him. Elias aimed his flare gun to the sky.

I'm sorry, he mouthed.

He pulled the trigger, and with a crack the message tube was lost to the clouds.

An eerie peace fell as the soft crackling of fire filled the absence left by the formerly churning engines, at least until Morris' scream penetrated the calm with an intensity that would have unnerved Elias even on his better days.

"Stop me," Morris pleaded to nobody in particular.

With no clue as to what the young man meant, Elias watched the three ships line up and fire a final barrage.

The explosion hurled the wind merchant over the bow railing and into thin air.

CHAPTER ONE
The Convergence

TEN YEARS LATER.

"I LOVE YOU, BUT THIS ISN'T WORKING FOR ME," RAS VEIR SAID, pulling down his welding goggles and flicking on his torch.

The Copper Fox rarely surpassed first impressions. Equal parts gasbag relic and salvage-yard special, the airship's mind was set on hanging dead in the sky. Inside its dank hold, sparks flared as a begoggled young man in his early twenties welded a metal plate over the most recently ruptured pipe. "Don't worry, nobody's going to notice," he said, inspecting the messy patch job. After all, it looked right at home within the context of its cobbled together surroundings.

"Atta girl," Ras said, flicking off the torch and standing to stretch his legs. A low-hanging pipe sounded an atonal clang as it connected solidly with the back of his head. Stars flooded his vision, punctuating the fading glow of the retina burn from his arc-welder.

"Not your fault," Ras said through gritted teeth. He gingerly removed his welding goggles, releasing a sweaty, tangled mess of dark brown hair into his face. He brushed it away, and as he did so, he caught his distorted reflection in the one redeeming feature of his ship: the massive glass container filling half of the hold.

Ras had mixed feelings about the inherited wind collection tank. The replacement part was the last vestige of his father's lost ship, *The Silver Fox*, and reminded him that his entire vessel was a slapdash homage to his father's legacy. From the stained patchwork balloon to the third hand engines, his ship felt like a child's scribble compared to a lost set of blueprints.

Extricating himself from the pipes, Ras walked to one of his twin scoop engines. He crouched and twisted the valve from the newly patched pipe, restoring the flow of Energy-filled air from outside to the machine. With a pull of a lever, the iris inside the steel barrel opened and shut, throttling the Energy feed. He allowed himself a moment of celebration even though another pipe would likely need his attention later in the week.

A win is a win, he thought, flicking on both engines before climbing above deck.

With the reassuring rattle of the engines once again filling the air, he let the cool wind whip his hair and ventilate his baggy third-generation clothing, drying the sweat worked up in the hold. At moments like this, Ras appreciated that his grandfather and father weren't small-framed men. After sufficiently cooling off, he cinched up the thin leather straps at his elbows and knees to avoid letting the wind play with the extra fabric.

Staring out at the open horizon of white, fluffy clouds, he imagined the days long gone when a wooden ship like his didn't need the gasbag to travel from place to place over the…big thing made of water.

He could never remember the name of anything below Atmo.

The tension eased from his shoulders when he took a moment to appreciate the subtle beauty of the clouds, knowing that nobody would ever see them quite this way again.

It was such a shame they would kill him if he ventured too low.

The very first time his father took him down to the cloud level, the proximity to the abandoned world below became his favorite part of sailing. It sparked his imagination with possibilities from an early age, but gaps to peek below were rare after The Clockwork War.

The constant presence of the clouds reminded him of a time when his father was the breadwinner for the family, and the responsibility of providing for he and his mother didn't weigh so heavily.

Ras lowered the ship's collection tube to let it troll just above the cloud level. He prided himself on being a traditional wind merchant, but was painfully aware that it was only because he lacked the means to acquire the more modern Energy hunting tools.

Up on the bridge, the monitor beeped, alerting him to a shift in the local Energy Level. On good days he would happen upon a

Level 3 source, but most days provided a 2. Level 1 meant he didn't eat. He climbed the stairs to the bridge to read the monitor. "C'mon, four," he said as if asking the wind for Energy had ever worked.

Level 2.

"Better than one," he said, pressing the button to begin pooling the wind in the collection tank.

A chill swept over the bridge, causing Ras to hug his arms for warmth, rubbing some life back into them. The cold was a telltale sign there was less Energy in The Bowl to warm the wind, and he had put off spending money on a warmer coat for too long. The trend frightened him. Having a bad economy was one thing, but having that economy literally powering his city's engines was another.

The radio squawked to life at a jarring volume, the sounds garbled and static-filled. "*Gomer Tassy. Ow obo eye? Nober.*" The phrase repeated itself, picking up speed with each iteration before Ras unplugged the power to the box, killing the spiraling loop. He plugged the box back in before saying, "Hold a tick, transmitter's on the fritz. Over." He gave the device the usual thwack with the palm of his hand and brought the comm unit back to his mouth. "Come again, please. Over."

"I just want to know how you haven't fallen out of Atmo yet, Rassy," said a jovial voice.

Ras sighed. The voice belonged to Tibbs, one of his few remaining childhood acquaintances. He preferred Erasmus to Rassy as his full name didn't prompt memories of schoolyard chants starting with 'Gassy.' "Send me your coordinates, I'll be right over."

"Stay where you are, Rassy. I don't need repairs," Tibbs said. "Got something for you. I'll be right over...Over."

Ras searched the skies for Tibbs, who found dangerously close buzzbys far more humorous than his targets did. *There.* Off the port bow a gleaming silver ship came careening in and clipped just above *The Copper Fox*'s balloon, forcing Ras to steady himself against the turbulence. The new airship made a lazy circle and sidled up next to its wooden-bodied brother as both vessels slowed to a halt.

Tibbs never quite lost his baby fat no matter how much time he spent working out. Those unfortunate enough to brush against his short temper knew not to make his size a point of conversation again, but he never held a grudge, and his easy smile was usually enough to set folks at ease again. Sauntering over to his railing, he waved for Ras to do likewise.

"What are you up to, trolling for Twos?" Tibbs asked.

"Just patching collection pipes."

"Why don't you buy a new set? How expensive can they be?"

Ras knew Tibbs had never owned an airship long enough to need repairs, always swapping out for whatever new model looked the shiniest. He assumed Tibbs didn't actually know what a set cost. "I don't mind getting my hands dirty," Ras said, hoping to change the topic. "So you don't need anything fixed?"

Tibbs snorted a laugh. "Does she look like she needs repairs?" he asked, placing a loving hand on the metal railing.

Ras shrugged. "I heard steering on the new model favors to port."

"Now that you mention…no, she's fine. You know, you might look into being a mechanic back on *Verdant*," Tibbs said, "Welding goggles look good on you."

Ras chose to take it as a compliment, smiling politely. It wasn't easy. "My current employment suits me just fine, thanks," he said, knowing he might as well call himself a mechanic that dabbled in wind collection. A growing percentage of his income came from various repairs for stranded wind merchants. "You said you had something for me?"

Tibbs' eyes went wide with excitement. "Yes, yes, yes." He fished out a small wooden box from his cargo pocket and cradled it in his hands as though he held a rare commodity. "You heard about the new version of Helios' KnackVision, right?"

Ras nodded. He longed for a pair of the goggles that showed Energy flowing on the wind, not least because he knew he was in the ever shrinking minority of wind merchants still flying blind.

Tibbs removed a shiny set of brass goggles from the box and placed them atop his head. "Ta-da!" he said with a flourish, jutting both hands out and spun slightly so Ras could appreciate the sides and back of the strap as well. "Just arrived this morning! With this version you can actually see the level of Energy on the wind, percentage of potency and all!" Tibbs said, quoting the promotional material.

"That's ah…really handy, I'm sure," Ras said, disappointed that what Tibbs had to give him looked to be little more than a demonstration.

"All the benefits of being a Knack without the pesky exploding part," Tibbs said. "Not that you'd have to worry about that, right Rassy?"

Ras hated how well known his inability to sense Energy was among the wind merchants in *Verdant*. Ras' grandfather was a true Knack who claimed he could actually see the Energy flying by, but he had run afoul of a concentrated amount, killing him. Elias had inherited his sixth-sense for finding potent currents, making him a fine wind merchant.

And then there was Ras, whose resounding deafness to the element gave him occasional difficulties with discerning port from starboard. "Ras or Erasmus, if you don't mind."

"Sure, sure, Ras, I got it," Tibbs said. He dug a small cloth bag stitched with the Helios logo out of his other cargo pocket. "My cousin Errol said you spent the afternoon with him yesterday after he blew his engines."

"All I could manage was getting him limping back home."

"He said you wouldn't let him pay you."

Ras shrugged. "He's going to have enough to worry about with two full rebuilds."

"You should have charged him. He's good for it," Tibbs said.

"I'll remember that next time."

An awkward pause hung in the air before Tibbs said, "Well, I don't really need two sets of backups, so I thought you might like these." He pulled a pair of goggles out of the bag.

Ras knew the model instantly. An identical pair had been taunting him from behind a pawn shop's counter while he saved up: the original model of KnackVisions crafted by Foster Helios before either young man was born.

It was difficult for Ras not to show his exuberance at the idea of finally owning his own pair of KnackVisions, even if they were old, even if they didn't work half the time, and even if they smelled like Tibbs lost them in his ship's septic system for a month.

"They don't keep a charge well, but if you want them..." Tibbs said, wiggling them in his hand as if the wavy motion could make them more appealing.

"I don't know what to say, I—" Ras stopped as Tibbs lobbed the goggles across the chasm between the two ships. Whether due to a gust of wind or Tibbs' lack of effort, it looked like the KnackVisions would come up short. Ras jumped up to the rope rigging and reached as far as he could before he noticed a rare clearing in the clouds, showing him exactly how far he had to drop if he fell. Instinctively, he pulled back to steady himself on the ropes. The goggles plummeted, vanishing into the great below. Ras involuntarily imagined himself in their place.

"Really?" Tibbs shouted at Ras, who clung the rigging for dear life with eyes squeezed shut. "Those were practically heirloom."

Ras hung there for a moment as waves of vertigo swept over him. "I would consider it a personal favor if you didn't tell anyone about this," said Ras, slowly opening his eyes and shakily lowering himself from the ropes. A flood of relief overwhelmed him at the feel of the creaky wood underfoot.

"The wind merchant afraid of heights? It's not exactly a secret," Tibbs said. "Listen, Ras…I know it's tough to hear, but maybe being just a mechanic would be a good life. You'd be the go-to guy instead of—"

"Instead of what?" Ras asked. He could feel the warmth filling his cheeks.

Tibbs changed the subject out of what Ras assumed to be pity. "Hey, I gotta go drop off my haul back at The Collective's station. You might check inside Framer's Valley…there was more in there than I could collect myself. Probably want to catch it before it gets drained."

"Son of a Remnant," Ras said, "Framer's? Are you insane?"

"Oh, c'mon, the old sky pirate nest has been empty for months," Tibbs said. "I'm sure Bravo Company probably moved on or got blown up."

"So you saw their base?"

Tibbs laughed. "Like I'm going to fly through the sky mines to look at it. I just went to the Valley. Pulled a Fiver."

"Seriously? I haven't scooped more than a Two in…I don't know how long. Port authority says The Bowl might be running dry."

"Don't tell me you believe the Diver Team conspiracies," Tibbs said. "Nobody's down there destroying our livelihood. Who could even get that close to potent Energy? Besides, if there's a Fiver in Framer's, *Verdant* should have plenty to run on."

Ras nodded and paused. "Hey, Tibbs?"

"Yeah buddy?"

"Is it true the guys started calling me a Lack?" The question held a hint of desperation, begging Tibbs to lie, and he knew it. The wind merchants back on *Verdant* had a leader board—irreverently called The Knack List—of who brought in the largest hauls, and the unfortunate soul holding the bottom spot unofficially received the title of Lack. More often than not, Ras found himself at the bottom of the list for long enough stretches that he feared the nickname had stuck.

"Framer's Valley. Only trying to help," said Tibbs. "See you back on *Verdant*?"

"If India Bravo doesn't get me first," Ras said.

"What's she going to do, gum you to death?" Tibbs asked, flapping his jaw for effect. "She's like, what, one-hundred?"

"I don't know. Still young enough to run Bravo Company," Ras said. He knew she was only fifty years old, but wasn't interested in yet another conversation devolving into stories about how his father marshaled *Verdant*'s forces to route the sky pirate assault. "See you later, Tibbs."

The ships drifted apart and Ras watched the shiny new airship shrink in the distance before he set his course for Framer's Valley.

EVEN FACTORING OUT SKY PIRATES, the valley held a reputation for claiming more than its fair share of wind merchants. The steep cliffs jutting above the clouds made it more a canyon than a valley and the further down one traveled, the narrower and more twisted it became. If one ventured too far, a strong gust could damage a ship enough that even an incredibly potent haul would only pay for repairs.

Ras had grown up with warnings from his father that only an idiot looking to prove his flying abilities would dare risk a ship in Framer's, but the only person he knew who had successfully navigated it was both incredibly handsome and talented. Ras' mother usually threw something at Elias after the advice and amended that her husband was only right about the idiot part.

Elias never disagreed on the point.

But today Ras would have to brave Framer's to make up for his lost morning.

Returning to the bridge, he opened the throttle and set the course he would travel for the next hour. Word of where to find the best collection points spread quickly among non-guild wind merchants, and Ras hoped Tibbs hadn't shared his info with anyone else yet.

Nearing the maw of Framer's, the roiling clouds beneath *The Copper Fox* turned an ugly gray. The cliffs jutted too high for ships to fly above them, and Ras wondered how impressive they must have looked from the ground, disappearing into the clouds above.

He slowed his ship to a crawl at the entrance. Off in the distance, specks in the sky indicated the active sky mines surrounding the cliff-side base of Bravo Company. There wasn't another ship in sight, which both encouraged and concerned Ras. Nobody would be around to tow him out if his ship careened into one of the walls. The entrance was wide enough for half a dozen airships to share, and he would be safe as long as he didn't venture in too far.

Tibbs said the collection point was inside Framer's, so inside he went. The storm beneath sent strong winds whipping around, and Ras only relented his death grip on the wheel to pull the lever lowering the collection tube.

The trolling sensor took a moment to scan the area, then blipped at him. *Level 4.*

"Yes!" Ras exclaimed. Only once had he ever stumbled upon a Level 4 haul, and it had not only placed him halfway up the The Knack List for about a month, but also had given his mother a well-deserved break from working herself ragged to compensate for her son's flagging ability to provide. She had sold too many of her possessions already to make ends meet, but to her credit she never brought it to her son's attention even when he noticed the items absences in the house.

Making a mental note to thank Tibbs later, Ras smacked the collection button on the console, prompting the vacuum to begin filling the tank. *The Copper Fox* drifted further into the canyon, but Ras didn't want to pull back in case he lost the current. Filling his tank usually took ten minutes, and he felt reasonably certain his choke hold on the controls would keep him out of trouble for that long.

However, halfway through collecting his Level 4 haul, the trolling sensor blipped out another spike.

Level 5.

It would be a personal record, but it would also mean dumping his current haul and starting over so as not to dilute the Fiver. He would need to fly into the canyon a bit further to chase the higher potency, but a Level 5 collection would surely erase the Lack title for at least a couple months, and if he could come back tomorrow and pull back to back Fives, he could afford a used pair of KnackVisions. He pressed the button, jettisoning the Level 4 air.

Beep. Level 6. The canyon narrowed.

He chuckled nervously as he restarted the collection process again. It had been years since anybody in *Verdant* pulled in a Level 6 haul and Ras noted Tibbs probably only pulled a Fiver because he wasn't willing to risk a few scrapes on his shiny ship.

A loud shriek of wood scraping rock made Ras' skin crawl as a gust pushed *The Copper Fox* against the cliff to port. Ras told himself the damage was still worth pulling in a 6, and rationalized how he would point to the scrape as part of a war story from "*Framer's.*" Granted, he would need to say, "*No, not that one*" several times, but it would still be worth it.

The wind's howl began resembling a wailing chorus. Ras decided it was time to turn the ship back toward the entrance and wrap up the rest of his collection process before the valley became too narrow to maneuver.

As he spun the wooden wheel to bring *The Copper Fox* about, the indicator beeped Level 7. Seven could buy a new airship, but Seven would most likely get him killed.

The high readings raised the question of what lay in the heart of the canyon, giving off such concentrated amounts of Energy. Before Ras could give it more thought, he spotted a large gash in one of the cliff faces and imagined the size of the vessel that had collided with it. Thinking about the ship wedged somewhere deep in the dark below unsettled him.

The momentary lapse in attention caused Ras to overcompensate his turn, setting him perpendicular to the canyon's path while the wind pushed him deeper into the valley. The nose of *The Copper Fox* careened off one of the cliff faces, jarring the ship and spinning it the remaining ninety degrees until it was flying backwards down Framer's Valley.

Ras threw the throttle forward to battle his way out of the wind tunnel, but the engines failed to respond.

The canyon began to curve to starboard and Ras frantically tried to remap his mind to steer the ship counter-intuitively as the force of the wind pushed him deeper into the canyon. Having the right gut reaction when flying forward often proved difficult enough, but this orientation forced him into an outright panic. He attempted to rely on his often incorrect judgment, which briefly brought success, then panicked when he second guessed which gut-reaction to mistrust.

An incorrect spin of the wheel slammed the ship into an outcropping, knocking Ras into the wheel and pushing his ship down into an unexpected dive toward the clouds. He righted the ship just before dipping into their midst, but finding equilibrium proved to be impossible. With the ship in a terrible tailspin, all Ras could think about was how his father would never have been greedy enough to place himself in a bind like this.

After another half-turn, the bow and stern of *The Copper Fox* lodged against each cliff face of the narrowing canyon, throwing Ras to the deck. He struggled to his feet and clambered down the stairs from the bridge toward his quarters. The ship shuddered and scraped a little further down the canyon with each gust. He threw open the door and dashed into the upheaved room. Sliding down beside his bed, he reached underneath to pull out an arm brace that ran from wrist to shoulder. Spools of wire and metal blocks attached all along its forearm exterior.

His grapple gun.

Ras had modified the 'gun' so it could be loaded with either magnetic or traditional spiked grapple cartridges that dragged a cable behind them once fired. The gun could also connect with a surface and then shoot the opposite end into something else if there was enough cabling left.

Ras heard rocks crumble from one of the cliff faces. *The Copper Fox* lurched from its lodging and Ras scrambled out of his quarters. He hastily secured the grapple gun's straps around his left arm and torso, then loaded two spike cartridges.

He aimed the device at the deck and squeezed the palm-activated trigger. The cartridge fired and the spike lodged into the deck of his ship. He lifted his arm, spooling a bit of cabling with the movement, and lined up a second shot into the cliff to port. Before the ship could swing into that wall, Ras repeated the process on the starboard cliff, anchoring his ship.

This isn't going to hold, he thought. He ran over and slid down the ladder into the hold to inspect the engines. One was making a horrible grinding noise while the other spewed steam, heating the cramped room.

Flipping the switches on the wall to shut them both down, he noticed a piece of metal debris lodged in the gear-work of the grinding engine. Ras tried to heft the piece free to no avail. The wind above deck howled louder as the ship bucked against its tethers.

He grabbed a heavy wrench hanging on the wall nearby and returned, giving the offending debris a stern whack to send it clattering to the floor. The engine grumbled back to life after a cycle, but before he could plug the leak on the other engine, a cacophonous screech gave way to a concussive blast, and the decking above him sheared away to reveal the bouncing balloon.

Ras wished he had questioned the wisdom of placing the two grapples so close together.

Freed from its moorings, *The Copper Fox* bounded forward, sending Ras tumbling in a small room full of sharp and hard machinery, earning him a collection of small cuts and a myriad of bruises to come—if he were to survive this. One engine was better than none, and Ras regained his footing enough to stand for a moment before a series of strong gusts flung the ship from port to starboard, then dove. He watched his feet leave the flooring of the engine room as the ship dropped out from underneath him. He shot through the newly created hole in the deck until his back hit something soft: the balloon.

Bouncing backwards, he saw *The Copper Fox* leaving him behind. Ras instinctively pointed his left arm at his ship and squeezed the palm trigger to fire off a spike at the hull. The line pulled taut, straining the strap around his midsection with a jerk, and Ras tumbled behind his ship like a lead kite as they fell toward the cloud level.

A powerful updraft ended the nosedive of *The Copper Fox*, stopping Ras just short of dragging his legs through the dark clouds before swinging him back up toward his ship. He pulled himself into a ball before colliding with the underbelly, almost knocking him unconscious. The pendulum motion left him dangling helplessly, watching his ship careen along unmanned.

His eye caught some light ahead…the end of the canyon. Ras watched his ship scrape against a cliff wall one last time for good measure before bouncing into the open area.

He entered a large, circular arena walled in by a grove of mountaintops. The wind swirled around *The Copper Fox*, gently spinning the vessel.

Ras took a moment to collect himself until he realized his ship was slowly losing altitude, bringing him dangerously closer to the hissing and crackling clouds. Light flashed and skittered beneath his feet, followed by a deafening boom which echoed throughout the canyon, scaring him witless.

"No, no, no!" Ras said as he began climbing the cable up to his ship. His ungloved hands were raw from holding onto the cable so tight, and each hoist shot bursts of pain through his arms. He looked up and spotted a ship hanging high above the canyon walls, higher than he'd ever seen a ship fly. It had a familiarity to it, but one that was difficult to place when he was busy climbing for his life.

"Help!" Ras shouted to the ship, his voice straining. He knew they probably wouldn't hear him, but he had to try. He climbed faster, barely staying a foot above the black swirl.

The young man's arms burned with exhaustion until he finally slipped, falling into the clouds. *The Copper Fox* drifted in after him, erasing any evidence of Framer's Valley's latest victim.

Ras closed his eyes and hoped the process would be quick.

Sensation flooded his body and Ras cried out until he realized he wasn't disintegrating…he was getting soaked from head to toe. Having fallen beneath the cloud layer, he looked up and shielded his eyes from the droplets of water cascading onto him. The sensation reminded him of a dew bath on *Verdant*, only the water here was extravagant. He knew people used to have a name for water falling from clouds, but the joy of not dying overrode any memory of his history lessons.

A jubilant laugh erupted from him, but a flashing streak of bright white light stopped his outburst and illuminated the area below in a brilliant momentary flash.

Beneath him lay a circular field of something green waving back and forth with the wind. Nestled in the green laid the remains of a derelict airship, grown over with some sort of vegetation.

Just beyond the ship where the cliff met the field, a green glow emanated from the dark maw bored into the rock.

In a matter of minutes he floated down and landed with a gentle thud in the wavy substance, too tired to do anything but just lay in the soft stuff. It reminded him of the pictures from before man took to the skies, but he never learned the name of it.

The strangeness of being on land finally caught up with Ras. There was a stability he appreciated, and for the first time in a long while he felt at peace.

Is this what my great-grandfather felt like? He wondered if he was the first person from Atmo to touch the ground in eighty years. *But why am I still alive?*

He didn't want to watch his ship crash but there was little he could do to stop it. He just lay enveloped by the green, wondering how many ships had fallen prey to Framer's, and how the ship he saw earlier could fly higher than the canyon—

"*The Kingfisher!*" It finally dawned on him where he recognized the mystery ship from. It fit the exact description of the ghost ship wind merchants told tales about. The stories about the ship hadn't begun as ghost tales, but since sightings were still reported one-hundred years after *The Kingfisher* and its crew ended The Clockwork War, the tales evolved.

Some said *The Kingfisher's* captain, Halcyon Napier, was the first wind merchant because he discovered The Origin of All Energy. No two versions concurred about where the man was from, but they all agreed he was single-handedly responsible for turning the tide against the clockwork automatons known as The Elders.

The grapple gun tugged on his arm and Ras realized he hadn't heard a crashing noise yet, but before he could move, the tugging evolved to dragging, and soon he began parting the sea of green. Ras' fumbling fingers worked the release latch on the device and the cable whipped away, leaving him lying in the field.

Picking himself up, Ras glanced over to see what had become of *The Copper Fox* and found it drifting lazily a hundred yards away, bobbing in the breeze and bumping gently into a cliff wall.

Ras waded through the tall undergrowth after deciding water falling on him was a unique but tiresome sensation. He headed toward the decaying airship, wondering what fate had befallen the crew until his attention was ripped away by what lay inside the rock.

A nebulous, floating sphere of Energy ten yards around exuded brilliance and danger, casting a green light all around it. It was the most beautiful thing Ras had ever seen, and also the saddest.

Ras knew he had found Framer's source of Energy: a Convergence. Aside from The Origin of All Energy, Convergences were the only things capable of putting off raw Energy onto the wind. The difference between the two was the Origin's Energy emanated from the ground, while a Convergence was composed of the absorbed essence of any man, woman, or child with an Energy sensitivity who got too close to a potent amount of the resource.

In the last years that humanity spent on the ground, Convergences had obliterated densely packed city populations, causing those sensitive to Energy to erupt, destroying city blocks and continually adding new sources of Energy to the wind. The higher levels triggered the less sensitive to follow suit, forcing the depopulated world to erect what defenses they could. And just when it seemed everyone that could succumb to the curse was gone, the next generation proved Energy sensitivity to be genetic.

Ras sometimes wondered if Knacks took up lives as wind merchants as a penance for The Great Overload, or just because they didn't want to be around cities. Regardless, the irony was not lost on anyone in Atmo that Knacks now sought Energy in survivable quantities to keep the world running.

Nobody knew where the first Convergences came from other than they arrived shortly after The Clockwork War. Most considered them a weapon of The Elders—a parting gift after they failed to subjugate humanity.

Ras guessed his insensitivity to Energy was the only thing saving him from the same fate as the poor souls from the wrecked ship, and for once he didn't mind being a Lack.

The high Energy readings from the canyon made more sense now. He estimated the Convergence put off a Level 8 rating if not a 9, which required a guild-approved license to sell the haul because collecting such Energy-rich air was extremely dangerous.

But not to Ras, for whatever genetic fluke.

A smile crept across his lips. He was going to be a hero, and better yet, a rich one.

Convergences usually flitted about on the wind, necessitating that wind merchants find new collection spots. Whether something was beneath the clouds destroying Convergences or they were simply being blown out of The Bowl, Ras wagered he was looking at *Verdant's* last fuel source.

This Convergence wasn't going anywhere, and nobody would be fool enough to risk flying through the canyon to find it. *Verdant* could relocate to Framer's Valley and have enough Energy to run indefinitely.

He would need proof, though. The amount of Energy *Verdant* would need to burn just to move was more than the benefit of hovering over any vagabond Convergence. But if he could show them a partially filled tank of Level 8 or 9 wind, then maybe—just maybe—he'd be able to convince them that this one was stationary. He could both save his home city and ensure nobody ever called him a Lack again.

He made his way to *The Copper Fox*, grappled to the railing, and with a little effort hoisted himself up to begin repairing the second engine and patching the balloon.

It took a few hours and several salvage trips to the wrecked airship, but at last *The Copper Fox* was in mostly working order. Ras flew it near the mouth of the cave, lowering the collection tube. The sensor read Level 9, but all Ras required was a sample. Even that would be worth a small fortune.

He mashed down the collection button. He didn't know if harvesting too much would destabilize or dissipate the Convergence, so he decided to only fill his collection tank up to ten percent.

"Seven...eight...nine...ten!" Ras pressed the button to stop collecting.

Nothing happened.

*Twelve...thirteen...*Ras' eyes went wide with horror. "No-no-no-no-no!" He ran down to the hold to shut off the valve at the collection point himself, but the rusted old valve wouldn't budge as he had never needed to stop Energy from entering the tank before.

He moved to shut down the generator powering the collection unit. It stopped, thankfully, but the vacuum process had already begun, and if he broke the tank or pipes, he would only release an unstable Convergence into his ship.

Thirty-four...thirty-five...

Ras bounded out of the hold and slid down the collection tube. A horrendous screaming noise assailed his ears, as if a choir had been set on fire. His stomach knotted and heart plummeted as he watched the perfect sphere of Energy start to fluctuate in shape.

He landed inside the cave and tried to pull the tube away from the Convergence, but the sphere pulled the tube back.

Within moments, the Convergence collapsed into Energy on the wind to which Ras was completely blind.

He knew without a shadow of a doubt he was now the richest man in *Verdant*. He also knew he'd just sunk her.

Chapter Two
The Floating City

CALISTA TOURBILLON SUCCESSFULLY EVADED THE SECURITY GUARD on all three of his rounds. The echoing clunk of the deadbolt securing the University library's heavy double doors signaled her glorious newfound solitude.

She celebrated at an appropriate volume.

While most students were packing up for the term and heading home to await notice of their grades, she decided to prolong her first year away from home for as long as possible.

Peering from behind one of the dozens of dusty bookshelves, she confirmed the guard's exit. She liked old Samuel, even though he had discovered most of her hiding places, forcing her to enact more and more elaborate plans for staying after hours.

Clutching a book to her chest, she lithely skipped barefoot down the hardwood aisle, long red hair flowing behind her. Freedom. She loved the spacious vaulted ceilings and stained glass windows that spilled in various colors of light along the path to her destination.

In the back corner of one of the reading areas, a particularly appealing golden swath of light bathed her favorite overstuffed arm-chair. She greeted the old friend, then pivoted and fell backwards over the upholstered arm into the well-worn seat. Dust plumed and danced about lazily in the rays as her hair draped over the armrest, nearly gracing the floor.

She closed her eyes tightly, fighting a headache. It clawed at the back of her mind, demanding her attention, but she wouldn't let it spoil this perfect moment like it had so many others.

Slowing her breathing, she whispered to herself a countdown backward from five and imagined securing heavy locks and chains on a metal door keeping the monster at bay. ...*three, two, one...peace.* Satisfied with the result, she cracked open the book, savoring the scent of the old paper.

She adored all things antique, or at least anything that had survived the move to the skies. Books contained stories of the land before The Great Overload, stories of adventures, dashing knights on quests and fair maidens locked up in towers. She related to the plights of the latter far more than she liked to admit.

The whole of *Verdant* was a prison as far as she was concerned. The flying city was her inescapable island, and her only consolation was having access to a library whose books she hadn't already read a dozen times.

She wasn't ready for that window of opportunity to shut.

The stories in those dusty tomes did little to slake her thirst to see the world. All of it. Not just above the clouds, but the forgotten realms, the places nobody spoke of anymore for simple lack of remembering or reverence.

The longing to explore had embedded itself during her first and only airship ride when she was five years old. Her family had just moved to *Verdant* under doctor's orders and she spent the next fourteen years cooped up in a basement due to her headaches.

Traveling beyond that basement, even if it was a five minute skiff-ride away to the University, had been a dream come true. Her parents' one condition was that she must remain indoors as much as possible, which Callie found acceptable, given the size of the library. The University was her favorite part of *Verdant*, since it was the city's only structure directly transplanted from before the launch of the Atmo Project. She loved wandering its halls, pretending she lived with everyone else on the ground by walking where they walked.

She softly hummed one of her mother's little melodies as she flipped through the pages, finding her secret bookmark. One chapter remained unread and as much as she pleaded with the librarian, it was strictly against University policy to let a book stay loaned out over break. Granted, it was a history book and part of an incomplete anthology, but a girl had to have principles, and completing a book once begun fell well within those bounds. Plus, she needed as much research as she could get on The Origin of All Energy for the book she had begun writing.

Her eyes soaked up the descriptions of multi-wheeled vehicles called trains. She had difficulty understanding why they gave way to four-wheeled vehicles called cars, but understood that they mostly resembled the ground-bound skiffs she saw zipping about the streets of *Verdant*.

The jangle of heavy keys at the entrance sent her heart racing. Barely a page completed and her time was up already. It wasn't fair. She had half a mind to try to sneak the book out, but she knew theft would lead to sleepless nights, and an eventual tear-filled confession to her father. She prided herself on being a storyteller, but drew the line at flat-out lying.

Speed read. There was a creak of the heavy door and what sounded like two sets of boots clattering louder as they approached. She ran her finger along the page, giving it more a glance than a thorough read. If she was caught, she was caught, but that only meant she'd need to read more quickly.

"Callie!" a familiar voice bellowed.

Daddy. She tucked in her legs tight, hoping the wingback would sufficiently hide her.

"I locked her in here, she should be around somewhere," Samuel said, erasing any pride Callie had in her subterfuge abilities.

Another two pages down, five to go.

The footfalls grew louder as her pulse raced. *The invention of type-writers, the predecessors to modern airships, the first discovery of relative time, The Clockwork War and*—the last two pages were torn out. It seemed she couldn't find a single book that contained information on The Great Overload. Her frustration only fed the monster that wouldn't stop charging the door the way it did in her nightmares.

The wingback chair tipped backwards. Callie let out a yelp, tumbling onto a rug in a most unladylike fashion and rolling into the legs of her father. Looking up through a mess of red hair, she saw her father's offered hand. "Time's up." Callie sheepishly accepted, and he hauled her small frame up with little effort the way he always had.

Samuel waited for her to relinquish the contraband. She gave the elderly guard her most pitiful look, but he just sighed and shook his head. He didn't understand he was taking the last vestige of fresh material she would see in the next three months.

"I'm sorry, Mr. Samuel," she said, placing the book in his aged hands.

"At least you don't get drunk and fall off the clock tower," he said. "I'll take playin' hide-n-go-seek any day."

The pounding in Callie's head suddenly intensified and the room spun wildly. She began to sway.

"Callie?" Mr. Tourbillon asked. He knew the dizzied look on her face and reached out his strong arms for her in a practiced motion.

The mental door holding back the pain finally gave way as the room disappeared into blackness.

VERDANT WASN'T PARTICULARLY FAR from Framer's Valley but it was the longest flight Ras had ever endured.

Underneath the cloud level, Ras discovered a far less dangerous path that didn't involve the main canyon. He took a tunnel offering the promise of daylight out of Framer's, and he desperately wished he had known of the path earlier. *The Copper Fox* was hobbled despite his best efforts to get it back up and running.

It wasn't until Ras had set his course above the clouds that the chill of the wind announced the new tears in his clothes. His threadbare outfit would need another set of patches, but such details felt frivolous.

Hours later Ras caught a glimpse of the floating city of *Verdant* glittering on the horizon. The sun peeked through its modest skyline, setting the clouds ablaze in a brilliant orange. It already looked as though the circular, ten-mile-wide city hung a little lower in the sky, but Ras hoped it was just his mind playing games with him.

Maybe Verdant *didn't rely on this particular Convergence,* he thought. *Maybe if I bring the load in front of the city council they'd know how to turn it back into a Convergence.* It was unlikely, considering the creation process of Convergences, but he hoped ignorance of some special process might be his salvation. The city wouldn't fall immediately as long as the emergency Energy balloons beneath the city weren't depleted, but he didn't know how long the city's reserves would last.

Ras queued up *The Copper Fox* behind several wind merchant vessels waiting to have their hauls appraised at The Collective's Energy refining station. Even though The Collective was the closest thing to a universal government in Atmo, the wind merchant guild had no jurisdiction over any of the fourteen remaining sovereign cities—but it was illegal to enter *Verdant's* borders with a full haul of Energy lest the city suffer repeat of The Great Overload.

He hated selling to The Collective after every haul. Mr. Planks, the frail collections officer, took full advantage of being the sole Energy buyer in The Bowl after the city of *Merron* fell eleven years back in a sky pirate attack.

Planks and his assistants had never come aboard *The Copper Fox* when Ras said the hold was empty, but the man had a nose for Energy. Knack sensitivities manifested themselves differently to different people. Some saw Energy in green swirls, others tasted or smelled something out of place. From the way he would scrunch his nose upon each inspection, Ras guessed the latter.

Idling forward and stopping again, Ras came close enough to hear bits of Mr. Planks' routine sales pitch to the pilot in front of him. "Have you considered swapping your scoops to Helios engines?"

"—The price of fuel is well worth the peace of mind knowing you'll never have to worry about dropping out of the sky," Ras recited, finishing the sentence in an affected nasal tone, then covered his mouth when he realized Planks could probably hear him. The whole system was rigged. Scoop engines allowed an airship to fly free, powered by the Energy it encountered on the wind. The idea of buying the ability to fly from anyone was preposterous until The Collective built the monstrosity called *The Winnower* to act as a filter over The Origin of All Energy. After all, with no way to test Energy sensitivity that didn't render the test subject debilitated one way or another, neutering The Origin was "a necessity."

The platforms outside each city ferried the raw Energy captured by wind merchants to *Derailleur* to keep up with fuel production.

The Collective's stated goal was to reduce the level of Energy to a livable quantity so man could return to the ground without fear of exploding, which was all well and good, until the process began choking the cities that ran off scoop engines.

But luckily for Atmo, The Collective just so happened to build a new type of engine designed to utilize the fuel created by *The Winnower* after it processed the raw Energy, rendering it harmless. It was obvious to most that The Collective attempted to make the new system more palatable by naming the new engines after the man who created The Atmo Project: Foster Helios, Sr..

The whole Helios Engine propaganda campaign played off the fears of parents by painting a picture of children as precious little time bombs.

Two cities rose up against The Collective, and both nationalities were branded as sky pirates and hunted down on sight by the fleet still equipped with the weapons from The Clockwork War.

Verdant was one of the final holdouts about swapping its engines from scoops to Helios, but whether the city's stance was a matter of principles or finances, Ras didn't know.

The Copper Fox took its turn in front of Mr. Planks, who didn't bother to look up. "Have you considered swapping your ship out for an entirely new one?" The gaunt, middle-aged man chuckled sharply, then sniffled and rubbed his nose. "What'd you collect?"

"Nothing I can sell," Ras said.

Mr. Planks sneezed.

"Bless you," Ras said in too polite of a tone. "Collection system got gummed up after I hit a cliff in Framer's."

Planks surveyed *The Copper Fox*. "Just one?"

"C'mon, Planks. I don't have anything for you. Just mark it zero."

Planks exaggeratedly swooped the circle on his clipboard. "It's quite charitable of you, continually saving the rest of The Knack List from humiliation."

Ras smiled in mock amusement, half wishing he could tell Planks to take a look in his hold and see exactly where he belonged on the list, but if The Collective took his supply, they wouldn't give him anything for it besides grief. "Thanks."

"Guess we can't always have a Veir at the top," Planks said.

"Are we done?"

"We were when I saw you fly up." He scrunched his nose, then reached up to feel a small amount of blood before wiping the rest away with the back of his hand.

Ras said his goodbye by jamming his throttle forward. The ship lurched, backfired, then puttered toward *Verdant*, lacking the dramatic effect Ras intended. He tried to ignore the hearty laughter coming from the crew of the collection station.

Thanks to the beating *The Copper Fox* had taken back in Framer's, the usual ten minute trip to the docks lasted an hour, giving Ras a long, hard look at his home city. He always thought *Verdant* looked like a gently rotating ship's wheel, with docks for airships at the edges, followed by traders, merchants, and stores with main avenues along the eight spokes. Other business and offices made up the next layer in, then homes, and at the very center stood *Verdant's* University, which tripled as the capital building and a park for children.

With everyone living more-or-less on the edge of Verdant Park, families spent time together and had enough isolation from the fringe trades if they desired, although there was less and less business as of late. Travel to the city was notoriously difficult because of the mountain passes, and with a dwindling Energy supply, fewer merchants included *Verdant* in their trade routes.

In the overall geography of Atmo, *Verdant* was its most southwestern settlement. The mountains comprising the borders of The Bowl constituted a natural Energy-trapping structure since The Origin wasn't too far away from the main mountain pass. Before *Merron* sank, The Bowl thrived with trade between the two cities.

Imagining *Verdant* lying desolate and empty beneath the clouds like *Merron* broke Ras' heart. With the influx of Merronian transplants living in *Verdant*, the city had become cramped. Ras wondered how crowded the cities outside of The Bowl were, and if they would even be capable of taking on the refugees of *Verdant*. With seven of the twenty-one cities downed and no real opportunity for expansion, where would everyone go? Ras had heard of some smaller settlements atop mountain ranges or townships comprised of bolted-together airships, but it was no way to live.

The dull roar of *Verdant's* engines grew as *The Copper Fox* approached the crowded old wooden docks. Ras' eyes easily found the empty slip designated for the Veir family. An older man creaked back and forth in a decrepit rocking chair, waiting.

Old Harley Hollister. He stood as Ras brought up a thick rope to moor the ship.

"Don't you have other slips to patrol?" Ras asked the man in the faded Port Authority uniform, tossing the rope for Harley to tie to the dock.

"Your momma's worried about you," Harley said, taking the rope and effortlessly securing it. "Looks like she had good cause, too." He paused, taking in the damage to *The Copper Fox* in the waning light. "I hope it was worth it," he said with true concern in his voice.

Ras walked down the extending gangplank, not even looking up at the old man.

"Hey, hey." Harley intercepted Ras, halting the young man. "What's the matter? You get into a fight?"

He had almost forgotten about the bevy of scrapes and cuts he displayed. "Cliff face: one, Ras: negative twenty."

Old Harley thought for a moment. "Cliff face…You know better than to go out to Framer's," Harley said. "That Tibbs boy came back bragging about pulling a Fiver from there."

"I didn't get a Fiver," Ras said, fixated on his boots. "Hey, could you do me a favor and make sure nobody messes with *The Fox*? I know she looks like a junker."

Old Harley stood at attention. "On Old Harley's honor. At least until I get off duty tonight." He smiled. "You want the weather report for tomorrow?"

Ras shook his head and walked past his friend, patting him on the shoulder. "Not going out tomorrow."

He opted not to take one of the public transit skiffs back to his home. *What should I tell mom? Hey, sorry I'm late, I was just off dooming our livelihood.*

Walking along a mostly depopulated main avenue, a street vendor tried to interest him in some sort of bird on a rotisserie. Ras wordlessly waved him off. *I don't get dinner tonight,* he thought.

His mind began playing the perverse game of wondering if each person he passed would be able to leave *Verdant*. The city wouldn't fall immediately, giving those with ships a chance to escape.

He walked past a tavern, one of the few popular businesses left, and stared through the large window into the Energy-lamplit room. Tibbs sat at the bar, surrounded by a handful of wind merchants. He made wide gestures, sloshing his drink back and forth before he spotted Ras. Tibbs motioned for Ras to come inside until the other wind merchants shot him a hard look.

Everyone knew a Lack was bad luck.

Just wait until you have a real reason to hate me. He continued down the avenue as night folded in around him and the streetlights slowly glowed to life as one. The artificial light guided Ras to the residential zone lined with various colored cottages on either side of the street, all identical in structure. After all, one couldn't exactly pluck building materials from the skies.

He came to the light blue exterior of the Veir home. His mother had inadvertently selected the color after mistakenly ordering a surplus of paint for Ras' nursery, and couldn't persuade the merchant to give her a refund.

Quietly working the key into the lock, he opened the door, which sounded the piercing creak he never did remember to remedy. The house remained dark as he waited for his mother to flick on the lamp next to her chair as she did so often during Ras' teenage years.

The sound of slow, heavy breathing came from the couch in the middle of the living room. Emma Veir slept soundly, her small frame huddled in a ball, and her head of long, dark chestnut hair lay on a pillow. The peaceful expression on her face erased the usual lines of worry, making it difficult to guess she had celebrated her 40th birthday just a month prior.

The slight chill in the house prompted Ras to retrieve a blanket from the hallway closet and carefully drape it over his mother. She stirred.

"Mmm…Eli?"

"I'm sorry mom, just me," he whispered.

She pulled the blanket tight and once again left the waking world.

Ras ascended the stairs, knowing this would probably be the last night in his bed for a long while. In the morning he would hand himself over to *Verdant*'s city council.

It seemed like Ras spent most of his night awake, feeling his bruises and aches settle in. The kaleidoscope of colors across his body was as impressive as it was painful.

The smell of something baking in the kitchen told Ras his mother was up. After a dewbath and gingerly scrubdown, he dressed in a loose-fitting white work shirt and a crumpled pair of tan pants adorned with only a few patches.

He walked down the stairs to find his mother setting a fresh batch of biscuits to cool on the stove.

In the daylight, the house looked more sparse than he remembered. It was always a sad game trying to guess which things had last disappeared from the house, but Emma always said if he didn't notice its absence, it was probably something they didn't need.

"I hope biscuits are all right again," she said, pulling a tray from the oven. "What time did you get home last ni—" She paused, finally getting a good look at her son, who stood a good eight inches taller than she. "Night."

"About midnight." Ras sat down at the kitchen table, letting his hair hang in front of his face to hide a few of the more grievous cuts near his left temple. He winced as Emma pulled the hair back.

"Who did this to you?" she asked.

"I hit some turbulence while I was in the engine room," he said, pursing his lips.

"Some." She cocked an eyebrow. "You all right?" she asked, taking a seat on the stool across the table from him.

Ras appreciated that she asked about him before *The Copper Fox*. He didn't know if he should tell her anything yet, but a 'no' or even a hesitation would earn him an interrogation.

"I banged up *The Fox* and didn't collect anything I could sell," he said.

"How banged up are we talking?"

"Nothing I can't fix eventually. The tank is fine."

Emma's eyes glassed over the way they usually did when she calculated what she would need to sell to pay off the bills when Ras didn't profit from his last run.

"Oh! I have something for you." Emma gave her best distracted smile and went to their refrigerator to extract a cake. She set it on the table in front of her son for him to read WELCOME HOME CALISTA in big blue frosted letters.

"Mom, Callie's dorm room isn't that far from her house."

"Well, she's home for the summer and might like to see an old friend," she said innocently. She never made any pretense of her preference that her son marry the girl next door.

"She's not going to think I made her a cake." Ras looked at the frosted words again. "Did you try to imitate my handwriting?"

She had.

Within ten minutes Ras bandaged himself, dressed in his one set of patch-less clothing, and found himself holding a cake on the front porch of the Tourbillon home. The family had selected the house for its basement due to Callie's special allergies. They had moved in when Ras was six years old, and the little red-haired girl with brilliant blue eyes and the fairest skin he had ever seen had captivated him from day one.

If he had to show himself before the council and be locked up for his crime, he was all right with Callie being the last person he saw.

Ras knocked on the door to no avail. He felt stupid and over-dressed, and Callie would instantly know he had been set up. He was about to knock a second time but a very faint "*chick-chicka-chink*" stopped him. Callie was home.

The sound carried from the side of the house, so Ras walked over to the ankle-level basement window. He sat the cake down in front of it and rapped on the window four times. *Tap-tap-tap.* Pause. *Tap.* Their code. He stepped to the side so she couldn't see him. The typewriter stopped.

A latch clicked open and the window swung out. Ras watched the porcelain hand reach out and pause; then another hand swiped a finger-full of frosting from the side of the cake.

"Now who could have left me a cake?" a familiar, playful voice wondered aloud. "I certainly hope it's not poisonous...but I suppose there are far worse ways to leave this world." The hand with the icing on it withdrew; a moment later, the one holding up the window did likewise. The window re-latched. The cake remained.

Ras sighed, smiled, and rapped once again on the window. This time he stood next to the cake. Still no response.

He went to his hands and knees to peer through the dirty window and saw a sparsely furnished basement with a pre-Atmo iron type-writer with black, circular keys on a table in the place of honor in the center of the room. But no girl.

"Erasmus Veir, you no good peeping Tom!" Callie did the best impression of her father that a nineteen-year-old girl could muster. The effect was comical, but still startled Ras, whose posterior stuck in the air as he froze, peering through the window.

His face flushed as he stood, and saw the little girl he had looked forward to seeing every day of his life. She had grown up since leaving for University. Now she stood with impeccable posture that he guessed her classmates mistook for snobbery, but Ras knew she feared becoming stoop shouldered for all the hours she spent reading and typing. Her long wavy red locks fell to the middle of her back but for a few strands cascading over her shoulders, and she wore a loose white sundress that both accentuated her fairness and proved she wasn't purely white as a sheet.

"I see you found the poisoned cake someone left for me," she said, playing with an errant lock of hair.

"I chased him off. Had a hook hand," Ras said, crooking a finger and mimicking the fabled intruder.

"Looks like he got you a few times," she said, causing Ras to chuckle and then wince. "Grab the cake, I want to show you something." She bounded back around the corner to the front of the house and Ras followed.

"So how was University?"

"Took my last final yesterday." She held up crossed fingers. They entered the living room as Ras' eyes darted about. "Don't worry," she said, "daddy's not home."

It was no secret that Mr. Tourbillon had stopped liking Ras upon discovering that the boy had started sneaking over to spend time with his daughter. The relationship worsened when Callie began reciprocating and sneaking out to visit Ras. The clandestine meetings had ended when Callie passed out on her way to Ras' house one night and had been found the next morning in her nightgown on the Veir lawn. She was only twelve at the time, but the past seven years hadn't softened her father's opinion of Ras.

"How were the headaches?" Ras asked, following her down into the basement.

"Never as bad as they were when I was little, but they're usually there." She arrived at her typewriter. "Right now they're gone."

Ras always wondered about her chronic headaches. She'd get them and collapse when she was out and about, but whenever he was with her she seemed fine. He had once accused her of faking when they were young and she had given him a two-month silent treatment.

He never dared to voice the thought again.

For whatever reason, she had fewer headaches in the basement, which she preferred to refer to as her library since the walls were lined with shelves upon shelves of books.

She slid into the well-worn desk chair and pulled the paper from her typewriter, placing it on a stack of pages. "I was just finishing the first couple chapters of a story I'd like you to read." She took the pages and straightened them with a few thumps on her desk. "If you have time, I could really use a friend's honest opinion."

A friend. That's all Ras had ever been. And her number one fan.

"Don't go easy on me. If it's bad, it's bad, and better I hear it from you—"

"I'll be honest, I promise," Ras said. "Where did you get the paper?"

"I saved up," she said proudly. "Well, I had to use the gifts I got for University too, but look at it. Isn't it so clean?"

Ras admired the fresh, white paper, and suddenly felt that no amount of hand washing would make him worthy to handle such a pure thing. There was no place on *Verdant* that made it, and most paper in Atmo was recycled to a mottled grayish blue hue. Mr. Tourbillon used to sneak her typo'd scraps from the capitol building until she began writing stories about the people on the front of the government documents. "Where's it from?"

"*Derailleur*," she said. She smiled widely and offered him the stack, then withdrew it. "We should probably bind these so pages don't go flying away when you're waiting on the next big haul," she said with no hint of sarcasm.

"What's it about?" Ras asked.

"The white train," she said simply.

"You're finally writing it?"

Callie nodded. "How many times can I dream about it before it's obvious I'm supposed to? Maybe writing it down will finally get it out of my head."

Over and over Ras heard the recounting of Callie's dream of being on a railed vehicle she called a train. She would describe in detail things she saw along the trip that baffled Ras. Her father chalked it up to reading too many pre-Overload novels and an overactive imagination.

"How's the life of a wind merchant going, by the way?" she asked.

He preferred to keep the conversation centered on her but she had the annoying habit of caring about what went on in his life. "Let's just say I have plenty of time to read between collections."

"That a good or bad thing?" she asked.

Ras hesitated. If ever there was someone Ras knew that appreciated a good story, it was Callie, and he'd rather tell her what happened than have her hear it from second-hand sources, or worse yet, her father.

"I fell beneath Atmo," Ras blurted.

Callie's eyes shot open wide as she held her hands up to her mouth in shock, then dropped them and shot him a look of disbelief. "Shut up. No you didn't."

Ras pointed to his head bandage. "Does this look like a face that would lie about crashing?"

She eyed him warily, a smirk growing. "All right, what did you see?"

"Green wavy stuff—"

"Grass! You saw grass?" she asked, excitedly pacing the room. "Did you get to touch it?"

"Laid in it. Really tall stuff. Soft," Ras said, enjoying how each minute description sent her over the moon with excitement.

"I knew it'd be soft!" she exclaimed. "Wait. Hold on." Her eyes narrowed. "How are you not dead?"

"Great question. I was probably ten meters from a Convergence."

"Erasmus Veir," she said, enunciating every syllable, "now I know you're lying."

"Callie, if ever there was one thing I need you to trust me about, this is it."

"Ever? As in forever and ever, ever?"

"Forever and ever, ever," he said, placing his hand to his heart.

"You realize, by law, I get to never trust you again if you're lying."

Ras knew there was no such law, but nodded anyway. It was as good as law to her.

Her demeanor lightened. "So they've been lying to us about The Great Overload..." A grin spread wide. Callie loved a good conspiracy theory.

"I don't think so—" Ras began.

"You know you're taking me with you," she said, "Today."

"I can't."

"Why not?"

The room shuddered slightly and books fell from shelves. It felt like when something went wrong with *The Copper Fox*'s engines, but on a massive scale.

Suddenly the entire room fell. The drop was only a couple of inches, but it was quick enough that both Ras and Callie braced themselves instinctively.

"What happened, Ras?" Callie asked. It wasn't an accusatory tone, and he appreciated her for that.

"I sort of…collected a Convergence," Ras said. "Accidentally."

The corners of her lips edged into a grin, which he knew didn't indicate amusement so much as that she didn't know how to respond to the news. She knew what it meant for *Verdant*. "Can you put it back?"

Ras shook his head.

"Then let's find another one!"

"I don't think there is another one in The Bowl," Ras said.

"You just flew below Atmo for the first time! Who knows what else is out there?" The prospect obviously excited her, and she had a point. A point that didn't involve Ras turning himself in and losing his ship.

Upstairs the front door opened. Heavy boots stomped around and Callie whispered, "That's daddy. We'll talk later."

Ras was two steps ahead of her, moving toward the basement window with a practiced motion, unlatching it, and opening it.

"Callie?" A deep voice boomed from above and the footsteps aggressively grew closer.

"Yes, daddy?" she called back sweetly.

Ras struggled to squeeze through the small window. "This was a lot easier when I was eight," he wheezed. He felt a shove on his boots as Callie did her best to push him free, allowing him to grasp further along the ground, but gained little purchase. Ras heard steps clomping down the stairs when he felt one last push that gave him enough force to free himself.

He rolled away from the window, safe.

Ras watched Callie feign interest in something outside as he heard Mr. Tourbillon arrive downstairs. He panicked when he spotted the dirty, man-sized boot print on her otherwise spotless white sundress. He tried to motion to her stay where she was, pointing to his own thigh.

"Callie, have you seen Erasmus?" Mr. Tourbillon asked. Callie turned to face him. "I was just over at Emma's and she said—"

Ras sat up and scurried back toward his house but ran straight into a man wearing a deputy's uniform, who shoved him into the arms of another deputy with handcuffs at the ready.

"Well, this doesn't look good." A middle-aged man with peppered temples and a square jaw sauntered up to Ras as one of the deputies worked the cuffs. Sheriff Pauling. He turned his head to see Mr. Tourbillon as he joined the crowd. "Good call. Poor boy was so surprised he didn't even put up a fight."

"What's this about?" Ras asked, doing his best to feign ignorance.

Emma Veir stomped out of the house shouting at Sheriff Pauling, "Let him go! You know he wouldn't do something like that!"

"Something like what?" Ras asked.

"Erasmus Veir, you are under arrest for the attempted murder of Harley Hollister."

CHAPTER THREE
The Sentence

SHERIFF PAULING WASN'T A CRUEL MAN. RAS HAD FOND MEMORIES of the Paulings being dinner guests in the Veir home occasionally, but looking at him through steel bars felt very different from sitting across a dinner table from him.

The stale smell of regret and half-cleaned sick in the cell was difficult for Ras to ignore as he worked out a plan.

Pauling looked over at Ras, reclining back in his chair across the small room. "You ready to talk or would you like to keep stewing?"

"I wouldn't hurt Old Harley," Ras said.

"Witnesses saw him climb aboard your ship last night. He was found there this morning after he didn't show for his shift. Unconscious, burns and bruises all over his body. Your mother said you told her you got home around midnight." The sheriff stood and began pacing in front of Ras' cell. "What can you tell me?"

"I asked him to watch the ship for me, I—"

"Why'd you ask him to watch your ship?"

"I didn't want scavengers mistaking it for a junker after it was torn up."

"Ras," Pauling said, "you dock in your family's port. People here have too much respect for the Veir name to do something to your ship."

Ras slumped as Pauling pulled up a chair and sat. He remained silent until Ras met his eye. "You're a good kid, Erasmus. Eli raised you right. Don't prove me wrong."

"Is Old Harley going to be all right?" Ras asked weakly.

"Was it self-defense?" he asked.

Ras flinched at the thought of himself attacking the family friend. Then it dawned on him. "Old Harley's a Knack, isn't he?" Ras asked, immediately wishing he hadn't voiced the question. He didn't want anyone getting close enough to blow themselves and his ship to bits, and hadn't considered Old Harley would snoop.

"Did you not deposit your collection before docking?" The Sheriff sounded noticeably relieved.

"No," Ras said, burying his hope beneath his shameful expression. If all it took to get off the hook was taking his ship out of dock to head to the Collective's drop-off station, he could make a run for it to find another Convergence. He could even feign engine problems and dump the collection once he made it close enough to the cloud level that it wouldn't hurt *Verdant*.

"It's not that bad, Ras," Pauling said. "It's not a big fine and I'm sure Harley won't press charges. Just be smart about it next time, all right?" He walked back to his desk to start filling out the paperwork.

One of the two deputies Ras met earlier bolted into the room, caught sight of Ras, and stared daggers into the young man.

"Sir?" The deputy waited for Pauling to look up. "We searched his ship, and the same thing happened to Robins. The kid brought enough Energy to light up *Verdant*."

THE GAVEL SLAMMED DOWN to quiet the overcrowded courtroom as the Council of *Verdant* began their sentencing in the case of the "City of *Verdant* vs. Erasmus Veir." The general public had great interest in seeing the son of Elias Veir brought low as the destroyer of *Verdant*.

Ras stood alongside his court-appointed lawyer as the Chief Justice read the counts. "On the charge of one count of first degree city sabotage, we find the defendant: not guilty."

Jeers and accusations shot forth from the crowd, requiring several more rounds of gavel pounding and threats of expulsion.

"On the charge of one-hundred and sixty-thousand, nine-hundred and twelve counts of attempted murder by the releasing of Convergence-grade Energy within city limits, we find the defendant: not guilty."

For once, Ras' reputation of incompetence worked in his favor. Throughout the proceedings, nobody seemed to honestly believe he held any ill-intention for the citizens of *Verdant*, but the prosecutor played up the need for repercussions for destroying the Convergence, even if accidentally. Ras sighed as the last of the charges that held hard time were behind him.

"On the charge of third degree obstruction of Energy and fueling, we find the defendant: guilty."

The crowd murmured an approval. The defense lawyer leaned over and whispered, "That carries community service, you'll be fine." Being able to verifiably reproduce the conditions of the malfunctioning collection system saved him from a second-degree charge.

"On the charge of bringing Level 9 Energy into city limits without declaring it, we find the defendant: guilty."

Ras felt the blood drain from his face.

"I hereby declare that the sentence is three weeks of community service in *Verdant's* engine per level of potency, resulting in no more than twenty-seven weeks," the Chief Justice said. "The Energy in the hold is to be confiscated and fed to the engines of *Verdant* to prolong its life. In addition, a fine will be imposed equal to the scrap value of *The Copper Fox*, and the court permanently revokes your collection license with no opportunity for appeal as of today."

With the drop of the gavel, Ras flinched as his future disappeared. He fell to his chair, numb to the shouts of the men and women behind him, suggesting he be locked away forever or tossed over the side.

Bailiffs roughly picked up Ras, escorting him past the throng that could no longer contain their vitriol toward him. He could see his mother in tears, and for a moment thought he caught a glimpse of Callie before he was shoved through the side door. It pained him to imagine the headache she must be suffering just to come out to watch the trial. He struggled not to pick out words like "useless," "incompetent," "idiot," and worst of all, "*Lack*," filtering into the hallway from the courtroom.

How many cities have been destroyed by one mistake?

Ushered in behind Ras, Emma strode next to her son as he walked down the long corridor. The shouts gave way to the clacks of boots on the hard floor as the entourage escorted Ras toward the side exit of the courthouse. Upon reaching the doors, Ras was met by a throng of reporters and some of the crowd from the courtroom that had already rushed outside to catch one more glimpse of him.

Just before he reached the bottom step, he stopped and turned around to address the crowd. Cameras began snapping wildly and the crowd hushed to hear his statement.

Ras took a breath to speak, held it for a moment, then simply said, "I'm so sorry." He could already see his picture with those three words atop it on the front page of tomorrow's newspaper.

Emma stepped into Mr. Tourbillon's borrowed skiff that awaited them. Ras followed, then shut the passenger door, drowning out the shutter clicks and accusations.

"And with the press of a button, the world hates me," Ras said.

Emma looked over her son for a moment. "I've never told anyone this…but you're not the only Veir to destroy a Convergence."

Ras turned his attention from the window to his mother for a moment, waiting.

She continued, "I don't know how your father found it, but it got us through our early years together. He never told anyone he would dip below the clouds, but little by little, he'd collect enough to not make anyone suspicious. Paid off the ship and house before he killed it."

Ras didn't know how he could have gotten so close, being part Knack. "Was it an accident?"

"No. It was intentional. Your father got it in his head that Convergences were collections of poor Knack souls that were bound together, waiting to be freed to return to The Origin."

He had heard that theory from his father before. Since Elias wasn't sure of it, Ras remained skeptical. "So Dad would have thought I did the right thing?"

"Maybe," Emma said, starting the skiff's engine. "This was a few years before *The Winnower* was built, of course, so we weren't expecting The Collective to take away our ability to stay in the air forever." She pressed on the accelerator, leaving the courtroom behind them. "There's someone I think you should talk to."

OLD HARLEY STRUGGLED to sit up in his hospital bed. "Come in, sit, sit!" He coughed, gesturing for Ras and Emma to enter. "It's good to see you!"

Ras hadn't believed that he could have felt any worse than he already did, but the sight of Harley's ashen complexion somehow managed to sharpen his shame. "Harley, I'm so sorry—" he began.

"Oh put a cork in it kid. All week long it's been reporters, deputies, or doctors. It's nice to see a familiar face. I kept telling them if I hadn't have been such a busybody, I would be fine right now. Serves me right," he said. "You know who should be sorry? The Collective."

"Why's that?" Emma asked, taking a seat.

"With *Verdant* sinking and no more Convergences in the area, they're pulling out. Who are the wind merchants going to sell to now? The least they could do is install their Helios engines so we could buy fuel, but it's like they're punishing us for not buying from them in the first place. They hiked up their prices on their engines and fuel too! All on account of the skirmish they got going on with the sky pirates." He scoffed. "Load of malarky, I tell you."

The beeps from the machinery were the only sound filling the room for the next few minutes.

"How much do you think The Collective would charge to swap out *Verdant*'s engines?" Ras ventured at last.

"Oh, I don't know. More than anyone around here's got, and probably all put together. Your father saw this coming. That's why he split."

"Harley!" Emma said, angered. She softened her expression and shook her head when Ras looked at her for clarification. "He did not '*split*.' He went to find a solution for *Verdant* that wasn't going to stuff the pockets of The Collective," she said in a phrase Ras heard many times growing up.

"Emma, the man said he had a mission from Hal Napier himself."

"What?" Ras asked.

Emma stood up. "That's enough!"

"The boy needs to know sometime." Harley protested.

"What exactly did Ras need to know? The rumors you hear third or fourth hand at the docks? If he wants to know more about his father he can ask me, not some deckhand," she said, then stormed out.

The two men sat silent for a moment. "Your father was a good man, Ras. I overstepped my bounds," Harley said, not meeting Ras' gaze.

"Do you believe he met Hal?" Ras asked.

"That's a hard thing to say. I think it's possible he met someone that flew *The Kingfisher*, but that ship would have to at least be one-hundred years old or more. That part's plausible."

"I think I saw it. *The Kingfisher.*"

Harley shifted in his bed, then peered out into the hallway before looking back to Ras. "Where?"

Ras lowered his voice. "Way above the Convergence in Framer's. I didn't get a long look, but how many other ships can fly above the mountains there?"

"Have you told anybody?"

Ras shook his head. "People would just think I was crazy."

"You flew beneath the clouds and collected a Convergence. You have a little wiggle room for discussing the impossible," Harley said. "I think I upset your mother a good bit. Would you pass along my apologies?"

Ras nodded and stood. "If that was Hal, or even the same person that my dad met…do you think they could help *Verdant?*"

"Couldn't hurt to ask," Harley said.

Without a ship, Ras didn't know how he'd be able to make it out to find *The Kingfisher*, let alone fly up to meet it, but opportunities to put things right for *Verdant* weren't exactly jumping into his lap. He'd find a way. Bidding goodbye to Old Harley, Ras turned and left the room to find his mother.

Emma had reached the main entrance of the hospital before Ras caught up with her. She wiped away smudged makeup while Ras kept pace with her short strides.

"I'm not asking you to talk about it," he said.

"I'm fine talking about your father," she said. "It's just some people have very inaccurate information about why he left."

"If he knew *Verdant* was in trouble, why didn't we just move to a city that ran on Helios engines?"

Emma stopped. "Because he didn't know how to quit when it came to helping others."

"Should he have?" Ras asked.

She took a deep breath before shaking her head. "It was one of his better qualities. *Verdant* would have been overrun with sky pirates if he had quit. It's just a shame—" she started, but restrained herself.

"What's a shame?"

"We were going to raise you on *The Silver Fox*…not be tethered to any Helios-built system. It's just a shame that's not how it worked out."

"Why didn't it?"

Emma half-smiled. "There were just some things your father needed to do on his own."

"Like work for Halcyon Napier?" Ras asked.

"I don't know what Harley was talking about. There were a lot of rumors about why your father left, but it wasn't for some long dead war hero."

"Mom?" Ras asked. "I'm sorry I lost the ship."

She embraced him tightly. "I still have you. Forget the ship."

THE FIRST DAY OF COMMUNITY SERVICE in the guts of *Verdant* made it very difficult to simply "forget the ship."

Gone were the clouds, replaced by flickering lights and dank pipes that smelled of stagnation. Ras meandered down the long corridors lined with cables and wires, his boots clanking on the iron grated walkway.

Three engineers passed Ras in a half-jog, ignoring the newcomer.

Leaving the world plastered with newspapers showing his name and photo was a surprisingly welcome respite, even after enduring one morning of walking to his new job.

Bronze signs pointed Ras in the direction of the dimly-lit main office. The eight-walled room consisted of twenty blueprint laden desks and one woman with a mop of curly hair poring over one of the sets. She looked to be in her mid-forties and filled out a jumpsuit that had once been a sky blue but now more resembled a patchwork of grays, greens, and browns with the occasional hint of its original color. The mostly white name patch read "Billie."

"You the new grunt?" Billie asked, not looking up.

Ras mumbled something resembling an affirmation.

"Good, glad they gave me someone with spunk," she said. "C'mon, I'll show you to your station." She began to walk, and Ras followed.

"How long have you worked down here?" Ras asked.

"Well, I was born down here, so you do the math," she said. Ras had heard of some communities that lived within *Verdant*, underneath the top layer. The rumor was they originated from groups that either hated heights or sought seclusion.

"Do you go up top much?"

"Occasionally. My father was a Knack so he was forced to live below ground when *Verdant* launched."

"Forced? I didn't know that."

"Yeah, most people chose to forget that tidbit or didn't pass it on to their kiddos," Billie said. "A few became wind merchants, but the rest wound up here." They took a turn down a corridor that looked exactly the same as the one they left. Ras could already see himself getting hopelessly lost on a regular basis.

"How do you know where you're going?" Ras asked.

"Most people who work down here are children or grandchildren of Knacks, so some of that gets passed down. We can sense where the engines are and how the Energy flows through the city," she said, gesturing to the conduits and valves all around. "Foster Helios designed the cities to give Knacks a special purpose and to keep them safe."

"Because we didn't know how much Energy was above the clouds?"

"No, because everyone hated us for destroying the world. Well, not us...my grandfather's generation. Not that they could help it," she said.

They stopped at a small supply closet. Billie opened it, extracted a mop, bucket, and gas mask, then handed Ras the lot. "Sub-level Four had an oil leak that needs cleaning up after."

"I'm sorry, I thought I was supposed to be working with the engine."

"You are," she said. "Underneath we refer to everything and everyone as 'the engine.' We work together to keep the city flying, no matter what. You up for that?"

Aside from making it onboard *The Kingfisher*, Ras couldn't think of any other way to begin balancing the scale, but this was by far the more practical way to help *Verdant*.

Sub-level Four greeted Ras with an acrid smell that prompted him to immediately slap on the gas mask, which did little to shut out the odor. He saw a dozen other masked workers already cleaning the corridor. "Lunch break is at noon on Sub-level Two," Billie said, the gas mask muffling her voice and forcing Ras to strain in order to hear her. "Did you bring anything?"

Lunch was one of the many small-picture things that had slipped Ras' mind lately. He shook his head, wiggling the mask and distorting his vision.

"There's a cafeteria you can buy something from, but I don't recommend it." She paused. "I have an extra sandwich if you'd like."

The generous offer struck him. "Out of curiosity, do you know why I'm down here?" It was a loaded question, but Ras had grown weary of waiting for the other shoe to drop.

"I do," she said, "Just about everybody does."

"Why are you being so nice?"

Her mask lifted slightly, indicating a smile. "Down here we come from a line of people accused of ending the world by accident…but we're still alive, and I figure we'll still alive after all this gets sorted out," she said. "Of course you'll run into some folk that aren't going to enjoy their job getting harder, but everyone down here appreciates a good second chance. Don't waste it." She placed a hand on Ras' shoulder, then shoved him out of the elevator. "Now, off to work with you."

The morning passed quickly. Nobody spoke to Ras, but he also imagined nobody knew who he was in a jumpsuit and gas mask, so he didn't take it personally. The work was tedious, but necessary, and Ras took a small amount of pride in the part he played.

At noon he left to find his way to Sub-level Two, and after a few errant turns, he found his way to the crowded mess hall, which was filled with long benched tables. Billie sat at one in the corner, and beckoned Ras over before reengaging two men in a spirited debate.

A fiery red haired man in a white lab coat gesticulated wildly with an unlit pipe. "Forget The Collective! If *Verdant* won't fit through the main pass of The Bowl, then all we need are wind merchants willing to collect outside The Bowl to feed her engines!"

"Have you ever been outside The Bowl?" A man with an eye patch and a short military-style haircut spoke with a gruff voice. His dark green jumpsuit held a patch that read "8", and Ras wondered what it meant. "Wind merchants have gotten soft, trolling around…half of them probably couldn't navigate the mountain passes out of here, let alone fend off India Bravo to bring back what little they do find."

"Well, do you have a better idea?" the red-head asked.

Ras sat down on the bench facing the wall next to Billie and she introduced him, "Ras, I'd like you to meet my two best friends: Finn," she said, nodding toward the red-head. "He works in our medical wing."

Finn extended his hand. "Ras."

Ras accepted the handshake and found his hand vigorously shaken twice before release.

"And this gentleman is Guy," she said.

"That's generous," Guy said. The man with the eye patch managed to make a point of not extending his hand, but acknowledged Ras' presence with a nod. "At least you showed up."

Billie slid a wrapped sandwich over to Ras as Finn continued. "Yeah, but the only reason they got soft is because The Collective did the dirty work, fighting the pirates. Thanks to the kid here, they've finally buggered off and we can go back to being self-sustaining."

"We're never going to be self-sustaining with *The Winnower* just sitting there. I mean, I don't remember getting to vote on building a giant dome over the Origin," Guy said.

Ras took another bite of his sandwich, taking in the exchange. He swallowed and said, "What if they took away *The Winnower* and just used it as a refinement plant to bring collected Energy?"

Guy shook his head. "What business would start paying people for what it already gets free? Besides, it's how they fuel their war with the sky pirates. Little fear goes a long way, and most people can still sleep easy in their beds if a few cities fall from the sky as long as they feel like someone is keeping them safe."

"They set themselves up nice," Finn said. "Opposing them means being for the sky pirates." He sighed. "We don't want to rape and pillage, we just don't want to fall from the sky."

"I just want to know," Guy said, jutting a thumb at Ras, "How someone like him flew below the clouds."

"Easy on the new guy," Billie said, shooting Guy a menacing look. "He's been here a whole four hours. We've got six months with him—"

"Chief is saying the city's Energy reserves are only buying us one month if we don't get a new influx," Finn said, inspecting his pipe.

"Then we have a month to get to know him. Maybe we can make it two or three. Maybe more. He's here to help us eke out every ounce of efficiency we can out of the old girl, and that won't happen if we don't work together."

One month, Ras thought. *Wonder if they knew that during sentencing.*

"I'm fine taking my chances on the ground," Finn said, nodding to Ras. "If they're saying there's no more Energy in The Bowl, why not?"

"Yeah, that's great, let's just pretend a Convergence won't come flying by and kill us all. Or maybe you'd like to get torn apart by Remnants!" Guy said, picking up his tray and slamming it on the table before storming off from the bench.

"Don't mind him," Finn said. "He likes you."

"Really?" Ras asked.

"No. I was just trying to be nice."

The rest of the afternoon, Ras made a point of avoiding Guy even though Billie placed him on Guy's maintenance crew. His duty consisted of running any errand for the twenty men and women assigned to the well-being of Engine Eight. When not being sent out, he observed the crew's personal sign language to overcome communication barriers while working around the large, droning beast of an engine that stood at least sixty feet high.

Some signs were easy to understand, like '*wrench,*' and '*break.*' Other's like '*I want you to go to Engine Three and ask for a three-quarters inch thick lead pipe,*' took a lot more work and usually broke down to scribbling on a piece of paper Ras had begged for from Billie during one of his trips. After his fifth trip request to retrieve a specific tool from halfway across *Verdant*, it became apparent his job was to get out of the way for long stretches of time.

Upon returning from his seventh trek, he found an entirely different crew working on Engine Eight. He looked down to his watch and saw his shift had ended twenty minutes prior.

The main office was filled with staff when Ras found it, and he spotted Billie, a handful of curly hair clenched in her hand as she stared at the documents on her desk. Ras stood silent for a few moments, then coughed politely.

"I see you," Billie said, still reading.

"Do I need to sign anything to check out?" Ras asked.

She looked up. The hair she had been holding stuck up at an odd angle. "No, I got you."

Ras nodded and began to turn around, but stopped. "Can I ask why you put me on Guy's team? All I did this afternoon was run around."

"They're just getting you acquainted with the city in their own way," she said, giving a tired smile. "It'll probably be the same tomorrow."

"What does Guy have against me?" Ras asked. "Besides the usual?"

"That's something you'll have to talk with him about." She waved her hand in a dismissive motion. "Shoo. I've got an engine to run. I'll see you first thing tomorrow."

WITH HIS BLUE JUMPSUIT DOFFED and slung over his arm, Ras leaned his weight on the heavy metal door leading back to *Verdant's* streets. The door creaked open, revealing a street lamp lit square populated with one inhabitant: Callie.

He didn't want her to see him like this, but those feelings couldn't override the grin she brought to his face. She even looked cute engulfed by her father's overstuffed brown coat.

"Walk me home?" she asked as if she needed to.

Ras offered his arm before remembering he probably smelled of engine grease and sweat, and hoped Callie wouldn't notice. She graciously accepted and they began their trek to the residential district.

"What brings you out this way?" he asked. He noticed the streetlights were dimmer than usual, which allowed for the stars to make a more prominent appearance in the sky.

"I thought you could use a friend." She walked along the sidewalk in an uneven pace as though following the rhythm of some song in her head. "How was it?"

"Made a few friends, I think," Ras said. "How are things up here?"

Callie shrugged. "Fine if you don't listen to the news reports. Everybody keeps talking about what happened when the city of *Worick* lost their Energy source just after *The Winnower* started up."

"*Worick* sank?" Ras asked.

"No, they bought Helios engines, but it didn't stop the people from panicking and throwing people over the edge hoping they'd overload and make a Convergence," she said.

Ras could feel her shiver and hug his arm tighter. "How sky pirate of them," he said. "I thought Convergences strong enough to support a city were made from tens of thousands of people from The Great Overload."

"Logic wasn't their strongest suit," she said. "At least that's not happening here yet."

He tried not to imagine the citizens of *Verdant* panicking and throwing wind merchants and Engine workers overboard as a last ditch effort. "Does your dad know you're here?"

Her laughter cut through the chill of the night. "I might have mentioned it."

"Might have?"

"I'd give it a five percent chance," Callie said.

"You're trying to get me killed, I hope you know that," Ras said as they turned a corner to walk along one of the main avenues. He took note of a man with a dark, wide-brimmed hat watching them silently from underneath a drugstore stoop.

She slipped her arm out from his crook and stepped up to a raised walkway, playfully balancing with arms extended and keeping pace with Ras. "You still haven't told me what the Convergence was like."

Every time Ras looked back to check on the man with the hat, he was met with a stare. "Ah, how about you tell me about your book first?" he asked. He didn't want his distracted explanation of a Convergence alerting her to the man interested in them.

"You're still going to read it, right?"

"Of course, I'd read it even if it's about an untalented wind merchant named Russ that accidentally crashed his city."

"Oh, come on, you're not untalented," she said, shooting him an accusatory look.

"I'm talking about Russ. Did you think I meant me?" Ras asked, feigning hurt feelings. "Seriously though, I know it's about the train from your dreams, but what's the story?" He looked back to see the man with the hat now walking on the sidewalk twenty feet behind them. He picked up his pace, and was relieved when Callie instinctively quickened her step to match his.

"Well, I'm having to do a lot of research to make sure it's as accurate as possible," she said.

"History piece?"

"Set during The Clockwork War."

"I'm already interested," Ras said, distraction creeping into his voice.

"There's nobody named Russ in it, but I can fix that if you like," she said, hopping down from the ledge. "Anyway, the train is carrying children away from cities that The Elders are bombarding."

"Uh huh," Ras said, checking over his shoulder once more. The man wasn't there. "So where do they go?"

"You'll have to read it," Callie said.

They rounded the corner to the entrance of the residential zone and almost bowled into the man with the hat.

A gray mustache accentuated his gaunt face, and he bore the haughty look of a man accustomed to having authority. His disquietingly blue eyes looked down a long nose at Ras. "Erasmus Veir?"

Ras paused for a moment and gently reached out for Callie's arm. "Can I help you?"

"Yes, yes you can." His tone held a roughness to it. He wrinkled his nose as though Ras offered an offensive odor. "If I could borrow you for a word."

Ras glanced over to Callie and said, "I'm afraid I promised to get her home. Perhaps another time." Ras couldn't imagine a stranger having good news for him and thought it more likely the man would lead him to a waiting lynch mob.

The tall man narrowed his eyes. "I am a patient man, Mr. Veir. I can wait." He stepped aside to let the pair pass.

Ras and Callie took their cue and continued walking, remaining silent until they were well past the man.

"Who—" Callie began.

"I have absolutely no idea."

"Creepy," she said.

"All right, maybe we should take a skiff," Ras said.

"Can't. The city is cracking down on Energy usage. It's not much further." She hugged herself for warmth. "It's kind of thrilling, isn't it? Being followed."

One thing Ras always admired about Callie was her incredibly romantic imagination. The few days Ras had spent cooped up inside his own house led to pure boredom, but somehow Callie never got bored. She read and she wrote, and Ras imagined this moment being an addition to whatever book she was planning on writing next. "I suppose thrilling could describe it. What happens next, oh worker of fiction?" he asked.

"Well, the couple unsuspectingly—"

"Couple?" Ras blurted, wishing desperately to pull the word back.

"...yes, couple. Two people makes a couple. Three makes a few.

What does four make?" She hid well whatever embarrassment Ras caused.

"A crowd, I think."

"Or death, classically."

"Then let's hope Mr. Hat hasn't brought a friend," Ras said.

They glanced over their shoulders to see the man keeping pace with them, not caring about being detected. "Nope, still a few." She resumed walking, "Where was I? Ah, so the couple doesn't suspect that the reason they're being followed is because he has a secret mission for one of them that the other can't know about." She narrowed her wild eyes, reveling in her storytelling.

"You doing spy work on the side?" he asked, arching an eyebrow.

"Wouldn't you like to know?"

"Hah, I knew it."

"What?"

"All your books. They're just secret ciphers you're sending out to The Elders or The Clockworks."

"Same thing," she corrected.

"Hmm…that's something a spy would know."

"Or someone who didn't sleep through history classes," she said.

"Or that," he said, "So what sort of spy job are you getting this time?"

"No clue. I'm not the one he wanted to talk to, remember?"

He did remember, and began to wonder about the old man's reason for pursuing him. They were only a block away from Callie's house and the man still followed them. "Hey, if I'm missing in the morning…"

"I'll put it in my story that you put up a heroic fight, but in the end were no match for an old man."

"Thanks, that's exactly what I was hoping for. Just give me more muscles in the story."

"Your muscles are fine." An awkward moment. "I mean, unless of course you wanted to further the irony," she said.

They made it up to her porch, and Ras turned to see the man across the street, staring. "Maybe if I get to be a spy, your books will start making more sense to me."

She crinkled her nose. "Now you're just being mean," she said, opening the front door. "See you tomorrow?" She rested her head on the door and gazed at him with blue eyes that sparkled in the porch light.

"Wouldn't miss it. You'll have to show me the secret spy handshake." He smiled. "Good night, Calista," he said. He usually called her Callie for the familiarity of it, but he liked the way Calista rolled off the tongue.

"Good night, Erasmus," she said, and gently closed the door.

Ras would have savored the moment more if he hadn't felt the bore of the man's stare on the back of his neck. He turned around to address his stalker only to see an empty sidewalk.

CHAPTER FOUR
The Engine

CLUTCHING HIS SACK LUNCH, RAS CLOSED THE FRONT DOOR TO HIS home. He eyed the horizon for any men with wide-brimmed hats, but failed to find anyone walking along the streets.

Checking his watch, Ras saw he had a very small margin to stop at his favorite basement window before the morning shift began. He stepped off his porch step toward the Tourbillon home, and a deep voice from the neighboring front porch made him jump.

"The Engine's the other way, if I recall," Mr. Tourbillon said, setting a newspaper neatly in his lap as he continued to rock in his chair.

Ras looked over his shoulder as an excuse to not have to talk over the rush of his thumping heart. "So it is. I just thought—"

"While I've appreciated that you've finally begun thinking, I'd recommend none of those thoughts correlate with my daughter," he said before pulling up a mug of coffee and taking a long sip.

Ras glanced toward the window. He saw a bit of motion, but nothing he could focus on without earning further ire from Mr. Tourbillon. "I was trying to help *Verdant*."

"I remember you saying so during the trial," he said, unblinking. The infrequency with which the man blinked disquieted Ras. "It's a shame intention didn't stack up with reality."

The front door opened, and Mrs. Tourbillon stepped out with an unmarked wooden box. She stared at Ras as she set the box on the chair next to her husband. "Erasmus."

"Ma'am," Ras said. Mrs. Tourbillon usually treated Ras with more warmth than her husband, but not today.

She turned to Mr. Tourbillon. "We're going to need at least a dozen more of these for the odds and ends."

"I'll see what's left at the office today," Mr. Tourbillon said, "We'll probably have to unload the boxes we have on the ship and reuse them."

"You're moving?" Ras blurted.

Mr. Tourbillon sighed, otherwise leaving Ras' inquest unaddressed. "I'll be in to help in a moment." He watched his wife collect his empty coffee mug and return into their home.

"But you can't leave," Ras said. He opened his mouth again but couldn't come up with any particular reason for them to stay.

"The other cities are going to grow rather crowded with *Verdant* refugees. I intend to not embarrass my family by being one of the last ones to realize help isn't coming."

"But the University—"

"My daughter will have her pick of Universities that remain above the clouds." Mr. Tourbillon stood and looked at his watch. "We're leaving tomorrow," he said, opening the door and crossing the threshold. "I'll make sure Calista says goodbye."

Ras jerked slightly at the sound of the closing door. He knew the arranged good-bye was primarily for Mr. Tourbillon's sake. Picking up into a jog toward the Engine, he lost himself in considering which words were appropriate when seeing someone for the last time. The circumstances of every other person previously snatched away from him didn't allow for such planning, which felt merciful now with the dull ache growing in the pit of his stomach.

Would telling her how I feel about her be selfish? He couldn't offer her anything but a sinking city, and wasn't even certain what would happen to his mother if the city ran out of its reserve Energy.

The jog turned into a run when Ras came to the populated market square, but even lessening his time around others didn't leave him unscathed by passing curses. He knew they felt helpless because of him, and he couldn't entirely fault them for their unkindness.

By the time he reached the main entrance to the Engine, he glistened with sweat. Even with the extra effort, he reached Billie's office a few minutes late.

"Sign," Billie said, handing Ras the clipboard and a clean jumpsuit. She looked Ras over, noticing his clothes sticking to him and sweat matting his hair. "You sick, boy?"

"It's not contagious," Ras said, avoiding Billie's gaze by looking for his name in the list. The number next to his name indicated he was already clocked in half an hour early. "It says I got here—"

"I said I only needed your signature."

"Thanks," Ras said. He dangled the brown bag. "Where should I...?"

"Oh, smart boy. Leave it with me. Volunteers don't get lockers," Billie said. The charitable way she said 'volunteer' struck Ras oddly.

"Hey, Billie?" Ras slipped his feet into the legs of his jumpsuit. "What are people in the Engine going to do when...*if* the Energy reserves run out? Some people on the surface are already leaving." He slid his arms in and fastened the buttons up the front of his uniform.

"Don't rightly know," she said. "We've been promised several airships to ferry us away if it comes to that, but they'll be hard pressed to find anyone willing to board."

Ras furrowed his brow. "How's that?"

Billie shrugged indifferently. "If some of us leave, it makes it harder for the rest of us. The old girl needs a lot of love after decades of making do with patchwork repairs and a distinct lack of replacement parts."

"Nobody's drawn straws to be on a skeleton crew?" Ras asked.

Billie's chuckle lacked amusement. "Hon, we *are* the skeleton crew."

Verdant shuddered with a groan and the room tilted slightly. Billie reached out to keep the paperwork on her desk from sliding away, then pulled a small wooden ball from a pocket and placed it atop her desk. It rolled toward the wall marked with a large "8" etched onto a single tile. She shot a look to Ras.

THE SCRAPING OF THE ELEVATOR against the metal of the angled shaft made Ras' skin crawl. By the time he arrived at Engine Eight, some of the crew were fighting a losing battle with a hissing pipe. He donned his goggles out of habit.

About fifteen workers hung back, watching a smaller crew, led by Guy, attempt to seal off the spewing pipe. The team became harder to spot as the haze filled the corridor.

One of the workers, a blonde woman maybe a few years older than Ras, gestured something rude until he remembered seeing it used the previous day as a sign for an inquiry.

"What's going on?" Ras shouted, barely able to hear his own words.

She shook her head, then pointed to the balled up bit of wax stuffed in her ear. Pointing to a pipe running along the wall, she then traced it down the corridor. Turning back to Ras, she brought two fists together before snapping them away in opposite directions.

Broken.

"Where's the shut-off valve?" Ras asked, then waved his arms dismissively. He couldn't follow her series of more intricate gestures and turned his attention to two workers moving toward Ras, each with the arm of a third, badly burned cohort around their necks.

An explosion of steam shot out from the pipe, filling the corridor with a dense fog. The crowd disassembled, running away and knocking into Ras in the process.

They're Knacks, Ras realized. He slid through the retreating group and pelted down the metal walkway into the oppressive heat. The steam spurted in arrhythmic fits around the edges of the unsealed metal patches, and Ras found himself barely able to see in front of him. The thick air forced him to choke out a cough.

"Hello!" Ras called out to no response. He continued his jog only to tangle his feet in the arms and legs of downed workers. The fall brought him crashing to the grated floor. He mumbled an apology before realizing the ground remained cooler than the air above, but its temperature still rose.

The idea of dragging these men to safety crossed his mind, but with the Energy filtering in through the cracked pipe, he might only save one or two before the rest died. He needed to cut it off.

Crawling forward, his hand reached the ankle of a man still standing. Ras hauled himself up into the boiling temperature to see Guy torquing a wrench around a clamp in pure defiance.

"What are you doing here?" Guy shouted. "Get out! There's too much Energy spilled!"

"Where's the shut-off valve?"

"Further down, but don't you dare go down there—"

Ras bolted further down the corridor, hunching low and losing the shouts of Guy in the hisses of steam. He reasoned if a Convergence didn't kill him, some leaked Energy wouldn't be a challenge.

However, the heat remained an issue.

He didn't know how long the corridor went, but running seemed a better idea than taking his time crawling along the ground. With each footfall his heart pounded and blackness ebbed in the corners of his vision. He panted, but gulping the hot air only made matters worse. He followed the pipes along the walls, the spurts of steam shrinking in volume as he continued his dash through the fog.

His hip struck something, sending his balance off-kilter. Reaching his hands out to break his fall, his right arm hooked through a large metal wheel and caught at the crook of his elbow.

Taking long, slow breaths, Ras eyed the three-foot wide metal wheel. It burned against his arm, forcing him to quickly extricate himself from it and he wished he had a pair of thick gloves. Unfastening the top of his jumpsuit, he pulled his undershirt off and wrapped it hastily around both hands before hauling on the large wheel.

The metal burned but didn't sear his hands as it protested against his tugging. Another heave gave a promising creak, but he didn't know how many more tugs his body would allow as sweat poured.

"C'mon!" he shouted at the machinery the way he'd chastise his ship on days it wouldn't behave. He brought a booted foot onto one of the spokes and leveraged his weight against the device. It groaned in protest but began its slow motion to the right even as it sent a blast of steam into Ras' face. He tried to cry out in shock only to find his voice stolen by the searing heat.

He continued the process, hand over burning hand, until the cessation of the hiss down the corridor alerted him that he had done enough. Slumping to the ground didn't bring the relief from the temperature, as the metal grating itself had heated considerably.

The state of exhaustion only allowed Ras to shamble toward where he had left Guy. If anybody were to come looking for bodies, he needed at least to make it back to the men attempting to seal the pipe before passing out. His heart, working overtime, thumped in his ears as he forced himself onward.

"Ras!" a voice shouted out. "Where is he?"

"Ran off. Steam probably got him," Guy's voice said before coughing.

Ras tried to speak, but his throat wouldn't obey. He almost raised his hand until he realized he wouldn't even be able to see it himself once fully extended.

His legs wouldn't carry him any further. His body fell to the hot metal grating, and rolled to his side, unable to catch his breath. Pulling his goggles off brought stinging tears to his eyes. He slammed them against the metal floor, then repeated the motion until he established an erratic rhythm.

"You hear that?"

"Probably the pipes settling."

Don't write me off! Ras thought, letting out a faint rasp in place of a scream. He continued the tapping until he heard one of the goggle lenses smash and clatter.

In desperation, he threw the goggles into the fog and rolled to lie on his back. If he was going to cook, it would at least be evenly.

Gasping for breath, Ras found himself moving as two pairs of hands grabbed him by his shoulders and began hauling him away. He mouthed a silent thanks as a third person took up his legs.

Ras gave a weak smile before his head lolled back to see the path before him bobbing upside down. He avoided succumbing to motion sickness by focusing on the pain at hand. Burns would heal, but not being able to say goodbye to Callie hurt far worse.

The dimly lit medical station for *Verdant's* Engine was a relief for Ras. The men cautiously deposited him onto one of the propped up mattresses, and all Ras wanted was to slip away from the waking world.

"Trying to get out of community service early?" a raspy voice asked.

Ras opened his eyes and looked at the bed to his left to see Guy sitting on the edge of the next bed over, staring back.

Finn re-entered the room, carrying an unconscious man with the help of a couple other Engine men. "Oh, come off it," he said to Guy. "I'd be a lot busier if it weren't for him." He walked to Ras' bed and looked the young man over. "What is that, your shirt?" he asked, tapping on the cloth still wrapped around both of Ras' hands.

Ras nodded, offering up his hands to let Finn gently unravel the cloth, revealing a set of freshly pink palms.

"That's not so bad. Let me get a salve for that," Finn said, striding away to a cabinet across the room. "Try not to move them."

"I told you not to go down there," Guy said, barely masking his agitation. "That should have killed you is what it should have done."

Attempting to speak brought little more than a faint squawk from Ras, then a frustrated sigh. He made a motion to his throat.

"Hey Finn, we got a steam swallower," Guy said.

Finn returned with a brass jar of pale green ointment. "I do suppose he wouldn't have learned when to keep his mouth shut from you," he said with some satisfaction, not looking at Guy. "You should get your voice back when the swelling in your throat goes down." Dipping two fingers into the salve, he began slathering it onto Ras' palms.

The sting gave way to a numbing sensation that tingled slightly. Ras nodded his thanks.

"What's this I hear about you sending him to shut off the valve?" A new, angry voice entered the room before Billie did.

A rare flash of fear played across Guy's face as he began his defense with hands outstretched. "The kid wouldn't listen. You know I know protocol, woman."

"He saved your life," Billie said, storming into the room.

Finn leaned in toward Ras and whispered, "Lesson number one: don't make mother mad."

"We wouldn't need to use the pipes from the Energy reserves if it weren't for him," Guy said. "We've never had to use them before, and you can bet we're going to have outbursts like that all across this city sooner or later, if we even get a 'later.'"

"I specifically told you to watch out for him," Billie said.

"It's not my fault he thinks he's Energy-proof," Guy said.

"He may just well be," Finn said, looking over Ras. "These are just steam burns. I'm not seeing any signs of Energy poisoning."

Ras furrowed his brow, giving a confused look.

"All right," Finn began. "As best as the medical world understands, everyone succumbs to Energy overloading, it's just a matter of threshold."

"He'd make a good sky pirate," Guy said.

"You're not a part of this conversation," Billie said. A stern look ensured he didn't protest the new rule.

Ras mouthed the word '*pirate*.' He knew the most feared pirates were the ones composed of crew members that were less likely to succumb to Energy. Initiation into certain crews was rumored to involve taking a cheap jetcycle beneath the clouds, and the longer one could last, the higher the share of the haul they garnered.

"Well, even the most resistant shipman will come back with at least some Energy poisoning," Finn said, unraveling some gauze to wrap Ras' hands. "Usually causes an ashen skin tone, but you're about as hale and hearty looking as someone who locked themselves in a sauna overnight."

"Is he going to be all right?" Billie asked.

"He's a little cooked. Hydration and rest should do the trick," Finn said, continuing to wrap Ras' hands. "I'll check on these later."

"What about him?" Billie nodded back at Guy.

"Aside from a lungful of hot air, he's fine. He's just making sure the kid is all right."

Guy growled his disapproval of Finn's assessment before exiting.

"He's lucky Ras was there, he just won't admit it," Finn said to Billie.

Billie pulled up a chair next to Ras' bed. "If you hadn't contained the leak when you did, we might have lost a week's worth of reserves. As it is, we only lost a day or two."

Ras made an approximation of a writing motion to Finn.

Finn looked hesitant. "You really should let your hands rest."

"How is he supposed to communicate?" Billie asked, receiving an appreciative nod from Ras.

"Blinking," Finn said with a chuckle until he realized nobody else found humor in the suggestion. "C'mon, it's not like we couldn't use a bit of levity." He pulled a pen from his lab coat and flipped his notebook of heavily recycled paper to a clean page. "Knock yourself out, but no complaining if your hands keep hurting, you hear?"

Ras accepted his new tools for communication gratefully. The writing was clumsy, and his penmanship was never terribly good to begin with, but with the pen wedged between his thumb and palm, he wrote '*Thank you*' in broad strokes.

"Don't mention it," Finn said with a grin. "I'll check back after my rounds, but don't be surprised if Guy sends someone after you if you aren't back on your shift in half an hour."

Billie watched Finn attend to a patient a few beds down and reclined a bit in her chair. "You know you don't have to be your father, right?" She waited for Ras to begin writing, but after a moment decided to continue. "Is that why you ran into the Energy?"

Ras considered it for a moment. He hadn't thought much about the ramifications or what motives might be assumed of him for his actions. He shook his head.

"Good," Billie said. "No sense in getting yourself killed trying to be him. Nobody expects it of you."

He wrote '*Shouldn't expect impossible*,' and showed the pad to Billie before resting his head on the pillow and staring at the ceiling.

"Hey, look at me," she said with an intensity that surprised Ras. "We don't have time to feel sorry for ourselves, so I don't want to see that out of you. People would have died if you weren't at Eight today. Just keep doing what you can, and I'll do the same." Billie stood, surveyed the wounded, then exited.

Ras clumsily flipped the paper over to a clean sheet and began drumming up everything he wished he had said to Callie. He hated that the letter she would have to remember him by would look like a child wrote it.

The blank page stared at him. He didn't know where to begin. He wasn't even entirely sure of the goal of the letter.

A new visitor entered the room and made a direct line for Ras' bed. The blonde girl from Eight stood expectantly at the foot of his bed. "Guy wants me to make sure you—how did he put it—make yourself less useless while you're resting."

Of course he does, Ras thought. He began writing a response before the girl waved to grab his attention.

She held her hand up to her forehead and saluted. Then she placed her hand flat over her chest and moved on to some intricate gestures that Ras couldn't follow. "Hello, my name is Kiria," she said, translating.

With his mitt of a hand, Ras saluted back. He at least knew how to greet someone with sign language.

"Good. Welcome to the rest of your day," Kiria said, signing along with her spoken words. She walked over and sat in the chair Billie left. "We'll focus on what you need to know to do your job on Eight, but if we have time we'll move on to other things."

Kiria began her lesson with the alphabet, which she quickly abandoned after it became apparent Ras couldn't learn them without replicating the shapes with his own hands.

Ras imagined Guy particularly enjoying the irony, but he quickly learned how to signal if he understood the sign or needed a repetition. After a couple hours of moving through basic conversation and engine parts, it became obvious he was giving the lessons his minimal attention.

"You do understand you can kill someone if you don't follow signed orders correctly," she said.

Sorry, Ras signed. It was a simple enough gesture and one he knew he'd need to learn early on. *Again?*

"What's the sign for '*hungry?*'" Finn asked, returning from his rounds.

Kiria turned and demonstrated by making a cupped hand that ran from her throat to her stomach.

"What about '*I'm hungry?*'" Finn asked.

She pointed to herself and repeated the previous motion.

"Good. Me too. Care to join us for lunch?"

Kiria blushed a little bit, and began signing a response before she caught herself. "I'm supposed to stay with Ras."

Finn rocked on his heels. "I wasn't using a royal 'us.' I was planning on stealing your star pupil here."

With Kiria's back turned, Ras offered a signed *thanks* to Finn, who simply replied with a wink.

Kiria turned to see what Ras did to prompt the wink, which allowed Finn a little celebration dance that made Ras grin. She signed, *what?*

He happy, Ras signed.

Why?

Ras thought for a moment how to craft a response with his limited vocabulary. *You fuel his engine.*

A grin spread across her face as she stood to leave the infirmary.

"Hold on, what are you telling her?" Finn asked.

"I'll see you both in the mess hall," Kiria said before slipping through the doorway.

"You should know the medic-patient relationship requires a lot of trust both ways," Finn said.

You welcome, Ras signed.

MUCH TO FINN'S DISMAY, his lunch date with Kiria turned into another sign language lesson for Ras, even with the absence of Guy and Billie.

Why sign here? Ras asked. *People talk here. No engine.*

"You need practice," she said.

I need... he signed, then looked down at the empty space on the table before him and mimicked a chewing motion, pointing to his mouth.

"Food," she said, displaying the far more elegant and more correct version of the sign. "Did you not bring anything?"

No. She has it. Ras didn't know how to sign Billie's name or even if Kiria knew Billie.

"Who is 'she?'" Kiria asked.

Ras looked over to Finn for help. He moved his hands in circles to indicate Billie's curly hair.

"I think he's talking about a crazy lady," Finn said, eliciting a glare from Ras. "Am I not being helpful? I feel like I'm not being helpful."

"Billie," Ras croaked out in a soft whisper that made his throat itch and sting. Being able to finally produce a sound was an improvement upon the morning.

"Oh, Billie!" Finn said. Then he lowered his voice and shook his head in mock chastisement. "Billie's not crazy. Be nice."

"I think Billie has his lunch," Kiria said.

"You want to go to Billie's office?" Finn asked. It was more of a suggestion than a question. He turned to Kiria. "He'll be right back."

"That's fine," she said.

Ras stood, nodded to Kiria, and tried not to laugh at Finn, who drew his hands apart in a wide motion. *Take as long as you can.*

Leaving the mess hall, he noticed a dozen workers from Eight meandering in, but no sign of Guy. A few men nodded to him with a bit less malice than before, which encouraged Ras a little. He hoped the story of the valve would spread around the Engine, but couldn't imagine one event swaying popular opinion.

Using a shortcut he had accidentally discovered on one of his previous fool's errands, Ras made his way through a dark passageway leading to the main office.

Billie sat at her desk, studying reports. She looked up as Ras entered. "Oh, sorry. After the pipe blew it's been nothing but paperwork. How's the throat?"

"Fine," Ras squawked. "I barely—"

"Stop. It hurts just hearing you," she said. "Lunch is on the cabinet."

Thanks, Ras signed.

The radio on Billie's desk burst into static cacophony that settled on a man's voice. "Mayday! Mayday! This is Thomas Carnes of *The Cirrus*. India Bravo has returned! I repeat, India Bravo has returned. Bravo Company is heading toward *Verdant* and—No!" The transmission cut off sharply, leaving the room silent.

The handful of men and women that hadn't left for lunch yet all stared at each other for a moment before Billie spoke. "They transmitted to the wrong channel. That should have gone to the capitol building." She looked about at the others in the room. "I don't know where else that was sent, but for now that information does not leave this room, everyone clear on that?" She turned back to look at Ras. "We need to verify its origin, and we don't need to panic everyone."

"I have the message transcribed," a balding man several desks down said, lifting a sheet of paper in the air.

"Eric, relay the message to the capitol," Billie said, pointing to the balding man. "Ramsey, radio port authority and verify *The Cirrus* and have them look up Thomas Carnes to see if he is a member of the crew." The office buzzed with activity.

"Ma'am, I don't need to verify," Ramsey said through a clenched jaw as though releasing the tension would cause him to fall to pieces. "Thomas is…was my brother-in-law. I'm sure he knew I'd pass it along."

Ras froze. If Bravo Company was coming, then the Tourbillons' move would be a day late. Without further thought, Ras dashed toward the exit with sack lunch in hand, ignoring the protests from Billie.

Running crew members weren't entirely out of place in the Engine, but twice he had to hold up his sack lunch to security officers, feigning an important delivery.

Once up top, the bright sun momentarily blinded him as he attempted to survey the skies for sky pirate ships. Not wanting to waste time letting his eyes adjust, Ras took off toward the residential zone.

The people he passed looked as though they hadn't heard any news of impending doom yet, which relieved Ras, but if one ship ran afoul of the inbound fleet, then surely more broadcasts would soon come.

Halfway to his goal, Ras felt the effects of the dehydration start to kick in. His legs felt sluggish and his swollen throat made sucking in air nearly impossible, but he couldn't give up now if it determined Callie being around when Bravo Company inevitably bombarded *Verdant*.

As he continued his run, his mind flitted to his mother. He didn't know how he would convince Mr. Tourbillon, but he needed to get Emma on their ship. Ras was the only family she had left.

All plans immediately dissipated when he saw what was parked in the middle of the street directly in front of the Tourbillon home.

The gleaming white vessel with silver accents looked like a hybrid between a giant skiff and an airship without a balloon. Its wingspan reached easily across both sides of the road and Ras guessed it used the flat surface as a runway. The elegant design reminded Ras of *The Kingfisher*, but on a much smaller scale.

Most ships in Atmo were based primarily off their sea-faring forefathers, but this ship's cabin was fully enclosed. The entire cockpit lacked any hard edges, making the machine look like its designer was inspired by a cloud.

Shouts snapped Ras' attention away from the vessel. Mrs. Tourbillon stood on her porch, engaged in a loud argument with a man on the other side of the threshold. The man held a wide-brimmed hat in front of him, gesturing occasionally and speaking in low tones that didn't travel far.

Ras changed course, walking on the other side of his house and back around behind to avoid detection. From behind his house, he could spot Callie's window and cautiously made his way over to the side of their house.

He peered inside to see Callie with her hair tied back, halfway through boxing up her bookshelves. He eased himself down to his hands and knees before rapping gently on the window.

Callie looked over, giving a brief, but sad smile at the sight of Ras before walking over to unlatch her basement window. "Daddy said he talked to you this morning—what happened to your hands?"

Ras waved away her concern, then whispered in a husky voice that scratched with every syllable. "Pirates. Coming. Today."

Her eyes grew wide. "What? Why haven't they sounded the alarm?"

"You have to go, now," Ras said. No other five words had ever caused him more pain. This was not how he imagined their last meeting.

Callie turned and ran across the room before disappearing up the stairs. The argument in front of the house ended abruptly and Callie came tearing around the corner as Ras stood. She threw her arms around his neck as she bowled into him. "I don't want to leave."

Ras watched the man with the hat as Mrs. Tourbillon came to the edge of the house and just stared at them. He was grateful that Mr. Tourbillon wasn't present. "It'll be okay," he said, unsure what that even meant anymore. "Where are you moving?"

"We don't know yet. Maybe *Kenus*, maybe *Derailleur*," Callie said.

"We're not going anywhere until your father gets here," Mrs. Tourbillon said.

"Nobody is going anywhere," the man with the hat said. "Not unless they're leaving in that thing." He pointed a long finger back at the vehicle in the road. "The sky pirates will attack anyone trying to flee *Verdant*, and almost certainly have forces at the entrance to The Bowl."

Callie released her grip around Ras' neck. "Where is it going?"

"Nowhere," Mrs. Tourbillon blurted, narrowing her eyes at the man with the hat. "Nowhere with us on it. Callie, I need you to keep packing. We might have to leave as soon as your father gets home."

"Mom, who is this?" Callie asked.

"An old acquaintance trying to call in a favor larger than he deserves," she said.

Callie turned back to Ras. "Promise me I'll see you again before I leave," she said, anger welling. "You still owe me a critique on those chapters."

Ras nodded, and watched her walk slowly back to her mother. The two women disappeared back around the corner, leaving him alone with the mysterious white-haired man.

"If I could borrow you for a word," he said, imitating the tone from their previous meeting.

Ras walked toward the man. "What do you want, Mr...."

"My name is hardly of consequence, Mr. Veir. It comes to my employer's attention that you appear to have…dug yourself a hole of a certain depth from which you cannot escape unassisted," he said as though the phrase were one he had heard spoken but had not understood himself. "Am I correct?"

"Everyone's employers know that."

"That may be the case, but not everyone's employers can offer you assistance like mine can."

"Is his name of consequence?" Ras asked.

"Oh, of the highest." He smiled broadly, stretching the mustache wide across his face. He slid his hat on easily and said, "Mr. Halcyon Napier has asked me to gauge your level of interest in saving *Verdant*."

Chapter Five
The Kingfisher

THE SMALL VESSEL'S INTERIOR CONSISTED OF LITTLE MORE THAN A pilot's seat and an upholstered bench with restraints for three passengers. Ras found himself absentmindedly running his padded hand over the impeccable workmanship of the silver trim set in a sparkling white pearlescent material. The instrumentation gave off a purple hued glow.

"So," Ras said, finally breaking the silence. "You fly on *The Kingfisher*. The *Kingfisher*."

"Is there another one I should be aware of?" the man inquired, genuinely interested. He flicked three switches to engage the engines. The sudden noise caused Ras to jump.

"Uh, no," Ras said, fumbling to secure his restraint and readying himself to be shoved back into his seat. "It's just said to be a ghost ship."

"That's very…interesting to hear. Brace yourself." He pulled a lever and a steering wheel telescoped from the dashboard to meet his hands. He tilted the controls back and pressed a button on the console. With an explosive hiss, the ship shot directly upward.

Having prepared for a launch forward, Ras nearly slipped out of his seat but for his restraint. He didn't recall seeing any rotors atop the ship, and as the vessel reached its apex and began to drop, he realized it didn't have any.

The man pulled back a lever and the ship rocketed forward, slamming Ras back into his seat. The back of his head smacked into the high padded back of the bench. He guessed it was an intentional feature.

"And so your employer is Hal Napier...the Fourth?" Ras asked, trying to be casual as he watched *Verdant* zip beneath them at a rate he found both exhilarating and terrifying.

"No."

"Fifth?"

"No," he said more sharply this time. "And may I suggest you refrain from that line of questioning when you meet him. If you would like something for your throat I can prepare a tonic once we've reached our cruising altitude."

"That...that would be nice," Ras said. "Thank you."

Through the wide, curved windshield, Ras could see the grand vista of clouds, including dozens of airships racing toward them. Ras recognized them as standard merchantmen moving at a much quicker pace than usual.

The man pulled the ship into a climb to avoid colliding with any of the merchant vessels, giving him perspective on what caused the wind merchants to flee.

Bravo Company.

Their flagship, *The Dauntless*, was an old dreadnaught from The Clockwork War, body corroded black and rigid balloon painted red with a crude rendering of crossed axes and a grinning skull. The ship itself was nearly a mile long, and bristling with guns.

A score of smaller airships and biplanes with the same logo emblazoned across their hulls accompanied *The Dauntless*, idly chasing and firing their weapons at the slower wind merchant vessels as they neared the floating city.

"How is Hal going to save *Verdant* from India Bravo?" Ras asked.

"He has his ways," the man casually said. "But *Verdant* is too valuable to her to sink."

"How are *you* going to save *us* from India Bravo?"

The man hefted back on the controls, gaining altitude until the fleet below became tiny specks.

Ras' ears popped as he looked out the window, then recoiled back. He had never been up this high, and wondered if a cannonball could even reach them. "How?"

"I pulled back on the controls. I thought you of all people would be familiar with flight mechanics," the man said before leveling off after a minute of hard climbing. He unfastened his restraints and stood, nearly grazing his white hair against the ceiling. "Tonic?" He reached into a small box and pulled out a glass bottle with a screw-on cap. The label was in an unfamiliar language.

Ras turned his attention from the window to his bandaged hand as the man pressed the bottle into his mitt. The idea of actually meeting the man his father had told bedtime stories about boggled his mind. He wasn't certain what he was going to see or if this Hal was an impostor, but it occurred to Ras that whoever this was it might be the same person that his father had claimed to have received a mission from, if Old Harley had heard his rumors right.

There was little to nothing he could do for *Verdant* right now, aside from helping out in the Engine for damage control. A twinge of guilt gnawed at him, but he forced it to the back of his mind by telling himself he would do more good by meeting with Hal. He just wished he could explain his actions without being deemed insane.

He undid the bandages on his hands before unscrewing the bottle cap to take a swig of the burning liquid. His eyes watered and throat tingled, prompting a cough. After pounding his chest with his fist to drive away the tickling sensation, Ras managed to croak, "You wouldn't happen to remember a man named—"

"Elias Veir?" The man let the moment sink in. "I had wondered when you were going to ask that."

"But—"

"Who else were you going to ask me about, honestly?" He flipped a lever and spoke into the comm unit in a foreign language before receiving a confirmation. "Yes, I knew your father for a brief time. You are sitting where he did when I ferried him to Mr. Napier." He pulled back once more, forcing the ship to climb, deepening the sinking feeling in Ras' stomach. "Ah, here we are."

Ahead gleamed the white ship Ras recognized from the brief glimpse in Framer's Valley. *The Kingfisher.*

In what seemed to be no time, the shuttle made a landing—no, a rejoining—with *The Kingfisher*, becoming one with the larger vessel. After a surprising snap-hiss that made Ras' ears pop again, the airtight seal sent wind rushing in to fill the cabin, and a light purple glow emanated from the ship.

"Mr. Veir, if you would be so kind as to follow me," the man said.

Ras obliged and stood, stretching his legs. He walked from the shuttle to the corridor lined with a half-dozen rooms on either side of the hallway. Between the doors hung artwork of landscapes, ranging from crude to masterfully done. Clouds, mountain peaks, plains, bodies of water...Ras had to make sure not to linger on the pre-Atmo artwork. Callie would have loved it, but the thought of her staying on *Verdant* drained any joy from the thought of him describing the paintings to her.

They came to a door at the end of the corridor. "Mr. Napier awaits," he said, bowing slightly as he pulled the door open for Ras. The circular study was filled with books, models of airships, and a very impressive telescope that cut through the center of a domed ceiling. Glass walls flooded the room with sunshine.

In the center stood a man looking to be in his early sixties. He hunched over a painting on an easel, scrutinizing the brush strokes, applying a few more. He wore a dark brown smoking jacket and had a neatly trimmed white beard that continued into a short haircut for a matching set.

"Mr. Napier," the man guiding Ras said, announcing his presence. "May I present to you Mr. Erasmus Veir."

Halcyon Napier looked up from his painting, standing to a height at least a head taller than Ras. He appeared as virile as a man in his forties. He smiled and leisurely strode over to Ras with his hand extended.

"About time," he said, grabbing Ras's half-extended arm and giving his hand two firm pumps, forcing Ras to contain a grimace. He motioned to a couple of wing-backed chairs next to the easel. "Come, please have a seat." He turned to the man with the hat. "Thank you, Dayus. You may retire until I have need of you."

"Very good, sir." With that, Dayus left the room.

Ras sat uneasily in the leather chair. It creaked loudly but was the softest leather he had ever felt, considering there hadn't been an easily ready supply in a century.

Hal sat across from him, then leaned forward. For a few moments he studied Ras from head to toe. "You got big," he said.

That phrase always confounded Ras. One summer when he was thirteen he had shot up six inches, but hadn't grown at all since, yet people throughout his teenage years kept asking how much he had grown recently. All that aside, it was a peculiar conversation starter, and Ras had no clue how to respond.

"Your father showed me a picture of you ten years ago."

"*Verdant* is under attack," Ras said. "Right now." The clarity in his voice surprised him. The tonic had done more than he expected.

Hal's disposition slid from welcoming to grave. "I am aware."

Ras turned and pointed to the door Dayus had exited. "He said you could do something."

"Straight to business. I can appreciate that," Hal said with a nod.

Ras studied Hal's response. Whomever sat in front of him definitely resembled the pictures of Hal Napier from the history books. "Dayus," Ras said as though trying out the name, "also mentioned there was a way to save *Verdant*."

"That's an entirely different type of saving, but we'll get to that, don't you worry." He leaned over to a side table and picked up a newspaper with a photo of Ras on the courthouse steps with the words "I'M SO SORRY" in dark, bold print, as if Ras needed a reminder. "I am told you are neighbors with the Tourbillons. How are they?"

Ras shot up from his chair. "Sir, with all due respect, people are dying out there and you're trying to make small talk."

"The talk I make is never small," Hal said. "Now, please, sit. I've already put in a call to The Collective to put a stop to it."

"You can do that?" Ras asked, his frustration allayed for the moment. The Collective's absence from The Bowl made him wonder how long it would take for them to arrive, and how much damage *Verdant* would suffer in the meantime.

"Indirectly." A shallow grin crept across his lips. "*Verdant* is not without its defenses either. She will survive this." He waited for Ras to sit before he continued. "Now, the Tourbillons."

"They're on *Verdant*, how good can they be right now?" Ras shrugged. "How do you know them?"

Hal rose from his chair and began walking toward one of his book displays. "Would you care to wager a guess as to why I'm in *Verdant*?"

Ras thought for a moment. "Because *The Kingfisher* has a scoop engine and got stuck after I killed the last source of Energy in the area?"

Hal laughed. "That's a good guess, but no. Let me simply say that I'm always looking for a good man, and you've captured my attention."

"What specifically are you looking for?"

"Redemption," he said, then after a pause, "for you." He picked up a book from the shelf, idly flipped through its brittle pages, then tossed it back onto a desk. "For me, I'm looking for a properly motivated wind merchant with enough grit to retrieve what I need. For a great reward."

Ras cocked an eyebrow.

"You should probably hear what I need before you fill your head with possibilities." His voice darkened, yet remained kind. "Erasmus, have you ever traveled outside of The Bowl?"

"Once when I was little."

"Then you should well understand that there is a big world out there with many things that defy one's understanding; that can challenge a way one believes the world to run."

"Like magic?" Ras asked.

"No, not like magic. Well, yes, *like* magic, in that you don't understand it, but not magic. If you'd like, you may now ask the obvious question you've been holding in," Hal said casually.

"How are you still alive?"

"*How are you still alive?* An excellent question and one that should indeed be asked. The short answer is that *The Kingfisher* keeps me alive." He paused. "Well, that's not entirely true. It helps, though." Hal appeared to lose himself in thought for a moment. "I was born one-hundred and sixty-four years ago, if that sets the stage."

Ras let out an inadvertent laugh. "I'm sorry, I just have a hard time believing that."

"Your belief does not determine the truth of me," Hal said, stifling any pithy response from Ras. "Your father also had difficulty believing everything, but he believed in what I offered."

"Which was?"

"A solution," Hal said. "Very similar to the solution you are after for your problem. Out of curiosity, how did you destroy the Convergence?"

"I collected it with my ship," Ras said.

"Simple as that?" Hal asked, snapping his fingers.

"I think so. Why?"

"It's poetic, is all," Hal said. "What I need is a full tank of wind."

Ras chose not to go into bothersome details like his ship being sold for scrap. "Why do I sense this wind isn't easy to track?"

"Oh, it's not going anywhere," Hal said. "But getting to it is the challenge. Are you familiar with The Wild?"

"Nobody is familiar with The Wild. Not since The Clockwork War, and I doubt anyone was even before that," Ras said. "I heard all of the mountain passes into it were collapsed after the war."

"I do remember mentioning it being a challenge. I wouldn't offer to save *Verdant* for a menial task," Hal said. "I need a full tank of air from a very specific set of coordinates within the borders of The Wild to filter into this ship. My last batch is…running thin."

Ras suddenly became aware of his breathing. He wished he could feel the difference from breathing air from The Wild, as though whatever medicinal properties it contained could be sensed and described.

"If you're wondering, this isn't going to make you live forever," Hal said, swirling a hand to mimic a current. "It doesn't work like that. Besides, the air in here has been recycled far too many times."

"But you sealed The Elders up in The Wild—"

"Not entirely sealed," Hal corrected. "No, you can't fly higher than those mountains, but there is still one mountain pass, narrow and winding, that leads into The Wild. For years I had wind merchants bring me tankfuls of wind from The Wild by taking up whatever poured out of the pass, but my last several couriers…failed their missions."

"The air wasn't concentrated enough at the mouth of the pass?"

"No. They just never returned."

"I'm not trying to put myself out of a job here," Ras said, "but why don't you just fly this thing over the mountain range?"

Hal smiled. "I used to. The Elders didn't appreciate my presence."

"So you need me to fly into The Wild and collect a concentrated amount of whatever it is on the wind that keeps you young?" Ras asked.

"I'm sorry, who is giving this job offer?" Hal retorted. Ras wondered if he had crossed a line by saying that Hal *needed* anyone. "But yes, that is the overall gist of what I'm looking for."

"Why didn't my father return?"

"Of that I cannot be certain. The Elders are…very territorial."

"They're just clockwork men though," Ras said. "Shouldn't they have wound down after a century?"

"That's a very rudimentary assumption," Hal said.

"I'm just curious why you think I could do something that killed my father."

"As I said, I look for properly motivated wind merchants."

"You mean those desperate enough to attempt a suicide mission," Ras countered. The job began to lose its sheen.

"Was your father a desperate man?" Hal asked rhetorically. "Forgive me. Elias sought me, not the other way around. After *The Winnower* had been completed, he was one of the few that saw the expiration date stamped on his city. But he was one of the rare breed bold enough to do something about it."

"How can you save *Verdant*?" Ras asked.

"One does not discover The Origin of All Energy without making sure one is properly invested in the right places." He smiled. "Compound interest is a beautiful thing."

"As is living one-hundred and sixty-four years," Ras said.

Hal blinked, then focused on the world far below. "The merits of that are debatable," he said coldly.

Ras caught Hal's reflection in the glass. For a moment he wondered if Hal earned the steel in his gaze from living through The Clockwork War and The Great Overload. "But money doesn't make a Convergence."

Hal let a dark chuckle escape, lost in a memory. "Let us hope not." He turned to look back at Ras. "Helios engines," he said with renewed vigor. "Helios engines to keep *Verdant* aloft are what this situation calls for. As little as I care for the system the Helios family crafted for Atmo, it far outweighs the loss of life required for a Convergence."

"But what about fuel—"

"I am willing to pay for a supply of fuel from The Collective as long as I am alive, which is a better offer than most can make."

"Hold on, how much of The Collective do you own?"

"Not enough to make any business decisions, but enough to put a dent in them if I pull out," he said. "I used to be more involved before they lost their way."

"I have one more question," Ras said.

"Yes?"

"Why offer this to the guy that caused his city to start sinking out of ineptitude? Every wind merchant left on *Verdant* is properly motivated."

"I think you're trying to put yourself out of a job again, Erasmus."

Ras thought. "No. I just want to understand your motivation."

Hal Napier smiled with a hint of sadness behind his eyes. "There's just something fitting when a man puts right his wrongs." He let the silence linger for a moment. "How soon will your ship be ready?"

Ras felt his heart begin to pound. He stood from the chair and stuffed his hands in his pockets so Hal wouldn't notice them shaking. "I'll need a week to get my affairs in order," he said with no idea where he would find a functioning wind merchant vessel or collect the means to procure it.

"Three days," Hal countered. "My air is running thin."

Ras felt Hal was being unreasonable, but it wasn't like he had any bargaining chips. "All right."

"But if I don't see you in three days, I'll be sending Dayus to find someone else." Hal extended his hand. "Do we have an understanding?"

THE SHUTTLE'S RETURN PATH avoided Bravo Company by keeping a high altitude until it was high above the tiny, glowing speck of *Verdant*.

Smoke trailed away. A third of the city was in flames.

While no ship actively attacked *Verdant*, Bravo Company hung in a sphere around the city, dissuading any escape attempts. Several ships lay wrecked, leaving scars of debris through buildings and streets.

Ras tried to spot if his neighborhood was one of the areas on fire and breathed a sigh of relief when he saw much of the residential zone remained untouched. The docks had been targeted, and many of the ships suffered for it.

"Let us hope your ship is all right," Dayus said.

"Can you put us down in front of my house?" Ras asked.

The shuttle dove, but pulled up with a deafening release of steam to pad its landing. Dayus turned in his chair, offering Ras a slip of paper with coordinates to *The Kingfisher*'s location over the next three days, and warned Ras not to tell people of his meeting with Hal as Hal didn't want his presence in the area known.

The cabin's sealed door opened, letting in the sounds of chaos. The low rumble of a fire mixed with screams and shouts in the distance unnerved Ras. A lot had happened in the last couple of hours.

"How am I supposed to make it past Bravo Company?" Ras asked.

"I was under the impression you had no difficulty flying underneath the cloud level," Dayus said. "They're interested in overtly showing their strength, not risking their lives by hiding."

"Right." Ras turned and began to exit the shuttle. He stopped, looked back at Dayus. "How old are you?"

Dayus scoffed. "Old enough."

The door of the Veir house opened and slammed shut, drawing Ras' attention to his mother running out to the street.

"What are you doing?" she shouted as she ran up to the door of the shuttle, focused on Dayus. "You get out of here."

"Ma'am," Dayus said, nodding a civil greeting.

"I don't care how bad things are getting, you can't have him too."

Dayus simply looked over to Ras. "Three days."

Ras stepped out of the shuttle to be with his mother, who threw her arms around her son.

"I thought I lost you," she said, tightening her embrace. "The Engine was hit hard." She released him, then began walking back toward their house. "You have a lot of explaining to do."

It took about ten minutes for Ras to relay the conversation with Hal to his mother, who sat stone faced at the kitchen table.

"No. Absolutely not. You won't have anything to do with that man."

"But this is a chance to save *Verdant*!" Ras said, gesturing wildly.

"That's what your father said, and I don't see *Verdant* saved, or him either. Let someone else go. I'm not losing you too."

"Mom, what if someone else goes and fails? What then?" Ras yelled.

"What if *you* fail?" she retorted. "You don't even have a ship! This is a moot point. You don't have a license, and nobody is going to give you a loan…and then what if you get caught piloting illegally?"

Ras narrowed his eyes. "Just tell me that you don't think I'm capable, or that if dad the hero was killed then little Rassy won't even make it past The Bowl."

"Honey, please don't make me lose you too," she said. She took a deep breath to steady herself. "You took after me instead of your father."

"What?"

"When your dad built *The Silver Fox*, I was going to be his navigator, but when we went out for our first few runs, he never found anything. We thought it was a fluke, but after a dozen runs with nothing to show for it, I moved back into this house and we had you. You're not a Knack like your father, you're—"

"Please don't say I'm a Lack," Ras said. "Maybe I'm not a Knack, and maybe I'll never be as good as dad, but I'm not going to spend the rest of my life knowing I turned down the opportunity to fix things after ruining so many lives. Don't let me die inside like that, because you know I would, and so would you." Ras stormed out of the kitchen and slammed the front door, almost running into Callie on the front porch. She looked at him wide-eyed as he tried to compose himself.

"I'm sorry," she said.

"How much of that did you hear?" he asked.

"As little as you need me to have," she said.

"Thanks. Is your family all right?"

Callie shrugged. "After the attacks, my dad went to the docks…a biplane landed on our ship, so we're not going anywhere for a while."

Ras felt guilty for feeling relieved. "Did The Collective come back?"

She gave him a confused look. "No. After about an hour of bombarding they just stopped." She paused. "So was Mr. Hat actually Hal Napier?"

"No."

"Oh. It would have made for a good twist though, right?" She offered a little smile as if encouraging Ras to give it a try. "So he really wants you to go to The Wild?"

Ras met her eyes. There was always something excited behind them when things went wrong. It wasn't that she enjoyed pain or suffering, but the idea that real life could look like the stories she read often mixed with the bit of naivete that told her everything would turn up all right by the end. He took a deep breath and let it go slowly. "I need a ship first," he said. "Keep your eyes open?"

"I won't blink."

Chapter Six
The Search

Before beginning his search for the ship, Ras felt an obligation to see what had become of The Engine during his extended lunch break. He wasn't sure if simply lying that he got lost in the attack, or a crazy-sounding truth would do better with Billie, Finn, and Guy.

The main entrance to the Engine was partially obscured with heavy iron debris, but the doors had been blown off their hinges, allowing Ras to easily climb over the wreckage and inside.

Overwhelming heat met him as he entered the main corridor. The acrid burning smell of overworked machinery mixed with the coppery scent of blood filled the air. Bulges in the bulkhead walls indicated the area had suffered major structural damage.

Workers busily lined the wide corridor with what Ras assumed to be bodies under sheets. The skeleton crew was shrinking, and all Ras could do was blame himself for provoking Bravo Company to swoop in on the ailing city.

Billie's office was dark, save for the sparks jumping from some of the dangling light fixtures.

"Billie?" Ras called. "Anyone?" After waiting a few moments in the dark to collect himself, he made his way to Engine Eight to find a quarter of the crew patching pipes and running about.

Kiria spotted Ras and immediately changed course to approach him. *Where were you?* she signed with aggressive gestures.

Where... Ras began signing, but didn't know how to sign Guy's name, so instead held a hand over his eye.

I don't know.

Ras turned to leave, but Kiria grabbed his arm.

Help us. Her scared expression broke Ras' heart.

I am, he signed before turning to head to the medical unit.

Shouts of agony met Ras before he reached his destination. Scores of men and women all cradling lesser wounds stood in the hallway, either waiting to be assessed, or for one of the beds to become unoccupied.

Ignoring protests that he was cutting in line, Ras walked past everyone and peeked inside to see medics bustling and every bed full.

"You!" Someone Ras didn't know shouted from one of the beds with a gash in his temple. He pointed accusingly at Ras. Two of the orderlies moved to restrain him as he attempted to get up from the bed. "This is all your fault! They wouldn't have attacked if they didn't smell blood!" He wrestled against the two men. "Let me go!"

Finn turned and noticed Ras. Striding over, he said, "I can't have a riot in here." His voice held more sympathy than Ras expected.

"Where's Billie?" Ras asked, eyes flitting among the patients.

"She manned one of the cannons," Finn said.

Ras knew *Verdant* had its own defenses scattered throughout the perimeter of the city, but didn't know where to find them. "Is she still down there?"

"The sons of Remnants targeted the city's weapons. I haven't received anyone from there yet, and I don't expect to." Finn bowed his head for a moment, the cries of pain beckoning him back into the ward. "Please go."

"What Sub-level?" Ras asked.

"Fifteen. Why?"

Ras bolted back into the hallway. He had to get to the defense platform, but found every elevator to be either packed or disabled. Finding a door labeled stairwell, he burst through it and began his descent down the spiral staircase.

He had to fight the crowds bringing the injured up to the medical center. He kept an eye out for anyone resembling Billie, but had no luck.

Sub-level Fifteen's stairwell door took a hefting to open as the top hinge had broken loose already. He scraped the door open just enough to fit himself through and saw a mostly collapsed ceiling; apparently Sub-level Fourteen had fallen through, scattering an array of broken pipes and sparking wires.

In the non-collapsed portions of the corridor, Ras could make out a row of large, seated cannons and piles of cannon balls in barrels bolted to the floor next to them. Daylight flooded in where some of the cannons had moved out to a platform outside of the corridor.

Reaching the first cannon, he saw a man seated atop the weapon, slumped over its controls. Next to it dangled a harnessed person whom Ras guessed to be the cannon loader.

"Billie!" Ras called out, scrambling over bent girders and pipes that spat steam irregularly.

"I haven't found her yet," a voice shouted back, its owner hidden in the wreckage further down the bay.

"Who's there?"

Guy stepped out from behind one of the cannons, caked with dust and blood. "Oh. You."

Ras trudged forward, occasionally tangling his feet in the debris as he walked toward Guy. "I thought she worked in the office—"

"Who sent you down here?"

It was difficult to know what sort of response would set off Guy's temper, so Ras answered quickly. "Nobody. Where would she be?"

Guy hoisted a thin sheet of metal bulkhead that had collapsed down over a body, and he swore before gently lowering the wreckage.

Clearing a wrecked cannon, Ras came close enough to see the bulkhead covering up a bloodied arm. "Is that…"

"No," Guy said. "Her name was Rin, not that you'd care."

"And why wouldn't I care?" Ras felt his temper flare. "I'm as much a son of *Verdant* as you are."

Guy huffed in grim amusement. "I'm Merronian, you idiot." He paused. "And where were you when all this happened, huh? Hiding?"

Ras became very aware that he didn't bear a single battle scar from the attacks. "No, I was…" He stopped, avoiding the bait. "Never mind." He turned his attention to the next section of wreckage.

"I already looked there. Where were you?" Guy narrowed his eye at Ras. "You weren't at Eight when we needed you."

"I was trying to figure out a way to save *Verdant*," Ras said.

"And how'd that work out?" Guy asked, gesturing to the wreckage.

"I can get Helios engines installed."

Guy stared at Ras with a blank expression before throwing his head back in a laugh. "Well, why didn't you say so? Did India Bravo offer you that?" He spat. "Or how about Foster Helios III himself? Oh, wait, let's make it a crazy Veir family tradition and say it was Hal Napier."

"Shut up!" Ras reached forward to shove Guy, but quickly found his forward momentum used against him and he hit the ground. He spun around, launching himself at Guy before being thrown back down in the same fashion. "You don't get to talk about my father!"

"Why not? He let *Merron* sink. He did everything he could and then some to stop Bravo Company from taking *Verdant*, but when his next door neighbor faced the same threat...nothing." Guy looked down at the young man. "And he could have. He could have so very easily fought that fight again if half of what everyone says about him was true. But he let India Bravo slaughter half the city and push most of the second half off its side just to see if she could make a Convergence."

Ras considered continuing the fight, but knew that every moment spent squabbling was another that Billie might need to survive.

"Bet nobody told you that story, huh?" Guy asked. "Did you ever realize that he skipped town just after the Merronian refugees arrived? He wasn't on a mission from some long-dead savior, he just couldn't live with himself after looking into the faces of everyone he let down." Guy clenched his jaw. His fists shook in anger. "So where were you when we needed you?"

Ras picked himself up and stared at Guy, then beyond. Looking out the open bay doors, Ras saw one of the cannons outside on the gunnery platform, and a mop of curly hair adorning the gunner. "Billie!"

Guy turned to look and they dashed toward the open bay doors.

Ras stopped immediately upon seeing the five-foot-long rail system leading to the cannon wasn't designed for people to walk on it, and the fact that the cannon hung in midair at the end of the rail certainly didn't make him feel any more confident. He looked down at the foot-wide beam, and the sea of clouds below blinded him momentarily, as his eyes had grown accustomed to the dark of the sub-level.

"Are you all right?" Ras shouted. He couldn't tell if her head moved or if it was the wind just shifting her hair around.

"There's a lever on the cannon that calls it back in," Guy said.

"Why don't you pull it?" Ras asked.

Guy pointed to his eye patch. "I don't do depth perception."

Against his better judgment, Ras stepped one foot on the beam leading out to the cannon, then another. He cautiously walked forward until a gust of wind made him lose his balance for a moment. Waving his arms wildly, he caught himself before lunging forward to grasp the back of Billie's seat. Pulling himself up and then alongside the cannon, Ras nearly bumped into a harnessed young man slumped against the weapon.

Billie's glassy eyes peered down at Ras as her left hand clutched the dark spot surrounding a bullet wound in her chest.

"She's alive!" Ras looked around the small platform until he spotted a lever. He disengaged the safety and pulled it back. The cannon ratcheted back into *Verdant,* and the bay doors slammed shut behind it. He clambered up to Billie as she slumped in her seat. "Hey, hey, stay with me. Let's get you to Finn, all right?" She moved her eyes slowly to look at Ras, whom Guy quickly pushed aside.

Guy unfastened her restraints to ease her down to the ground with Ras' help. "Don't you dare leave me," Guy said, cradling her head.

Billie said something too softly for Ras to hear so he pulled in close.

"What's that?" Ras could smell the blood, sweat, and grease mixed in with the tang of the gunpowder.

Again she mouthed, this time with a faint smile. "Home."

Billie went slack.

Guy gently closed her eyelids. "She didn't deserve this."

The world spun on Ras. His staunchest defender was gone. Tears formed and he made no pretense of strength. "I don't care if you believe me or not, Guy, but I talked to Hal Napier."

Guy remained silent.

"He was the one who stopped the attack on *Verdant—*"

"Not in time."

"I know," Ras said, then paused. "I'm sorry about *Merron,* and I'm sorry about Billie."

"Don't say her name," Guy said, shooting a glare at Ras.

Ras continued, unflinching, "But my father wasn't a coward. He died trying to save *Verdant.*" He thought for a moment. "And I'm probably going to follow in his footsteps, but that isn't going to stop me from trying."

Guy continued to cradle Billie, his breathing slow and labored. "I don't want to see your face again unless you make good on that promise."

The ache of Billie's loss had fully settled in by the time Ras reached the salvage yard. Years ago he had selected all of the components for *The Copper Fox* from there when he built her. Slade, the owner of the yard, rubbed his old, bald head, leaving a smudge of grease atop it.

"Sorry Ras, I knew how much she meant to you," Slade said, kicking a small compression coil back to one of the massive piles of scrap. "I'm not saying who I sold the parts to."

"I just want to see if I can buy one part back for sentimental value," Ras said.

"Never heard of someone trying to buy a bad luck charm. Besides, how'd you like it if you had half a dozen guys chasing you down trying to get back the parts you had picked for *The Fox*?"

"If they made me decent offers..."

"No, Ras. You lost your ship for good reason. You're lucky I don't contact the guy that bought your ship to warn him you'll be by."

Bought my ship... not ship parts...

"All right Slade, you win. Sorry I asked."

Slade swallowed hard. "You know Ras, you really did a lot of us a bad turn. Some folk sell little things like books or hats. They pack up their shop and set up somewhere new. How am I gonna move any of this stuff anywhere?" he asked, gesturing to the piles of parts.

"I don't know, but I'm doing everything I can to put things right."

Slade grunted and spat on the ground.

Searching the undamaged sections of the docks for *The Copper Fox* would take at least a full day, as they made up eighty percent of the perimeter of *Verdant*. There were thousands of slips to check and to even begin to start looking in the right area, Ras would need a guide. He needed Old Harley.

Ras considered checking the hospital before deciding to see if Old Harley wasn't already back home on his ship, and if that ship hadn't been decimated during the attack.

It took an hour on foot for Ras to make his way to the Western docks while safely avoiding anyone from Port Authority. Old Harley's decrepit airship was more a house than a wind merchant vessel ever since he removed the collection tank to make way for a living room. Atop the ship, the man himself sat in a wheelchair, surveying the smoke billowing from *Verdant*.

Ras pulled in close alongside the ship and softly called up, "Harley!" He could hear the squeak of the wheelchair inching to the edge.

"Who's there?"

"Harley, I don't have much time. Someone bought my ship and I need to convince whoever it was that I need it to save *Verdant*."

"Erasmus?" Harley asked, poking his head over the railing.

"You were right. My dad had a mission from Hal Napier and if I can get my ship and do the job for him, he'll replace the engines on *Verdant*."

"I knew it!" Harley exclaimed a little too loudly.

"How do I find my ship, Harley? Quickly."

"Oh! Go to the dock registry terminal at Southport," he said as two members of Port Authority walked by. "Good afternoon, Shane. Caedmon." He nodded to the men, then waited until they left. "Look at the ships added in the last week." Harley said, "Whoever bought it probably renamed it."

"Thanks Harley," Ras said.

"Now hurry up before I report you," Old Harley said with a smile. "Give my regards to Hal."

Another half hour brought him to the Port Authority terminal with the log book. Most men were busy putting out fires on some of the airships, and Ras ran up to the book, flipping to the end of the log.

There had only been one new ship registered at the docks in the past week. Name: *The Onlo Ann*. Registrant: Freddie Tibbs.

RAS MADE THE LONG WALK to the Southern Docks and arrived at *The Onlo Ann*'s slip at about five-thirty. He passed by the space reserved for the Veir family and remembered how his mother used to take him there as a small child to see Elias off before each collection run. He'd hug Elias' leg, begging him not to leave, and Emma would comfort him, telling him that Daddy would be back before he knew it. So little Ras would plant himself on the dock after *The Silver Fox* had left and then he would call "Dad?" every time an airship passed by until Emma had to explain to him that he would be gone for days, not minutes.

Seeing the empty slip made those emotions well up. He now understood why his mother had accompanied Elias to the dock before every trip to kiss him goodbye.

In a matter of minutes, Ras arrived at the slip for *The Onlo Ann*. There sat *The Copper Fox*, garishly decorated with party lights and some deck furniture. He could hear a muffled rhythm from inside as he approached the gangplank. *Music?*

"Tibbs?" No response. Ras called out again. The music coming from below deck softened before the footsteps grew, and out walked Freddie Tibbs, whose outfit consisted of a dingy bathrobe, shorts, and sandals. The drink in his hand completed the ensemble.

"Slade said you'd probably be by," Tibbs said, a touch inebriated.

"I'm just glad she wasn't chopped up," Ras said, trying to ease his way into the inevitably awkward question he knew he had to ask.

"Chopped up, no. Gutted, yes," he said, uncaring. "Couldn't get the tank out though. Too big."

Ras' fists tightened, and the pain fed the frustration. "Ah, yeah… had to build the ship around that. What happened to your old ship?"

"It's a few slips down. Dad said I needed to get my own place and this thing was dirt cheap."

"Your old ship doesn't have a Captain's quarters?" Ras asked, trying to hold back his anger.

"It does, but who wants to live and work in one place? Gets old fast," Tibbs said, then motioned for Ras to come aboard. "I'm being rude, want anything to drink?"

You don't want me compromised right now. "No, I'm good."

"Suit yourself." Tibbs watched Ras walk across the gangplank. "I thought about fixing her up to sell to one of the pilots that lost their ship in the attack…demand's high right now…but y'know, there's something reassuring about having a backup."

"Beats no ship at all," Ras said.

"Or I might use her as a transport. People would pay well to get a ride off this city." He eyed Ras, gauging what reaction the suggestions would bring. "Slade said you wanted to buy a piece of her for nostalgia."

Ras remained silent.

"Tell you what, if it won't make the ship fall apart by prying it loose, it's yours. I wanted to redecorate anyway," he said.

"How about the keys?" Ras said, half-joking.

Tibbs let out a big belly laugh. "You lost her fair and square, Rassy. Besides, you can't even fly anything bigger than a paper airplane without a license."

"I was offered a job."

"Oh? You want to save up and buy her back? I'm not *that* attached."

"I'd need a ship, but if I do the job, then The Collective will replace the scoop engines on *Verdant* with Helios ones. *Verdant* will be safe."

"Just in time for Bravo Company to take over," Tibbs said. "Do you think I'm stupid enough to believe a story like that and just loan you the ship? You know what? Never mind. She's not on the market. You screwed things up for everybody and now you're trying to steal my house. You should go before I call Port Authority."

"Why? You invited me aboard."

"For skipping on community service," Tibbs said.

Ras shook his head and began to walk away.

"Tell your mother I'll give her a discount if she needs a ride off this forsaken city. I know she needs it," Tibbs said. "Well, I guess there are other ways to get on ships."

Something broke. Ras spun on his heel and threw a fist into Tibbs jaw. The larger wind merchant fell back a couple of steps, then planted himself back on the deck, tripping over his own feet. He blinked dumbly as Ras shook out his hand.

"I'm calling the Sheriff!" Tibbs shouted.

"Good," Ras said. "Maybe I'll get an extra month. I hear seven is lucky." He turned to walk back to the residential zone. Day one was coming to a close and he was quickly running out of ideas of how to legally procure a ship.

As Ras walked back to his house, he spotted a fair face peeking at him from the basement window before it disappeared. Soon Callie ran out to meet him.

"Any leads?" she asked.

"Tibbs has *The Fox*, but he'd never sell it to me," Ras said. "Not that I have any way to buy it from him."

Callie looked lost in thought for a moment. "I talked to some people from University, but nobody had a ship they're willing to loan or part with," she said. "Ras, nobody expects this from you except you. I'm not saying you should give up, just don't ask too much from yourself, okay?"

Ras nodded.

"Maybe I can go talk with Tibbs."

Ras was about to protest when the front door of the Veir home swung open. Sheriff Pauling and three deputies exited. "Erasmus, how's your hand feeling?"

"*Verdant* is burning, and this is what you're focusing on?" Ras asked, earning a forceful cuffing from one of the deputies.

Emma mouthed a silent *I'm sorry* to Ras.

The ceiling of the jail cell was becoming far too familiar as Ras lay on the hard wood cot, staring up. Sheriff Pauling had tried several times to get the young man to talk, but Ras' silent treatment had finally earned him his solitude and Pauling went home to his family.

Evening turned to night, which brought fitful sleep and half-remembered dreams of a giant Tibbs picking up *The Copper Fox* and pulling it apart the way a toddler would a toy too complex for him.

At about four o' clock, *Verdant* faltered for a moment, jolting Ras awake in the middle of a falling nightmare. Sleep didn't return.

The second day passed with no visitors and no sure answer from Pauling as to how long he would spend in the cell. His only consolation was the absence of more attack sirens.

On the morning of the third day, the Sheriff's office came to life around seven-thirty. Pauling walked up with a set of keys. "Bail's posted."

Ras eased his sore body from the cot, massaging a crick in his neck as the cell door ratcheted open. He looked up at Pauling, confused, until the Sheriff stepped aside, revealing Emma. She stood with her hands folded as Ras left the cell. "We need to talk."

Emma had borrowed Mr. Tourbillon's skiff to come to the Sheriff's office. As they both climbed inside she said, "I don't blame you."

Ras didn't know if she meant for *Verdant*, wanting to take Hal's mission, or skipping community service. He hoped all three.

The skiff took off with a high pitched whine before Emma spoke. "I think we try to control everything we can so life works out how we want…but you can only control yourself, and even then it's not simple."

"Mom, I don't have a ship. I'm not going."

Emma didn't say anything until they arrived at the Engine entrance. She pulled a sack lunch from the back seat and handed it to Ras. Her eyes began to tear up. "I love you, Ras. Don't forget that."

He accepted the brown bag, wishing he understood this new wave of emotion. "Never have, never will."

She grabbed his hand and squeezed it as though she was doing it for the last time before letting him exit.

The full day of work consisted of Ras cleaning up an oil spill, this time alone. *This is their version of solitary confinement*, he thought, and wondered if it was for his own protection.

He wasn't allowed to eat in the mess hall. He wasn't even allowed to have more than ten minutes for lunch, and when he asked for a bandage after cutting his forearm on an old pipe, his request went ignored. When the names of those who died in the attack were broadcasted throughout the Engine as a makeshift memorial, it was all he could do but not feel personally responsible for every name read.

He was grateful for his solitude when Billie's name was read.

Flexing his hands, which were sore from too many hours clenched tightly around a mop handle, he left the building to go home. Ahead, he spotted Callie waiting for him.

"How was your day?" Callie asked innocently.

"Better now," he said, starving for a friendly face. "You didn't have to come out here."

"I wanted to. Are you up for a walk?"

He wasn't, but obliged anyway.

"I never got to ask; what was Hal Napier like, and—"

"How is he still alive?" Ras finished for her with more energy than he knew he currently possessed. "He said he's one-hundred and sixty-four years old, but he looked like he's sixty. Had eyes that bore straight through you when he was mad or annoyed."

"Did you make him mad?" Callie asked.

"I was…challenging from time to time." Ras looked around and realized they were heading east. "Where are we going?"

"I have a small package to pick up and I wanted you to be there when I do," she said.

"Can I guess?"

"Sure, if you like."

"Any hints?" he asked.

"Nope. You've always been too good at guessing when I give clues. It's annoying."

He had to concede that point. When they had played the game as children, she would always come up with wildest guesses while Ras' more pragmatic deductions hit closer to the mark. "Is it a book?"

"No."

"Typewriter ink?"

"Why would I want you there when I picked up typewriter ink?" She laughed. It was a valid question.

"I don't know, maybe you're branching out to blue and it's a big moment for you." Ras laughed. It felt good to laugh again. It felt like a moment stolen away from the oppression of India Bravo's looming fleet.

"This is bigger than blue ink."

"Oh, a clue?"

"Hardly. Most things are bigger than trying blue ink," she said, pushing him.

"Jewelry?"

"Hmm, I suppose it could be," she said. "You can stop guessing."

They stood outside a hardware store. "Your first socket wrench set. Big moment."

She made a sour face at him. "Stay here, I'll be right back." She disappeared inside the door and returned within three minutes with a small brown paper sack. Something clinked inside it as she walked.

"All right, out with it."

"Hold on, this requires a little decorum," she said.

Ras looked around at the shopping center and couldn't imagine a less worthy place for decorum.

"Erasmus Veir the Third—"

"First."

"Third sounds more important."

"Also sounds more inaccurate."

"Fine. Erasmus Veir the First," she said, affecting a formal accent that Ras didn't recognize.

"Yes, Calista Tourbillon?"

"Before I show you what's in the bag, you have to answer three questions."

"All right," said Ras.

"First, do you solemnly swear that you would do everything within your means to save *Verdant*?"

The request of an oath brought him back to his trial a little too easily. Ras cocked his head slightly. She was being serious. He took a quick breath and said, "Yes, I do."

"Second, do you absolutely promise that if you saw me in danger you'd save me from whatever it was?"

A million times over. "As long as it didn't kill me first," he said. "Yes."

"Last one. If I offer you what's in this bag, will you promise me something that you can't say no to?"

Ras had to think for a moment as to where she was going with this. He still didn't know what was in the bag but he would find some way to jump over the moon if she were to just ask. "Yes, I promise."

She reached her hand into the bag, then stopped. "Remember, you can't say no now."

"I know," he said.

From the bag she produced a key ring with a set of airship keys. "You're taking me with you."

Chapter Seven
The Mission

Now was not the time for rational thought over how Callie had acquired the keys; it was enough that she had managed it somehow. Her broad smile worked its way over to Ras like an infection. He hugged her and spun her around, eliciting a small squeal.

"But, how?" Ras asked, setting her back down.

"I talked Tibbs into selling *The Fox* to me yesterday."

"But he gutted it."

"We got Harley to tell us what we needed," she said.

"We?" Ras' head swam.

"C'mon, I'll show you. We're running out of time." She began bounding toward the docks.

The East docks weren't far, and as Ras and Callie approached he saw Emma and Harley, who rolled out in a wheelchair and greeted them.

Tied to a dock stood a ship that looked more like *The Copper Fox* than Tibbs' party house. The more severely damaged pieces of paneling had been replaced from other ships, giving the familiar vessel a new sheen. It was a perfectly beautiful mess.

"How did you afford this?" he asked.

"Well, three years of University tuition was just about enough—"

"Callie, no!" Ras said, boiling with anger at Tibbs. He didn't have the heart to tell her that a ship like this should have only cost one year of tuition. He assumed she'd told him how much she had and he had taken every last bit.

"Ras, I went to the University so I could someday get out and see the world. Think of it as…graduating early," she said with a smile kinder than Ras could handle. "Your mom bought Harley's engines."

Harley wheeled forward. "They don't make them like they used to."

"Mom, what did you sell?" Ras asked. The house was the only thing they owned valuable enough to buy a set of engines.

"Don't worry about it," she replied.

"Mom?"

"You weren't getting anywhere without engines. I'll be fine," she said.

Old Harley pointed a withered hand at Ras. "Don't worry, her first month's rent is free. You bring me those engines back and we'll call it even," he said with a wink.

"But what about your ship?" Ras asked.

"This city is my ship," Old Harley said, challenging Ras to argue.

Emma turned to Callie. "You bring me my boy back."

"Yes ma'am," Callie said, nodding.

Emma picked up a heavy duffel bag sitting behind Old Harley's wheelchair and handed it to Ras. "I found this while packing up the attic today."

Ras unzipped the bag, revealing Elias' grapple gun with his father's name stamped on the side. The model was a much nicer version of the cheap one Ras had last used, as Elias' grappler could retract the cable back into itself. As a boy, Ras had used it for target practice and would occasionally misplace it, forcing Elias to collect Energy without the device. Before Elias had left on his mission for Hal, Ras had lost it and he often imagined his father dying because of his missing safety measure.

Underneath Eli's grapple gun was their last family portrait, taken when Ras was ten. Little Ras had an awkward bowl haircut and hadn't lost his baby fat, but thankfully he resembled Elias more now.

Emma gave Ras a long, tight hug. "You can do this," she said, sounding like she needed to hear the words more than her son did.

He nodded as they ended their embrace. He took in an eyeful of *Verdant*, unsure if he'd ever stand on it again. With the day having waxed far into evening, Ras said, "We better go before Hal finds someone else."

Ras and Callie waved to Emma and Harley as they walked up the gangplank. Ras took his place at the helm, running his hand over the familiar spoked wheel. Pressing the buttons, he retracted the gangplank and roused the engines.

Callie called up from the main deck. "I renamed her!"

Ras furrowed his brow. "She's not *The Copper Fox* anymore?"

"The name was already taken when I tried to register her."

"I'm afraid to ask," Ras said.

"She's *The Brass Fox*."

"Copper mixed with…?"

"Tin," she answered.

"I like it. *The Brass Fox* she is. Good name."

"I thought so," Callie said, beaming.

The ship glided out of the dock, and the tiny crew of *The Brass Fox* waved to the two on the dock.

"Wait," Ras said. "How did you get your father to agree to this?"

Callie climbed the steps to the bridge. "I left him a letter."

A horn blared as Mr. Tourbillon's skiff pulled up to the dock and Callie's parents exited, shouting out to her.

"Bye, mom! Bye, daddy! I've got to go save *Verdant*! Love you!" Callie turned to Ras. "Punch it," she said casually. Ras obliged and *The Brass Fox* dropped beneath the clouds, well on its way for its maiden voyage.

RAS HAD NEARLY WRITTEN OFF EXPERIENCING THE WIND pushing on his face and tussling his hair the way it did out on the open air. Callie, on the other hand, struggled with the reality that if the wind wasn't in her face, her hair was.

"None of my books mentioned this happening to girls' hair," she said, brushing an errant lock out of her face. "It's not terribly romantic." She pulled her locks back with her left hand to end the struggle and stared over the railing to the great below. "This. Is. Amazing." She beamed. "You should come see!"

"Your face is going to stick like that," Ras said.

"I hope so," she said.

"It's bad luck for the pilot to leave the wheel," Ras said, making up the poor excuse on the spot. It was one thing to have clouds just below him, but another thing entirely to see the ground and be reminded of just how far up he flew. As far as he knew, Callie was ignorant of his fear of heights, and he figured that if he wanted her to continue to trust him as a captain, she should remain in that ignorance.

"How dangerous is it for me to be under the clouds?" she asked, not taking her eyes away from the ground.

"With what little Energy is left in The Bowl, not very," Ras said. "We should probably stay on the safe side after we pass Bravo Company."

Callie pushed off the railing, then looked up to Ras. "Do I have time to get changed?"

"Uh, sure. I'll let you know if we're getting close to Framer's." He watched Callie disappear into the Captain's quarters beneath him. He hadn't considered that there would be only one bed on the ship unless Tibbs had made some changes. He'd address that when the time came, but for now he had to make it to Hal's ship before sundown. He opened the throttle as the sky began filling with the orange hue of the setting sun.

He looked above at the clouds to notice a series of shadows he assumed belonged to Bravo Company, then surveyed the skies to see if they left lookouts for any Verdantian willing to risk overloading.

As soon as he felt they were a safe enough distance beyond Bravo Company, he brought the ship back up into the clouds until he peeked over to see their ships as tiny specks behind him on the horizon, then pulled *The Brass Fox* just above the clouds for safety. In a few minutes Ras heard the door open to the Captain's quarters and looked over in time to see Callie reach the railing and toss something overboard. He glimpsed something red and gossamer flitting about on the wind behind the ship and did a double-take.

Callie shook her head, running her fingers through her newly cropped hair. "How's it look?" she asked, cringing slightly.

Ras was speechless. She wore tall leather boots over a pair of tan corduroy pants held up by brown suspenders strapped over a white long-sleeved ruffled shirt. Her brilliant red hair fell just below the nape of her neck when the wind wasn't picking it up. She looked stunning.

"I look stupid, don't I?" she asked.

"No, it's great. You look like the navi of *The Brass Fox*."

"Navi?"

Ras nodded. "Navigator." They were almost to the other side of the canyon, having taken the long route. "Is your head all right?"

"I'll be fine."

"When we go through the tunnel into Framer's, I'll need you to keep an eye out for *The Kingfisher*."

"Aye-aye, Captain," she said.

"You really don't have to call me that," Ras said.

"Yes, sir!" She stood at attention, then broke into laughter as Ras made a face at her. "*The Kingfisher* is the one on the propaganda poster in your room, right?" she asked, "Stop the Clockwork!" she quoted the poster in a mock deep voice.

"That's the one. Should be easy to spot."

"Why's that?"

"It'll be the only one above us."

Eventually *The Brass Fox* glided toward the cliffs that made up Framer's Valley. Ras brought the ship through the tunnel and into the circular opening covered in the wavy green. Ras looked mournfully at the cave.

"The Convergence was in that cave over there—"

"Is that *real* grass?" Callie exclaimed, leaning once more over the railing. "I just want to roll around in it!"

"Uh, yeah…it's pretty great," Ras said, distracted. He brought the ship up above the clouds and began searching for *The Kingfisher*.

Callie rotated to leaning her back on the railing to stare beyond *The Brass Fox*'s balloon. "Ras! He's still here!"

"All right, let's see how high she can go." Ras engaged the controls, pulling up on the wheel to pick up altitude until it capped out well underneath what *The Kingfisher* could manage. He retrieved his flare gun from underneath the ship's console and loaded up a charge before firing off a red flare into the sky. It erupted into a star pattern.

"Ooh, pretty," Callie said.

They waited for a moment for the ship to descend down to their level. Then waited another minute.

"What other colors do you have?"

"I think just red…I've never used one before," Ras said.

"Don't different colors mean different things?"

"I thought they all just meant '*hey, over here,*'" Ras said as he looked at the box containing two other flares. He didn't want to waste them and wondered if Hal was testing him. He grabbed the duffle bag and extracted Elias' grapple gun. The leather straps were worn but form fitted to his father's arm. Fastening the straps from wrist to elbow, he then loaded a spike-to-magnet shot. He fired the first part into the hull of his ship, then took aim and shot at *The Kingfisher*, spooling out a healthy length of cable.

"What are you doing?" Callie asked.

A satisfying metallic clank rang out. Ras smiled. "If he won't come to us…"

"What if it moves?" Callie asked, sounding like she didn't want to question Ras' intelligence, but needed to make sure the obvious was stated.

"It won't…shouldn't," Ras reassured. "But just in case, we should move quickly."

"We? You want me to go up there too?" Callie asked.

"I promised to protect you, right? Can't do that if you stay behind. Besides, it's just a couple of old men up there. They'll probably give you candy." From the bag Ras pulled a harness attached to a locking mechanism with a crank. He tossed the harness to her. "Here, put that on, legs in those holes…"

She did so dutifully and Ras began equipping a harness himself. He heard a delicate *clink* and looked up to see Callie connected to the crank already. "Like this?"

"You been taking climbing lessons?"

"No, but once I read a book about rock climbers where the author went into painful detail about how the characters prepared for a climb…and the gruesome details of what happened to them when they fell. I felt it worth remembering."

A gust of wind gently rocked *The Brass Fox*, causing the part of the deck attached to the spike to creak loudly.

"Let's lock you in," Ras said, attaching Callie's crank to the cable. "There we are. You're going nowhere," he said. "Now, we'll turn this crank to ascend and descend." Ras fiddled with his harness when he heard a deafening crack and a piercing scream as Callie shot up and away from *The Brass Fox*, trailed by the loose piece of deck.

"Ras!" she cried out as she slipped away, rising with *The Kingfisher*.

He stood dumbfounded for a moment. "Idiot!" he muttered to himself. "Hold on! I'm coming!" Ras loaded a rappelling hook into the gun and fired it high into the nearby cliff well above his ship. He ran over to the railing and climbed atop it, almost losing his balance, then pushed the button to start retracting the cable and swung off the side of the airship.

He landed hard against the cliff face, still needing to ascend. Callie's screams continued. Taking the cable in his right hand, he disengaged it from the gun, then loaded another rappelling hook. He fired, listened to the cable *fwip* away, and felt the line go taut. Testing his weight with a quick tug, he then let go with his right hand and began retracting the cable. The next ascension led him to the rock face at an altitude even with *The Kingfisher*'s. In the distance, Callie dangled below the ship. "Hold on! I'm coming!"

Ras repeated the ascending process once more on the cliff face, pulling him high above the ascending ship. He only had one more charge, but it had a magnetic top on it, which was perfect. He looked down at the ship and did a little calculation before noticing Callie being hauled onboard the ship by a few men on the deck.

He took a breath, swallowed hard, and squeezed the firing mechanism in his palm, watching the magnet connect to the siding of the ship. "I'm going to regret this," he said, throwing caution and himself to the wind. He fell like a stone past *The Kingfisher* before jerking underneath the ship as the cable wrapped around the underbelly, rounding out his descent and shooting him up the opposite side.

At the inception of the plan, he had imagined himself landing squarely on the deck with a heroic tuck and roll that would have impressed Callie.

He didn't anticipate bouncing off the dirigible.

Rebounding from the balloon, Ras lost momentum and fell past the side of *The Kingfisher*'s deck. In a brief moment of clarity, before the cable jerked taut, he tried to recall why he had forgotten to fasten the strap around his torso.

Snap.

THE ARTWORK ONBOARD *THE KINGFISHER* made it difficult for Callie to keep up with her elderly escorts. She didn't dare stop, but made a mental note to request a tour if time would allow.

The door to the circular study slid open, spilling light from the hallway onto the room's sole inhabitant. The man reclined in a dark leather chair, well worn to its master's form. Without conceding defeat to the ceiling in their private staring contest, the man acknowledged the entrants. "Dayus."

"Sir?" Dayus asked, standing at attention.

"Am I to gather by the absence of a certain young man behind you that you've found a replacement?" the recliner asked, breaking his gaze from the ceiling, turning his attention to Callie. "Oh, who have we here?"

Callie's mouth went dry as the legend from her illustrated books stood before her. She began to speak, but opted to curtsey beforehand. "Calista Tourbillon, sir. Thank you for having us, Mr. Napier," she said shakily.

"Us?" Hal asked, directing the question to Dayus.

"Erasmus is being fetched from underneath the ship," Dayus said with a mixture of amusement and apology.

"Is he now?" Hal asked, then swept an arm toward his desk. "Miss Tourbillon, if you would join me, I believe we have business to discuss."

Callie found herself half paying attention, lost in the stacks of ancient books lining the walls. "Yes, business..." she said, fully distracted and not stepping forward to join Hal.

Hal traced her eye-line and chuckled softly. "I don't think those would be of much use to you, I'm afraid."

"Are they blank?" Callie asked, aghast.

"Oh, no, my dear," Hal said, "just in a language unfamiliar to most."

Callie's shoulders sank slightly and she stepped away from Dayus to take one of the seats facing Hal's desk. Her eyes were drawn to a small model of a white train sitting next to some papers. "Scale replica?" she asked hopefully. The object seemed plucked straight from her dreams.

Hal sat across from her, then picked up the train, inspecting it. "I should hope so," he said, grin widening. "I wouldn't envy the difficulties of travel for such small people."

"I mean, it's based off of something real, right?"

"A relic of a bygone era, yes," Hal said, gently returning the model to his desk. Some soft voices murmured in the hallway, drawing Hal's attention. He looked across the room to Dayus, raising an eyebrow.

"It appears, in his theatrics, Mr. Veir has managed to dislocate his shoulder, rendering himself unconscious," Dayus said.

"What? Where is he?" Callie asked.

"Just…hanging around at the moment," Dayus said. "So I'm told."

"Dayus," Hal chided, attempting to hide a smirk. "Not everyone appreciates your sense of humor. Let us treat our guests with respect."

"It's not like he's going to hear me," Dayus said. "I'll see what we can do to ease his pain." With that, Dayus left the room, leaving Callie alone with Hal.

"It looks like business may have to wait," Hal said.

Callie thought for a moment. "Not necessarily," she said. The opening twinge of a headache made her steady herself.

"Do you have a proposition?" Hal asked.

She shook her head. "A request, if you're willing."

Hal leaned back in his chair, giving approval with his silence.

"How did the Great Overload happen?" Callie asked.

Hal ran a hand through his bristly hair. "That is quite a large request."

"Weren't you there?" Callie asked.

"If I were there when it happened, suffice it to say I wouldn't be here," he said.

"But you do know how it happened?"

"Why are you so keenly interested in such a morbid blot on our world's timeline?" Hal asked.

Callie shrugged. "I guess I've always thought if we knew how it happened, then someone could figure out how to reverse it."

Hal took a deep breath. "I'm afraid those that have gone on have gone on for good."

"No, I'm sorry, that's not what I mean," Callie said, "I mean, make the land livable again. It's only a matter of time before the last Atmo city falls, right?" The headache gnawed at her once more, but she closed her eyes to focus on battling it back.

"Ah, there we have a noble endeavor, indeed," Hal said, offering a sad smile. "As best I understand, the Great Overload was a construction of the Elders, whose antidote—if ever there was one—has been lost to time."

"Oh." Callie's shoulders fell in disappointment.

"But, just because we don't know doesn't mean we can't find out," Hal said, nodding until she mirrored the motion.

Dayus entered the room with two other elderly men, carrying Ras' limp form at waist height. "Sir, where would you like this deposited?"

"On the fainting couch," Hal said. "That feels appropriate."

With Ras draped over the furniture, the men nearly exited the room before Hal called out to them, "I do believe it to be well past time for supper, Dayus. If you would be so kind as to prepare something for Miss Tourbillon and myself to enjoy in the study, I would be most obliged."

Dayus nodded, then promptly exited the room.

Callie stared at Ras' limp form before turning back to Hal. "What about him?"

"If he rouses, we'll have a third plate made up," Hal said, "but for the meanwhile, you look like you could use a good story."

The snap returning Ras's left arm into its socket brought him back to consciousness with a scream. He shot up from the fainting couch in Hal's parlor.

"Would you care for some painkillers?" Dayus asked as he knelt next to the couch.

"Yes!" Ras said, still half screaming. "For the love of corn that is a… that is a…yes to painkillers, please." The words didn't come out of his mouth exactly how his brain had formed them.

The door from the hallway corridor opened and in walked Halcyon Napier. Ras' blurred vision cleared enough to see Hal towering over him. Dayus rose to leave, and Ras attempted to stand but immediately fell back down on the couch.

"No. Please. Sit," Hal said with a touch of sarcasm.

Ras looked about and realized it was fully daylight outside. "Where's Callie?" Ras demanded.

A voice spoke directly behind him. "I'm right here, Ras. I've been here all night," she said.

Ras whipped his head around to see her and had to steady himself for a moment as the room spun. She sat in a nearby armchair with one of Hal's books sitting open in her lap.

"Yes, we had a riveting discourse over your disjointed body," Hal said, "She's quite the curious one."

"Dayus mentioned painkillers," Ras said, feeling nauseated.

"I believe he has already supplied those. He was likely asking retroactively for permission. They're quite strong. I'm sure you'll find your footing soon enough," Hal said.

"I was telling Hal how you procured a ship so quickly," Callie said.

"Oh, were you?" Ras said, concern creeping into his voice. For all her merits, Callie could be a bit of a storyteller and the truth didn't always interfere with the details.

"Who knew you would save an entire orphanage and receive a vessel in return?" Hal said, amused. "Funny how you didn't mention you lacked a ship when we spoke last."

Ras turned and shot an incredulous look back at Callie, who proudly smiled, then returned his attention back to Hal. "My dad taught me that someone else should toot your horn. Wait, that's wrong," Ras said, feeling the effects from the medicine.

"Sage advice either way," said Hal. "I'm impressed with your tenacity. It will serve you well in The Wild. Is your collection tank amply sized?"

"It is *so* ample," Ras said. "Am I getting worse? I feel like I'm getting worse. My fingers feel…backwards."

Callie interrupted. "Maybe you should lie back down."

Hal turned to address Callie. "Miss Tourbillon, have you had time to practice with the device?"

"I think I'm getting the hang of it," she said. "What do you call it?"

"It doesn't have a name. Very rare. An old friend made it for me."

"Whassat?" Ras asked.

Callie produced a brass sphere about the size of a snow globe from beneath the book. There were three holes where she inserted her thumb and first two fingers, activating the device. From within came a high-pitched whine of gears, and from the top, an arrow attached to a metal rod lifted. The arrow clicked into place and turned slightly to the left and downward, pointing east.

"It's a compass that follows the trail to the mountain pass into The Wild," Callie said.

"It reads the trace amounts of the element on the wind that comes from there," Hal added.

Ras stared wide eyed at it the way a drunken toddler would. "Wow," he said, over-enunciating. "Can I try?"

"That wouldn't be wise, Ras. The device attunes itself to its user and another's touch might cause it to stop working properly for Callie," Hal said.

Ras nodded solemnly. "Don't touch the shiny. Got it."

"Precisely. Don't touch the shiny," Hal agreed as though Ras had just divulged a great secret.

"How long will he be like this?" Callie asked.

"Days, months, thirty more minutes…these things are hard to say." Hal winked at her. "Dayus is preparing breakfast as we speak. Can't send you off on an empty stomach, now can we?"

"No, we cannot," Ras said in agreement, looking up at the ceiling as though Hal were standing on it.

"If you excuse me, I'll have Dayus fetch you both when breakfast is ready." With that, he exited the room.

"Ras, are you all right?" Callie asked.

"Aside from my arm attempting to exit my body, never better." He slumped on the fainting couch, looking at Callie upside down. "How *you* doin'?" He frowned. "That came out wrong."

She looked a bit flustered. "It's just a lot to take in. Hal told me so many stories last night."

Ras righted himself. "What kinda stories?"

"About The Wild. I think we might have gotten ourselves in over our heads."

"We'll be fine," he said before slumping. "When I have two working arms I can sink entire cities," Ras said. "I'm…*dangerous*. But I promised to save *Verdant*, protect you, and bring you with me. We're in this thick as…thick as…butter."

"Thieves, Ras. Thick as thieves," Callie corrected.

"Or butter. Look it up. It's a thing." He inspected his fingernails, biting one. "I'm sure of it." Not caring for its taste, he made a face. "So what's in The Wild?"

"Pockets of frozen time, for one. That's what he wants us to collect, Ras."

"That would make a great birthday present," he said matter-of-factly. "Why is that?"

"'*Surprise, little Timmy, now you get an extra long birthday!*' Kids will go nuts over it."

"More like, '*Surprise, little Timmy, now you're stuck in time as the rest of the world ages around you until the sun explodes,*'" Callie countered.

"That sounds considerably less marketable."

"I don't want to get frozen in time," she said, looking legitimately worried.

This sobered up Ras. "I won't let that happen, okay? We stick together, and I have absolutely zero plans to get frozen in time forever. That breaks promises number one and three, plus it keeps me from number two, okay?"

She nodded.

"Is that a page turner?" Ras pointed to her lap.

"I've just been admiring the illustrations. Hal wrote it," she said.

"He definitely has enough time on his hands. What did he say was in The Wild?"

"Elders that aren't frozen in time pockets—"

Dayus opened the door and announced that breakfast was served. Callie helped Ras to his feet, careful not to aggravate the mending arm as the pair shuffled toward the door.

"So when did you become a cliff-diver?" Callie said, teasing.

"That was my first time, if you'll believe it," Ras said, missing the jab. He turned to Dayus as they passed him, "What's this mesid… medic…medi…drug called?"

Dayus responded with a word Ras didn't understand and most likely couldn't pronounce when not under its effects.

"Fun."

Hal sat at the end of a long wooden table with twenty place settings. Including Ras and Callie, only eight seats were occupied, and the other four crew members that Ras had not yet met were all older than Hal, looking to be either in their seventies or eighties.

Ras giggled slightly when he saw prunes in a bowl. He caught himself and stopped, tucking his lips between his teeth to avert a smile. The effects of the medicine slowly began ebbing away as he took in the smells of the food on the table. Toast, eggs, bacon, more eggs, toast with butter, and something that Ras figured to be yet even more eggs in an unfamiliar format were laid out before them. It was apparent that Dayus' cooking repertoire was limited, and thus Ras assumed one of the empty seats formerly belonged to their late cook.

Ras was grateful to have some protein in his diet for a change and he filled his plate with scrambled eggs, two pieces of bacon, and a piece of buttered toast. He assumed Dayus knew where to find the rare mountaintop farms.

"So, Hal," Ras said around a bite of toast. "How did you stop Bravo Company from attacking?"

Hal smiled. "I sent word to The Collective I was on *Verdant*."

"Why would that stop sky pirates?" Callie asked.

"Not every member of The Collective wears a uniform," Hal said, "and they have a keen interest in knowing what I know."

"Then why are sky pirates fighting a war against The Collective?" Ras asked.

"Have you heard any news of Bravo Company fighting in that war?" Before letting it sink in, he changed the subject. "So, Ras. Tell me about *Verdant*."

Ras choked on the mouthful of eggs he had overzealously stuffed into his mouth. "But, Bravo Company…"

"*Verdant*," Hal said, his stare challenging Ras to continue inquiring about the sky pirates.

"Ah, well…It was built in The Bowl about eighty years ago because The Bowl trapped Energy naturally—"

"I'm not looking for a history, my boy," he said with a chuckle. "I *am* history. I'm more than familiar with how things came to be in the last century."

"Oh. Sorry."

"Quite all right. What are the people like?" Hal asked, inspecting the toast and selecting a piece.

"Well, people like to talk a lot. Catch up on things they missed while out on collection runs. People move there and stay, I guess because they like it there. I…don't really know how it's different from the rest of the world," Ras admitted.

"Are the people happy?"

Ras had to think. "When not bombarded by sky pirates? I remember when I was little, people laughed more, but when you're little people tend to hide the sad things from you. But since *The Winnower* put a lot of wind merchants out of work…we make do."

Hal looked over to Callie, "What about you? What do you think of the people?"

She sheepishly smiled. "I…I don't know."

"Come now, you must have an opinion," he said.

"Aside from my last year at the University, I've spent most of my life in my family's basement or in doctors' offices."

Hal looked over to Dayus before nodding somberly as though he fully understood. Ras picked up on why he was asking about the people. He lived vicariously.

The old man probably hasn't been outside this airship in over one hundred years. No wonder he's the youngest on the ship full of people who occasionally leave, Ras thought.

"What are you waiting for?" Ras asked bluntly.

"Pardon?" Hal asked, affronted by the abrupt tone.

"One-hundred and sixty-four. That's a lot of time."

"Yes."

"The world thought you disappeared after you shut The Elders into The Wild," Ras said.

"I did, in a way."

"I mean no disrespect, but feasibly you could live for, say, at least a thousand years, right?" Ras asked. "But you stay on this ship writing and painting. It seems like a self-imposed prison sentence."

Hal firmly placed his water glass on the table. "Let me ask you this: When would you step off the immortality train? Hmm? When would you decide you've lived long enough and it was time to stop taking your medicine?" Hal's eyes narrowed. "You speak of things you don't understand. I hired you to bring me my medicine and you question why I choose to take it? You just concern yourself with repenting of your sins and I'll do the same."

Breakfast was concluded.

THE KINGFISHER DESCENDED all the way down to *The Brass Fox*'s altitude and sidled up to the other ship. Ras and Callie stood inside the control room next to Hal.

"I don't know why I expected more out of a ship found in three days," Hal said, surveying *The Brass Fox*. He pressed down on the intercom button. "Dayus! Bring something from the treasury for Flint." He turned to Ras. "If you're going to be outrunning Elder ships, you'll need better engines than that."

"Hey! My mother sold our home for those engines." Ras said, his eyes narrowing.

Hal sighed and inspected the engines as though to see if she got her money's worth. "I'll send Dayus to fetch her if *Verdant* is to sink."

Dayus arrived in the control room with a stack of bound currency that Ras didn't recognize. Hal flipped through it and approved. "Fly to *Derailleur* first and find a mechanic named Flint. His shop is on the first level in the main channel."

Slipped into the band of money was a piece of fine paper with a set of coordinates written on it. Hal pointed to it. "Once inside The Wild, that's where you will collect the air. Don't let these numbers or Callie's device fall into the wrong hands. There will be other interested parties," Hal said. "Do you understand?"

Ras nodded. "Got it."

"I've had Dayus take the liberty of adding to your food supplies. You have quite the trip ahead of you."

As Ras and Callie were ushered back over to *The Brass Fox*, there were so many things Ras felt he should be asking Hal, but he didn't even know where to begin. He watched *The Kingfisher* ascend into the clouds, and kicked himself for forgetting to ask Hal what allowed his ship to fly so high. He wished he hadn't spent most of his time aboard the fabled vessel with his faculties dulled by the medicine.

It dawned on him just how little he knew about the world outside of The Bowl, and he was about to cross the entirety of it.

Chapter Eight
The Great Below

Foster Helios III watched with little interest as the movers skittered about his father's mansion, packing up boxes and lugging them out the massive front doors to be packed into an air transport parked on the front lawn. It was the seventh ship of the day.

It all had to go.

After a month of living with austere portraits and busts of his late father staring him down, he had called the movers. He didn't know where they were taking everything and he honestly didn't care. Here in *Derailleur* there were committees, sub-committees, and foundations devoted to preserving the legacy of his father: Foster Helios II, the richest man in the Atmo, who couldn't buy himself another second no matter how hard he tried. And he tried.

Echoes filled the mansion now. The emptiness wasn't for want of money, as The Collective had compensated young Foster amply ever since he was old enough to command the attention of his father. He would make his own way, filling the mansion with the mementos of his conquests, and he would have many opportunities as he commanded The Collective fleet to wipe the sky clear of pirates. He was already thirty-five, which meant it was high time for a Helios man to save the world again.

A man wearing The Collective's insignia on his arms dashed into the main foyer and saw Foster standing on his interior balcony. "Sir!" he called up.

"What is it?" Foster said, more interested in guessing the length of the foyer than speaking to the man.

"*The Kingfisher* was spotted with another ship outside of *Verdant*!"

"What? Intelligence said he was on the city."

"I know, sir, but a dive team stayed behind to investigate the residue of the Convergence and—"

"Did we capture Napier?"

"No, sir, he flew higher than we could follow."

"What about the other ship?"

"A junker. We don't have a ship in the area that's not a diver or one of Bravo's," the lackey said.

"Send one of the *Derailleur* detachments. I want the Captain of that ship brought directly to me."

"Yes, sir!" The man left the mansion as quickly as he had entered.

Foster looked at one of the paintings of his father that had not yet been packed up. "You search your entire life for the ageless Napier and he falls into my lap just after you ran out of time… Looks like I won't need a son to carry on the Helios name after all." He smirked. "After all, sons just throw away what their fathers spent their lives building so they can make their own name anyway. What good are they?"

RAS' ONE MEMORY of flying through the main pass leaving The Bowl had frightened him as a small boy, but at least he had had the reassurance of his father being at the helm. The wind tunnel effect jostled the ship, but back then he knew without a shadow of a doubt that they would never crash as long as his dad had the wheel firmly in his capable hands.

Having cliffs on either side of him once again drew Ras' mind unwillingly to Framer's, but he was determined not to let another *Fox* fall prey to further scrapes if he could help it. If the main pass to The Bowl was wide enough to let a dreadnaught like *The Dauntless* through, he could literally fly in circles and be fine.

Callie stood next to Ras, gripping the railing near the helm tightly, laughing nervously with every bobble. "So, what's the number one rule of being on an airship?"

"You want rules?" Ras asked.

"I want to make sure I know what I'm doing," she said. "I just figured there was a list of rules for wind merchants."

"Let's go with 'don't fall off,'" Ras said.

"Good rule." A current rocked the ship quickly to port and Callie wrapped her elbow around the railing for extra support. "Let's follow that one."

"The second rule of being a wind merchant is when you see sky pirates, you run," Ras said. He spun the wheel to starboard, correcting their altered course. "More often than not they're interested in the ship instead of a ransom." He looked over to see Callie's eyes fixed on the grand horizon unfurling before them as the cliffs gave way to the end of the pass.

"Sky pirates, bad. Got it," she said absentmindedly as the last of the turbulence subsided. She released the railing, taking in the vista. "This is magnificent," she said, raising a hand to her mouth.

Looking at the clouds with Callie present made Ras feel like he was seeing the world anew. Her excitement passed to him, almost overcoming his nervousness about spending the foreseeable future with her. "It's a big world out here," he said, looking back to the opening of The Bowl. The last vestiges of home fell away, and he knew he couldn't face himself if he saw those cliffs again without a full tank of Hal's air. He pushed the throttle forward, flexing Old Harley's engines on the open sky. They responded sluggishly, but reached a top speed higher than his old set.

"What else are we going to see?" Callie asked.

"I don't know. Floating cities, more clouds...hopefully not sky pirates. What about all of your books, don't they talk about Atmo?"

She shook her head. "New books are kind of hard to come by."

"Because paper is hard to make up here?"

Callie shrugged, transfixed on the horizon. "Partly, but when the cities were built, they couldn't take everyone that survived the overload, so they focused first on taking doctors, scientists, engineers—basically the people they felt could keep humanity afloat—and since everyone else had to make it into one of the cities by lottery, not a whole lot of writers made it onboard."

Ras didn't quite remember learning that lesson in school. "Is that why you're writing your book?"

"Kind of," she said, drumming her fingers on the railing. "Can I tell you a secret?"

"It's just you, me, and the wind, so I'd say it quietly," Ras said.

"I set my book during The Clockwork War so I could investigate why The Great Overload happened without getting kicked out of the University," she said.

Nobody liked talking about The Great Overload. The concept of millions of people exploding into vapor throughout cities deeply frightened Ras, and rightly so. Most parents avoided telling their children about it for as long as possible. Ras was eight when Elias sat him down and explained what happened as best he knew. "What's the popular theory there?"

"All the professors would do was refer me to books in the library that were continually checked out or had the important pages missing," she said. "I think someone is trying to cover up why it happened."

"Well, that makes sense. If it was man-made and they survived it, I'm sure they wouldn't want to go down in history as the destroyer of mankind," Ras said, locking the wheel to set course for *Derailleur* before leaving the console.

"Where you going?" Callie asked.

"To check the rigging and the engines. I just want to make sure everything is running all right before we get too far," Ras said, "So, you were saying about ripped out pages..."

"Yes, that's why I think it wasn't an accident or a natural occurrence. There were a lot of books with pages missing," she said, following Ras down the stairs to the deck. "If someone didn't want people knowing why it happened, they'd have to rip pages out of way more books than just the ones on *Verdant*."

Ras tugged on the ropes securing the balloon to the body of his ship, inspecting the knots. "How are you going to continue your research?" he asked as he unfastened one of the knots and began retying it.

"We have to get our engines upgraded on *Derailleur*, right?" she asked in a tone Ras recognized as one usually preceding a request.

He finished the knot and turned to face Callie. "Yeah...but if Hal was right about India Bravo being in The Collective's pocket, we're going to need to lay as low as we can there."

"Well, I hear libraries are excellent places to lay low," she said, shifting her weight back and forth playfully. "And *Derailleur*'s is the biggest of all of them. Very easy to hide in."

He considered it. It wasn't a bad idea, but he didn't like being apart from the ship while it was being worked on. Leaving Callie alone to wander by herself in the metropolis wasn't an option either. "We'll see how things are when we get there this evening. For all we know your father has radioed out to every bounty hunter with an open channel to bring back his kidnapped daughter."

"He wouldn't do that," Callie said.

Ras lifted an eyebrow.

"All right, he'd probably do that," she said. "But would they really let a bounty hunter waltz into that library?"

Ras considered it. Hiding in a place that made Callie happy beat out being trapped in a waiting room at Flint's. "All right, we'll check out the library. Carefully," he said, holding up his index finger as a warning.

"If you can't be good, be careful, Mr. Kidnapper," she said playfully.

"You do know you're going to have to clear all this up with your father when we get back, right?"

Callie sighed. "I'd prefer not to think about that until I have to."

Ras checked a few other knots, satisfied with their security before heading toward the ladder down to the hold. "So, what's got you interested in The Great Overload?" he asked, lowering himself below deck. He stood at the base of the wooden ladder and held out a hand to assist Callie in reaching the floor.

"Well, if we can figure out why it happened, then maybe there's a way to reverse it," she said, opening her eyes wide to drink in the little bit of light from the porthole in the otherwise dark hold.

Ras pulled the Energy bulb's slender chain, bringing the room into illumination.

"What is that?" Callie asked, nodding toward a vehicle sitting next to the collection tank. The single seater open-air skiff sat with a wheel almost as tall as Ras at either end of it, but didn't need to be propped up. Its bronze finished gave it a classic, sleek look, and its small wings were currently folded back into its body.

"It's a jetcycle!" Ras exclaimed with a laugh. "Oh, my mother would absolutely kill me if she knew it was in here. It must have been Tibbs'."

"I had him throw it in. Happy birthday," Callie said.

"But it's not—"

"I know when your birthday is," she said, giving him a playful shove.

"How did he get it in here?" Ras looked over until he saw a new control panel and a hydraulic system that outlined the side of the hold. "I just thought this was a patch job, not a bay door."

"He was going to use it as a patio…or something," Callie said with a shrug. "He said you'd have to flush the engine a few times to break it in. I assume you know what that means."

"More or less," Ras said absentmindedly. It was a new model, just like anything else Tibbs ever bought. He threw a leg over the body, straddling the seat. The odometer read all zeroes. "He never flew this thing."

The idea of a jetcycle had honestly scared Ras to death growing up. Several wind merchants he knew had died in accidents when their motors clogged and fell out of Atmo, never to be seen again. But having another transport option if something happened to *The Brass Fox* made him feel safer.

"Thank you," Ras said. "You didn't have to do this."

"I know," she said. "You helped me escape *Verdant*. I owed you."

Ras dismounted and walked over to her, taking her up in a hug. "Your math is fuzzy." He squeezed her tight before releasing. "Now let's see what Old Harley left us." He walked over to one of the Windstrider scoop engines and squatted down, running a hand over the dusty metal casing before wiping his palm onto his pant leg.

"Are they any good?" Callie asked.

"Oh, they're fine. Well past their prime, but what isn't?" Ras asked. He felt the cabling along the underside, pulling it into the light to inspect. "Corroded."

"That's another reason I want to find out if the Great Overload can be reversed," Callie said. "I don't think we were meant to fly. Not that there is anything wrong with it, but even birds can't stay up forever."

Ras retrieved a wrench stuck to a magnetized metal bar on the wall before moving to an upright toolbox. "Could you flip the left switch by the ladder?" He rooted around until he found old cables comparable to the corroded set.

At the flick of a switch, one of the engines fell silent and the ship tilted a little to starboard.

"Are we turning?" Callie asked. "Should I flip it back on?"

"We're fine. I'll correct course after this. Might as well keep moving forward," Ras said. He moved to position himself on his back underneath the engine and began loosening the nut securing the cabling system. "Do you not like flying?"

"Oh, I love it out here," she said. "It's just…"

"Clouds get boring?"

"Nothing is boring compared to that basement," she said. "It's just that I want to see lakes and rivers and mountains and forests full of trees. It's all going unappreciated right now."

Ras carefully removed the corroded cable, but oil immediately spurted across his face. *This would happen in front of her, wouldn't it?* He wiped his mouth before berating the engine. "I don't care what anybody says, that was not a feature. You deserved to be updated, you know that?"

"Are you all right?" Callie asked.

"Fine. Just reminding myself what oil tastes like." He turned his head to spit a greasy strain of saliva. "Sorry. You were saying, about those things that all sound like they're words you know and I don't. Rakes and livers and whatnot."

Callie laughed. "It would just be nice to see them, is all."

"Energy poisoning and exploding aside…you're not afraid of Remnants?" Ras asked.

"That's not a nice way to refer to them," Callie said.

"What do you call them?" Ras plugged the hole with the new cables, fastening the nut.

"They're just people that got left behind…assuming anybody is still alive down there."

"Oh, they're down there," Ras said, pulling himself out from underneath the engine and wiping his blackened face with a hand-kerchief. "My dad knew a few pilots who weren't afraid to dive for relics. Months later he later saw their ships crewed by pale men with ragged clothes that didn't know how to fly. Probably murdered the pilot."

"You talk about them like they're bogeymen," Callie said. "You missed a spot." She pointed to her forehead.

Ras rubbed his forehead with the rag. "I mean, it's not their fault Atmo cities couldn't hold everyone…I just wouldn't want to meet the kind of people that are slowly poisoned by Convergences generation after generation. That has to do something to them," he said. "Besides, imagine not knowing if your baby would be born a Knack—"

"I get the picture," Callie said. "But wouldn't it be amazing to find a way to fix things?"

"You think they'd let us land? They probably hate us for leaving them."

"Maybe they've figured out why the Great Overload happened." Callie shrugged as she watched Ras step beside her to flick on the engine. It sputtered, then backfired in a concussive blast that belched black smoke into the hold.

"No!" Ras put the rag over his mouth and ushered Callie up the ladder before flicking the engine off and climbing up after her. The smoke billowed up out of the hold behind him as they reached the deck. "Half a house, up in smoke!" He coughed. "Make that another day to *Derailleur*."

After the smoke cleared, Ras spent the remaining daylight hours tinkering with the engine while Callie steered and kept a watchful eye on the horizon for sky pirates or The Collective.

"I can barely see where we're going anymore," Callie's muffled voice filtered into the hold from the bridge.

Ras looked out the porthole to see pitch black and checked his watch to confirm his stomach's assessment that it was well past dinnertime.

He lobbed the wrench to the wall, and it stuck against the magnetized strip with a clang. Climbing the ladder to the deck, he looked up to see Callie softly illuminated by the console's faint blue light.

"Crescent moon's out tonight," she said, pointing to the horizon.

Ras looked back over his shoulder at the sliver of white barely illuminating the clouds. "We could probably keep flying if the moon was full. But at least we'll get to see some stars." He watched Callie crane her neck to stare up at the sparkling sky.

"Remember when you used to tell me their names?" she asked.

He did. Reciting incorrect names for constellations to the pretty neighbor girl was the closest his nine-year-old self ever got to flirting. "How old were you when you figured out what they were really called?" Ras asked. Stepping up to the bridge to join her, he gently moved her aside so he could resume command of the vessel.

"I already knew, but I think I liked your names better." She looked back down to him and smiled. "Besides, I don't think anyone owns them, so who's to say your names weren't just as good?"

"Right. Because Megastar was more elegant than Cassius."

"There's nothing wrong with Megastar," she said, laughing. "It's very descriptive." She took in a deep breath and let out a heavy sigh.

"You all right?" Ras asked.

"It's nothing. I'm fine," she said, plastering on her best fake smile.

"C'mon navi, out with it." Ras meant to sound playful, but his words had more of an edge than he anticipated.

"I just had a rough headache while you were working on the engine. I'm fine now."

Ras nodded. The concept of the trip keeping her constantly away from a physician's care wasn't something he had considered. He imagined her falling unconscious onto the wheel, throwing the ship into a dive while he was down in the hold. "Will you promise to tell me when those start?"

"Yeah," she said. The usual joy that accompanied most of her facial expressions was now absent for a moment before she changed the subject. "I think I'm going to go see what food Hal gave us. Any requests?" she asked as she began descending the stairs to the deck.

"I'm not picky, I'll eat whatever." Ras smiled. "Fair warning, I only know how to make windcakes."

"Dare I ask?"

Ras laughed. "It's like a pancake, but the mix is different. Thicker. I think they find whatever grain they use on the mountains. It's easy for wind merchants to just keep a bag of dry mix next to the stove if they want a hot meal. Just add water."

"So I'll be cooking for the entirety of this trip," Callie said half to herself before opening the door to the quarters.

"Unless you want windcakes," Ras called over the railing.

She stopped and looked up at him. "Is that all you ate when you were out collecting?"

"Like I said, not picky." He watched her disappear into the room beneath him.

Ras wasn't entirely certain how they'd be able to afford restocking with what little money they had between them, or even how long the trip would last if more engine difficulties arose. He'd need to be frugal with Flint when it came time to barter for the engines.

Looking over the horizon, not a single mountaintop peaked through the cloud floor. Ras hoped to anchor down to a mountain for the night, but wasn't finding any prospects. He didn't want to risk setting down somewhere with wind potent enough to overwhelm Callie's Energy threshold, but he also didn't want to let *The Brass Fox* drift aimlessly into the clutches of a band of nocturnal sky pirates.

At the pull of a lever, the collection tube lowered into the clouds. The dash beeped. *Level 1.* They would be suitably safe for the night.

Ras pushed the wheel forward, dipping the nose forward until clouds spilled over the deck. A clanging noise from the quarters and a shout of surprise reminded Ras to ease the descent. "Sorry!"

Callie exited the quarters and began to inquire what was going on until she saw the clouds quickly engulf her. "Why are we going below cloud cover again?" she asked before disappearing in the fog.

"We're going to have to lay down anchor soon."

"But, the Energy—" she began.

"We're in Level 1 territory. It'll be like walking around on *Verdant*," Ras said, just as *The Brass Fox* exited the clouds to the dark world below. What little light escaped through the clouds allowed Ras to barely make out some of the topography. It didn't shimmer, so he at least knew they weren't over a body of water.

"Do you think anyone is down there?" Callie asked.

"Maybe. I doubt a Remnant would climb up our anchor if that's what you're worried about."

"I hadn't considered that," Callie said, becoming lost in thought. A long moment passed before she snapped herself out of it. "Dinner should be ready soon," she said before disappearing once more into the room.

Once *The Brass Fox* descended low enough, Ras abandoned his position at the helm to work the anchor's crank, lowering the hunk of metal until the chain went slack. He looked over the side to see it resting in what appeared to be a grown-over field of some crop long since allowed to run wild.

He shut down the remaining engine, its drone giving way to the teeming sounds of nature so unfamiliar to his ears. He heard a low roar from somewhere in the distance but couldn't discern its origin.

It didn't sound like an animal or an airship, so he let the mystery rest until morning and made his way to the Captain's quarters for the first time since his ship had been called *The Copper Fox*.

It took Ras a moment to recognize the usually disheveled room. For once, it was spotless, something he attributed more to Callie than Tibbs. From the makeshift mini-galley to his left he smelled something savory cooking.

Ahead, Callie faced the door, occupying one of the four chairs circling the table in the center of the room. She stood, carefully removing the typewriter from the table, and placed it atop a set of maps on the rolltop desk behind her.

The flimsy bed Ras avoided sleeping on whenever he could afford to sat in the back corner to his right. He wished Callie had something more substantial to rest on for their voyage.

He walked over to the old wardrobe he had long ago bolted to the wall, desperately needing a towel to wipe off the grime of the day. He wondered if his mother had brought his clothes aboard. Opening the double doors, it took Ras a moment to realize he was staring at some of Callie's more delicate clothing items hanging in place of his.

"Hey!" she shouted. "Your stuff is in the drawers," she said, flustered.

Ras quickly shut the doors. "Sorry. Won't happen again," he said as he crossed the room to grab a dishrag from the galley. He scrubbed at his face in an attempt to hide the blush.

The whole room glowed warmly under the Energy lamps that hung from the ceiling. By nature they glowed green, but Tibbs' orange fixtures over them cast a more natural hue.

"Thanks for cleaning the place up."

"Had to. I can't concentrate on writing if there is clutter."

"I'll remember that," said Ras, lifting the lid to reveal red soup with steam rolling from the surface.

"I hope you're a fan of the world famous Tourbillon tomato soup," she said as she stood. She walked to the galley and grabbed two mismatched bowls and a ladle from the pantry.

"Who wouldn't be?" he asked genuinely. He spotted himself in the mirror. He was a complete wreck. Mostly dry clothes hung off of him, his left pant leg was ripped from snagging it on the engine earlier in the day, and he was certain Callie was being polite and not mentioning the smell of smoke from the repeated attempts at starting the failed engine.

He slumped into the chair facing the galley so he could see Callie. For a moment he wondered if this was what it would look like if they were married, or if this was what it looked like on those few voyages where Emma went out on runs with Elias during their first years together.

"You're staring," Callie said, teasing.

"Sorry. Long day," he said with a lopsided grin. "Thanks for dinner."

Callie brought the bowls to the table before she sat. "At least we're on our way." She held up her spoon ceremoniously. "To seeing the world."

It took a moment for Ras to realize she wanted him to clink his spoon the way two would toast a happy occasion.

"Hear, hear." Ras tapped his spoon against hers and dug in.

"Did it turn out okay?" she asked as soon as Ras had his first taste. "Sorry, I always ask when the other person's mouth is full."

Ras swallowed eagerly to answer, then winced as the heat of the soup burned its way down to his stomach. "It's great, really."

A couple minutes passed with nothing but the clanks of spoons on bowls before Callie broke the silence. "Have you ever been to *Derailleur?*" she asked.

"My dad took me once when I was eight. It's a least ten times the size of *Verdant*. I once heard that almost a quarter of all the refined fuel from *The Winnower* goes to feed its Helios engines."

"No!" she said in disbelief. "Do you think we'll see *The Winnower?*"

"Maybe," Ras said, scraping the last of the soup from the bowl, its warmth having escaped. "Since it covers The Origin, I doubt the Energy will be terribly thick around it. We might be able to dip down and see it."

"Would you like some more?" she asked.

He shook his head. "Need to save what we can when we can. Thank you, though." He stood and brought his bowl to the galley to clean. "Nobody's going to climb the anchor."

"What?"

"The chain is too long for anyone sane to climb," Ras said.

"Oh, yeah, of course it is," she said. "I knew that."

He walked to the door. "Good night, and thanks again for dinner."

"Wait, where are you going to sleep?"

"I'll figure something out," he said before ducking out the door and into the night.

Outside was peaceful. The cloud cover kept the stars from peeking through, but at least sky pirates and The Collective wouldn't be searching for them this low.

After one more cursory check of the rigging and the anchor, Ras descended into the hold and grabbed a tangled bit of rope netting he once used as a hammock on a particularly slow collection day. He untangled the mess, securing it between the engines. Satisfied, he balled up his jacket as a pillow and eased his way into the makeshift bed.

Ras drifted off, wondering if Hal would be able to keep Bravo Company from attacking again.

The dreamless sleep ended after an indeterminate amount of time as Ras bolted awake to Callie shoving him. "Ras! Ras! Fire!"

CHAPTER NINE
The Clockwork Metropolis

RAS WOULD HAVE FLIPPED OUT OF THE HAMMOCK ENTIRELY IF IT weren't for his leg tangling in the netting. A dull roar filled the area from every direction. "Where?" he shouted as he slipped out of one of his boots to expedite his extraction.

As the world came into focus he spotted Callie sitting on the floor hugging her legs. She pointed up. "I don't want to blow up!"

Blow up?

Ras scrambled up the ladder to get above deck and squinted at the sudden rush of light as the sound grew louder. His eyes adjusted to the daylight, allowing him to notice the small green tongues of flame showering down around the ship. They sizzled when intercepted by falling drops of water. As best Ras could tell, the ship wasn't on fire. Ras leaned over the edge to spot the source.

A Convergence drifted high above the ship.

Rain pattered on Ras' face and one of the green tongues of flame dissipated as it almost came into contact with him. "Are you watching over us?" Ras asked, half to himself.

Peeling his attention from the burning sky, Ras looked out and spotted a cascade of water pouring down into a larger pool. *That explains the sound from last night.* He wished he was more cognizant of his surroundings to appreciate them, then remembered the terrified Callie below deck.

Sticking his head down into the hold, Ras said, "It's all right. We're all right." Not garnering a response, he climbed down to meet her. "Hey, it's just a Convergence." Ras was fairly certain that phrase had never been uttered before. He kneeled down next to her huddled form.

"You shouldn't be near me!" she said, tears forming.

"What's going on—" Ras began, not moving.

"I'm a Knack, Ras! I'm a Knack and I'm going to blow up!"

"You can't be," said Ras.

"Yes, I can! That's why I have my headaches! That's why my parents put me in the basement! The doctors say I'm so sensitive to Energy that I could go at any minute, and a Convergence is right above us!" She sobbed, her body heaving with each gasp of air.

Suddenly the basement prison made so much more sense. She was Mr. Tourbillon's supposed time-bomb baby. Ras wrapped his arms around her instinctively. "Hey, hey, it's all right. You're not a Knack, trust me."

"Why do you keep saying that?" she asked.

"Because you're closer to a Convergence than anyone has a right to be, and you haven't blown up," Ras said. "Look at yourself, you don't even have Energy poisoning." He unwrapped one of her arms from her legs and brought her hand up in front of her. "Your skin turns gray before you blow up. What color do you see?"

Callie took a deep, shuddering breath. "Not gray."

"Not gray."

She smiled sweetly and tears began forming in her eyes again. She wiped one away, laughing. "For the longest time I wouldn't let myself really believe I was a Knack, but until you know for sure, there's still a little part of you that wonders if the next moment will be your last…I guess that settles that."

"I'd say it does. Breathe deep, Callie. There's a new, old world out there with nothing to be afraid of. Well, at least not from the wind," Ras amended, releasing the embrace and patting her on the shoulder. "C'mon, the fire is really pretty if you don't think it'll kill you."

He stood and offered his hand. She looked up and suppressed a laugh as she noticed Ras' wild hair.

His morning bed-head was something Emma teased him about relentlessly, and having Callie see him like this was its own special brand of mortifying. He quickly tried to tame it by licking a palm and running it over the hair that couldn't pick a direction. "I call it *windswept*. All the wind merchants are doing it."

"Uh-huh." She giggled as she accepted his hand and stood.

Above deck, Callie gave names to everything, pointing out the waterfall pouring into the river. "Is there a chance we could ever go down to the ground?"

"Let's save *Verdant* from sinking first," Ras said, "But how about you find where we are on the map, and I promise I'll take you here after everything's finished."

"A fourth promise?"

"As long as you don't tell anyone about…this," he said, circling a finger around his hair.

"Deal."

They stared at the waterfall through the tongues of flame for another minute before Ras asked, "So, the headaches don't mean you're a Knack."

She nodded. "Maybe someday I'll figure out what's wrong with me."

"I'm not seeing anything," Ras said before leaving to clean up and prep *The Fox* for the flight to *Derailleur*.

After a quick breakfast and raising the anchor, they returned to their positions on the bridge. With a sub-cloud course plotted, Ras propped the wheel and took a brief walk to stretch his legs to pass the time and gaze at the lush world below.

Clouds were simple in their grayscale palette until the sun set them ablaze, but having stared at them his entire life, the changing vista of the ground was a feast for the eyes.

Ras felt much safer flying where few dared to tread, bolstering his hopes that as long as he could continue to stay beneath the clouds, their trip might be healthily uninteresting.

Callie used the next five hours to display her knowledge of the world below, educating Ras on what everything they could see was called, and even tossed in some animal names.

"Honestly, I always wondered what a fox was," Ras said.

"They're cute," Callie said. "With their little paws and white snouts."

"Cute, huh?"

"And cunning," Callie said, attempting to dissuade any thought of renaming the vessel. "People used to think of them as sly."

"I guess that makes it better."

They watched the landscapes change from lush to arid, noting the occasional shadow cast on the clouds above, and even the rare wind merchant collection tube trolling through.

Ras pointed to a small circular gap in the clouds far ahead. The sky just beneath it shimmered in a heated distortion.

"What is that?"

"*Derailleur*. Its engines push so much it's one of the few places in Atmo you can sneak a peek at the ground."

Ras remembered his father telling him the exact same thing. As a young boy afraid of heights, he imagined the massive city falling through its self-manufactured hole. Then again, the young boy also thought the clouds were solid and bouncy.

"Do you see what it's connected to?" Ras asked, using a finger to draw a line in the air, pointing out a cable that looked thin as a thread from such a distance. It reached down to what looked like a domed version of a floating city sitting on the land.

"*The Winnower*," Callie said reverently, "So that means..."

"Underneath that thing is the Origin of All Energy. Trapped," Ras said. "They relocated *Derailleur* here after building *The Winnower* to fuel the city more efficiently...and cut off sky pirates from the resource."

"And choking *Verdant*," Callie said.

The large glass dome of *The Winnower* glowed a vivid green, filtering out whatever Energy the Origin would have normally kicked out to the winds. The ground surrounding the structure looked dead and barren.

"We're still probably half an hour out," Ras said, eyeing the distance. "It's going to look that small for a while," he said to Callie before making his way to the helm to pull back on the wheel.

The Brass Fox climbed steadily above the cloud level, joining a cluster of airships on their way to the city. If any of the caravan was surprised by the newcomer, thankfully none of them showed it, or else they just chalked up the surprise to a wearying journey nearly concluded.

The city itself was admittedly magnificent with its towering skyline above a stabilization ring, as though it were two cities mirrored. It was truly ten times the size of *Verdant*, if not more. Ships queued up in long lanes for trade and sightseeing at the hub of Atmo, and *The Brass Fox* had to slow to a crawl and wait for its turn to enter the city.

"Oh my dear sweet goodness," Callie said in a gasp, holding her hands over her mouth. "I feel so small."

"Just wait until we get closer," Ras said, happy to play tour guide. Seeing the city again through a pair of fresh eyes was amusing, but having not seen the city in so long, the sense of wonder was not wholly lost on him, either.

"My dad used to bring me pocket watches from here when collection runs took him this way," Ras said. "I bet it'd be impossible to find the shop he went to."

"What made you want to collect pocket watches?" Callie asked.

"It's what he brought me so they reminded me of him."

"Oh, I'll be right back!" Callie said before running down to the Captain's quarters.

The Brass Fox was queued up behind a much larger luxury tour vessel painted green, and behind her were a couple of personal skiffs. Ras had never seen skiffs that could fly like a ship before, as all the ones on *Verdant* could only fly five feet from the ground. *Must be a new kind of motor.*

Ras observed the traffic patterns closely as they entered the main channel of the city. He didn't know the rules of the skies when it came to flying through the city as he was used to just flying over one.

He gawked at the levels upon levels of walkways lining the channel and the oddly dressed people going about their day. Brightly colored shop signs made their best attempt to draw in customers who weren't waiting in lines for public transport.

Someone's yelling at Ras snapped him out of his sightseeing. He jerked the ship to starboard to avoid collision with what looked like another wind merchant vessel. The unfriendly gesture the other pilot gave indicated there was no spirit of brotherhood.

Callie stepped out in what Ras guessed was her attempt at a disguise. She wore a black bowler hat and one of Ras' jackets, swimming in the dark green fabric. "I hope you don't mind," she said.

"No, it's not a bad idea. I just think a walking pile of clothes might draw more attention," he chided.

"Hey, this isn't *Verdant*. Just look around…I'm not going to stand out like this." She gestured to the people walking on the streets, and Ras saw that was right; it would be difficult to stand out. He had never seen such a diverse group of people living so packed in together.

Billboards and advertisements hung from tall buildings and promoted products ranging from the newest model of Helios engine to a bizarre item that Ras couldn't discern if children were supposed to play with or eat.

"Don't you just want to live here?" Callie said, soaking in every new, weird, and fascinating detail *Derailleur* had to offer. She waved like she was on a parade float. She spotted a little girl dressed head to toe in a deep royal blue who was walking along the channel with her mother. The little girl smiled and waved back until her mother pulled her along.

Ras wrinkled his nose at some new offending odor. "This doesn't feel...crowded?"

"Of course it does! It feels alive!" She took a deep breath in and choked a little. "Well, no place is perfect."

After an hour of crawling traffic, they finally saw the opening to the eastern end of *Derailleur*. On the right stood a massive statue of Foster Helios, Sr., holding an outstretched hand as if about to pluck a star from the sky. It was in the courtyard for the headquarters of The Collective.

Callie turned to Ras. "Did Hal realize where he was sending us?" She pointed down the way at an illuminated sign on the building next to The Collective's headquarters that boldly read FLINT'S.

"That's...inconvenient," Ras said, grimacing. There was little they could do but putter past the building and hope that Flint didn't ask too many questions.

FOSTER HELIOS III SAT at his desk on the sixty-fifth floor of The Collective's headquarters. The office, like the mansion, had its decor stripped and lent the white room an austere feel. He pored over the report on his desk, acknowledging the man entering on the opposite side of the room with a slight lift of his hand. "How many ships do we have out looking for them?" Foster asked.

"A full detachment, scattered in a three-hundred mile radius between *Derailleur* and The Bowl," the uniformed man said, stopping at Foster's desk.

"And nothing," Foster said, closing the folder. "Did you send a dive team to search beneath the clouds?"

"No, sir, I didn't imagine they would risk—"

"What, then, do you imagine they did to evade two-hundred ships?" Foster asked.

"We do have a lead on who is aboard the ship, sir," the man said. He placed two sheets of paper with sketches on Foster's desk. "There have been reports of a kidnapper leaving The Bowl, and the vessel matches the description of the one that met with Napier."

Foster nodded, then dismissed the man with a shooing gesture. "Put out a bulletin across all Collective ships. We want Miss Tourbillon returned safely to her father. Flyers, billboards, newspaper ads...blanket it. I want everyone to know her face."

"A REFERRAL! I LOVE REFERRALS," Flint said, scratching his bushy beard before ushering Ras and Callie into his office.

They followed the mountain of a man wearing greasy overalls and a smile through the doorway to his office. He led them into the mostly-windowed room, motioning for them to sit in the iron chairs in front of his desk.

"Who sent you? I'll give them a discount next time," he said with a beaming smile that crinkled his dark brown eyes.

"I'm afraid we can't exactly say," Ras said.

Flint plopped the bag of money on his desk and made quick work of the purse strings with his thick hands. He reached inside and extracted a note. In impeccable penmanship it read, '*Please accommodate my friends as best you can, Flint.*' He chuckled. "Nice friend you've got." He tucked the note into a pocket next to a dingy red rag and dug deeper into the bag to see what sort of budget the young couple had. Satisfied, he looked out at *The Brass Fox*, which was held in a suspension rig. The vessel was dwarfed in his repair bay. "Let's have a looksee."

"One of the engines won't start," Ras said.

"Sure, sure. I'm surprised you made it all the way from..." He turned back to the pair sitting on the couch. "Where did you say you were from?" He asked as he fanned through the stack of bills.

"I'm afraid we didn't," Ras said.

"Then I'm afraid you might have to pay a higher discretion fee."

"Discretion fee?" Callie asked.

"Sure! I have nosy neighbors, and anything not done on the level winds up costing me extra...grease money." He shrugged. "It's not like I get to keep the money, but I also don't like getting shut down. Besides, I doubt your friend wouldn't have sent you here with a bag of money if I wasn't the best."

"You're asking us to sell ourselves out?" Callie asked, prompting a groan from Ras. "What?"

"It's fine if you don't want to say," Flint said, standing and walking to his office window. "Just know I charge extra if I find out I'm being lied to. But let's focus on what you need first and then we'll see where we stand." The cordial grin returned. "Now, are we looking to fix that engine or replace the set?"

"It was requested that we upgrade," Ras said.

"Do you disagree?"

Ras shrugged. "A lot of sacrifice went into getting those engines."

"Well, they're classic Windstrider scoops. Nothing beats 'em if they're flying low or below cloud cover, but who does that, right? Won't fly you very high though. Are you looking for Helios engines?"

"If that's the best option…"

"I've never heard of a man less excited about free upgrades," Flint said with a laugh.

"What's wrong with Helios engines?" Callie asked.

"Well, they have a bad habit of breaking if they get too much raw Energy around them," Flint said. "So you better not fly too low. Plus you have to buy fuel." Flint paced, causing the floor to creak. "How about I leave the working Windstrider as a backup and put a couple Helios in?"

"Flip that," Ras said. "Add a Helios as a backup and fix the broken Windstrider," he said resolutely. "I don't like paying for fuel and flying low doesn't bother me."

"Brave man. But a rebuild of the Windstrider costs more than a new Helios. To be honest, I don't know how they make them so cheap."

"It's because they make them cheap," Ras said, deadpanning.

"They do, don't they? But there ain't enough money in this bag for a rebuild plus a Helios…plus the discretion fee."

"C'mon," Ras said, protesting.

"C'mon, nothing," Flint said. "You've still got my interest piqued… how's about you tell old Flint who sent you my way and I'll make sure a little bit stays in the bag? You won't even have to tell me your names or where you're from."

Callie looked over at Ras, arching an eyebrow. "Nobody would believe him."

"All right, deal," Ras said.

Flint grunted an approval.

"You know a Dayus?"

"Can't say I do," Flint said.

"He works for..." Ras leaned in close, prompting Flint to do the same. He whispered, "Hal Napier."

"Hal!" Flint bellowed. "I haven't seen that old coot in at least a dozen years! Needed some work done on the old *'Fisher*. Well, now the sack of money makes much more sense."

Ras stood. "If you get a chance, the steering to port is a bit sluggish."

"Don't worry, you won't even recognize her when you pick her up. Give me about seven hours and I'll have her turned around for you... just be sure to put in a good word for me with Napier. I'd love to get my wrench back on *The 'Fisher*."

The wind merchant and his navigator became cautious tourists as they left Flint's. Ras procured a map and the second order of business was to hand it to Callie before she snatched it from him after three time-wasting wrong turns.

After half an hour of taking in the sights, sounds, and smells along Callie's correct route, they arrived at the library.

"It's bigger than the entire University!" she exclaimed. The building's marble columns shot to the sky at the top of the stairs they began to climb, giving the structure an otherworldly feel.

"You know," Ras said breathlessly, placing a hand on the thick marble column to steady himself after their ascent, "you don't realize how little you move when your entire job revolves around a steering wheel and some buttons. You feel like you're going everywhere...but you're really not." He looked up to the non-winded Callie. "Don't give me that look."

Callie just smiled as she walked through the threshold of the tall double-doors and into the foyer. Her shoes lightly echoed on the ornate tile floor and she stared up to the tall stained glass windows that failed to let any light through them. Frowning, she looked back to Ras. "I'm guessing when this thing was built, there weren't skyscrapers next to it."

Ras took a deep breath. "I think that's a fair assessment." He looked ahead of them to the rows upon rows of books. The vaulted ceiling in the foyer showed the beginnings of two more floors. He looked around nervously and felt exposed in the open even though nothing pointed to anyone taking a particular interest in them. "Where do we begin?"

Callie began walking into the maze of dark bookshelves and dusty tomes. "First stop: history." She traced a finger along the guide at end of one of the bookshelves. "2H, section 8."

"Second floor?" Ras asked, craning his neck to the right in an attempt to read a few spines. "Why would they have cookbooks here?"

"Why not?" Callie shrugged, but her smile was permanently affixed. They continued deeper into the library, occasionally coming across a sparsely populated reading area until they reached a matched pair of spiral staircases.

Ras looked up to see they reached high above into a taller section of the library that seemed to climb a dozen floors, if not more. They walked to the stairwell, ascending each metal step in a corkscrew until they reached the second floor. Callie began looking around at the ends of the bookcases for their designations.

"Can I help you, miss?" an elderly gentleman pushing a metal book cart asked. He wore a frock bearing the library's logo and smiled eagerly at the opportunity to be of service. "You have that look about you."

"Do I look lost?" Callie asked. She looked down at the man's name tag: Wilfrid.

"No, no, no. You look plenty at home, young miss. You just have the look of someone who's ready to begin but might need to be pointed in the right direction, is all." Wilfrid tried to comb down the wild white wisps of hair into something more streamlined, but failed.

Ras leaned in, "We should probably—"

"He'll save us some time," Callie said, still smiling. "Yes, I'm looking for a good book on the weapons the Elders used during the war."

Wilfrid gave a soft chuckle. "Now that's a first. And you, young sir?"

"I'll have what she's having," Ras said, jutting a thumb at Callie.

"Two orders of military history, coming right up…if you'll follow me," Wilfrid said, spinning the cart with a squeaky wheel and disappeared down a set of aisles.

"I like him. He's cute," Callie said.

"Like a fox?"

"Hopefully not like a fox." Callie walked toward Wilfrid, waving her hand for Ras to follow. They caught up with the old man momentarily, easily tracking the squeaky wheel.

"Now, I thought the University was on break. Did some sadistic professor give you an assignment for next term?" Wilfrid asked, raising a wispy white eyebrow.

"Oh, no, sir, just naturally curious," Callie said.

He stopped the cart and turned to look at Callie. A grin spread wide. "Good on you. Now, you might find better luck learning about The Elders in the folklore section." He reached out and pulled two red leather-bound books with golden edges on their pages. "But these are the crowd favorites on The Clockwork War. That should get you started while I go find something out of folklore."

Callie graciously accepted the books, her hands trembling slightly as Wilfrid tottered off with his cart. Clutching the books to her chest, She half-skipped to an area with four stuffed chairs surrounding a table before plopping into the one facing the atrium. "Best idea ever." She ran her hand over the cover that held the embossed title: *The War of Time, Volume I.* She looked down at the author's name.

Dayus Ofanim.

"Ras?" Callie handed him Volume II as he approached. "How many Dayuses do you think there are?"

"Are or were?" Ras asked, inspecting his book as he sat in the chair left of Callie. "It might be him. He was in the middle of everything, after all." Ras cracked the book open. "And now he makes eggs."

"I tried asking Hal everything I could about the war while you were unconscious," Callie said, "but maybe Dayus will be a bit more helpful." She flipped to the first few pages. "Ooh, a first edition."

"What am I looking for?" Ras asked.

"Most sources say the Great Overload didn't happen until The Elders were shut into The Wild. Some say it was before that. I'd start with the last battle over Treding and see if the book mentions the city of Bogues erupting first," Callie said, already half lost in her book.

Ras turned to the table of contents and ran a finger down to the last chapter. "*The Battle of Bogues.* Sounds promising."

Callie looked up, eyes dancing with excitement. "There wasn't a Battle of Bogues. The war ended after Treding."

"Or did it?" Ras flipped toward the end of the book, fanning the paper until he hit the final chapter. The pages were blank.

Ras held up the open book to show Callie, who reached over and snatched it from him, flipped back a few pages to scan the passage about Treding, then forward to the blank pages.

She shut the book and inspected the binding. "The gilding on the paper is a different shade of gold. Someone actually went through the trouble to bind and paint it so nobody would notice the missing pages."

"Hey, at least you know you're on to something. We just need to figure out what happened in Bogues."

The squeaky wheel announced Wilfrid's imminent arrival. Callie shot up from her seat, rushing up to him with blank pages exposed.

"Well now, what's this?" Wilfrid asked, examining the paper.

"Someone rebound blank pages here," Callie said, offering the book.

Wilfrid took it, stacking it atop two other books. He then carefully placed his reading glasses atop his nose and furrowed his brow, inspecting it. "Perhaps it is a misprint. I can check with the front desk to see if we have another edition in the archives. My apologies," Wilfrid said with a serious nod. "In the meanwhile, I've brought you a book on folklore from one of the territories closest to The Wild: *The Demons of Bogues*." He offered a cotton-bound purple hardback. "And a children's book."

Callie looked at the illustrated cover Wilfrid still held. It showed two clockwork Elders, one with decidedly feminine features, and a smaller clockwork, all standing above the title. "*The Littlest Elder?*"

Wilfrid chuckled. "I'm afraid The Great Overload didn't leave much time to...document the subject." He placed *The War of Time, Volume II* in his cart and turned to head down to the front desk.

"What'd we get?"

Callie tucked *The War of Time, Volume I* underneath an arm and held up each book for Ras to see.

"I call the one with pictures," Ras said.

The sound of footfalls clapping on tile echoed through the library. Ras and Callie turned their attention to the man in a Collective uniform running up to the information desk, arriving just before Wilfrid.

The man in uniform placed two stacks of posters with dark black print atop each.

"What does it say?" Callie asked. "My eyes aren't the best."

Ras squinted. "One says…wanted. The other…Oh no."

"What?"

"Kidnapped." He could only assume whose faces were sketched underneath. "We have to go, now."

Before Wilfrid could study the posters, Ras pulled Callie into an unoccupied aisle. He heard a muffled sniffle beneath the hat and oversized green jacket, and he lifted the front brim of the bowler to see Callie's wet eyes look up at him.

"What have I done?" she said in a whimper.

"You didn't do anything."

"Exactly. If I had laid everything out in front of my parents instead of just leaving—"

"You'd still be stuck in a basement in a sinking city," Ras whispered. "Just look at where you are now."

"I'm in the library I've always dreamed of but can't enjoy because that sweet old man is probably going to realize who he was talking to any second now and we'll be trapped." She sniffled. "I'm sorry."

"Let's just add this to the list of places I'll take you, sound good?"

She took a deep breath, let it out slowly, and nodded.

"We need to get to the first level. I doubt there are any exits from here up." Ras led Callie to the spiral staircase and quickly descended and hid behind the nearest bookshelf.

Ras peeked out to see two security guards walking in from outside and setting up a post at the entrance. He ducked back into the aisle. "How about a very quick tour to see if there's a back exit?" His eyes darted around as he tried to imagine a best course of action, and they fell on Callie. "Good call on the hat."

They walked to the end of the aisle away from the entrance and information desk, then turned, following a side wall deeper into the building. Ras caught a glimpse of more security guards amassing around the information desk, taking flyers and studying them.

"So much for friendly librarians," Ras said. He ducked low and looked ahead of him to see a set of tables for readers before the bookshelves resumed. The gap would leave them exposed.

There were a few readers scattered about the tables, so crawling underneath would surely alert the guards.

"Swap me jackets," Ras whispered. Callie obliged and they swapped as quietly as possible. "And the hat." Ras donned the hat, tucking all his hair underneath.

"I guess looking different is a start," Callie said.

"I'll walk across first. They'll be trying to spot two people," Ras said. "If I make it across unnoticed, wait a moment before you follow."

"Wait, what do I do if they chase you?" she asked.

"I don't know, throw a book at them or knock over a shelf."

She looked at him like he had just asked her to skin a kitten with a dull spoon.

Ras picked a particularly large book off of the shelf and cracked it open. He began walking as casually as he could manage with his head down, checking to make sure that he at least held the book right side up, and pretended to read.

Heavy footsteps indicated the guards breaking off from the information desk, but Ras didn't look up to give them a free glance at his face. Thankfully, none of the footfalls seemed to be heading toward him.

Making it across the open area, he placed the book on a nearby shelf. He looked back at Callie, who held a stern expression, gesturing something about taking a book off the shelf, and Ras realized she was getting onto him for misplacing the book. Ras did his best not to roll his eyes and motioned for her to cross over. She slowly made her way out to the open area but was only a few footsteps in when a guard shouted. Callie froze.

"Hey, stop her!" a voice from above shouted.

Ras ran over to Callie to grab her. He looked up to the balcony to see the guard wasn't facing them at all.

A thunderous crash resounded and dust flew up from the opposite side of the room a good distance away. The crash was followed by another, then another. Ras watched the tops of one bookshelf after another topple in a cascade.

"All those books," Callie murmured.

"Look at the front door," Ras said, pointing as security guards filed in toward the commotion and away from the front door. "That's our cue."

Ras looked over and realized that the bookshelves would topple and eventually cut off their exit. It became a race to see if they could get back before the final bookcase fell, blocking their escape.

They darted back through the same aisle that led to the staircase as the crashing sound grew louder. At some point the cascade doubled in two directions and the toppling bookcases took a shortcut toward the front door.

"Run!" Ras shouted as they entered the foyer, joining into a mix of other frantic citizens. The increased frequency of the crashes concerned him as they still had two-hundred feet to clear and only three bookshelves left to outrun. Ras saw a book cart and began to push it.

The next to last bookshelf collided into the final one by the door. Ras shoved the cart forward as the final shelf toppled, and did so just in time. The bookcase crashed down on the metal box, and the remaining gap gave about three feet of clearance through which to escape.

Ras slid down to his hands and knees and began to crawl over a pile of books underneath the heavy bookshelf. The wheels on the cart snapped, dropping the shelf by half a foot. Ras flinched but scrambled out and spun around to offer a hand to Callie, who hesitated as the metal cart's sides began to creak and bend.

"C'mon!" he shouted to Callie. She shook her head as the cart groaned. "Now or never."

Clutching the books to her chest, she got down and began to crawl forward. Ras reached underneath and hauled her out just before the cart fully buckled and collapsed under the weight of the shelf, effectively blocking the entrance.

"What was that?" Callie asked weakly.

"Let's let them sort that out," he said, then pointed to her books. "Smart move on keeping those."

"Oh no! I didn't check these out," she said. "I'm a criminal…"

Ras gently grabbed her shoulders and guided her away from the building. "I'm sure we'll return them on the way back," Ras said, perking up at the sound of sirens. "I doubt the police will be cross-checking the stamps in the books."

They descended the marble staircase as quickly as their adrenaline-filled legs would carry them, catching up with the rest of the escapees and blending into the commotion as the *Derailleur* police arrived. The uniformed men seemed far more focused on whatever was going on inside the library.

In the distance, they heard glass shattering and more shouting coming from the direction of the library.

"We should probably just wait it out at Flint's," Callie said, disappointment hanging heavy on her voice.

"No, we don't have to." Ras took the hat off and gave it back to her. "Looks better on you," he said, "besides, there might be people waiting for us at Flint's now. Worse comes to worst, we'll sneak onboard and steal the ship back. Either way, I don't want to spend my day in one place afraid we're going to be found," Ras said.

Callie attempted a smile, but failed. "Why don't we check out the shop your dad used to bring you back pocket watches from?"

"That'd be nice."

They walked along a sidewalk far enough away from the library that things seemed peaceful once again.

"Help me!" The cry pierced the calm.

Down the alley to their left, three figures brawled, or more correctly, two large men kept a small woman from escaping by throwing her against the nearby dumpster.

Chapter Ten
The Piper

"I'm sorry!" the young woman cried. "I don't have anything else." She whimpered as one of the thugs shook her violently by her collar before throwing her to the ground.

Ras watched for a brief moment before he changed his course and made a direct line toward the scuffle. "Wait here," he said over his shoulder.

"But, I—" Callie sputtered as Ras left.

Ras walked along the right edge of the alley as quietly as he could so as not to be noticed by the two men. One held a wrench ready to strike the woman, while the other, a balding man with a mustache, grabbed her.

"Anyone?" she cried desperately. The woman looked to maybe be all of five feet tall and had shockingly white short messy hair. Her frame made a large boom as the mustached man slammed her hard into the dumpster again. She let out an involuntary cry when she hit. Her lip was already bleeding and she was wide-eyed with panic.

She slumped to the ground as the mustached man let her go. She noticed Ras approaching but tried not to make it obvious by turning her attention back to the two men. "Can I just say one thing?"

"Wot?" the mustached man said with a grunt. He heard footsteps quickly approaching and turned to see a blur sprinting toward him, but before he had time to react, the blur had already wrapped its arms around his waist, planting a shoulder into his rib cage. The two crumpled to the ground with a hard thud followed by a sickening crack. "Harris!" he shouted before focusing on sucking in air and cradling his ribcage.

Ras stood, catching his bearings just in time to duck out of the way of a large wrench aimed at his head. "Go!" Ras shouted to the young woman.

She stood, but instead of running, she placed a swift booted kick to the mustached man's midsection, expelling what air he had collected in the finest curse he knew.

Ras flung himself at Harris in an attempt to wrestle the large wrench away, but recognized too late that it was a trick and quickly found himself flipped over the thug's shoulder, landing squarely on his back. Ras looked up to see the wrench swinging down and rolled out of the way just in time for the wrench to strike pavement instead of skull.

Spinning on the ground, Ras solidly planted his heel into Harris' shin, eliciting a scream of pain. He could see the small woman digging around in the jacket pockets of the mustached man but didn't have time to wonder what she was doing.

Ras tried to evade Harris' next swing by rolling out of the way, but he went the wrong direction, planting himself into the side of the dumpster and halting his escape. With nowhere to go, the wrench connected hard with Ras' left arm. He cried out in pain as the big man reached back to swing again.

"Ras!" Callie called out.

He heard a clattering sound grow louder as a metal pipe rolled down the alley, stopping against his leg. Ras dove to collect it and avoided the next swing of the wrench.

Picking up the pipe, Ras swung low at Harris, connecting with his leg. Harris faltered from the blow and fell to one knee. Ras took the opportunity to jump onto Harris' back and pressed the pipe against the man's throat.

Harris flailed wildly in an attempt to remove Ras and swung the wrench over his shoulder like an oversized flyswatter, almost connecting with Ras' head. The wrench instead slammed into Ras' shoulder. He winced but pulled the pipe even tighter, and Harris collapsed into a heap before he could swing the wrench again.

Ras looked up to see the mustached man down for the count as well. He shakily came to his feet, looking for Callie, who stood fifteen feet away, clutching her books.

"Are you all right?" she asked Ras.

Before he could respond, the small white-haired woman stood up from behind the dumpster and launched herself at him.

"Thank you, thank you, thank you!" She wrapped her arms around him, then put her hands on the sides of his face, stood on her toes, and kissed him full on the lips. "You saved me! Oh, I could kiss you! Wait, I just did. I'm sorry, I just got caught up in the moment," she said rapidly with an almost childlike voice.

She released his face, freeing Ras to touch his lips, still in shock. He felt a slight stickiness and pulled his hand away to see a bit of the woman's blood.

Callie unclenched her jaw before speaking. "What happened here?"

The sprite-like woman turned on her heel to face Callie. "Oh, not just here, about half a dozen of them attacked me in the library. These two were just the most persistent." She leaned over, grabbed the wrench from Harris' hand, and offered it to Ras with a deep bow. "A trophy to commemorate your great victory and to remember the day you saved Dixie Piper!"

Ras hesitantly accepted the makeshift weapon.

Dixie offered her hand next. "People call me Dix, Dixie, Pip, Pipe, or Piper, and I hate all but two of those, so choose wisely." She winked.

"Ras. Pleasure," he said, still a bit shaken from the wrench strikes. He took her hand and gave a nod.

"Pleasure. Say, can we not be here when these two wake up?" Dixie asked, pointing a finger and oscillating it between the two men.

"So the library was you?" Callie asked.

"Indirectly," Dixie said, chagrined. "Again, may I stress the importance of not remaining here?"

"Yeah, we should…we should go," Ras said, still a bit stunned. He shoved the wrench under his belt and began to walk back toward the alley entrance. He looked over to see Dixie walking quickly to keep pace.

She was clad in tight-fitting, gray pants draped with a couple belts over her slender waist, a white shirt marred with a few drops of blood, and a fashionably-cut purple leather jacket.

"Why were they attacking you?" Ras asked.

"Oh, them? They don't like me," Dixie said dismissively.

"Any reason in particular?" Callie asked.

"I kinda got their boss put in jail," she said. "Sky pirates. Hate 'em. You two aren't pirates, are you? Of course not, you don't look the type. Besides, sky pirates don't help people in alleys that are about to get killed." The speed with which she spoke dizzied Ras.

"Ah, Dixie? Sorry to interrupt your conversation, but do we need to get you to somewhere safe?" Ras asked.

"Me?" she asked. "I am somewhere safe. I'm with you," she said with a winning smile. They made it back to the sidewalk outside of the alley. "And I dare say that I owe you something of a favor."

"That's not necessary, I was just trying to help," Ras said.

"And you succeeded, so now I'm trying and hopefully I'll succeed as well. Are you from *Derailleur*?" she asked.

"Do we look that out of place?" Ras asked, keeping an eye out for more flyers.

"Oh, no, no, no, not that. Just most people aren't from here, and I am something of an immensely talented tour guide if there's anything you're looking for," Dixie said.

"What happened in the library?" Callie asked unsympathetically.

"Ah, yeah, that. Well, one of them grabbed me from behind so I kicked off a bookshelf to break free…which worked, but then I started climbing a shelf and when they grabbed me by the ankles to pull me down…book avalanche." She made a sound with her mouth to replicate an explosion. "And mass destruction. Might as well cut up my library card, huh?"

"Do you know of any pocket watch shops?" Ras asked to pull the subject away from Callie's ire.

Dixie lit up. "Ooh! A request! Excellent. Let's see…pocket watches, pocket clocks…there's Crimens, Badger & Fount's, The Gear Outlet, Orville's, The Golden Calendar—"

"Wait," Ras said. "The Orville one. Where's that?"

"That's about two miles away. Bit of a walk," Dixie said. "Back on 8th and Holloway."

Ras looked at his watch. "We have time."

Dixie stopped walking and almost caused Ras and Callie to pile into her. "Let's just take my skiff!"

"Oh, we wouldn't want to impose," Callie said.

"No, really! Stay right here and give me ten minutes. I'll swing by in the channel." She was off and lost to the crowd almost instantly.

Ras and Callie stood awkwardly for about a minute. "What if she sees your wanted poster?" Callie asked.

"I don't think she's big enough to drag me into a police station," he said. "You know, unless she drives us there unwittingly while telling us we're heading to a pocket watch shop..." Ras trailed off. "We should probably go."

"Good call," Callie said as she fished out the map.

"My dad used to tell me about how it was a clock shop with no ticking," Ras said. "They started the watch when you bought it. It was like starting a moment, but my dad would always bring me watches that hadn't been started and ask me what I wanted most. We'd wind the watch together and he'd tell me if I worked hard, it'd just be a matter of time before it was mine."

"That was sweet of him," Callie said, her demeanor finally softening to the usual state.

"Yeah, but life doesn't exactly work like that."

"No, but having a father who encourages you goes a long way," she said as she pulled out the map. "C'mon, we can at least see if she wasn't lying about Orville's being on 8th and Holloway. You can tell me on the way what little Ras wanted most." She put her arm through his and they began walking.

Telling her what he wanted most would make for a long and awkward trip across Atmo if she didn't reciprocate the feeling. "I'm afraid I can't," he said. "It doesn't come true if you tell anyone."

"That's birthday candles and shooting stars. You already said all it takes is time." She nudged him and all he could smell was the intoxicating scent of strawberries and vanilla. "You just don't want to say."

"I think a boy is entitled to his secrets," Ras said. "What about you? Any falling star wishes you never told me about?"

"I always wished I would leave the basement and see the world, but that's not a secret." She looked up at him with her perfect blue eyes. "You want to know a secret?"

"Sure."

"You can't tell anyone."

"That's how secrets work, I hear."

"Well," she began, "if anyone was to kidnap me, I'm glad it was you."

It was the nicest, strangest compliment Ras had ever received. "You've been a perfectly pleasant prisoner. No annoying escape attempts, no running to police. You've really made my first kidnapping a positive experience," he said, laughing. "You know, my arm really hurts."

"It was a rather large wrench...Do you think it's broken?"

"No. But, I've seriously got to start taking better care of this arm." He lifted his left shoulder, wincing.

"You've got to start taking better care of you."

"I don't do that well, do I?" he asked.

"It's not one of your stronger suits, no."

IT TOOK THEM ALMOST AN HOUR to find Orville's, as 8th and Holloway held three different vertical levels. Orville's was on the bottom level, which was a small mercy; at least they wouldn't be out in the open.

A clock face comprised the O in Orville's sign, which wasn't terribly clever, but gave any passerby a clear idea of what to expect inside.

Callie opened wide one of the shop's ornate brass doors, sweeping a hand with great ceremony.

"Oh, stop it," Ras said. "It's just a—wow." Ras' eyes went wide as he passed through the threshold. The thirty foot tall walls appeared to consist entirely of clocks. Hundreds upon hundreds of devices hung so densely packed that the walls only peeked out in various places where a purchased clock had not yet been replaced. But, just as Elias had described, there was absolutely no ticking, which Ras found both eerie and fascinating.

The showroom held glass displays full of watches, pocket clocks, and other assorted geared items with tiny price tags attached.

"This place is incredible," Callie said, her fingers lightly brushing a display.

The sound of winding and a faint ticking noise drew their attention to a balding man standing behind the counter. His thick glasses gave his face a pinched appearance. Smiling, he placed the newly wound watch in a velvet box for the customer in front of him. "I'm sure she'll love it. I wish you both luck," he said.

Ras watched the only other customer in the store pass by with his new purchase before the door chime marked his exit. The large room once again fell silent until the man behind the counter called out. "How can I help you, young sir?"

"Are you Orville?" Ras asked, and was met with a nod. "My father always told me about your shop, so I thought I'd see it for myself."

"I'm pleased you did," Orville said. "May I ask your father's name? I have a rather encyclopedic memory."

Ras approached Orville's counter. "It's been a while since he shopped here."

"Hold on, you look familiar," he said. "Do you take after your father?"

"He doesn't think so," Callie said, "but he's wrong."

"Hmm. Give me a moment." He studied Ras' face carefully. "Are you wearing a Parkman 51 with a brown leather strap on your left wrist?"

Ras pulled back his jacket sleeve, revealing the watch, which looked small for his arm. The inappropriate size wasn't enough to have discontinued use of the last birthday present from his father.

Orville closed his eyes. "It's due for a cleaning, Erasmus Veir. I told Elias it requires maintenance every year, but…the second-hand is sticking, isn't it?"

Ras smiled. "It waits three seconds before it ticks, but it keeps time."

"It's well past its warranty, but if I may?" Orville held out a hand.

With the watch surrendered, Orville held it to his ear, then gently placed it on a black felt cloth and pulled out a small set of fine, shiny tools. He adjusted a pivotable magnifying glass for a better look.

"I have something to give you, Erasmus, but it pains me to do so," Orville said as he popped the back of the watch off and went to work.

"Why is that?"

"Because your father would place an order for you on his trip out, I would build it to his specifications—he always provided me with such challenges—and he would pick up the finished work on his way home."

"I didn't know that," Ras said.

Orville adjusted a gear, held the watch to his ear, then replaced its back before returning it to Ras. "Almost good as new." Without requesting payment, he turned and disappeared into a storeroom.

Ras gave Callie a perplexed look.

"Ah, found it," Orville called out and returned, holding a small box with a couple envelopes taped to the bottom of it.

"What's this?" Ras asked.

"The last assignment Elias gave me." He slid the box across the counter. "I'm sorry. I'm sure we both wish he was the one picking this up. Your father loved you dearly," Orville said, then took a moment to compose himself. "He lit up when he spoke of you and would always tell me how you'd react when he came home with the latest—"

"Orville, please."

The old man nodded knowingly. "My apologies, young sir."

"Are the envelopes for me?"

"One is." He smiled sadly. "Would you like me to wind up the clock for you?"

"I'm afraid what I want most right now isn't possible." Ras picked up the box, which had a surprising heft to it. He slid the top off of it, revealing a clock like he had never seen before.

It was a glass ball with a brass porthole on its perimeter. Inside, the clock had a graceful design, and if the hands had been moving, they would have looked as though they were swimming in glass.

"It's beautiful…you made this?" Callie asked.

"One of a kind," Orville said.

Ras picked up the envelopes. One said 'Ras,' the other, 'Emma.'

The shop didn't feel like the proper venue to read his father's final words to him, but he wasn't certain what venue would feel right.

He slid the envelopes into his jacket pocket. "Did he leave a letter every time?"

"No. Just the one in case you eventually visited," Orville said, "which you did. I do feel honored to have been entrusted with such a thing, but I am also glad that I lived long enough to see it through."

Ras lifted the round glass ball of a clock. If one didn't look at it directly, the curvature of the glass would obscure the face the way that looking at the side of an eye showed the iris differently.

"Do I owe—" Ras began.

Orville waved dismissively. "Paid in full. Elias was always up front in his dealings."

Ras placed the clock back in the box. "Thank you," Ras said quietly.

Back at the entrance, the door squeaked on its hinges. Over some of the taller displays a bit of white hair quickly bobbed forward.

Dixie turned the corner, continuing her quick strides. She was not pleased. "I offer you a ride and you ditch me? Can't a girl return a favor?"

"We thought a walk would do us good. See more that way," Ras said as he slid the box into his pocket to join the envelopes. He noticed Dixie's eyes track it. "Sorry about that, but we wound up here all together, so you're off the hook."

"Trust me, you don't want me to be off the hook right now. If you don't let me give you a ride right now, we're both liable to be on sharp, pointy hooks for a long, long while and nobody wants that… except for the people with the hooks."

"Pardon?" Callie asked.

"Look, I saw the posters," Dixie said, "so I get why you ditched me, but if we keep talking here, we're going to see about a dozen boys in blue and my hands aren't entirely clean after the whole library debacle. I don't have to be here, but I take favors seriously. So, if you would kindly come with me so I can get us out of here…"

"Where's your skiff?" Callie asked.

"Just follow me," Dixie said.

They began to leave and Ras looked back at Orville. "Thank you for everything."

"You come back and get that cleaned every year now," Orville said. "None of this 'ten years later' business."

Ras smiled sadly and nodded.

They made it out of the shop and onto the busy sidewalk. Ras spotted a squad of *Derailleur* police forcing their way through the crowd, and as soon as they spotted Ras, Callie, and Dixie, they began aggressively shoving people out of the way.

Dixie ran up to the ledge of the airship channel, unhesitatingly planted a hand on the railing, and vaulted herself into the abyss. Her disembodied voice shouted, "Jump!"

Ras and Callie looked over the edge to see a small four-seater open aired skiff idling below the railing. Callie began climbing over the railing with Ras' assistance. She dropped the five feet ungracefully into the backseat as her bowler hat blew off into the deep below.

Watching the hat made Ras freeze. All of the shouting from the police, Dixie, and Callie became muffled and he found himself acutely aware of his heartbeat. He had five seconds before the closest officer would reach him.

Dixie huffed, pulling up on the controls to raise the skiff to the railing's level. Ras climbed onto the rail just in time for one of the officers to get a fist full of Ras' pant leg. The alteration of balance kept him from doing anything but grasping the rising skiff's door handle as it continued to lift.

Ras ascended with the small ship. His hold was tenuous as he kicked free from the officer, and his legs flailed wildly as Dixie's skiff accelerated.

"Dixie!" Ras shouted. He looked down and fought the urge to black out as the skiff sped forward. The wail of sirens grew behind them.

"Hold on tight, then don't!" Dixie said.

"What?" He tightened his grip on the handle as best he could. They weaved through airship traffic when suddenly the skiff rolled hard counterclockwise and Ras immediately found himself on top of the sideways vessel.

"Let go!" Dixie shouted as she shunted the skiff into a nosedive.

Ras lost his grip completely. He grasped fistfuls of air as the vessel leveled out and shifted to starboard. The top of the passenger door connected with his ribcage, halting his fall.

Callie didn't miss a beat. She grabbed Ras' hand, hauling him inside.

"Sorry," Dixie said. "That should have gone better."

Ras fought the urge to hyperventilate as Callie grabbed his seat's restraints and buckled him in. "There, you're safe now," she said. The sirens grew louder.

"I wouldn't say that yet," Dixie said. She threw the ship down another avenue, then dove through the lowest level of traffic. The air around them grew hotter as they continued lower and pulled even with *Derailleur's* gigantic engines. Four police skiffs dove in pursuit.

"If we go any lower the exhaust will boil us!" Ras shouted over the deafening roar.

"Then we won't go lower!" Dixie shouted.

The engine array of *Derailleur* would have fascinated Ras under more serene conditions. Over fifty engines working in league with humongous fuel reservoirs kept the city afloat.

"Each major city section is given its own engine and then bolted to its neighbors in case of a regional failure," Dixie shouted.

"What does that have to do with anything?" Callie asked.

"Just thought you might find it interesting. I said I was a great tour guide!"

Ras looked around in an attempt to spot the four pursuing skiffs, but the heat emissions distorted anything underneath the engines.

"Just so you know, I don't exactly have a place to hide!" she shouted.

"I thought you lived here!" Callie said.

"Nope! Where's your ship?"

"East side, Flint's!" Ras barely got the word out before Dixie slammed the steering wheel hard to starboard and pulled up to ascend back into the city. The drone of the engines dulled as they rose.

"Do you think Flint is going to be finished with the upgrade by now?" Callie asked, pressed firmly into her seat, her fingers digging into the upholstery.

"If he isn't, we might not get much further," Ras said. He leaned forward to talk to Dixie, who had just merged in with traffic on the second level of the three vertical intersections. "What about you? What are you going to do after you drop us off?"

"Well, I'm probably just going to have to give them a bit of a chase so they don't follow your ship, now won't I? Maybe by the end of this you'll owe me a favor," she said with a peal of laughter. "You two are a lot of fun. You'll make beautiful children." She lifted the ship to the top level of the vertical intersections, once again throwing Ras and Callie back into their seats.

"Wait, what did she say?" Callie asked.

"Oh, she and I, we're not...you know," Ras said, stammering.

"Why not?" Dixie asked.

Flashing lights began reflecting off buildings and airships as they sat in gridlocked traffic.

"That's kind of personal," Ras said. He looked over at Callie, who blushed.

"Why aren't we moving?" Callie asked. "They're getting closer."

Dixie looked over the side of the skiff, calculating something. "I'm not moving until one of you two tells me why you aren't together."

"Dixie!" Ras shouted.

"I'm doing you a favor, hon," she said. "One of you spoken for?"

More police skiffs flew above the traffic for a good vantage point and would spot them at any moment.

"No, we're not, now will you please move?" Callie asked. "You're risking the lives of tens of thousands of people with your stupid game."

"I'm logging that one under things to ask about later," Dixie said. Turning to Ras, she said, "C'mon, ask her out before I ask you."

Spotlights popped on, blinding them and a voice came over the loudspeaker ordering them to stay where they were.

"Fine!" Ras yelled. "Callie, let's get dinner sometime."

"That's not asking," Dixie said.

"Callie, would you do me the honor of having dinner with me?" Ras asked with more sincerity than he expected. The police continued to shout over their loudspeakers.

Callie looked frozen.

"Well?" Dixie asked, once again staring over the side of her skiff before she cut power to the engines. They began to plummet past the second intersection's traffic, almost clipping an airship, and down to the first intersection where the skiff struck a floating traffic sign but managed to miss everything else. She turned the key and their fall halted just before they reached the burning engine exhaust. "Callie, what d'ya say?"

"I say you're insane," she said, eyes narrowing.

"Callie, it's okay," Ras said. "She was just buying time so the police would have to push through three intersections of traffic." He turned to Dixie. "Can we please just get to Flint's?"

The skiff turned east. "You got it," Dixie said with a sigh. "I really thought that was going to work. I really did."

It was a two minute flight to Flint's, and as Ras suspected, police skiffs were parked outside.

"Really?" Dixie said, smacking the steering wheel. "Let's see if we can't sneak in the back. No, wait. Better idea! Get out." She pulled up to the sidewalk a block away from Flint's. "Go on. Freebie on me for what I did earlier."

"What are you going to do?" Ras asked.

"I'll draw them away and you get back on your ship." She smiled. "Maybe we'll see each other again someday." Dixie nodded to the curb. "Mind your step."

Ras unbuckled and stepped out, followed by Callie, who hadn't said much since the drop. They stood beside the skiff as Dixie winked at them, then jetted forward on a collision course with the police skiffs, sideswiping each of the parked vehicles.

They watched police file out of Flint's. Dixie stood in her driver's seat waving at the men, blowing them kisses as they piled into their damaged vehicles. She sat back down and scooted away as the police gave chase.

"Why do I get the feeling that skiff isn't hers?" Callie asked.

THEY APPROACHED FLINT'S CAUTIOUSLY in case any more officers were still posted inside. Ras decided to enter through the repair bay instead of the main office doors.

Above them hung *The Brass Fox*. Nobody was working on it, and Ras reasoned that the police would frown on Flint aiding criminals.

They weren't more than a few steps into the hangar before a mechanic spotted them. "Hey," he whispered, waving them over.

Ras spotted two policemen patrolling the catwalk up by Flint's office, still ignorant of the intruders, so he led Callie along the wall over to the mechanic.

The man had a buzzed haircut and a name patch that said 'Sarks.' "About time you two showed up. Flint wants to talk," Sarks said, leading them toward a door marked 'Employees only,' then pushed it open.

They walked into the dark room with Sarks bringing up the rear. He flicked on a light switch and the door closed behind him.

Ras' eyes adjusted to the light just as two mechanics grabbed his arms, both restraining him and reminding him exactly where the wrench struck him back in the alley.

A dozen other workers in mechanic jumpsuits lined the walls of the locker room, and Flint stood at the center.

Ras chose not to struggle.

"What's going on?" Callie demanded.

Flint towered over her, holding the wanted and kidnapped posters. "Both have rewards attached to them." He took another step toward Callie. "Care to explain?"

Ras began to speak, but a mechanic twisted his arm, turning his words to pained grunts.

"Not you. Her," Flint said.

"He didn't kidnap me. *The Fox* is technically my ship. Check the title. I bought it to retrieve something for Hal so he would save *Verdant*."

Flint gave her a hard look, then flicked his gaze to Ras. "Is he the one that killed the last Convergence in The Bowl?"

"Yes," Callie said. "But if you turn us in for a reward you're sinking an entire city, and I'll tell everyone—and I mean everyone that will listen—exactly who acted like a sky pirate and stopped the city's last chance for survival over a little reward money." She stood resolute as Flint's eyes returned to her. "And I doubt you'd ever get another chance to work on *The Kingfisher*."

Flint glared at her for a long moment, then looked to Sarks. "Get them some jumpsuits and back onboard their ship. Distract the cops."

"Thank you," Callie said.

"You drive a hard guilt trip, missy," said Flint.

With a quick outfit change and an entrance through the bay door to the hold, Ras, Callie, and Sarks walked onboard *The Brass Fox*.

"We didn't have time to test the Helios engine," Sarks said. "But we'll release the ship from the mooring after I leave the hold. You'll hear three clicks. On the third, you'll be pushed forward. Stay below and we'll act like it's an accident. Just turn on your engines once you've cleared the building and you should be good to go."

"You're being a lot nicer about this than Flint," Ras said.

"I'm a Verdantian, born and raised. Got family still there I'd like to go back and visit sometime," Sarks said. "I'm rooting for you."

With that, Sarks left the hold. Ras walked over to inspect the Helios engine. It was covered in a shiny but flimsy chrome encasement with Helios logos stamped all over. The solid metal Windstrider engines were twice its size and looked like they would easily outlast the Helios.

Click. The ship rumbled, and Ras braced himself against an unfamiliar barrel next to the engine. Ras had never seen refined Energy fuel up close.

Click. Another shake. Ras looked at Callie. "You ready to be a navigator?"

Click. They began to drift and shouts came from outside.

"No, but I'll get there."

"You'll be great," Ras said, smiling at her.

Outside, the shouts continued and Ras could hear Sarks yell, "Stop it! It's almost completely outside!"

"Subtle," Ras said, then climbed the ladder to get above deck. Once up top, he maintained the ruse of being one of Flint's staff by shouting, "Hold on, I got it!" He ran up to the helm and started the engines. They roared to life with a vigor Ras didn't know was possible, and *The Brass Fox* took off with an uncharacteristic start.

Flint's men had done their job well. Ras bobbed and weaved through traffic the short distance to the Eastern Entrance. "I'm going to need a Navi!" he called out to Callie, looking back at *Derailleur*. He couldn't spot any obvious pursuers.

They looked to be in the clear, finally.

FOSTER HELIOS III's FACE BURNED WITH ANGER. "We worked very hard to ensure that every cop sent to Flint's was in our pocket! How did they get away?" The lackey walking down the hallway with him began to speak but Foster cut him off. "What have we learned from Flint?"

The man in uniform paused awkwardly. "He spoke nonsense."

"I'll take the information unfiltered, thank you," Foster said.

"He said the pilot had a deal with Napier—"

"Burn his whole operation," he ordered. "Make sure *The Halifax* is prepped for departure, and in the meanwhile, see if we can't find out where they were headed."

"Sir, your ship is supporting the engagement against the sky pirates outside *Nalon*. Pulling away now would—"

"I am well aware of the ramifications. I'm telling you where it needs to be. Now!" he barked. "I'll just have to find them myself."

CHAPTER ELEVEN
The Local Legend

THE BRASS FOX HUNG MOTIONLESS ABOVE A SEA OF PERFECT WHITE clouds, completely alone. What little wind existed gently rocked the ship but did little more than bring tidings of aimlessness.

"I don't know why it's not working," Callie said, "I've been practicing." She held the small brass ball perched on three fingers, but the metal arrow wouldn't budge.

Ras paced around her, examining the device from all angles. "I still don't get how you can practice using a compass."

"Hal said it has to connect with me or something."

"So you're its battery?"

"Right now I'm not. Either that or there's nothing for it to pick up." She held it high as though a few extra feet would give it what it needed before resting her arm. "The Wild is east of here, can't we just start heading that way?"

"That's what we've been doing, more or less." Ras rhythmically tapped his fingers on the big wheel. "But the pass could be far north or south along the mountains bordering The Wild. We could be doubling our travel if we fly blind." Frustration crept into his voice, and he hoped Callie wouldn't suggest dipping below the clouds once more to see if she could pick up a heading down there. They had already tried it four times, up and down at various altitudes. "I'm going to go down and see if I can't get the jetcycle running. Just let me know if that thing starts working."

Ras descended into the hold as Callie started walking toward the front of the ship. He looked over at the vehicle that his mother would have killed him for owning. Elias used to have one, but had sold it as soon as Emma announced she was pregnant.

Dad. Ras reached into his pocket with the clock in it, fishing out the envelopes. He stuffed the one for his mother back in and pulled up an overturned bucket for a makeshift seat. He gently tore open the side of the envelope, and when he turned it over to fish out the letter inside, a picture fluttered to the floor.

He stooped down, collecting the small rectangle and brought it close. The photo was a candid shot his mother had taken. Elias was in his 30s, had longer hair than Ras ever remembered him having, and was leaning down to give little ten-year-old Ras his first flying lesson.

RAS HADN'T BEEN ABLE TO SLEEP the nights leading up to his first outing and was convinced that if he didn't touch the controls just the right way that *The Silver Fox* would plummet from the sky.

Elias had repeatedly told his son not to worry and that flying wasn't so difficult.

"Dad?" little Ras asked, not looking up from the broken scoop intake his father had let him tinker with.

"Yeah, kiddo?" Elias responded as he hauled another crate of provisions up the gangplank.

"Will I get my own ship someday?"

Elias sat the box down and climbed the steps to the helm. "You better, because I'm going to need this one for a while."

"How long?"

"Years, and years, and years." He ruffled his son's hair and it fell in Ras eyes. "Better tell your mother you need another haircut before I get back."

"I don't like bowl cuts," Ras said. "Why do you have to leave again so soon?"

"Because this time everyone in *Verdant* needs me to."

"Did you get in trouble? You can tell me," Ras said.

Elias laughed heartily. It was a deep and rich laugh and always made Ras feel like everything was right with the world. "No, no more than usual."

"Mom says you're in big trouble if you don't come back."

"That's usually understood," Elias said. He walked over and stood beside Ras next to the helm. "Ras, I need to tell you something."

Ras stopped playing with the machinery, and looked up at his father.

"People are going to say a lot of different things about why I'm going on this trip, but I'm going to tell you the real reason up front, all right?"

"Yeah, dad."

"It's because I love you and your mother."

"You don't have to go for me to know that, though."

Elias hid his tears by embracing his son. "Ah, that's a very good thing to know. A very good thing indeed."

Placing the photo on his knee, Ras removed himself from the memory. He took a deep breath and extracted the letter.

He didn't want to read it.

There was always some comfort left that his father's final, perfect message was out there waiting for him, but this was it. Elias the hero would have spoken his last, for better or worse. Best to treat it like tearing off a bandage. Ras began before he could overthink it.

My dear boy,

> *It is my chief wish that you never read this letter, and that it rot in the storage room of Orville's shop until the end of time. But I find writing this necessary as I can't guarantee what the wind holds for me...but therein lies the adventure of life and all its uncertainties.*
>
> *The one certainty is that if you are reading this, then my time has come and gone. I can only hope that I made it count for the right things. That I stood for truth, took care of your mother, and imparted the necessary building blocks so that you, in your ripe old age, could be proud of the man you became.*
>
> *I need you to take care of your mother now. She'll still care for you of course, but she's always struggled with being alone. If ever she meets someone new, please do your best to make sure he's a good man.*
>
> *There are so many paths your life can take you, and most will lead to the unexpected, but I would be remiss if I didn't warn you that you will find following in my footsteps as a wind merchant difficult, if not impossible.*

Your grandfather was a full Knack, and some of that was passed down to me, but as you probably know, I have failed to pass it along to you.

Your mother and I built The Silver Fox *to be wind merchants together. What I didn't know was that your mother has something about her that dulls the sensitivity of Knacks. I won't use the slang, but it made tracking Energy with her by my side impossible. She thinks she's bad luck, but that was the kinder of the options to tell her.*

I hate to tell you this, Ras, but you share this trait with your mother. I don't know if it is something you'll grow out of, but I hope shedding light on this will keep you from taking an unnecessarily difficult path.

You're smart, good with people, and can easily take things apart and put them back together far better than I ever could. You have such excellent strengths, Ras, and I hope you use them for a wonderful and successful life. No matter what, I have and will always love you and I wish I could be there to see the man you will become.

Be good, do good, love others.

Always,
Elias Veir

Ras let the letter drop.

I am officially a Lack. Dad always knew it, Ras thought.

It made so much more sense why he never had his bearings in the sky. He had never heard of someone who went so completely to the entire other end of the sensitivity spectrum as to be a detriment to those around them.

No wonder nobody took me on their crew when I was a teenager. His eyes began welling up. *Don't let mom be alone, don't try to be a wind merchant. Sorry dad, zero for two there.*

Ras considered crumpling up the letter but knew he would regret it. He couldn't tell Callie. He didn't want her to lose faith in her flawed captain. *She threw away her future betting on a Lack.*

A triumphant cheer erupted from above. "It's working! We have a heading!"

*   *   *

THE LITTLE ARROW POINTED EAST BY NORTHEAST, and it stayed constant even if Callie twisted the device or moved around. Ras locked *The Brass Fox* on its course and did his best to hide his red eyes from her, which was no easy task.

"Are you all right?" Callie asked.

"The hold was stuffy," he said.

"Well, I for one am so relieved that Hal didn't entrust this mission to a dud," she said, chuckling nervously, before lifting the orb and sighing with relief. "I think I even gave myself a bit of a headache trying to focus on getting it to work."

"I'm sure we just hadn't gotten a potent enough gust for it to register," Ras said, "or something."

"Wait, do I have to have this thing always on?"

"No, I don't think so. Maybe check every hour. Once we get closer, though, it might be good to check more often," Ras said.

"Do you mind if I pull a chair out here and read my library books?" Callie asked.

"Only if you read *The Littlest Elder* aloud and do all the voices." Keeping up a cheery demeanor around Callie proved more difficult than Ras anticipated, but he did the best he could.

Callie rolled her eyes and left the bridge, leaving Ras alone with his thoughts.

The revelation of truly being a Lack focused and tinted his memories. *No wonder I could get so close to a Convergence, but I had no business even chasing wind to get there. If I had read that letter earlier, would* Verdant *be safe?* He wondered what his mother would have preferred her boy become instead of a wind merchant.

The Captain's quarters' door opened and Callie returned with *The Demons of Bogues* and one of the dining room chairs.

"What about the others?" Ras asked.

"I've already read the history of The Clockwork War on *Verdant* and, spoiler alert, *The Littlest Elder* finds his way home before the main gate seals his family into The Wild."

Ras stared at the horizon as the winds began picking up. Below, the clouds moved quickly, turning more of a dull gray the further they flew. Hours passed and very seldom did he see the speck of another ship on the horizon. Callie would occasionally check the compass and Ras would alter course by one or two degrees.

With the sun setting, the black clouds skittering with light drew Ras' attention. Deep booms reverberated through his chest. "I don't think we're going to want to anchor below tonight."

"Are we going to have to fly through the night?" Callie asked.

Ras shook his head. "If there's a city nearby, we can dock. Maybe see if I can buy some new grapple gun charges if I'm careful. It makes me nervous flying without any."

"Won't someone spot *The Fox*?" Callie asked.

"Doubt it. She's based on a popular model," Ras said. "Besides, it beats getting struck by...what did you call it?"

"Lightning."

"That's it. I doubt the ship would react well to it." Ras locked in their course and pulled out a tube from underneath the console. He extracted a map from its container and pressed it firmly to the dash to keep the wind from whipping it away.

Callie closed her book and stood. "Anything nearby?"

"Well, we're coming up on *Crispin*, but Bravo Company downed it before attacking *Merron*." Ras said, pointing to a big X over the illustration of a city. Ras moved over slightly to let Callie investigate.

"Look, there's a little dot next to the X," Callie said, leaning in close. "*New Crispin?*"

"I don't know. Let's see..." Ras mused over the map. "We're maybe half an hour away if the wind's with us."

She held up the brass orb and compared it to the compass. "Looks like it's right on the path. Can we at least check it out?"

"*New Crispin* it is," Ras said.

With a new course plotted, they were able to rest easy for the remainder of the afternoon. Callie took breaks from reading to fashion a holster for Ras' new wrench. She had called the holster dashing when he first tried it on, which, unbeknownst to her, was a salve to his tattered ego.

The sun began to disappear beneath the roiling clouds as they approached a structure of several dozen vessels cobbled together. The mostly empty docks, if they could be called such, led to a settlement whose sole source of illumination was its engines.

"Why is this even here?" Callie asked.

Ras looked down at the Energy level indicator. "The air is rich here. I'm guessing even after they lost their city, wind merchants made this out of some wreckage so they could still pull big hauls," Ras said. "But The Collective isn't around anywhere to buy their Energy."

"That's good for us, I suppose," Callie said. "I'm kind of regretting reading *The Demons of Bogues* now. This place looks like a ghost town."

"If it was abandoned, it would have to have been recently. The scoop engines are still keeping it up," Ras said. "Might still be worth a scavenge while the storm passes."

The Brass Fox's engines shut off at Ras' command and the ship glided silently into an empty slip. A young man escaping his teenage years appeared from somewhere Ras didn't notice, wearing an odd looking checkered hat with ear flaps. He stood, ready to catch the rope.

"Hello," Ras called out, genuinely surprised to be met by a dock-hand. "What's the docking fee here?" He cradled the rope, ready to toss it to the teenager. No response. "Excuse me, hello?" he asked, snapping his fingers to draw the young man's attention. It looked like he was staring up at the balloon. Ras turned and called back, "Callie! Will you toss this rope to me? The dockhand is having a staring match with *The Fox*."

"The... *The Fox*?" The young man finally spoke as though pulled from his trance.

"Ah, there you are. Here." Ras tossed the rope to him. The young man made no effort to catch it. "Oh, no, let me," Ras deadpanned and hopped down to the makeshift dock, which prompted the boy to burst into a full sprint away from Ras.

"He's back! He's back!" the young man cried out, fleeing.

Ras picked up the rope and tied it to the dock. He looked at Callie, who walked down the newly extended gangplank. "What in Atmo is he talking about?" Ras asked.

Callie shrugged. "Free parking?"

They walked along the docks and Callie handed Ras the duffle bag she carried. It held Elias' grapple gun and his newly holstered wrench. "You might as well make sure whatever cabling you need will fit."

Ras tilted his head in agreement. "Good call." He extracted the grapple gun from the bag and placed the sleeve of it over his arm. It wasn't entirely out of fashion for wind merchants to wear them while off of their ships, and it protected his wrench-struck shoulder. The combination of an armored arm and large wrench made him look like an odd mix of mechanic and knight errant.

"For as empty as this place is, I think the deckhand might have been the King of *New Crispin,*" Callie said. Leaving the docks, they made it to the outskirts of the town to find absolutely nobody on the platforms they passed. They looked back to realize that the only other ships in the docks looked abandoned or in terrible disrepair.

The whole situation made Ras want to turn around and head out. They could find grapple gun charges somewhere else, and passing wind merchants were usually willing to make trades. He was about to voice his opinion when Callie stopped him by placing her hand on his arm.

"Wait, do you hear something?" She tilted her head. "Music."

Due to wind-whipped ears, Ras strained to hear what sounded like the faintest of piano music in the distance. It stopped abruptly, replaced by the sound of dozens of boots coming down the curving path toward them.

The light of handheld Energy lamps began giving a green glow to the area, their reflections bobbing off of shop windows and the light grew in intensity as the footsteps became louder.

"Should we run?" Callie asked, concerned.

"I'm not opposed." Ras turned to head back to the ship.

"Veir!" A voice shouted, accusatory and questioning at the same time. "Hold it right there!"

Ras looked at Callie, whose face was lit by the flickering lamps. He took a deep breath and turned to see the materialized mob.

"At least they don't have pitchforks," Callie said under her breath.

"What's a pitchfork?" Ras whispered.

A man with a white beard and bald head hobbled ahead of the crowd of thirty. He leaned on a crutch to help him manage on a peg leg. He held a lantern in his other hand and stopped ten feet away from Ras and Callie, prompting the rest of the group to halt as well. He studied Ras for a moment, then turned back to the crowd.

"You knucklehead, that ain't him!" he called out, prompting the teenaged dockhand to emerge from the group.

"But he called her *The Fox!*" the young man said.

"Had you considered he might have been referring to the red-head?" the older man countered.

"Hey!" Callie said.

"No offense, miss."

They think I'm my father. Ras shook his head. "You were hoping for Elias Veir and *The Silver Fox.*"

"Aye," the one-legged man said with a renewed vigor, "Know 'im?" he asked, adjusting his crutch.

"*Knew* him," Ras corrected. "My father died ten years ago."

Gasps escaped from the crowd, and the bearded man's shoulders slumped. "That's…that's a right tragedy, son. Your father was a fine, fine man." He turned back to the crowd and bellowed, "Tonight we drink to the life, legacy, and memory of Elias Veir!" This elicited cheers. He turned to Ras and asked, "What's your name, boy?"

"Erasmus—"

"And to Erasmus Veir! May he be even half as great as his father!" The crowd cheered and began shuffling back up the road.

"Yeah, already got that one covered," Ras muttered.

Callie nudged him. "He didn't mean it like that."

Ras looked down at the grapple gun and suddenly felt ten years old, wearing a wind merchant costume and pretending to be his father. He trudged up the street, coming alongside the bearded man. "I'm afraid I didn't catch your name."

"Oh, pardon my rudeness, Erasmus. Around here people just call me Pop," he said, shifting his weight so he could offer his hand.

Ras accepted the shake, and was pulled off balance by Pop's eager fist pumping. "Easy enough."

"And young miss, I do apologize for earlier," he said. "The boy is known to be uncouth."

"It's all right. My name is Calista."

"Lovely name, if I may say so," Pop said.

"Where are we going?"

"*The Silver Fox*, o' course." He smiled broadly. "We named the tavern after his blessed ship on occasion of him savin' the city."

Ras looked at Callie and raised an eyebrow. "*Crispin?*"

"Oh, no, *New Crispin*," Pop said, "But I bet if your dad had been around for the first tussle, you'd be standing on a much finer city."

The tavern was the only building lit up in the dark town. Draped above the outside entrance was *The Silver Fox*'s original dirigible canvas with the hand painted logo of *The Silver Fox* that Emma had designed for Elias.

As Ras approached the insignia he searched for every time his mother paraded him to the docks to meet Elias, he pointed up with a look of confusion.

Pop explained. "During the attacks, a cannonball went straight through, puncturing the ballonet. I'd never seen a pilot make it through losing their balloon."

"How'd he do that?" Ras' boyish grin broke through.

"Well, all he had was his Windstrider scoops, so when he dropped below the clouds we thought we lost him. But he used what was in his collection tank to stop the dive by fueling his engines. Then he skimmed by the Convergence below us to act as a scoop booster to shoot back up through the clouds, balloon-less!"

"How'd he land?" Callie asked.

"*New Crispin* caught him," Pop said. "Nobody liked that bakery anyway..."

They walked underneath the relic and into the tavern, finding the rustic, two-story interior of an old transport with a hearth built in the center, complete with crackling fire. Tables with mismatched wooden chairs were scattered around the hearth, and lining one side of the room was the large wooden bar. In the back, a man with a shaved head and dark glasses plinked away at a piano.

Applause erupted inside as soon as patrons realized the guest of honor had entered, but it was quickly subdued as those that had been outside informed others that the newcomer wasn't their returning hero.

"Gil!" Pop shouted to the piano player, "Something jaunty!"

"Yup!" Gil obliged, and the piano began filling the tavern with music.

Ras could feel the stares subside as Pop escorted them to the bar.

"Krantz, this is Eli's boy, treat him right," Pop said to the barkeep, a serious looking barrel-chested man with a beard and slicked-back hair. Pop looked back at Ras. "Ten years ago, huh?"

"More or less," Ras said.

"So he didn't make it back to you from here?" It was more an observation than a question.

Ras shook his head. "I didn't even know my father had been to *New Crispin.*"

"Then you're in for a treat," Pop said, gesturing for Ras and Callie to each pull up a bar stool. They obliged.

Krantz had already prepared two drinks and slid them along the bar.

Callie sniffed at the beverage, then recoiled, crinkling her nose. "Am I allowed to ask what's in this?"

The woman sitting on the stool next to Ras with long blonde hair spoke up, "He won't talk to you unless you take a drink."

The bearded barkeep grunted what Ras assumed to be an agreement.

The blonde woman laughed. "But even then, he's laconic," she said, prompting him to narrow his eyes at her, then let slip a grin. She blew him a kiss.

Ras took a swig of his drink and was surprised to find it lacked any alcohol but instead had a sweet, fruity taste—the kind that Emma used to surprise him with during the hot summers in his childhood. "You sure you didn't mix these two up?" Ras asked, pointing at their drinks.

Krantz stared at him. He was probably ten years Ras' senior. "Yup," he said as he cleaned a glass with an old rag. "That's what your dad ordered. Pirates were likely to strike at all hours so he wouldn't let himself get caught off guard."

"How'd you know my dad?"

"Flew with him once during the first raid," Krantz said.

The lights dimmed, and Pop made himself comfortable on a small stage composed of a couple crates sitting next to the hearth. He clanked his tankard with a ring on his right hand to quiet the crowd. Gil stopped playing and the room fell silent.

"Now, I know about six months back we had our 10th anniversary of emancipation, and we had a big to-do of it, but there's someone here that hasn't heard anything about this, which I find a crying shame. Erasmus Veir, would you wave your hand?"

Ras sheepishly obliged and heard every wooden chair creak as people turned to look his way.

"I'm afraid I have some very sad news indeed," Pop said. "According to Erasmus, Elias didn't make it home after his three months under our care." Murmurs spread through the crowd. "So I think it's fitting to tell his story to commemorate the man who gave us so much. Most all of you know it, but we could all use a reminder from time to time, I'd like to think."

Ras settled into his stool. He was practically able to recite the tales from the scuffles with sky pirates around *Verdant*, but this was his one opportunity at hearing this tale, and he wanted to relish it.

"As most know," Pop began, "the banner of India Bravo is enough to send most men back to their own engine wash, let alone her entire fleet of miscreants, who had set their eyes upon *New Crispin*."

"Did he say India Bravo?" Ras asked Krantz, who just shushed him and pointed at Pop.

"India and *New Crispin* had an uneasy agreement that none of us much liked, but once *The Winnower* was built and set up over the Origin, Ms. Bravo realized that Convergences were becoming far more valuable than ever.

"So the evening before the fireworks began, in flies *The Silver Fox*. Now, we don't oft get travelers around here, and especially not wind merchants since The Collective doesn't have many a person to do business with in these parts. We house mostly tinkerers, traders, and the like, so a wind merchant was a treat. Elias Veir was his name, and right over there is where he sat." Pop pointed a finger directly at Ras, then winked.

"Most wind merchants are natural storytellers due to the nature of what they see in their trade, but it's bad luck and bad manners to ask for a tale, especially when they are taking a respite from the skies. But Elias was kind enough to regale us with the tales about the Cliffs of Quinn, the Tunnels of Lacercie, and the time he squared off against the Red Band sky pirates." Pop paused, then said, "Erasmus, do you know those stories?"

"Bedtime favorites," Ras said.

"Lucky lad. Then I won't bore you by rehashing them, as I'm sure you could tell them better than I," Pop said. "Well, little did we know that India Bravo was waiting for night to fall before she struck, so Elias only made it halfway through the legend of Hal Napier and the secret pass into The Wild."

Callie leaned in, "That might be something to ask about later."

Ras nodded, his gaze transfixed on Pop.

A voice called out, "Get back to India Bravo!"

"Patience. A good story has to unfold. If I rush, you won't enjoy it as much," Pop chided. "Anyway, *New Crispin* shudders while we're all enjoying our suppers. We chalk it up to old engines, but the cannon ball ripping through the wall just behind me changed our minds rather quickly," he said, jutting a thumb over his shoulder. The crowd chuckled darkly.

"We make it outside and see dozens of ships surrounding *New Crispin* with *The Dauntless* sitting back, taking it all in. Well, Elias was as quick as a whip. He asked if we stored any Energy reserve balloons below the town, which we did, and told us to use whatever we could to attach them to our ships and open 'em right next to the sky pirate vessels. We told him most of us didn't have cannons, but he said we didn't need cannons.

"So, *New Crispin* is under bombardment and we have about ten able ships among us to collect the Energy reserve balloons. Next thing we know, Elias has dropped below the cloud cover in his ship and we worry we've lost him. We wouldn't have blamed the man if he had just run to let us fight our own battle, but he had Krantz and a few other able-bodied men aboard with him." Pop looked at Krantz. "My boy, you want to tell this part?"

Krantz just stared at Pop and the crowd burst into laughter.

"Suit yourself," Pop said. "Anyway, Eli was skimming The Convergence below about as close as anyone would dare, collecting a tankful of concentrated Energy. He led the charge toward India with nothing but Energy."

"How did he down 'em?" the teenage boy said, piping up.

"Joey, you've heard this a million times!"

"I know, but I was just trying to add tension for Erasmus," Joey said.

"Just let me do my job," Pop said, then muttered, "Knucklehead." He turned back to face Ras, "Where was I?"

Callie chimed in, "Charging India Bravo with—"

"Nothing but Energy, very good. So, the thing that Elias knew that we didn't was that the Bravo fleet were the only pirate ships around outfitted with Helios engines, and anyone that's flown with a Helios knows that they fall dead in the sky if their engines are surrounded with raw Energy…so that's what we did. We flew in, ripped the reserve balloons right next to 'em while we dragged them behind us. *The Silver Fox* reversed its collection process, gassing the engines of anyone stupid enough to fall behind its collection tube.

"We took down twenty of their ships, lost four of ours, before the shot burst through *The Silver Fox*'s balloon, but I already told you how he made it out of that one. Poor old Krantz hasn't stepped foot inside an airship since—"

"Unnecessary detail," Krantz said. He glanced at Ras, who had turned to look at him. "As you were."

"Well, being out of a ship wouldn't stop Elias Veir, would it?" Pop smiled broadly. "Now, nobody was around to see it, but the legend goes that he hijacked one of the pirate ships trying to board *New Crispin*, piloted it to *The Dauntless*, and became the reason India Bravo wears an eye patch."

A low, mechanical moan grew in the room, halting the story.

"Is that an engine?" Pop asked, inclining an ear.

Joey stood and ran outside as the pulsing sound grew. He ducked his head back inside and shouted. "It's *The Halifax*!"

The sounds of chairs scraping against the floor added to the noise as everyone scrambled to filter outside.

"What's *The Halifax*?" Callie asked.

"The Collective's flagship," the blonde woman said. "If it's here, it means trouble."

CHAPTER TWELVE
The Halifax

RAS AND CALLIE FOLLOWED THE BLONDE WOMAN OUTSIDE. THE suffocating heat of the engines from the ship above made it difficult to breathe and cast the whole of *New Crispin* in a sickly green glow.

The silhouette of the monstrosity blacked out most of the sky above except for four glowing orbs on each corner of its structure, where its engines burned. It was clearly larger than *The Dauntless*.

"What's it doing here?" Joey shouted to Pop over the thrum of the engines.

Pop shook his head. "It should be on the front lines. Must be retreating."

Tiny flashes of light caught Ras' attention from behind *The Halifax*. The growing howl confirmed cannon fire before little eruptions pocked the underbelly of the capital ship.

"Helios brought them here!" Pop said. "That son of a Lack!" He began hobbling toward the docks. "Everyone to your ships. Sky pirates inbound. Krantz? Where's Krantz?"

"On it," the surly barkeep said as he exited the building. "Addie, help me prime the cannon!" The blonde woman followed Krantz as he broke off from the crowd.

Above, a green light flashed from *The Halifax*'s port side with a familiar unholy scream that set Ras' skin crawling. A beam formed behind the ship, lashing out at one of the sky pirate vessels. The pirate airship erupted in an incinerating wash of green, illuminating the skies around the explosion to reveal the inbound swarm of sky pirates.

"What was that?" Callie asked, "That's horrible!"

Ras stared blankly before blinking away the bright line burned into his vision. "I don't know, but we have to go," Ras said. He clasped Callie's hand and began leading her back toward the docks before a hand caught his shoulder.

"We could really use your help, son," Pop said. "Will you fight with us?"

Ras struggled for words. He wanted to tell the old man he wasn't his father, that he didn't even have a cannon, and that he couldn't make a difference unless he made it to The Wild, but it all felt cowardly in the moment. He opened his mouth to speak before the sound of harnesses grinding against cable drew his attention above them.

A dozen helmeted men in Collective uniforms fell into the midst of the dispersing crowd with rifles at the ready, shouting orders over the din of cannon fire and engine wash.

Ras pulled the large wrench from its holster and held it at the ready.

"Erasmus Veir!" one of the soldiers shouted. "We're looking for an Erasmus Veir and Calista Tourbillon!"

Helping The Collective was a low priority for the residents of *New Crispin*. Everyone scattered.

"I think this is a little overkill for bringing in a kidnapper, wouldn't you say?" Callie asked.

Ras looked up at *The Halifax*, taking in its size. "A bit."

"Hey! You two!" one of the men in uniform pointed at Ras and Callie. "You need to come with us! This place is going to be overrun with pirates!"

Pop interjected himself between Ras and the soldier. "Not if that thing makes a stand for us!" he said, pointing at *The Halifax*.

"That's not our mission, now step aside!" the soldier leveled his rifle at Pop.

"You brought them here and you're leaving them with us?" Pop said.

"Step aside! That's your final warning!"

"It's all right, Pop," Ras said, stepping in front of the old man. "It's better this way."

"Good," the soldier said. "Strap into one of the harnesses—"

Before the soldier could react, Ras swung the large wrench, knocking the rifle loose. "Run!" he shouted, leading Callie toward the dock.

"What are you doing?" Callie asked breathlessly, stumbling into a run behind Ras.

"The longer it takes for The Collective to bring us in, the longer *The Halifax* has to fight the pirates," Ras said as the first warning salvo from the soldiers ripped past them and into a storefront's window. "Which means less pirates for *New Crispin*."

"They're shooting at us! I thought they wanted us alive!" Callie said.

The Halifax's weapon screamed again as they turned a corner to see *The Brass Fox* waiting at the dock less than one-hundred yards away. Thunderous crashing noises erupted, and Ras couldn't tell if it was from the storm below or the battle above.

"Look out!" Callie shouted, yanking back on Ras' arm and stopping him from running directly into the path of the half-airship on a collision course with *New Crispin*. The edges of the back half of the vessel were simply cauterized and smoldering where the front half used to be.

The wreckage crumpled, shooting wood splinters everywhere before screeching to a halt, effectively cutting off the path to the docks.

"There! Fire!" A pursuing soldier knelt with a tube over his shoulder.

Ras turned and wrapped himself around Callie before a mesh net knocked them off-balance, engulfing and dragging them to the ground.

The small squadron of Collective soldiers ran up and began securing ties into the netting before aiming the large gun at a descending Collective airship.

The gun fired, sending cabling out to strike the airship, and before Ras could attempt to cut his way free, the net lifted with a jerk and they were on their way to *The Halifax* as the battle over *New Crispin* began.

In his Captain's quarters, Foster Helios III wore a grin he couldn't have lost if he tried. The ornate brass sphere from Hal Napier sat in the middle of his desk. He placed a magnifying glass over it, inspecting the craftsmanship. The fine lines of filigree etched in the sides resembled a stormy sea of clouds. A product of a bygone era.

"Was this the only thing of note on their ship?" Foster asked the three officers standing across the desk from him.

"We pulled an old grapple gun that you might like for your collection off of the young man," one officer said.

"Yes, I should very much like to see that," Foster said, his eyes flicking to the walls of his Captain's quarters which were lined with artifacts from the earliest days of wind merchants, back before the adventure of saving the world had turned into board meetings on profitability and risk matrix analyses. "Where are they now?"

"We're running them through the battery of tests," the second officer said.

"Good. They should be nice and pliable when I speak with them." Foster placed his bare hand on the brass orb and held it high. "But what do we do with you?"

RAS LAY STRAPPED TO A GURNEY at a forty-five degree angle inside a glass dome. The worst part hadn't been the different gasses they subjected him to, or even the needles that forced him to fight the urge to vomit every time one unceremoniously jabbed him. Those came a close second and third to having Callie merely ten feet away from him in her own glass dome; scared, crying, and in pain as the two men in labcoats behind their console subjected her to the same treatment.

His voice had gone hoarse hours earlier from screaming at the scientists and trying to reassure Callie, who would look over at him but couldn't hear or understand him. The familiar hissing noise returned as air filtered into the dome again. This time a burning sensation tingled throughout his body before sending chills up his spine. Callie just cried. She looked over at Ras and mouthed—or maybe said; he couldn't tell—"Why?"

Ras violently shook the gurney, fighting the restraints to no avail. "Leave her alone!" he screamed repeatedly.

The scientists appeared to take special interest in one of their readouts and looked up at Ras with confusion, then delight. One of them twisted a knob, and the gas filtering in had Ras fighting to stay awake, as if he would somehow be more capable of protecting Callie if he remained conscious. The last things he saw before the blackness took him were her beautiful, tear-filled blue eyes, pleading with him.

* * *

THE VISION OF CALLIE MELTED AWAY into a gunmetal gray ceiling that provided absolutely no clue as to Ras' whereabouts. He was horizontal; that much was certain. He attempted to sit up, but his body failed to obey any commands. Looking around was the extent of his range of motion. His ears rang and a high-pitched, feminine voice spoke in muffled tones, its origin unknown.

In his peripheral vision, he could make out some straight black lines. *Metal bars?* His limited ability to look around hindered him from surveying the entire cell, but from what he could ascertain, he was alone. No Callie.

The voice became clearer. "Hello?" it said. "You look awake. Are you ignoring me, Ras?" The woman's voice was child-like. "Blink if you can understand me," she said.

Ras blinked.

"Oh, good, you're just paralyzed and not ignoring me. I hate when people ignore me."

He tried to speak, but his best attempt produced a hum.

"'Where's Callie?' you say? That's terribly romantic of you to be so concerned. Tell me you at least had that date before you wound up here."

Dixie.

Someone approached his cell, unlocking it. Two men entered. "Him?"

"Yeah, Foster wants him sobered up before they talk." A needle plunged into his arm.

A pinch and a burning sensation flooded through Ras. He could still feel everything happening to him. His whole body began tingling like a limb growing new nerves. The men left the cell, slamming the door.

"Wurru," Ras mumbled, trying to locate Dixie's position. He attempted moving his head but waves of nausea crashed over him.

"Yoo-hoo," Dixie said. "Next cell over. You're lucky they're speeding up your recovery. Took me the better part of a day before I could talk again. They haven't been able to shut me up since."

Ras didn't doubt it. "Ow yuher?" Ras slurred.

"What's that?"

Ras grunted in frustration. "How. Here."

"Oh, that's a horribly long story. It started about eighteen years ago when my father…"

Ras rolled his eyes, sending stars into his vision.

"Not that far back, no, of course not. What girl doesn't want her backstory skipped over? You are a captive audience in most senses of the word, you know."

He lolled his head to the left to see Dixie sitting on the floor in the next cell over, hugging her knees. She wore a plain gray jumpsuit. She cocked her head and wiggled her fingers at him.

"Hello!" she said. "Boy, they must have run you through the wringer back there. You look like death warmed over."

"What…they…do?" Ras asked.

"I have no idea. They're testing us for something. I thought The Collective just sold fuel. Silly me. Oh! How I got here…my escape attempt at *Derailleur* didn't go like I'd hoped, go figure. Police caught me and The Collective bought me." She stood and walked up to the bars, resting her forehead between two of them.

"Bought?" Ras was able to flex his arms slightly.

"Well, they bought the police, and I guess The Collective needs test subjects, so what if a prisoner with no family goes missing." She sighed. "Look at me, accidentally giving you details of my backstory. You'll care about me yet, Erasmus Veir."

Ras tried moving his leg and successfully swung it off the metal cot, inadvertently causing the rest of his body to awkwardly follow it to the floor. He crumpled on his side, his body awash with tingles.

"Up and at 'em, flyboy." Dixie cocked her head. "Did you really talk to Hal Napier? I overheard the guards making a bet and I'd love to get a piece of that action with some inside info."

"Where's Callie?" Ras said as he began to sit up slowly. The sensation started to subside.

"Probably still wherever they tested us, and if you wait long enough, she'll probably wind up in the cell next to you," she said, pointing to the empty cell behind Ras. "So, Napier. He'd have to be like five-hundred years old now, right?"

Ras eyed her. "You shouldn't believe everything you hear." He carefully reached an arm out to the metal bar to steady himself. "I take it you've already tried escaping."

Dixie laughed. "One doesn't escape *The Halifax*. I just wish I had a porthole…we won a battle while you were out, but I think they're at it again."

"We?"

"I count anyone not a sky pirate as 'we.' It doesn't mean I like The Collective," she said, idly running her fingers along the metal bars of her cell. "You know, they aren't the only ones fighting those sons of Lacks. Some of us wage our own private little wars."

"Why do you hate them so much?" Ras hauled himself off the deck and sat on the cot.

"Backstory! I knew you'd come around," she said, perking up considerably. "Well, I grew up with a bunch of wind merchants that built a city over a Convergence."

"*Crispin?*"

"No, but close. Same story, same pirates. Anyway, about nine years ago—" She stopped suddenly. "Aww, c'mon!"

Six armed guards approached from down the hallway and stopped in front of Ras' cell. They slid open the part of the door for Ras to put his hands through to be cuffed. "Foster Helios requests your presence."

"Requests?" He stood and offered his hands. The restraints ratcheted tight, digging into his wrists.

The door slid open and Ras looked over to Dixie. "Tell him I say hi!" she said as Ras fell into formation with the six men. He wondered how much trouble people went through to have an audience with arguably the most powerful man in Atmo.

After several long corridors and one trip up a stairwell, the burning sensation wore off, leaving Ras feeling oddly refreshed.

They reached a set of guarded double doors that swung open upon Ras' arrival to reveal a room roughly twice the size of *The Brass Fox*'s deck. An octagonal window running from ceiling to floor flooded the room with daylight and displayed the battle raging on outside. Ras wondered how long he had been unconscious in his cell.

From the ceiling and walls hung artifacts that would have made even the richest museum curator envious: original parts of an Elder airship, prototype sketches of blueprints for the Atmo Project, and trinkets of all sorts from history lost. Ras wondered if there was any-thing in the room that didn't have 'the first' in its description.

Foster Helios III stood from the desk in the middle of the ornate room. With outstretched arms and a broad smile he said, "Now, now, this is not how we treat our guests. Restraints weren't necessary." One of the men behind Ras removed the cuffs before all but two of the guards exited the room.

"I couldn't help but see you've noticed my grandfather's collection," Foster said, motioning for Ras to have a seat in front of his desk. "Inspiring, isn't it? I guess when you create Atmo, you get to keep the nice things for yourself."

Ras remained still. "You torture me and my friend and you want me to sit at your desk?"

"Torture?" Foster lifted an eyebrow. "Hardly. The Knack testing process is unpleasant, I'll concede the point, but I assure you it leaves no permanent damage." He smiled. "You'll even find your wounds will heal once the effects have worn off. Marvelous process."

"Why put us through it?"

"I can't have a Knack ignorant of his—or her—ability accidentally blowing up half of *The Halifax*, now can I? A lot of Energy gets thrown around in battle," Foster said.

"I noticed. New feature?" Ras asked.

"New war."

"My friend and I aren't Knacks."

"Your concern for Miss Tourbillon is noted, but I didn't make the rules."

Ras scoffed. "Why did you bring me up here?"

"Erasmus, I'll be upfront with you," Foster said, leaning against the front of his desk. "You have done what my father spent the latter half of his life failing to achieve."

"Cause a city to start sinking? Maybe he and I have more in common than you think," Ras said.

"No, Erasmus," Foster said, clearly annoyed, "you have met with Halcyon Napier and tasted the air that keeps him alive."

The Halifax shook slightly as its weapons fired on the sky pirate fleet.

"Shouldn't you be out on the bridge, winning the war?" Ras asked.

"This is more important, I assure you," Foster said, walking back to Ras. "Who is the first wind merchant, and why?"

"A history quiz?"

"Humor me, and I'll end Miss Tourbillon's tests early upon your word that she isn't a Knack."

Ras narrowed his eyes. "Hal Napier, because he discovered the Origin of all Energy."

"Exactly," Foster said. He pressed a button on his desk. "Yeardley, end the girl's testing." An affirmative crackled from his unit. "Better?"

Ras nodded.

"What if I told you that you could be the most famous wind merchant of all? Even more so than Napier."

"I can't exactly go and discover another Origin," Ras said.

"Can't you?" Foster asked playfully. "You've already met someone eight times older than you and you're discounting what's possible?"

"What exactly are you proposing, Mr. Helios?" Ras asked.

"That you take the same deal my father offered your father."

"Excuse me?"

"It doesn't surprise me that he didn't tell you. Publicly he was so outspoken against The Collective."

"You're lying."

"He actually came to my father, telling of Hal Napier's need for wind merchants to retrieve tankfuls of air from The Wild, then offered us the location of the source of this…fountain of youth in return for…something," Foster said, sliding into his desk chair.

Ras finally sat. "Which was?"

"Such things were never shared with me, but I do know what I can offer."

The battle raged on outside. Ras was amazed at how Foster didn't even take note of it. "Do you now?"

"Yes. If you lead us into The Wild, and I'm talking about just crossing the mountains, not even trying to find the fountain of youth, or Origin, or whatever it is; I will do three things: one, I will credit you as the wind merchant that discovered the new Origin."

"But I wouldn't have," Ras said.

"History has a selective memory," Foster said, gesturing dismissively. "Two, I will install Helios engines on *Verdant* with a lifetime supply of fuel."

Ras thought the offer oddly familiar. "Whose lifetime?"

"The Collective's," Foster said. "And three, I'll commission a new ship for you...how does that sound?"

"What happened to my ship?"

"You'd prefer to keep that old thing?" Foster asked. A distasteful look played across his face.

"So it wasn't destroyed?" Ras asked.

"Goodness, no. I ensured a team extracted it before *New Crispin* fell."

Ras heart sank. "I...how did it fall?"

"Sky pirates, of course."

"You led them here."

"And you led us here," Foster said, folding his hands politely. "I hope this underscores the importance of what I'm after, and how willing I am to compensate those who aid me in finding it."

Ras closed his eyes and couldn't escape the faces of Pop, Joey, Krantz, and everyone else his father had worked so hard to save. "Then it must be incredibly, incredibly important," he said slowly.

"I assure you, it is."

"You're looking for the fountain of youth?" Ras asked. He could feel himself shaking, but hoped it wasn't visible.

"My father was. He obsessed over it later in life," Foster said with a sigh. "I do suppose when nearing the end, one finds ways to distract oneself from the inevitable."

"What do you think is in The Wild?"

"Well, something is keeping Napier alive, is it not?" Foster asked. "But let's just say that from what I've learned, stopping at immortality is a touch...shortsighted." He smiled a devious smile. "Ras, you have an opportunity to surpass your father. You would even travel with the safety of our numbers." He slid open the drawer of his desk, and delicately pulled Callie's brass orb out, placing it on the table. "My grandfather invented this." He pointed a finger at some of the scrollwork. "It has his initials worked into the engraving here. I can only imagine it still works."

Ras fought his instinct to swat Foster's hand away from touching the orb. If Hal was right, Callie's tool for completing their mission was compromised.

"After a thorough searching of your ship and your person, the only coordinates found were well on the other side of the mountains," Foster said, "Hal wouldn't have been so careless as to simply leave instructions into what is presumably the only backdoor into The Wild in the hands of someone so…you." He picked up the orb, hefting it. "Hence this."

"So that's why I'm here," Ras said. "Nobody can make it work, so you need a guide."

"I don't need anything," Foster said, his temper flaring. "I'm offering you a fleeting opportunity. I have other methods of getting what I want."

"I'm thinking," Ras said.

"You misunderstand me. I'm not offering options, Erasmus, and 'thinking' tells me you're coming up with some excuse. Show me how it works, now, or I'll resume the tests on Miss Tourbillon," said Foster.

Ras reached for the orb a little too eagerly, and placed his fingers in the device like he had seen Callie do before. Several moments passed.

Nothing.

Foster's eyes narrowed. "You're just the pilot. It's the girl I need, isn't it?" He grabbed the orb from Ras's fingertips and motioned to the guards.

"No, no, I can use it. It just takes a moment to warm up," Ras said, backpedaling.

"Then why did you bring the girl with you?"

"She's…" Ras said, thinking, "entertainment."

The battle outside intensified as another sky pirate ship erupted in green flame and disintegrated.

"It's obvious you care more about her than that," Foster said. "She'll guide me and maybe provide me some entertainment as well." He addressed the guards, "Take him somewhere he won't stain anything."

The guards were almost upon Ras as he dove forward across the desk and grabbed the brass ball from Foster's grasp. He slid to the floor, orb in hand.

A clicking mechanism from underneath Foster's desk placed a pistol in Foster's hand, which he shoved point blank toward Ras' face. He pulled back the hammer on the flintlock to a full cock.

"Lack," Foster hissed, pulling the trigger with a spark of flame and expulsion of smoke.

CHAPTER THIRTEEN
The Lack

THE WIND MERCHANT LAY MOTIONLESS ON FOSTER'S CARPET, BRASS orb clutched to his chest. "I'm sorry, Callie," he whispered, and then it dawned on him that there was no possible way he could have spoken the words in the space of the bullet's flight. A misfire! His eyes shot open, but he was not prepared for what they were to see.

A small metal ball floated motionless halfway between Ras' nose and the gun, while a frozen plume of flame and smoke hung as if frozen from the barrel of the pistol. The disdainful expression on Foster's face had stuck like a molded mask.

Ras scurried backward out of the path of the bullet and stood to his feet. His heart was pounding in his ears, and as the rush of adrenaline overcame his caution, he reflexively crouched, bracing himself for the two guards. Only an instant before leaping, he realized that something was wrong and caught himself. The guards had stopped mid-stride, their rifles mounted and pointing at the ground.

The room sat completely still except for Ras' riotous heart, and as he began to walk, he struggled to hear his own footsteps for the stagnant quiet that had befallen the area.

He turned his head to the window and saw that contrary to the testimony of his ears, the battle was still raging on outside. A sky pirate ship lined up its broadside with *The Halifax* and fired its salvo directly at the bridge of the flagship. Ras dove to the floor with his hands over his ears.

A moment passed, then another as Ras' chest tightened with a wave of panic over his complete lack of understanding. The room should have been a picture of carnage by now. He hauled himself back to his feet and peered through the window. Twenty cannon balls hung in the air a few dozen yards away.

"What in Atmo!" Ras said. He only belatedly recognized the voice as his own; the words sounded hollow as they rang in his head.

He glanced around the room devoid of any motion, still unable to wrap his head around it quite yet. Looking down at the brass orb in his hand, he asked, "Did you do this?" He fought the urge to shake it, thinking it might accidentally reverse the thing possibly keeping him safe. "Some sort of time bomb?"

He was exiting the door when he noticed something familiar: Elias' grapple gun, loaded up with cabling and charges to make it look more authentic in its display. Walking up to it, he pulled the old friend from its wall mount with a little bit of effort.

"What else?" he asked himself as he surveyed the walls for things he might need to save Callie.

Ras burst into the hallway looking like a museum thief. His father's grapple gun adorned his left arm; a leather satchel filled with gadgets, goggles, and old dueling pistols was slung across his chest; and an antique sword led the way in his right hand. He was worth a small fortune but it was pointless if he couldn't find Callie and get off *The Halifax*.

Retracing his steps as best he could remember, he passed by halted crew members on his way back to the brig. *Two lefts, then a right?* He got turned around more than once, but time was on his side. He wondered how he was going to move Callie in a frozen state, but brushed the inconvenient thought aside.

Upon his successful return to the brig, he saw Dixie sitting on the floor of her cell with her arms wrapped around her legs. Just on the other side of the bars, a guard with a thick key ring dangling from his belt stood conversing with another man.

Ras didn't dare touch either of them, but he used the tip of the long, thin sword to try to lift the keys. They were stuck firmly on the guard's belt. *Interesting.* He had been able to remove the items from Foster's walls, but then again, he had personally picked them up. *Was that the trick?* If so, he'd probably need to avoid touching anybody.

He decided to chance reawakening the guard and reached out carefully to grab the large keyring. This time it came free. Then he reached his arms through the bars and tossed the keys toward Dixie, but they froze in place after leaving his grasp.

Satisfied with the result, he then pulled one of the antique dueling pistols from the leather satchel and soon it hung alongside the keys. Ras had no clue if the gun would even fire, but if Dixie kept her head, she'd know better than to expend its single shot and waste the intimidation value of a loaded weapon.

"Advantage, Dixie. You're welcome," Ras said, leaving the brig.

From there, Ras had no clue where to go next. He would occasionally catch updates via portholes on the growing number of cannon balls frozen in a radius around *The Halifax*. It began to concern him.

He followed a corridor that forced him to snake around an obstacle course of men in lab coats before it led him to a hallway filled with doors running along either side. Peeking through the windows, he saw large, burly men strapped down, looks of agony plastered on their faces as they received injections of some sort. *Soldiers?* Ras saw room after room of strapping young men, all somewhere in the process of being injected.

Ras made it to the door at the end of the hallway and found what he was looking for.

"Callie!"

He threw himself into the door but did little more than budge it open and dig the grapple gun into his shoulder. By leaning his weight into the door, he forced it far enough open to be able to slide through into the laboratory.

Based on the tearful expression on Callie's face, Foster had lied about stopping the testing. Surveying the room for a way to free her, he saw the two scientists standing behind their vast array of knobs and levers. He didn't even know if he could find the one to lift the glass dome, or if pressing a button would be too indirect an action to work on the frozen ship.

Looking back at Callie's state, he couldn't handle her being in pain when he could finally do something about it. Enraged, he ran up to the dome and swung the sword with all of his might at the glass. With a sharp snap the blade left the hilt, flying back over Ras' shoulder, just missing him. He looked back. The broken blade hung just above the floor a few feet behind him. As Ras stepped over to the blade, it clattered to the ground.

All right, that makes no sense, Ras thought.

Still, there was no time to consider the oddness. He had to see Callie. Up close, he noticed her eyes no longer looked blue, but violet. He took note of it, ran back to the entrance to fish out a pair of old goggles from his newly acquired satchel, and strapped them on. A display winked, showing a green glow etched in lines all about the room.

KnackVisions. He was using Foster Helios' original pair of Knack-Visions as safety goggles.

"Here goes nothing," Ras said, taking off into a dash toward the glass. He knew the collision would hurt, but he didn't realize how much until he crashed through the glass dome, creating a Ras-sized hole. Shards of glass flew everywhere, nicking and cutting him up. Pieces that flew over a foot away simply hung in midair.

He slowly picked himself up from the glass on the floor, shaking a few pieces from his hair. He placed the KnackVisions atop his head and moved to start unstrapping Callie from the gurney.

The sound of cracking and shattering glass was the first indicator that the spell was broken. Time appeared to finally catch back up.

Chaos erupted.

Ras threw himself over Callie to shield her from the collapsing dome, and her continued scream of anguish almost drowned out the rest of what was going on aboard *The Halifax*.

The lab erupted in sparks, splinters, and flying debris as two cannon balls ripped through the room. *The Halifax* shook violently under the stress of hundreds of cannonballs as they finally found their mark.

Ras undid the last strap and Callie collapsed into his arms, sobbing.

Another cannon ball careened through the room as warning klaxons blared. Ras could no longer hear the shouts of the scientists. Looking back, he noticed the control panel bore the brunt of the latest blast. The level above them groaned, ready to collapse upon them.

He scooped up Callie and carried her out of the lab. It was every man for himself in the corridors and nobody took much notice of the escaped test subjects.

"How did you get here?" Callie asked, nuzzling into his shoulder.

"I really don't know." He shifted her slightly in his arms.

"Where are we going?" Callie asked.

"As far away from here as we can," Ras said. "Can you put my goggles down on my face for me?"

She slid them down and the structure of the ship fell into view, highlighting the framework of Energy pulsing through the ship. He couldn't imagine how his grandfather got around seeing every breeze and power line without going mad. The Energy patterns of the ships docked on the underside of the behemoth showed where Ras needed to go.

The flow of people jostling and elbowing their way to safety made it apparent to Ras that the crew either had never drilled for such an evacuation or hadn't taken training seriously.

The Halifax jerked, and Ras almost dropped Callie down a flight of stairs as an Energy surge far below blew apart one of the engines. The explosion left the flagship limping at a slight angle.

A scuffle at the base of the stairwell backed up foot traffic. From halfway up the stairs, Ras could see a small white-haired figure launch herself onto the back of a guard. She viciously slammed the butt of a pistol into the top of the guard's head and disappeared from view as she rode the toppling man to the ground.

"At least she's making good use of it," Ras said.

"What? Who?" Callie asked as if stirred from sleep.

"Dixie!" Ras shouted. The jam cleared and Ras saw her once more. "On your six!"

The white haired girl popped up and whirled around as Ras approached her. She beamed as she shouted back a greeting. "Ras!" She spun and smashed the butt of the antique dueling pistol squarely into the jaw of another guard, dropping him. "You got a plan? Mine involves more violence than escaping, but I like having options," she said as she slung a duffle bag over her shoulder.

Ras caught up with her and stepped on the back of one of the guards who was attempting to pick himself back up, eliciting a groan. "We're heading to the docks."

"To the docks! Lovely plan. Is she okay?" Dixie asked before stooping down to pick up the unused musket of the downed guard and rejoining the flow of the crowd.

"I don't know yet," said Ras. The ship shuddered again, rolling slightly and forcing everyone to stand half on the floor and half on the wall to their right. It made for awkward progress as they shuffled down the last corridor to the docks.

The wind howled beneath *The Halifax* as the mob spilled out onto the hanging walkways leading to the docked ships. Sky pirate biplane fighters zipped by, taking potshots at escape vessels.

Ras blanched slightly when he saw the grated metal walkway with nothing but sky underneath it. The ship shuddered again, and several men in front of them fell screaming over the railing and disappeared beneath the clouds.

The tilting flagship made carrying Callie a challenge. Ras scooted along the handrail and surveyed the docked ships until his eyes fell upon *The Brass Fox*.

"Dixie! That one!" Ras shouted over the battle.

"The junker?" Dixie asked, prompting an angry look from Ras. "Got it!" She scurried down the metal pathway toward the ship. She didn't have the keys, but Ras suspected she wouldn't need them.

Callie looked around her and realized exactly where she was. She jerked and tightened her grip around Ras' neck, causing him to stumble and almost fall.

"Easy, easy, I got you," Ras said as he watched Dixie board *The Brass Fox* and run up to the helm.

Although faltering, *The Halifax* still volleyed green beams, wreaking a swath of havoc on three pirate ships swarming around it.

"Veir!" a deep and menacing voice shouted behind Ras. A small escape airship pulled up underneath *The Halifax*. Foster Helios III stood at the ship's railing beside his entourage of bodyguards, who were preparing to leap over to Ras. "The girl, if you will."

Ras attempted to hobble down the scaffolding, but couldn't move quickly without being able to use his hands freely. He looked around for another option. There was only one. "Callie," he whispered, pulling her closer. "I'm sorry, but hold tight and don't let go."

The bodyguards jumped from Foster's getaway ship onto *The Halifax* just as Ras conquered every sane impulse in his body and leaned backward, falling over the railing and into the abyss.

It took Ras a moment to spot *The Brass Fox* in a dive of its own, smoke billowing from its port engine. Extending his left arm, Ras fired a grapple shot at the ship. The cable whirred madly until the spike connected to the deck. Both parties continued to plummet toward the cloud layer until *The Brass Fox* began leveling off, causing Ras and Callie to swing wildly inside the clouds.

Ras struggled to work the mechanism on the grapple gun to begin pulling them toward the free falling Fox. As they burst through the stormy clouds, Ras felt the sensation of a downpour of water, soaking him through.

Below them, a Convergence whipped wildly about on the winds over the dark ground, which billowed in a constant state of motion.

"Callie! What's happening to the ground?"

She peeked one eye open then both eyes shot wide. "We're over an ocean!"

"A what?" Ras exclaimed. The cable pulled them closer and closer to *The Brass Fox*. A strike of lightning illuminated the skies, followed by a deafening peal of concussive force that shook Ras to his core. "Pull up!" Ras shouted to the white haired figure on the bridge.

They continued to fall.

The roar of the Convergence grew and Ras realized he was on a collision course with the sphere. He cursed himself for not having done something differently to alter his path, although he didn't know what he could have changed.

"Hang on!" Ras squeezed Callie tight as the Convergence screamed toward them. He knew he would be safe, but hoped he wouldn't watch the girl he loved evaporate away in his arms, lost forever.

Everything moved so quickly that Ras struggled to comprehend it all. Over the screams of the Convergence, he heard the engines of his ship engage. He felt a tug on his arm pull his center of gravity toward the ship, but the shift in momentum wasn't enough to swing away from the ball of Energy.

Ras braced himself for impact as the heated air fought to steal away his breath. Once he pierced the exterior of the Convergence, the roar of the green fire dampened. He gripped Callie so tightly he feared he was hurting her.

Green flame engulfed them. Swirling figures made of light danced around, but kept their distance. Within moments he shot through the bottom of the sphere and was once again doused by the crying skies.

Ras realized Callie was still clinging to him as their fall leveled off just above the spray of the ocean. He wiped away the wet, matted hair from his face and saw *The Halifax* burst through the cloud cover, its fiery engines struggling to keep it aloft.

An updraft took the Convergence soaring to meet the flagship, but the sphere began to fluctuate and lose stability along the way.

The Brass Fox pulled to a stop, and Ras found himself seesawing underneath his ship before the retraction of the cable dragged him and Callie over the side railing to the deck. Ras decided he had earned a moment to just collapse into a heap with Callie and rest.

Dixie bounded down from the bridge. "I don't want to interrupt… anything, but that ship might come falling on our heads any second now, so…yeah," she said, glancing over her shoulder.

Ache and exhaustion settled into Ras' body as the adrenaline ebbed away. Sitting up caused him to feel every muscle in his body screaming at him. Ras stood, then helped Callie up.

Pop. Pop. Pop, pop, pop. Dixie, Callie, and Ras walked over to the side railing, looked past the balloon, and saw *The Halifax* erupt in a series of small green explosions as it met with the Convergence, ripping the ship apart.

"What's going on?" Callie asked.

"They had Knacks onboard," Ras said.

"Oh my…so they're…"

"Overloading," Dixie said, "Being pulled into the Convergence."

Callie turned her head away. "I can't watch that."

The Halifax's engines failed completely as the ship erupted into a furious inferno and continued hurtling toward *The Brass Fox*.

"Do we have a magnet in us or something?" Ras protested. He pointed to Dixie. "Get her into the quarters and make sure she's secure," he said, running up the stairs to the helm. Dixie had lodged her hair clip into the ignition to start the airship. There was no time for amusement or annoyance. He jammed the throttle forward.

The Brass Fox jerked into motion, bringing shouts from the quarters. *The Halifax* blotted out the sky above him, blocking what light fell through the clouds onto the small wind merchant vessel.

"C'mon, c'mon!" Ras shouted at his ship, slamming the wheel to starboard. The ship barreled toward the edge of *The Halifax's* shadow.

He didn't let himself look back to see if he would make it, as there was little more he could do.

A groan of metal and a sizzle of hot engines hitting the water behind Ras finally piqued his curiosity. He turned to see *The Halifax* splashing down, creating a wave higher than *The Brass Fox* was flying. Ras yanked up on the wheel, giving the airship enough altitude that the wave merely clipped it. Still, the force pushed *The Brass Fox* forward and almost threw Ras against the wheel as the water roared over the railing and slammed against him.

Soaked, Ras continued to pull his ship into a climb and circled back around the burning wreckage of The Collective's capital ship. Smoke belched from the hull as the fires lost their battle to the flooding waters, and *The Halifax* descended into a watery grave.

HALF AN HOUR AND FIFTY MILES LATER, *The Brass Fox* was limping just underneath the clouds. Inside the upended Captain's quarters, Ras sat stunned in the chair next to Callie, who was resting her head on the small table next to her destroyed typewriter. Dixie paced around the ripped up mess of sheets, clothes, and cookware, her expression manic.

"I cannot believe sky pirates took down *The Halifax*. It's *The Halifax!*" Dixie said, continuing to pace. "Well, say something!"

"We'll get you another typewriter," Ras said, placing a light hand on Callie's shoulder. "I'm sorry." Ras' head swam. Nothing made sense.

"What were they doing to me?" Callie finally asked, still not looking up. "To us?"

"Like I told him, they were testing to see if you were Knacks," Dixie said.

Callie looked up and shook her head, then reeled before steadying herself. "That doesn't make sense. They had Knacks onboard already. You saw what happened when the Convergence hit it."

"Well, they were testing for something," Ras said, leaning over to pick up the old leather satchel, and carefully emptying the relics onto the table.

"Hold on, where'd you get that?" Dixie asked, walking up and snatching a small dueling pistol. She pulled its weathered and bloodied twin from the small of her back, then shot an accusatory finger at Ras. "You! I knew it!" she shouted. "I don't know what I know because it still doesn't add up, but I knew you had something to do with it!"

"What are you talking about?" Callie asked.

"One second I'm sitting in the brig, and the next thing I know, I'm strong-arming the guards with this," Dixie said, hefting one of the pistols. "What gives?"

Ras reached into the satchel and offered Hal's brass orb to Callie. "This thing, I think."

"You touched it!" Callie cried. She snatched away the device and inserted her fingers to start the mechanism. The arrow began to scope out, then stuck.

"I wasn't the first," Ras said, "Foster got to it before I did, and who knows who pulled it from our ship when they ransacked it?"

Dixie pointed at the orb. "How does that explain what happened?"

"It doesn't," Callie said. "It's supposed to just be a compass that leads to one place, but nobody else was supposed to be able to work it but me."

"I think it's more than a compass," Ras said, then hesitated. "I don't know how, but I'm starting to think it can stop time."

Dixie gave a hard laugh. "And you know that how?"

Ras sighed. "Everything around me stopped and I was the only one on the ship that could move. The pirates kept firing though…"

Callie stared blankly, lost in thought.

Dixie opened her mouth as if she had something to counter with, but her mouth shut and she gave a look of confusion. "I'd call you a liar, but…" She lifted the dueling pistol. "Why would something like that happen?"

"I thought stuff like that only happened in The Wild," Ras said to Callie, then waved a hand in front of her eyes. "Are you with us?"

She shook her head slightly, breaking the trance. "Right."

"Hold on, did you say The Wild?" Dixie asked. "Who knows anything about The Wild? It's not like anyone's been there in a hundred years."

"We're trying to break that streak," Ras said, then turned to Callie. "But how are we going to find the pass now with a busted compass?"

"Who in their right mind would ever want to go into The Wild?" Dixie asked.

"Our hometown is going to sink if we don't," Callie said.

"I'm going to assume there's a longer story attached to that," Dixie said. "What's your hometown?"

"*Verdant*," Ras said.

"I heard Bravo Company attacked it. It's still flying?" Dixie asked.

"When we left they were just surrounding it," Ras said.

"So if you go to The Wild and do whatever you need to do, it'll be a blow to Bravo Company, right?"

"They want *Verdant*, so yes," Ras said.

"Perfect! I particularly enjoy not giving sky pirates what they want. I'm in."

Ras shook his head. "Sorry Dixie, you're not going with us—"

"You've saved my life twice now, so I'm a little in your debt," Dixie said. "By personal obligation I kind of have to, and if I'm being perfectly honest, now I kind of want to."

Ras held up his hand. "It's a moot point. We don't know how to get into The Wild anymore."

Callie stared blankly at the wall.

"What's wrong?" Ras asked. Not getting anything further from Callie, he turned to Dixie. "Would you give us a minute?"

"Sure," Dixie said, "but talk quietly. These walls are kind of thin and I'm a bit of a snoop. Just a heads up." She exited, and Ras turned to Callie.

"Hal was telling me the truth," Callie said, half to herself.

"What about?"

"Me," she said. "Ras, I'm a Knack."

"We already know you're not—"

"I'm not an *Energy* Knack, I'm…" She clenched her jaw. "I'm a Time Knack."

"What in Atmo is a *Time* Knack?" Ras asked.

"According to Hal, there's an Origin like Energy in The Wild, only it regulates time. He said it's like friction. If it's thick in the air, things can't move," she said, looking into Ras' eyes. "The first Knacks developed their sensitivity by living close to an Origin, so instead of exploding when an Energy Knack gets too close to too much Energy, a Time Knack…"

"Stops time," Ras said, understanding. "And they were blasting us with something." *No wonder they let me go...* He ruffled his hair. "But you're not from The Wild. Nobody is."

"The Elders couldn't have built themselves, Ras. Maybe somebody in my family way back when was from there," Callie said.

"So, the headaches..."

"Maybe it's because I'm a Time Knack. I don't know," Callie said, then wrinkled her nose. "That still feels weird to finally say out loud."

Ras gently picked up the brass orb from Callie's hand. "So does this thing actually point toward Time?"

Callie sheepishly looked at Ras, then shook her head. "I just made it point whatever direction I wanted it to point, which was whatever direction I saw Time the most concentrated." She smiled an apology. "He made me promise not to tell anyone unless I had to."

"What, it's not like there's some super powerful leader of Atmo's Energy supply after someone like that, is there?" Ras asked with a half grin.

"I don't know, is there?"

"Oh, I didn't tell you about that. Yeah, Foster shot at me when he realized I didn't know how to use this thing," Ras said, inspecting the orb. "Your overload stopped the bullet, so...thanks for that."

"Really? Jerk." Callie said. "But wait...How were you able to move?"

Ras had an idea exactly how a Lack could avoid being affected by something coming from an Origin, but preferred to skirt the issue. He turned the orb around in his hand. "Maybe whoever holds this is immune to freezing?"

She furrowed her brow. "That doesn't really make sense, but right now not a whole lot does."

"Wait, so that means you can still get us to The Wild?"

Callie nodded, her tired grin spreading to Ras.

"I'm feeling excluded now!" Dixie shouted from the deck. "You two aren't being nearly loud enough!"

"Huddle's over," Ras said.

Dixie returned, rubbing her arms for warmth. "I don't know if you know this, but clouds are cold."

Ras stood and brought the tattered map draped over the bed to the table. "We'll have to check our coordinates against the stars tonight, but unless the battle moved, we should still be over *New Crispin.*"

"You mean *Crispin*, right?" Callie asked.

Ras turned, looked at Callie, and solemnly shook his head.

"Oh," Callie said, slouching slightly. "Wait, everyone was running to their ships. Maybe they got away."

"I hope so," Ras said. He turned his attention back to the map, tracing a finger east by northeast from *Crispin*. "It looks like the only city between us and The Wild is *Solaria*. We'll have to drop you off there, Dixie."

"Oh, will you now?" Dixie defiantly planted her hands on her hips and raised an eyebrow. "*Solaria* is on the opposite end of Atmo from *Verdant*. Did you fix that compass?"

"It's a little worse for wear, but it'll work," said Callie, looking at Ras.

"Well, you're not dumping me off on *Solaria*. It sunk just after it launched. How old are those maps?" Dixie asked. "If you're heading that direction, any respectable Atmo city is going to add days to your trip."

"How much longer does *Verdant* have?" Callie asked.

Ras did the math. "Three weeks. Maybe. I'm sure Bravo Company has been circling *Verdant* just to use up as much Energy as they can in The Bowl."

"But Pop said Bravo Company uses Helios engines," Callie said.

"No pirate uses Helios engines," Dixie said. "They'd have to continually raid Collective sources for it."

"Well, regardless, nobody is bringing extra Energy to *Verdant* from outside The Bowl. Three weeks, max. On top of that we have to think about getting back to tell…" Ras looked at Dixie, then Callie.

"So, you don't have time to spare," Dixie said, smiling. "Y'know, you two don't have the best track record when I'm not around. Besides, who gets to say they've been to The Wild and back?" She paused. "You are coming back, right?"

"That's the plan," Ras said.

"It's settled, then. You nice people wouldn't leave me to die alone on the surface at the hands of Remnants or a Convergence, so I'll help you get to The Wild and back. We'll call it even after that."

Ras took a deep breath and slowly let it out. "You need to know what you're signing up for. There are Elders still in The Wild."

Dixie shrugged. "So? There are sky pirates on this side. And now we've got The Collective after us. Give me antique wind-up toys any day. I know how to handle myself. I'm a big girl. Let me pay my debt."

Ras took a moment, letting the silence hang. "Do you know your way around a Windstrider engine?"

Dixie beamed. "Oh, definitely! I mean, I'm no miracle worker. We'll need parts to repair the one that took the brunt of that pirate's cannon ball."

"Hold on, when did we get hit?" Ras asked.

"Someone took a pot shot at me when I launched...You didn't think I expected you to go skydiving without a parachute off *The Halifax*, did you?"

"I didn't really have a lot of time to think about it," Ras said.

"Well, we should be able to putt along just fine under the clouds with one Windstrider, but I wouldn't bet on us in any races," Dixie said. "*Solaria* is old enough. Maybe we could find some Windstrider parts if it's not already picked clean by Remnants."

"I still kind of want to meet one," Callie said.

"Girlie, you don't want to run into a Remnant," Dixie said.

"Why? Have you seen one?"

"No, but you hear all those stories...some say they're cannibals; others say their skin is green and sickly, almost falling off their bones."

"Can we focus on getting the engine fixed?" Ras asked. "We'll fly out toward *Solaria* and at least see what our options are." He turned to Callie. "Can you get us a heading while Dixie and I look at the engine?"

"Aye-aye, Captain," Callie said.

Ras escorted Dixie to the hold. The cannonball lodged in the Windstrider didn't give Ras high hopes as he collected a few broken engine parts from the floor.

"Wow, this was a classic," Dixie said, resting her hand on the Windstrider. "If *Solaria* didn't fall too hard, it shouldn't be difficult to find what we need."

"Dixie, can I be blunt?"

"I usually don't ask, so go ahead," Dixie said.

"Don't you have something better to do?" Ras asked.

"Better as in...what? A job? A family to be with?"

Ras shrugged. "I just find it odd you want to come with two strangers on a mission most would consider suicide."

"One, I like you guys, and I feel like being here makes it a little less suicide-y," Dixie said with a wink. "Two, any opportunity I get to humiliate India Bravo, I'll take."

"Why?"

Dixie paused for a moment. "Bravo Company don't just sink cities, Ras. They also do unspeakable things to freshly orphaned little girls."

A silence hung in the air. "I'm sorry—"

"Don't be. You're not on their side," Dixie said, half of her usual smile returning, "Remember, I don't ask if I can be blunt." She walked from the engine across the hold. "At some point you'll have to tell me how going to The Wild fixes everything for you, but since you're going through all this trouble, and a cursory observation doesn't leave me thinking you're too terribly insane, I'll assume this mission of yours is valid." She ogled the jetcycle, then threw her leg over it. "I didn't take you for a jetter." The oversized machine made her look more childlike than usual.

"I'm not, really. It came with the ship."

Dixie looked down at the jetcycle, then scanned the hold. "Not exactly a matched set, are they?"

Ras shrugged.

"I could take this thing off your hands, if you like. That way your lady won't get too envious," Dixie said, caressing the machine.

"Not interested, but thanks," Ras said.

"Doesn't look like you're making much use of what you've got."

"Maybe after this whole thing blows over I'll take her out."

"I'm not just talking about the jetcycle, Ras," Dixie said.

"Me neither."

CALLIE SAT ALONE IN THE QUARTERS, allowing herself a moment to battle her brewing headache. The room sat in shambles around her. In one of the messier corners, her beautiful paper lay strewn, marred with the bootprints of Collective men.

It felt childish to tell Ras about the paper, but it broke her heart. She hadn't had the time to work on her book, and with the destruction of her beloved typewriter, several of the little round keys had been jarred loose. It looked like someone hadn't just knocked it over, but had actively hurled it across the room.

She slowly stood and walked to the back corner of the room to collect the paper, seeing if she could salvage anything. The fact that they destroyed something so rare and pure left her seething. They didn't care, and each time she found a piece that might have survived unscathed, she inevitably discovered a tread mark as though it were part of a thorough vendetta against her. Stooping over brought another wave of pain, forcing her to sit on the floor next to the pile.

Sifting through the paper revealed a ripped open envelope. A letter peeked out, inviting her to read more than just the words '*dulls sensitivity to Knacks.*'

She stopped, eyeing the paper. A moment passed. She looked over her shoulder, then listened for any approaching footsteps. It sounded like Ras was still with Dixie down in the hold. Letting curiosity get the best of her, she slid the letter free.

Her hungry eyes devoured each line as though she were in a speed-reading event and the judge might enter at any moment to disqualify her.

She was almost finished when a new wave of pain washed over her, pulling her into the blackness.

As NIGHT FELL, the remaining Collective forces mopped up the last of the sky pirates. Foster Helios III stared out the main window of a Collective gunship.

A dozen soldiers accompanied an approaching man in a white lab coat. The scientist spoke up. "Sir, they're ready."

Foster turned to address the soldiers standing behind him. "Thank you, Dr. Lupava," he said, nodding to the doctor. He began to inspect the soldiers. Their pupils were black and hollow, giving them a hungry, disquieting look. "What happened here is an example of the power of what we're after," Foster said, gesturing to the stormy sea below. The last vestiges of *The Halifax* manifested themselves as large air pockets bubbling to the surface.

"Imagine being able to stop your enemy in their tracks like that." He snapped his fingers, "But we've taken measures to safeguard ourselves…with you." He continued to pace around the line of soldiers. "You are all the first in the line of Time resistant soldiers. We weren't able to extract the essence of the girl, but even if we can't get into The Wild, she will suffice. Your mission is to find Calista Tourbillon and bring her back to me, as unharmed as possible. We already have what we need from her companion, and now you do too."

CHAPTER FOURTEEN
The Demons

THE SPEED AT WHICH THE WORLD ZIPPED BY THE LOCOMOTIVE'S windows belied the train's smooth glide. Callie knew better than to question the idiosyncrasies of her dreams, but the experience left her curious as to whether riding on a train truly felt like being whisked away on the wind.

She felt two sizes too small next to the other passengers, which remained a consistency in every dream. Standing on her seat only allowed her to peek out the window of the train at the blurry, lush landscape.

Something was different about the cabin this time. The faces of the other passengers remained blurred, but other details beckoned for her attention. A pattern comprised of crisscrossing diamonds was etched into the ceiling, and the carpet below mirrored the design in ornate threads of gold and maroon.

She tried to recall the paintings back on *The Kingfisher*, wondering if perhaps one of the works of art lining its halls might have spurred a deeper level of imaginative detail.

A giant man in a dull gray uniform walked up to her seat. The man was the only one whose face wasn't obscured. His expression remained sad yet kind, and his smile flared out his mustache the way it always did in her dream. However, when he spoke, Callie couldn't understand his gibberish.

"Could you maybe write down what you're saying?" Callie asked. She had never thought to go that route before.

The muddled voice of the caring man accompanied a bewildered expression. He patted Callie on the head with a large hand, then moved on to speak with other passengers.

Callie looked back out the window at the green scenery. Suddenly, all went dark.

CALLIE OPENED HER EYES. The world was a blur, but the familiar wooden ceiling coming into focus told her that she was still in the Captain's quarters of *The Brass Fox*. Absolved of her headache, she tried to sit up but found herself mildly restrained by bedsheets. An absence of light from the porthole let her know she hadn't slept through the night.

She was still fully dressed except for her jacket and boots, but there was no sign of Ras anywhere. Peeling away the sheets, she swung her feet over the side of the bed, connecting with something decidedly not the floor, as floors didn't say, "Ow!"

Callie jerked her legs up, sliding them back onto the bed. From the floor she heard a man's voice groan. "Ras?"

"You're up," he croaked. "How's your head?" The question was flat and lifeless, as if Ras had asked it more out of duty than anything else.

She peeked over the edge of the bed, looked down at Ras, then glanced over to the table in the middle of the room. His letter sat out in the open. "I'm all right now. It kind of came out of nowhere again," she said, trying desperately to maintain some degree of nonchalance.

Ras got up and wordlessly made his way over to the chair where his jacket was draped. He grabbed it, slung it over his shoulder, then turned to exit. "When you're ready, we could use a heading," he said curtly.

Callie began to speak, but the slamming door stopped her.

THE BRASS FOX SLID above the starlight-bathed cloud layer, its balloon peeking out first, then its whole body. Up on the bridge, Ras worked the controls using more force than necessary to restart the working engine, then half-folded, half-crumpled his star map. He heard noises from the Captain's quarters and assumed Callie was moving about. First shuffles, then clanking sounds.

An hour passed before the quarters door open and Ras watched Callie as she made her way up to the bridge.

"Where are we?" Callie asked, beginning with a safe topic.

Dixie peeked her head up from the hold before climbing onto the deck. "Look who's finally awake! Evidently The Collective had the same idea as you guys and headed east while we were aboard. Are you feeling any better?"

"A little, thanks," Callie said. "How much time does that save us?" She aimed the question more at Ras than Dixie.

"At least a day," Dixie said, allowing Ras a continued respite from speaking. "Assuming they were heading in the right direction."

"We passed *Solaria*," Ras said quietly.

Callie leaned in and whispered, "Can we please talk?"

Ras watched Dixie watch him and Callie. "Just let me know when you get a heading," he said.

"I thought we were going to pick up parts in *Solaria*," Callie said. "What happened to that plan?"

"*Solaria* isn't where we thought it'd be," Dixie said. "We checked."

"It must have moved before it crashed, and we don't have time to go searching for it," Ras said. "We'll have to limp around The Wild as best we can."

"But we're a day closer than we thought, so that's good, right?" Callie asked.

"Why did you read my letter?" Ras asked, his tone harsher than he had intended.

Callie stood stunned for a moment. "I was just cleaning up the cabin and I accidentally saw part of it."

"Then you accidentally saw all of it?" Ras asked, hurt.

"I'm sorry, I had to know."

Dixie raised a hand. "Can I interject?"

"Not now, Dixie," Ras said. He turned back to Callie. "What, you had to know that I'm a Lack?" His eyes welled up. "That I'm practically wired to make life harder for others?"

"That's not true!"

"Who *don't* I make things harder for?"

"Guys?" Dixie asked.

"What?" Ras shouted.

"Now might not be the best time, but I thought it worthwhile to mention that we're sinking. Just saying." Dixie pointed down to the hold. "Maybe I should go check on the engine?" she asked as clouds began to spill over the railing.

It dawned on Ras that the silence of the night had come at the expense of the other working Windstrider. He flipped the switch to restart the engine, but nothing happened.

"Me," Callie said, "You don't make things harder for me. I've had a theory for a long, long time, and that letter confirmed it."

"You thought I was a Lack too?" he asked. The instrument panel noted that the scoop wasn't taking in any Energy and automatically shut down to avoid damaging itself. He lowered the collection tube and the sensor indicated a Level 3 potency.

"No, think about it, Ras. Have you ever seen me with a headache?"

The ship shifted to port and their descent quickened to a pace that promised an unpleasant and hull-damaging landing. It was too late to engage the Helios engine since they were no longer above the clouds. It was a perfectly acceptable time to panic.

"Cut the ballasts! We're sinking!" Ras shouted. He couldn't see Dixie, but he could hear her swearing a blue streak.

"Maybe the headaches come because I can't escape Time," Callie said, "Maybe you keep me from overloading by dulling that sensitivity." As they cleared the cloud layer, Ras saw her beginning to tear up. "And I'm sorry that you're stuck with me."

He didn't have time to mull over a lifetime of memories to weigh against her theory, but he needed Callie to keep a level head. "Callie, I've never considered myself stuck with you, but if we don't offload enough weight, we're going to be stuck without a ship." Ras dashed over to the side railing to the nearest of the ballast bags. "We can talk about this after we don't crash, deal?" He fumbled with the rope, untying it as Dixie and Callie moved to other bags and did the same.

As the weights dropped, *The Brass Fox*'s descent didn't slow noticeably. They needed to drop something far heavier.

"Open the bay!" Dixie shouted, and without much time to question why, Ras obliged, running back up to the console, and jamming the new button Tibbs installed. He looked up to see a frightened Callie and no sign of Dixie.

The whinnying of an unfamiliar engine trying to cycle from beneath the deck caught his attention.

"Dixie!" Ras shouted. The howl of the wind flowing into the hold drowned out his voice. "Callie! Tell her it's not ready!"

"What?" Callie shouted back.

"The jetcycle isn't ready! Tell her to dump it!" Ras mimed a pushing motion.

Callie nodded, then descended into the hold as Ras did his best at the helm to stave off their descent by redirecting the collection hose and expelling the air in the tank.

The roar of an engine cut through the wailing wind and disappeared with a quickly fading exclamation of joy or despair as *The Brass Fox*'s descent tapered to a glide.

"Dixie! You did it!" Ras shouted to no response. With both engines dead and the Helios engine in danger of overloading underneath the clouds, the ship sat eerily silent save for the usual creak of wood and rope. "Callie?"

Callie climbed from the hold to the deck, her expression blank.

"It worked!" Ras said. "We're not falling nearly as much."

"She dumped the jetcycle."

"I suppose that's better than losing *The Fox*."

"She was still on it."

RAS' EYES HURT FROM SQUINTING, trying to make out movement in the inky night after his KnackVisions gave no indication of anything Energy-fueled beneath them.

"Maybe she got it working before it crashed?" Callie asked.

Ras shook his head. "She'd have flown back up here if she did."

"We should at least look for her when we touch down. Maybe the trees softened the fall enough?"

The thought of what they might find disturbed Ras. He nodded and trudged back up to the helm to steady the ship's slow and graceful descent.

The sun began to peek over the horizon, lending a bit of light to the world, and Ras could see they were floating high above a dense forest outside of a town built around something chillingly familiar. "I think we found *Solaria*," Ras said. Aside from some superficial architectural differences, the crashed structure reminded Ras of *Verdant*, giving him a glimpse of his city's grim future.

"Torches!" Callie said, pointing down. Beneath them, a moving line of two dozen twinkling lights blinked through the dense foliage. "Maybe they'll help her if she survived!"

"They're probably Remnants," Ras said, searching for a clearing big enough to land the ship.

In a matter of minutes, *The Brass Fox* settled neatly into a nearby clearing. Ras lowered the anchor out of habit, as though the ship might somehow take off without them.

Callie packed the leather satchel with provisions while Ras holstered his large wrench and strapped on the grapple gun, thinking it wise to bring even though they had no places from which to fall.

With a general idea of the direction of where they needed to go, Ras stepped off the gangplank and shortly realized he heard only one set of footfalls. He turned and saw Callie standing on the edge of the gangplank, satchel strapped across her body.

"If we're going to find her before the Remnants do, we're going to have to hurry," Ras said.

"It's just…" Callie began. "I've never touched the ground before." She gently lowered one foot forward to the grass. She tentatively shifted her weight, then took a few experimental steps, unsure of her new sensation. "It…doesn't move."

Ras nodded before turning around to head back into the woods. An hour of trudging through the forest only offered up the clue of a scraped chunk of metal that Ras recognized as part of the jetcycle.

"We can't do this all day. Maybe she made it into town," Ras said.

"But what if she's still out here and we gave up on her?" Callie asked. "Dixie!" she shouted, cupping her hands to her mouth.

"Shh! What if Remnants hear you?"

Callie sighed, looked about and continued walking. "Just ten more minutes."

Ras wanted to protest. He wanted to remind her that *Verdant* was still sinking as they searched; that he had no idea how they were going to avoid Remnants, find Dixie, and fix their engines; and that even if they were to successfully make it into The Wild, they still had Elders to dodge and a return trip filled with most of the same obstacles to navigate.

"Ras?" Callie crouched about fifty feet ahead, inspecting something. He quickly closed the distance and saw what interested her.

Blood.

Formerly white strands of hair lay matted in the small pool. Nearby, multiple sets of tracks headed off in the direction of the town.

"I don't know why they'd take a dead body. Maybe this is a good thing?" Ras asked. According to Dixie's theories, he actually had several gruesome ideas as to why they might take a dead body, but didn't feel it an opportune time to share.

"We're too late." Callie said, looking up at Ras, then past him. "Maybe not..."

Ras turned to see what she was looking at. The jetcycle hung lodged high between a couple of close growing trees. Still, it would have been a long way to fall. "There's no way I'm getting up there without that thing falling on me," he said.

Twenty minutes later and fifty feet higher, Ras was peeking out between green leaves for the first time in his life. Naturally, some part of his mind had decided that standing on the swaying branches was a sufficiently novel sensation to deserve an attack of the vertigo. He looked down at Callie, who stood near the base of the trees, and immediately regretted it. "I'd stand back. No sense in both of us being crushed if we can help it."

She obliged.

Merely five feet away from the jetcycle, Ras lacked an actual plan on how to get the thing started. He imagined getting the machine to run, only to career into another tree moments later. On the other hand, if the plan worked, they might have a chance at getting to the town before the torchlight party.

The awkward position of the jetcycle caused Ras to wonder about the merits of trying to start the machine while sideways to let the engine cycle. Letting the bike fall would almost ensure its inoperability, a state that Ras didn't wish to share by riding it straight down to the forest floor.

Climbing the last five feet, he pulled within grabbing distance of the right handlebar. The key was still in the ignition.

"Will it work?" Callie called up.

Ras looked down to respond and immediately tightened his grip on the branch, shutting his eyes tightly. "Don't know yet." Retrieving the wrench from his holster, he used it to press the ignition button. The engine cycled but didn't start.

He pressed the button again to the same effect. The sound reminded him of whenever *The Fox*'s engine scoop would clog. But with the intake on the bottom of the jetcycle, Ras realized he had climbed the wrong tree to access the guts of the vehicle.

After one last fruitless push of the ignition button to remind him that luck was not usually on his side, he climbed a bit higher than the jetcycle. The other tree offered a few branches to grasp, but none that looked likely to support his weight.

He set a foot lightly down on the side of the jetcycle's seat. It shifted slightly, but settled. He didn't know if Dixie could have survived a drop from this height, but if she did, she'd be showing meetings with every branch below, of which there were many.

Ras placed more of his weight onto the jetcycle, which now felt firmly lodged. He took a deep breath and pulled himself toward the opposite tree as the jetcycle rumbled to life beneath him. "No, not now!" Ras scolded the machine, but like a disobedient child, it throttled harder, shooting steam out behind it as Ras lunged for the controls.

The jetcycle shot free of its wooden prison and Callie gave a yelp of surprise as it came careening down straight for her. Ras grasped the left handlebar, pulling it back toward himself to alter the jetcycle's course. This also righted the vehicle, causing Ras to no longer be atop it but to dangle from the handlebar as the jetcycle picked up speed and leveled off just above Callie.

The sudden jerk upward caused Ras to lose his grasp and he spun like a ragdoll until he met the ground. Painfully.

The bike zipped off in the distance.

Callie came rushing to Ras' side. "Are you all right?" She felt around, looking for any obvious wounds. "Anything broken?"

"I got it out of the tree. Yay," said Ras flatly. He groaned. "I do entirely too much falling."

"I was meaning to talk to you about that." Callie smiled slightly as she brushed some of Ras' hair out of his eyes, revealing a scrape on his left cheek. Suddenly Ras no longer minded falling so much.

"Where's the jetcycle?" He tried to look around but the pain persuaded him to leave that to Callie.

Callie surveyed the area. "That's funny."

"I could stand to hear something funny."

"The jetcycle. It stopped." Callie stood, leaving Ras.

Ras fought to pull himself up to a seated position, but failed. His outfit was covered in leaves and dirt, and the nicks and cuts would soon be accented with bruises. He felt mostly unharmed, but experience taught him it was just the adrenaline. Rolling over to his side, he could see the jetcycle had come to rest mostly unscathed in a nearby clearing.

Its engine softly puttered as though inviting them to come play.

Carefully picking himself up, he approached the jetcycle. "Do you remember which way the torches went?" Ras asked as he slowly swung his leg over it, hugging its wide body for a respite.

Callie climbed behind him, pointing slightly to the left before gingerly wrapping her arms around his midsection. "Too tight?"

His head shook a negative although his tender ribs screamed otherwise at him. "Can't have you falling off." He gunned the throttle and off they went.

Zipping through the forest on the jetcycle was far more manageable than he had expected, and after only a few close calls with low-hanging branches, Ras gained a feel for flying the persnickety vehicle.

Judging by the speedometer, they were heading at a good clip toward the town. Callie kept an eye out for Dixie or any party of travelers that might have collected her, allowing Ras to focus on not killing them both. Dixie was nowhere to be seen, but keeping an eye on the tracks at that speed was near impossible.

Within twenty minutes they reached the edge of the forest and disembarked, covering the jetcycle with a mix of shrubs and downed branches which did little more than make it obvious that something was hidden underneath.

The town itself was surrounded by a dozen giant metal obelisks. The structures towered several hundred feet high.

"Did Remnants build these?" Ras asked.

Callie shook her head. "They're older than the Atmo Project. Helios invented these pylons to keep the cities safe." Callie said, nearing the tower and inclining her ear to the hum and crackle emanating from it. "It's still active."

"What are you talking about?"

"This was a stop-gap after the Knacks blew," she said. "Energy can't pass in or out of these fields. It kept people safe inside from Convergences."

"How did people travel between cities?" Ras asked.

"They didn't. The field would detonate a Knack passing through. Nobody wanted to find out if they were a candidate for joining a Convergence," Callie said.

"Hence the Atmo Project."

"Exactly," she said, "I just wish I knew what town this was."

"So, Remnants won't be inside, right?" Ras asked.

"Not unless they're willing to risk blowing up."

"Suddenly this town seems a lot more appealing."

"But that means Dixie won't be inside," Callie said.

"We'll cover a lot more ground with a working ship," he said and walked up to the crackling pillar.

"What if it doesn't discriminate between Energy and Time Knacks?" Callie asked. "I didn't bring Hal's sphere."

"I'm pretty sure I don't actually need that to move around if you overload," Ras said. "It's probably the only useful side effect of being a Lack." He walked past the pillar casually and turned to see Callie still standing on the other side.

"Don't call yourself that. You're special. You've always taken my headaches away…I just never told you because I didn't want you to feel pressured into being near me all the time." She met his eye. "I don't want you to feel obligated."

"I promised I'd keep you safe."

"I made you promise."

"I could have said no," Ras said.

"Would you have said no if you knew what we are?"

"What exactly are we?"

"A matched set."

Ras smiled. "I guess I thought that before we left *Verdant*." A pause. He walked past the pillar again to Callie and offered his hand.

She placed her small hand in his and stood near him. Inhaling sharply, she began walking forward with her breath held. As they passed through the field together, Ras felt tingles coursing through his body that he hadn't felt when passing through alone.

A quick expulsion of air from Callie panicked Ras until the laughter tickled his ears. He looked over to her and began laughing heartily, as Callie's red hair was standing on end in every direction. Ras tried to stop laughing. "I'm sorry, but your hair."

"My hair? *Your* hair!" she said, trying to smooth her own mane.

Ras patted his head to find that going through the gate with her left him with the same treatment.

"It didn't do that the first time..." The laughing hurt, but oddly enough Ras appreciated the moment of levity more for it.

The laughter died down, and Ras and Callie just smiled at each other. She quirked her mouth and squeezed his hand gently. "I'm sorry I read your letter," she said.

"It's all right," Ras said. He loosened his grip on her hand, but it remained attached to his. He looked down at their clasped hands. "We're through the field now. You know you don't have to keep holding my hand."

"Right, but we're also closer to The Wild. The headaches start faster if I get too far away from you," Callie said.

Ras fought disappointment. "Well, squeeze tight if you see anything."

They continued down the broken road, passing grown-over farms along the way before reaching the wreckage of the crumbled city. Half-fallen buildings lined the path, their debris strewn everywhere. A large sign, faded from time and neglect, welcomed and warned them.

It read: *The Township of Bogues.*

"Now might be a really good time to tell me what was in *The Demons of Bogues*," Ras said.

"Not Elders. I skimmed it," Callie said, a smile growing. "I don't even know where to begin..."

"What now?"

"Ras, the first Convergence was either made here or came here after The Battle of Bogues. Look," she said, pointing past the decrepit buildings to a more modest set of thatched-roof cottages, "They rebuilt after the Great Overload."

"But Bogues wasn't one of Atmo's twenty-one cities," Ras said, "So, what happened to the people that stayed inside the pylons?"

Callie stopped, jerking Ras' arm back. "Then people might be in those cottages." She held a hand over her mouth. "And they might know what happened."

"And they might be inbred cannibals."

"That's hardly a sustainable system," Callie said.

"I can't imagine a flying city falling on them left a sizable population," Ras said, "How about if we see someone and they don't look like they want to eat us, we'll stop and chat?"

As they continued down the path, the fallen city loomed larger, canted at a slight angle.

"Can we at least check inside one of the huts?"

Ras took a deep breath. "Real quick." He drew his wrench from his holster as they approached one of the small buildings. The cottages pocked the land in no particular pattern, and looked unkempt as far as Ras could discern.

Callie stepped up to the door and raised her hand to knock before looking at Ras, then the wrench. "Let's not scare them."

"I think strangers talking outside their front door already takes care of that," Ras said. He holstered the wrench and gestured for Callie to continue.

Upon Callie's first knock, the flimsy wooden door creaked open. Callie peeked her head in, then recoiled back with a retch before falling to her hands and knees away from the door.

"What is it?" Ras asked before he saw the remains inside. "Oh." With a foot, he pushed the door further open, shining daylight on a family of skeletons in tattered clothing.

"I'm sorry," Callie said, reaching for Ras to help her up.

Ras held her close and quickly walked away from the cottage. "I'm no doctor, but I'm going to say they're dead."

She pulled away, "Ras, those were people with family, and stories, and…" She sighed. "And now they're going to be in my nightmares, and I'm never going to find out why the Overload happened." She fought her irregular breathing with a quick inhale. "Let's just get the parts."

STANDING UNDER THE SHADOW of the crashed city's lip, Ras estimated the crater left at least thirty sub-levels exposed. A shelf eight feet above them held an open door that looked promising.

"I'll give you a leg up," Ras said, squatting down for Callie to step on his thigh. She steadied herself on some exposed pipe and as soon as she no longer needed his support, he climbed up the wrecked machinery to the ledge.

Pulling himself up next to Callie, he rested for a moment. "Are you all right to go in?" Ras asked.

"As I'll ever be," she said before disappearing into the black maw of the doorway.

The light only reached so far in, and after a minute they needed to open their eyes as much as possible to see anything.

"New rule: always bring a flashlight," said Callie.

"Good rule," Ras said, using the wall to half support himself along the angled hallway.

"So where's the most likely place to find what we need? Up top in the abandoned city?" Callie asked hopefully.

"I wish. Any engine parts are going to be salvaged from below." He patted the wall, causing a metallic echo. In the distance, a small green light grew, illuminating the long corridor. They froze. It faded, then pulsed back, continually repeating the pattern.

"Emergency system. We must have tripped a sensor," said Ras.

"You say that like it's a good thing."

"Seeing our way around is usually a positive." The dead city unnerved Ras more than he was willing to admit. It was one thing to compare the fallen city to *Verdant* from the outside, but another thing entirely to have an identical interior. For all the familiarity of The Engine garnered from his short stint in *Verdant*'s underbelly, he might as well have been walking the dead halls of his hometown. "But if this place still has emergency systems, it still has scoops."

They came to a fork in the corridor and Ras instinctively chose the left path, which pointed slightly downward. "So if *The Demons of Bogues* didn't have Elders in it, what did it have?"

"The usual. The boogeyman under the bed with green eyes that ate children if they didn't sing the right song," Callie said.

"How did the song go?"

"I didn't memorize it."

"Don't give me that," Ras said with a chuckle, "You memorize practically everything."

"I really don't feel like singing right now."

They approached an old elevator shaft. Green lights blinked down it, lighting it enough to show that if it had been vertical, it would have been a good three-hundred foot drop. Thankfully, it sat at an angle that would have made for the biggest playground slide ever.

Ras swapped out the grapple spike with a magnet charge on his grapple gun, then placed the magnet against the wall next to the elevator entrance instead of firing a charge. He spooled out some thick cable and tested his weight against it. The quality was far superior to anything he had ever stocked the grappler with before. "Mr. Helios didn't skimp on his displays," he muttered to himself. He looked up at Callie. "Climb onto my back."

"It'll hold two of us?"

"More than that. Not all wind merchants make exercise a priority." He turned for her to ease onto his back.

She stood on her tiptoes and wrapped her arms tightly around his neck, her breath warm against his skin. "Ready."

He swung out into the empty shaft, and one foot after the other, slowly began his descent alongside a long set of metal rungs. They looked to be a feasible alternative to the grapple gun, but Ras preferred to have the cable as a lifeline and a means to haul up parts.

A few odd noises clanked about high above them. Ras glanced up to see that the shaft went up at least another fifty stories.

"Emergency system, right?" Callie asked, tightening her grip ever so slightly.

"Yeah." They came to another open elevator doorway one floor down. "Hang on." Ras swung to the side a little, walking alongside the open entrance. In the corner of his eye he saw a blur of motion in the corridor as they descended. He decided it was just his fear playing tricks on his eyes and put it out of his mind until Callie's arms tightened to a chokehold.

"Ras!"

"I saw it," he said.

"It? *Them!*" She pointed upward. Pairs of glowing green eyes stared down from the open elevator shaft doors, including the one they had entered. There were dozens of glowing sets of eyes, with more appearing by the moment from above and below.

"P-please, don't hurt us," Callie said.

The eyes merely watched.

The cable began vibrating, alerting Ras to a creature above them that was starting to use some sort of tool on their cable.

"No, no, no let's talk this out, huh?" Ras called up. It continued hacking at the cable. "Callie, I'm going to swing us over to the rungs—"

The cable snapped, sending them sliding down the wall of the shaft at an alarming rate. Callie's screams pierced Ras' ears, making it difficult to focus. The rungs along the wall of the shaft sped by, and he made a grab for one but accomplished little more than repeatedly bashing his hand.

Ras passed by a dozen or so elevator entrances before he looked down to see less than a dozen left before they would meet some nasty looking machinery waiting to stop their fall.

He tried to maneuver his right hand over to load another grapple charge, but in the process accidentally knocked his elbow on another set of rungs. The continuing slide caused his stomach and thighs to burn madly from the friction.

Another doorway flew by.

Seconds left.

Ras twisted his body, pulling Callie above him to shield her from the machinery awaiting them below.

"What are you doing?" she said.

"Just close your eyes," Ras said, embracing her. He didn't know if she would survive either, but he would give her the best possible chance.

Something pried his left arm off of her, slamming it against the metal shaft so that it screeched a horrific symphony as sparks showered down the hole. His arm and shoulder burned as they dragged along the rough wall. Ras squinted to see what had happened.

The placeholders for extra magnets atop the grapple gun, which Ras had never been able to afford to fill, had drawn close enough to the wall to pin his arm against the shaft.

The quick shift in momentum left Callie dangling from around his neck, facing him as they continued to careen down level after level. The magnet holder eroded away, slowing their descent until they stopped with just one elevator entrance above the floor.

"You're smoking," Callie said, arms trembling but still holding tight.

Before he could address his friction-burns, Ras swung his body as best he could, reaching his right arm over to the set of metal rungs. "I think this is your stop," he said.

Callie reached over, taking the pressure off of Ras, who focused on prying his arm free from the grapple gun without falling the remainder of the way.

"I think I'm stuck," Ras said. He noticed a couple of silhouetted figures climbing up from the bottom level to grab Callie. She screamed in surprise and began kicking down, striking one of the figures in the face. One of the glowing green eyes cracked and winked out.

"Leave her alone!" Ras shouted.

More green-eyed figures appeared at the open elevator doors above her. Ras worked his wrench free from the holster, tossed it to her, then returned to untying the grapple gun straps.

Callie climbed above him. Suddenly the half dozen straps that ensured his safety were his prison. Two down, four to go.

A loud beeping noise began emanating through the shaft as machinery whirred to life all around. The express-elevator cables began moving at a rapid rate. Pairs of green eyes disappeared as the hot, dank air moved through the shaft.

"What is that?" Callie asked, watching her pursuers flee back through the open doorway.

"They're trying to crush us!" Ras had the third strap undone and began jerking his arm to save time. He offered his right arm to Callie. "Pull me free!"

She looped an arm through a rung and clasped his hand, then pulled with everything in her. Ras was slowly coming loose from the straps around his elbow when he saw the elevator screaming down at them. They had moments left.

Putting his feet up against the wall, he gave one last ditch yank to pull free. Slipping out of the grapple gun, he swung tenuously on Callie's grip as the elevator neared.

"Ras!"

He fell the last ten feet, landing hard on his back next to some of the sharp bits of metal. He watched Callie barely dive out of the way of the rushing machine and into the open doors of the bottom floor entrance.

As the elevator came down upon him, all went black.

CHAPTER FIFTEEN
The Doctor

THE WORST PART FOR RAS WASN'T BEING TRAPPED IN A SMALL, greasy encasement with a burned arm, nor was it being alone. No, the worst part was not knowing where Callie was, and there was precious little he could do.

Ras ran his hands in front of him, feeling a metal ceiling several inches from his nose, then a sharp tug of metal caught his hand. He felt the warmth of blood in his palm, causing him to recoil and knock his begoggled forehead against the elevator with a thud.

"I think he survived!" an old voice said. "Young man, did you survive?"

Ras almost demanded where Callie was, but he still held out hope they might leave him for dead, giving him an opportunity to escape.

"Young sir, I am leaving this machine here until you're ready to speak." A pause. "I can wait. I even have a comfy chair!"

The musty air tickled Ras' nose, and he fought valiantly to suppress a sneeze. He failed. The sneeze shook his body, and his forehead once again struck the elevator.

"Bless you!" the old voice said. "Would you be in need of a kerchief?" The voice seemed willing enough to please.

"Wouldn't you need to lift the elevator?" Ras asked.

"He speaks!" A panel opened in front of Ras' face and a white kerchief floated down, obscuring Ras' view before he could see who dropped it. "And no, I don't."

"Thank you, I think."

"You are most welcome," the man said, his voice once again muffled, "Now, what are you doing in my city?"

"Right now I'm lying underneath an elevator, wondering if my friend is all right." He wondered how one could own a fallen city.

"The girl? She took a spill but is being seen to, I'm told."

"Who am I speaking with?" Ras asked.

"I'm afraid it is 'with whom am I speaking?' You mustn't end a sentence with a preposition. That is something up with which I shall not put." He giggled.

"The elevator must have knocked the grammar straight out of me," Ras said, rolling his eyes.

"Quite. You are addressing Dr. Bernard O'Reisenbraun, proprietor and repossessor of what once was referred to as *Solaria*," he said.

"May I call you Dr. O?"

"You wouldn't be the first. My minions tell me you are called Ras. Is that short for Raziel or Rastiban?"

"Your *minions*?"

"You can't have missed them," he said with a scoff. "Minion number sixteen received a kick to the face from your friend. He was only trying to save her from the elevator."

"After trying to drop us down the shaft."

"You'll have to forgive minion number eight. He took my order to make sure you drop by my office a touch literally," Dr. O said sympathetically.

"Is there any chance we could continue this conversation elsewhere?"

"Oh, there is an excellent chance. All you have to do is tell me where you crashed your ship."

"Who says I have a ship?"

"Tut tut, Mr. Rastiban, please do not insult my intelligence. No Remnant would dare pass through the fence. Now please, the location of your vessel."

"Why do you need to know that?"

"Well, to be perfectly forthright, repairing a flying city takes an awful lot of spare parts."

The irony of Ras' purpose in the fallen city was not lost on him, but to be fair, he didn't know anyone had been planning on using these parts. "Funny, that's what I came down here for."

"Most do."

"My ship's engines are broken; I doubt they would be of use to you."

The elevator floor panel lifted again, revealing a balding, white-haired, bespectacled man leaning over from a wheelchair. "Not broken, I just disabled them." He grinned. The elevator lifted and two young, white-haired men clad with green glowing goggles stood at the entrance with rifles pointed at Ras.

Given that he was constantly moving from one dark place to another, Ras started to get used to functional blindness. The guards shoved him roughly into a pitch black room, causing him to trip and tumble over something that gave a guttural grunt as the door slammed shut. He scurried away, knocking into one of the walls before falling back to the floor. A decidedly masculine groan emanated from the unknown source. Not Callie.

"Hey, sorry about that," Ras said to his new roommate, picking himself up.

"Did you come to rescue me?" the voice asked. The tone contained no traces of hope, yet no sarcasm; it merely queried for information.

"Wish I could say I did," Ras said. "But, there's no reason we can't make each other's escape a secondary objective." Ras ran his hand along the smooth bulkhead. "Let me guess, your airship crashed too?"

"About a month ago, I think. I won't tell them where it is. Pretty sure it's what is keeping me alive," he said. "Name's Carter."

"Ras." He felt awkward not shaking the man's hand. "Nice little trap they set. Did anyone else come before me?"

"A couple, but that was probably a few weeks ago," Carter said, "I haven't seen them since they said where their ship was."

Ras pounded a fist against the wall twice, hoping for a response. None. "So, Carter, who are these people?" Ras asked, sliding over to find the next wall.

"Damonites," Carter said.

"That's funny."

"Why?"

"Sounds like 'demons' is all."

"Not far from the truth. They knock you out of the sky and drag you to the depths."

"How do they knock ships out of the sky?" Ras asked.

"Everyone I've talked to had the same symptoms. Engines suddenly going out and set out looking for parts."

"I'm curious how many pilots don't make it past the pylons." Ras pounded twice on the wall opposite the door. No response.

"What are you doing?" Carter asked.

"Looking for a friend. They might have her in another room."

"Ah, good luck with that. What kind of ship did you fly?"

"*Do* I fly," Ras said. "It's based off an old Rytrap model."

"Wind merchant, huh? Rytraps can't carry much besides collection tanks. Are you Collective?"

Ras scoffed. "Please. I'm about as far from that as you can get," he said, then immediately regretted it; he had no idea whether Carter was a guild member. "You?"

"No. Sky pirate?"

"Now that I think about it, that's probably what The Collective—" Ras' knee connected hard with something sharp and metal. He let out a cry of pain.

"Sounds like you found the cot."

"You could have warned a guy."

"Apologies." A pause. "Well aren't you going to ask about me?"

Ras finished rubbing his knee and navigated to the final wall. "Oh, yeah. Sure. Sorry, just…preoccupied. Tell me about yourself, Carter." He wished he sounded more interested for Carter's sake, but couldn't muster it. "What kind of ship do you fly?" He knocked twice on the wall and waited.

"Well, I flew a Tropo-capable—" Carter began but two response pounds on the wall quickly cut him off.

"Callie!" Ras shouted.

A high pitched muted voice came through the bulkhead.

"*That* won't attract attention," Carter deadpanned.

"Oh!" Ras said, "I'm such an idiot!" He felt for the KnackVisions perched atop his head. They winked on, crackled a bit in protest from their abuse, then showed him the dull lines of Energy coursing through *Solaria*'s emergency systems. The lines running behind the bulkhead walls showed him his boundaries, and the faint glow of green goggles moved toward the room he thought contained Callie.

The guards entered the room and appeared to struggle with something. Muffled shouts echoed down the hallway.

Two more guards walked down the corridor toward his room. "Carter?"

"Yeah?"

"Tropo-capable," Ras said. "Hold that thought. I think we've got a chance to break out. Two guards are coming. Hide in that corner, and when I say, rip the goggles off the face of the one close to you. Without them they're blind."

"Got it."

Ras stepped back to the opposite side of the small room by the metal cot, ready to leap.

The door slid open with a woosh. One of the guards said, "Erasmus Veir, we cordially invite you—"

"Now!" Ras shouted.

One of the sets of green eyes jerked violently away from the entrance, and Ras launched himself from the metal cot, bowling into the other guard. He tackled the guard, throwing them both to the ground. Once horizontal, Ras scrambled forward and pulled the man's goggles from his head. He clasped both hands together and swung his fists, solidly striking the minion and ending the struggle.

Ras donned the green goggles in favor of the KnackVisions and the world came alive in monochrome, now filled with a mountain of a man in a tanktop and goggles. Carter immediately dropped the upside-down guard he had been holding.

"Wow, you're tall," Ras said.

Carter shrugged and ran a hand over his short hair. "It's nice to see again. Did he say you were 'cordially invited'?"

Ras entered the hallway and found the cell next door empty. Dejected, he watched Carter stuff the unconscious guards inside it. He configured the two pairs of goggles in such a way that his right eye looked through the KnackVisions while his left looked through the night sight, allowing him to alter whether he saw the structure of the place or his immediate surroundings. Opening both just dizzied him.

He looked around and spotted the two bobbing pairs of Energy-powered goggles walking away on their level. He turned to see if Carter was following him. "You could have mentioned you were a wrecking ball."

"I'm small for where I come from," Carter said, easily catching up. "You're smaller than I imagined."

"Well, we can't all be giants," Ras said, turning his attention back to the two guards in the distance. They began rising evenly and started to mingle in with other sets of dots.

Ras and Carter turned down an empty corridor, heading unopposed toward the elevator at its end.

"So, where are you from?" Ras asked.

"Illoria."

"I can't say I've heard of it."

"That doesn't surprise me," Carter said.

They approached the elevator door and Ras' right eye told him the vacant elevator car was approaching. The doors slid open and they entered.

Unsure of which floor the guards exited, Ras looked over all the buttons. "Uh, let's try Sub-level 8?"

"Try?" Carter asked. "I thought you were leading us out of here."

"I'm pretty sure I mentioned I had a friend."

Carter grunted.

"A lady friend."

"Well, that makes more sense," Carter said. "Just remember you're not the only one that has someone to reunite with."

"Noted."

"Wife and kid."

"Doubly noted," Ras said as the elevator lifted. "Son or daughter?"

"Daughter. Less than one year old."

The elevator ascended in silence. Ras didn't want to contribute to another child's growing up fatherless. "Then let's get you back to your ship." The elevator began to slow, and Ras' right eye told him there were four sets of eyes waiting to board. "Uh oh. Wrecking ball time. Can you handle four?" Ras asked quietly.

"Going to have to, huh?" Carter asked with what sounded like a hint of relish.

The doors slid open and all four Damonites suddenly found themselves either on the ground or thrown against a wall by the lumbering wrecker. Ras moved quickly to relieve them of their goggles, then retreated back to the elevator with Carter. As the doors closed, Ras heard one of them calling for help over the radio.

They left sub-level thirteen and rode upward. Ras saw pairs of eyes mobilizing around the city. A voice crackled in over a set of speakers in the elevator.

"Now, now, Rastiban. I hold a banquet in your honor and you attack my minions? Hardly fitting, m'boy," Dr. O said.

"Who is that?" Carter asked.

"The old coot that runs the place," Ras said.

"Old? I can forgive 'coot,' but old? This is a two-way intercom, may I inform you," Dr. O said. "I would advise not engaging in future acts of violence. I don't care if you did me a great favor, you'll not be enjoying the banquet if you do."

What favor? "I'll come peaceably if I can guarantee safe passage for my friend," Ras said.

A long pause. "I'll change your reservation from plus one to two." The elevator chimed and the doors opened, revealing eight guards in two rows with muskets aimed at Ras and Carter. Dr. O's voice piped in again from the tinny speaker. "Now, will you be so kind as to grace us with your presence?"

For as dead and drab as the rest of *Solaria* had been, the banquet hall was opulent, well lit, and almost inviting. Paintings hung askew on the walls, indicating gravity's true orientation.

Ras once again wore cuffs. A set of goggle-less guards separated him from Carter. Their white hair and pale skin would have made Callie in her basement dwelling years look hale and hearty by comparison.

In the center of the room, an ornate wooden table stood lined with place settings. The only dinner guest was Callie.

"Ras!" she said, trying to stand from her seat near the head of the table. She wore an elegant green dress that Ras only saw half of as two men behind her forced her roughly back into her chair. The guards seated Ras across the table from Callie and stood at attention behind him.

"Nice dress," Ras said.

Callie gave a look indicating she was a little too frightened for banter and remained silent.

The head of the banquet table lacked a chair, and Ras wondered if they had been seated at the end of the table. The chairs next to both Callie and him remained empty, and Carter was seated half a dozen chairs down.

"Are you all right?" Ras asked Callie.

"About as much as I could expect to be." She looked beautiful. Seeing her dressed like that and imprisoned wasn't right. Ras felt his cheeks flush with anger.

Men in black uniforms entered the room and deposited trays in front of the three prisoners, the two empty settings next to Ras and Callie, and the one at the seatless head of the table.

The double doors swung open as two servers made a great show of the guests of honor: Dr. O'Reisenbraun in his wheelchair and a woman in a slinky black dress, the elegance of which was marred somewhat by her bandaged arms and slight limp.

"Dixie!" Ras said, and was reminded quickly of the roughly enforced 'no standing' policy.

"Hello, Ras," she said in an uncharacteristically docile tone. "I'm glad to see you're well."

A server pulled a chair out next to Callie for Dixie to sit on. Ras was too distracted with Dixie to notice the long-eared, four legged white creature sitting on the armrest of Dr. O's wheelchair. A server picked the small beast up and set it down next to Ras at the remaining place setting. Ras thought better than to ask why.

"There we are, Bartholemew," Dr. O cooed at the small creature.

Bartholemew sniffed at the covered tray until it noticed Ras staring at it, then stared back with red beady eyes.

"I have to say I'm getting very mixed signals," Ras said.

"Oh?" The old man cocked an eyebrow. "It's simple, really. I disabled the ship that was bringing my long lost granddaughter back to me, and for that, the very least I could do was provide supper."

Dixie looked embarrassed for what Ras imagined to be the first time in her life.

"So...Dixie...O'Reisenbraun?" Ras asked.

"Astrid, actually," Dr. O said, quite happy with himself. "Astrid O'Reisenbraun. We lost her at such an early age it's no wonder she picked a silly name like Dixie Piper. Astrid is so..."

"Regal?" Ras said. If the table were narrower he would have expected a swift kick from Dixie.

"Yes, regal. A fine name for a princess. Astrid."

Dixie made a face that looked like she was doing her best to agree. "It will take some getting used to...again," she said, half-smiling.

Carter just watched on from the other end of the table, sneaking a roll of bread from one of the bowls.

"Where are my manners?" Dr. O asked. "Bartholomew must be starving!" He clapped his hands twice and the servers removed the lids from in front of everyone. Bartholemew attacked the long orange stalks revealed before him.

Ras looked down at his plate. An ornate pistol sat in front of him. "Is this a test?"

"Life is a test, so, why not?" Dr. O said before cutting into the hunk of meat before him. "I will say there are some advantages to living on the ground for the time being."

"What is this?"

You've never seen a Forcible Engine Rebooter?" Dr. O asked. "Of course you haven't! I invented it!" He cackled heartily. "It reverses the signal I broadcast over this city that disabled your engine. I just repackaged it into something more portable."

"I asked…grandfather," Dixie said, choking on the word, "to spare you, Callie, and your ship for the sake of *Verdant*."

"And when that didn't work, she said it would be a suitable reward for bringing my dear sweet Astrid back to me!" Dr. O said. "I'm still on the fence about your Illorian friend."

"Carter?" Ras asked.

"Yes, the brute."

Carter spoke up. "I'm actually a cartographer."

"Same difference," said the doctor.

Ras noticed Dixie shooting him a furtive look while the mad doctor preoccupied himself with his meal. "So, how close are you to getting this city up and running?"

The old man smiled at the interest in his handiwork. "With the current rate of parts deliveries, I'd wager a few more years. If we weren't so far away from the trade routes we could be skybound in less than a year! Ooh, what I'd love is for one of those Collective dreadnaughts to have a reason to fly over us…" He stared off into the distance, his mind full of some new scheme.

"For Carter's release I could arrange that," Ras said.

"Excuse me?"

"You fix Carter's ship and I'll bring The Collective this way."

Dr. O laughed. "You're pulling my leg."

"Just ask Astrid," Ras said, "They're very inclined to have me and even detained your granddaughter once because of me. If they knew where I was, they'd come."

The old man eyed Ras warily, then looked at Carter. He turned to Dixie. "Is he being straight with me?"

She nodded eagerly. "Oh, they definitely don't like him."

"Wonderful!" Dr. O said. "The Illorian can go then. Minions! Take him back to his ship."

"I'd rather take him to his ship, if it's all the same," Ras said.

Dr. O chuckled. "It's not, but very well, don't trust me."

"Grandfather?" Dixie asked. "They still need to repair one of their damaged engines."

"Fine!" Dr. O said, throwing his hands up. "Prisoners are so demanding nowadays." His voice began to rise, wobbling its way to an unstable crescendo. "When I was your age a prisoner got gruel once a day and he was grateful!" He blinked twice, and when he spoke again, he had regained some of his composure. "Minion number Four!"

A white haired man with a scar over his left eye stepped up. "Sir?"

"Escort Mr. Rastiban and his friends come nightfall to the bone-yard so they may salvage from the remains."

Number Four nodded and supper continued. Ras almost brought up the fact that what was on his plate wasn't edible, but he didn't want to push any of the old man's randomly placed buttons.

"Sir?" Callie said in a small voice.

Dr. O stopped his fork halfway to his mouth. "She speaks," he said around a mouthful of steak.

"I was curious what you knew about the city surrounding *Solaria*," Callie said.

"Oh, yes. Bogues is it? Quaint little village," Dr. O said.

"Did you know about the battle here during The Clockwork War?" Callie asked.

Dr. O wiped his mouth with his napkin, leaving a grimace. "Such things do not make for polite dinner conversations, young miss."

Callie's eyes flared with life. "You're the first person I've met that has ever acknowledged something happened here."

"Well, being the epicenter of the Great Overload doesn't leave many left to tell the tale," Dr. O said, "But, Bartholemew is sensitive to violence, and I do not wish to damage his innocence."

"He's a rabbit," Callie said, frustration mounting.

"Excuse me?" Dr. O asked, his eyes narrowing behind his glasses. "What did you call him?"

"Callie," Ras said, trying to calm the situation.

"A rabbit. Floppy ears, long legs, eats carrots," Callie said as she pointed a hand across the table to the animal, who looked back at her, sniffing the air. "They're called rabbits."

Dr. O turned his attention to the animal. "Bartholemew...is it true? Is that what land dwellers called you? Rabbit," he said, wrapping his mouth around the word for the first time. "That's quite fun to say. *Rabbit*. Rabbit, rabbit, rabbit." He clapped his hands twice. "Four! Take Bartholemew and place him with the other Bartholemews...Rabbits," he said, nodding a thanks to Callie. "Learn something new every day, don't we?"

Minion Four stepped in, extracted Bartholemew and left the room post haste.

"Now that innocent ears are absent," Dr. O said, "Let us talk of Bogues." He placed his utensils carefully upon his plate. "My father fought in the war in the First Airship Brigade, commanded by Halcyon Napier himself. Seeing as we're so close to The Wild, Bogues was the first city subjugated by the Elders, and the last one for them to leave."

"Every book I've read said Treding was the last battle," Callie said.

"As far as proper give-and-take battles go, that's entirely accurate," Dr. O said. "Bogues was a massacre. Napier led the First in an aerial attack on the Elder's makeshift base, but those clockwork detonated a weapon of some sort, creating the first Convergence and destroying themselves in the process. The rest is history."

"That's not how it happened," Carter said, his voice echoing through the room as the rest of the diners turned their attention his way.

Dr. O laughed a little too loudly. "Are you calling my father a liar?"

"Perhaps not an intentional liar," Carter said, "but that's not the whole story."

"Then what is?" Callie asked.

"The Elders didn't have a weapon that made a Convergence," Carter said, pressing his napkin nervously in his lap, "Hal Napier used Energy-filled cannon balls—"

"Nonsense!" Dr. O shouted, "You go one lower than a liar and accuse my father of being an accessory to apocalypse. If you continue with these idiotic notions, I won't care if Rastiban brings in a dozen dreadnaughts, I'll have you rot in the belly of *Solaria* long after we're skybound."

The room fell silent, and Carter showed no further interest in speaking.

"There we are, settled," Dr. O said. "All this shouting has wearied me." He looked over to Ras. "Minion Number Thirty-Eight?" Dr. O asked, prompting a man in uniform to step up to Dr. O's side. "Put out a message that we have a Mister..."

"Erasmus Veir," Ras said.

"I like Rastiban better," Dr. O said. "Put out a message that we have a Mr. Erasmus Veir in our possession and would very much like to offer our assistance to The Collective."

"Yes, sir," the minion said, nodding and exiting the room.

"Now, Mr. Erasmus," Dr. O said, "you will wait in what I hope you'll find to be more agreeable quarters until we have confirmation that The Collective indeed holds an interest in you."

"I thought you said we could go," Ras said.

"You wanted the brute's freedom, and you wanted to personally ensure I upheld my part of the bargain," Dr. O said. "I don't see how you could do the latter if you left immediately."

Ras looked over to Carter, who gave a weak smile. *Wife and kid*, Ras reminded himself.

A SET OF GUARDS whose numbers Ras could only guess escorted him, Callie, Dixie, and Carter into a room that Ras presumed had been decorated by a doting grandfather with a five-year-old girl in mind. The expanse of pink was only occasionally interrupted by various colors of dust-laden plush pillows and googly-eyed stuffed animals.

As soon as the door shut behind them, Dixie addressed the three sternly with a more familiar tone and rate. "One, if any of you breathe a word about this room, I will end you. *End* you. You too, hulk," she said, wagging a finger at Carter, then looked at the intercom by the door and placed a palm over the speaker. "Two, you're taking me with you, and I don't care how it happens."

"But your family—" Callie said.

"That madman is not my grandfather, and amending my first-two points, you will also meet your end if I ever hear any of you say Astrid again."

Ras failed to suppress a laugh, collapsing into a pink bed half covered in pillows. It was the most comfortable thing he had ever experienced. "C'mon, this place isn't all that bad. Comfy bed, creepy green goggled minions, crazy old man that needs to keep up a fantasy that his granddaughter is alive—is this down? It feels like down." Ras patted the comforter. The oddness of the whole situation was well mitigated by his need for rest.

"I don't know. I haven't slept on it," Dixie said dismissively.

"Whatever it is," Ras said with a yawn, "I'm getting one. I don't care if it only comes in pink." He closed his eyes. "Oh, Dixie, Callie… this is Carter. Carter? Dixie and Callie."

"Where did you hear that story about Hal Napier starting the Great Overload?" Callie asked.

"My father," Carter said.

"Where did he hear it?"

"His father."

"You're not the most forthcoming fella, are you?" Dixie asked.

Carter pointed to the intercom box by the door, then tapped his ear. "I just want to get home."

"The doctor mentioned you were from Illoria," Callie said. "Where is that?"

"It was wiped off most maps many years ago."

"Oh," Callie said, "Does that make you…a Remnant?"

"No, he has a ship," Ras said groggily. The wear and tear on his body combined with the exquisite bed made a nearly insurmountable case for sleep. He tried to say something else, then quickly forgot it as his exhaustion excused him from the conversation.

Something heavy landed squarely on Ras' midsection, jerking him awake. He craned his neck up from the sea of dusty pillows and wrapped his hands around his father's grapple gun on his stomach.

Dixie stood at the entrance, once more in her regular clothing. "That's for stealing my bed."

Callie sat in a lavish chair next to the bed, also having changed out of her dress. "I mentioned you probably left it behind."

Ras' body protested when he sat up. Two falls in one day made a tie for his record, and his body begrudged him both. "I'm surprised it wasn't crushed by the elevator," Ras said, inspecting the device. The magnetic slide down the shaft gave its top a shiny yet worn appearance. Ras noticed a full spool of cable and new magnetic charges.

"Oh, it was," Dixie said. "The old man is a tinkerer...and I suppose bored when there aren't new pilots to terrorize."

"How long was I out?" Ras asked.

"Almost fifteen hours," said Callie. "You needed it."

"What did I miss?"

"Callie told me all of your embarrassing childhood stories," said Dixie.

Ras shot a betrayed looked over at Callie, who wrinkled her nose and shook her head in an amused denial of Dixie's accusation. "Carter told us Illorian folklore. It was fun."

A knock prompted Dixie to open the door, revealing the scarred visage of Minion Number Four. "It's time. The Collective is on their way."

THEY REACHED THE TOP of the dead city as the diffused moonlight brightened the cloud cover. Dixie sweet-talked Number Four into letting her say goodbye to her friends, and only after much protest and the threat of playing the maligned granddaughter card was she permitted into the skiff. Another minion, Number Thirty, joined to fill the vehicle to capacity with six riders.

Four pressed a button on the dash, and the skiff shot down the streets of *Solaria* until it ramped off the last airship dock. "Hang on."

The skiff fell sharply, its repulsion system not kicking on until the moment before they would have collided with the cracked streets of Bogues. They eventually gained enough altitude to fly over the obelisk gate and back into the foggy forest as per Ras' guidance. After a quick stop to collect his jetcycle, Ras led the skiff to *The Brass Fox*, which waited unmolested in the midst of the forest.

"You came from *Verdant* in that?" Four asked.

Ras muttered something uncharitable under his breath and parked the jetcycle within the ship. After lowering the gangplank, he asked Callie to man the helm and start the engine when prompted.

Four pulled out Dr. O's 'pistol' and pointed it at the engine to reverse the jammed intake.

"Can this also do the jamming?" Ras asked.

"You want to gum up your intake again?" Four asked, laughing, "Yeah, it'll work both ways." He tucked the gun in his belt behind him.

Ras called up for Callie to try to start the Windstrider. A moment passed and the engine chuffed in protest, then roared to life. Ras ran up to the deck, followed by Four and Thirty.

"All right, Carter, where to?" Ras asked with more energy than he had felt in quite a while. The sleep, coupled with captaining a ship again, made him feel almost like a new man. It was either that or knowing The Collective was once again on his heels.

"East. Just don't fly over the town," Carter said.

The Brass Fox limped back into the sky on one engine. The wind blew on Ras' face again, offering a stark contrast to the stale air in the belly of *Solaria*.

Within ten minutes, Carter navigated them to his ship, which looked unmistakably familiar. A sister ship to *The Kingfisher* if ever there was one.

"Is that..." Callie began to ask.

"I know," Ras said. "Carter...is that a typical design for an Illorian ship?"

"Nothing quite like them, is there?" Carter said proudly. "I'm surprised you've seen one before. Like I said, it's Tropo-capable, so most people don't spot them."

"Tropo...Troposphere capable." Ras smacked his forehead. Now it made sense why Hal managed to stay hidden for so long. "Do...do all Illorians stay up there? The Troposphere, I mean."

"Not necessarily, but most do," Carter said. "There aren't many of them left."

The Brass Fox landed next to Carter's ship. "You hug that wife and baby for me," Callie said. "They sound so sweet."

Carter nodded and extended a hand to Ras. "I'm glad you tripped over me."

"I'm glad I met a wrecking ball." Ras' hand disappeared into Carter's mitt. Carter, Four, and Thirty disembarked and shortly got his ship's engines back in working order.

Ras watched the minions return to *The Brass Fox*, and then Carter's ship took off.

"So, why is it called the boneyard?" Ras asked.

Further south, Ras found his answer. Despite the dense fog, Ras could see at least fifty ships in various states of disassembly.

"What happened to their crews?" Ras asked, turning to Four.

"They didn't deliver granddaughters," he said matter-of-factly. "Find something suitable and land. You don't have all night."

Ras surveyed the field, which consisted of transports, tankers, and a few ships emblazoned with pirate insignias.

"How about that ship?" Dixie said, pointing to port. "Looks a lot like this one."

Ras pulled the wheel to port and glided over to the ship she was pointing out. As he did so, a knot of dread began to twist in his stomach, but he forced himself to ignore it and continue.

The moon came out from behind a rare break in the clouds, illuminating the decrepit vessel, and Ras could no longer ignore his gut. "No," he whispered. He began shaking ever so slightly. "Not like this."

"What's wrong?" Callie asked.

Ras dropped the gangplank while *The Brass Fox* still glided along low to the ground. He abandoned the helm, forcing Dixie to take the wheel. Callie chased after him.

"Ras!" Callie shouted, "What's going on?"

He leapt off the gangplank, fell five feet and rolled. Callie stopped at the deck railing, her shouts nothing but an echo to him as his heart pounded faster. Dashing past a small transport, he arrived at the rusted shell of the vessel his mother faithfully used to take him to see off and welcome home.

The Silver Fox lay ruined.

CHAPTER SIXTEEN
The Lost Fox

EVEN WITH ITS BOW CRUSHED AND PARTIALLY BURIED, ITS TAIL lifted off the ground, and its partially deflated balloon draped over the starboard side, Ras would have recognized the ship of his childhood anywhere.

He collapsed to his knees, holding back rage and sadness, but his will to fight the two-fronted battle eroded.

The Brass Fox came to a stop and Callie stepped off the gangplank, hitting the ground running. When she approached Ras, he had already made it back to his feet and was manically talking to himself.

"No. He came back from worse. Disabled engines wouldn't have stopped him," he said methodically, walking toward the back of his father's ship.

"Who are you talking about?" Callie asked, running after him.

Ras stopped in his tracks and turned back to Callie with tears in his eyes. "He made it all this way and they knocked him out of the sky." He shoved a shaking, accusatory finger toward *Solaria*.

"What?"

Ras turned again and walked around the aft of the ship to the other side. "Maybe he left me something...a message, note...anything that might tell me where he was going, a—" The sight of a crumpled and black figure in the distance halted him.

Callie almost ran into Ras as she rounded the corner. "Ras, I—" She lost the words when she spotted the body.

Ras stood, paralyzed with fear. It was dark enough to allow him to doubt what he knew deep down to be true. He was staring at the corpse of his father. "I don't know what to do," he whispered.

"You don't have to do anything," Callie said, placing a hand gently on his shoulder.

"No, I can't walk away from this," he said. Each step closer offered more information as he recognized the bits of jacket that weren't charred. The body looked to have Elias' frame even though it lie in a fetal position.

Ras' heart plummeted when he saw the leather boots. He remembered the day his father had brought them home, retiring the oft-repaired hand-me-downs from grandpa Veir, which Ras currently wore.

Carefully kneeling beside the body with fear and reverence felt like the right thing to do.

After ten years out in the elements, the body was badly burned and withered. Ras slowly peeled off his jacket and placed it over the charred head and torso, allowing himself to imagine the face of his father without having to look at the blackened and grotesque visage staring at the clouds above. The visage he was certain that would turn dream to nightmare for the rest of his life.

Ras let out a scream he didn't know he had in him. "No! No! This is not how you die!" The tension released from his chest, then tightened again with another heaving intake of air. "I was supposed to find you and you were supposed to save *Verdant*, not me." He didn't care that Callie stood behind him. "I can't do this! Not like you could have. If you only made it this far, then how am I supposed to stand a chance?"

Callie kneeled down next to Ras.

"He wasn't supposed to die," Ras said.

"I know."

"He was so strong, and smart…he always knew what to do."

"I know."

"And I have no clue what I'm doing or where I'm going."

"That's not true."

"Yes it is!" Ras turned to look into Callie's beautiful, calming eyes. He took a breath to catch himself, then spoke softly. "If he couldn't save *Verdant*, then what hope does his failure of a son have?"

Callie looked at him sympathetically, remaining silent.

"I just…I wanted him back so badly for so long. I *knew*," he said, wiping his eyes with his sleeve, "I knew that he'd come through like he always did." Ras stared at the ground, then back up to *The Silver Fox*. "What do you do when the man you've looked up to all your life is gone? What do you do when your hero dies?"

Callie wrapped her arms around him, holding him tight.

"He knew I didn't have what it takes to be a wind merchant." Ras looked over at the body. "He just wouldn't tell me until it was too late. A mechanic couldn't destroy a Convergence."

"*Verdant* doesn't need a wind merchant, Ras. It needs you," Callie said. "How many times would a Knack have died where you've gone? You haven't let me down, all right? I still believe in you. I just need you to believe in yourself too. You've made it all the way this far without your father, and I'm sure he'd be so proud of his boy right now." She moved to hold him at arm's length, not speaking until he met her gaze. "You are a good man, Erasmus Veir. Don't you forget it." Tears glistened in her blue eyes. "Take however long you need."

Ras looked at the wise girl from next door for a moment. "Thank you."

"Any time." She hugged him for a good while, then gracefully stood and walked back toward *The Brass Fox*.

Once alone, Ras found a seat on the ground next to his late father. He sat silently for a few minutes, unsure of what to do, then finally spoke. "So...mom's doing all right." The words hung in the air. He knew what he must have sounded like talking to what remained of his father, but he needed to speak his piece. "It was tough for a while, but she's better now. Nobody new. She wouldn't even look at someone else. Every day we just expected you to come back, y'know?" He took a deep breath. "I wish I could actually talk to you. About life...ships...girls. Well, one girl, but you probably knew that," he said in a lower volume. "You know how they say it's like time stops when you meet the right person? I think they got it mostly right.

"Being a Lack has its upsides, I'm learning. When you're with the right person you don't feel the void so much. I guess it makes more sense why mom wanted you near. I probably reminded her of the void only you could fill." He sighed. "I wonder if you'd have made it further if mom had gone with you." Ras sat for several minutes, taking in the sounds of the night. He eventually stood and brushed off the dirt from his pants. "I know you did what you could."

The concept of burying a body was foreign to Ras. When people passed away on *Verdant*, they were set adrift among the clouds to find their ways through the fog to the abandoned ground. But now seeing what had become of his father, the only thing Ras could think of to get any closure was to bury the body.

Everyone lands somewhere, and underneath the shade of The Silver Fox *seems as appropriate as anywhere.*

He wiped away the freshly emerging set of tears, remembering waving to the ship years ago as it set off form *Verdant*. His mother would take shallow breaths to keep from crying for his sake. The imagery was too painful to dwell on.

His father needed burying.

Ras climbed aboard *The Silver Fox* where the nose met the ground, searching for the best tool he could find for digging up dirt. Rust and moss covered much of the dead airship. A large portion of the deck had been eaten away, most likely by fire, judging from the state of his father. The glow of the moonlit fog illuminated the gaping hole in the deck, showing the hold. The collection tank his father prided himself on lay shattered, its sharp edges glistening.

Tiptoeing along the railing, he made his way to the Captain's quarters' door. Its hinges creaked in protest as Ras pushed it open. The small sea of empty bottles collected at the front of the room clinked out a tune.

Dad didn't drink, Ras thought as he stepped inside. *At least not this much. Or in front of me.* He moved past the last of the bottles, turning and making his way to the upright wardrobe. Opening its doors, Ras coughed at the musty smell.

Most of Elias' clothes remained, reminding Ras of long summer days when he would raid the wardrobe to pretend he was his father.

He selected a long, dark blue coat that Elias had worn as a younger man in *Verdant*'s ragtag defense fleet. The coat was thicker than a wind merchant needed in Energy warmed skies, but Elias considered it good luck and wouldn't part with it despite Emma's prodding.

Ras had always thought his father looked like a hero from Callie's books when he wore it. Elias would let the coat envelop little Ras during their flying lessons.

He slid his arm into the sleeve, almost pleased that the coat once again could humor the boy pretending to be the hero.

Shouts in the distance snapped Ras from the memory. He slid back down to the bottles and through the door. He could see an argument breaking out on the bridge of *The Brass Fox* between Dixie and Four. He couldn't make out the words but the harsh tones filled in the gaps.

"Hey!" Ras shouted, garnering their attention. "What's going on?"

Dixie began to yell back, "They're trying—" until Four struck her in the head. She crumpled. Ras' eyes went wide and he dashed from the bridge down to the sloped deck. Upon reaching the ground at the bow of *The Silver Fox*, he saw Thirty exiting the bay door of *The Brass Fox*, clutching Ras' large wrench from *Derailleur*.

"Thanks for flying her to the boneyard for us. Makes the process so much easier," the white-haired man said.

Ras spotted Callie's frightened face through the Captain's quarters' porthole, and Four delivered a kick to the downed Dixie. Callie yelled Ras' name as she pounded on the window.

Ras' father lay unburied after the process these men hoped to repeat with him. Callie was trapped, Dixie was knocked out, his ship was soon scrapped, and he was unarmed. Something broke in Ras, and he had one thing going for him.

He was properly motivated.

Ras let out a war cry and charged toward Thirty, who held the large wrench at the ready. Ras didn't fear the wrench. He knew its pain and he was too filled with rage to let the idea of a broken arm or rib deter him.

The smug look dissolved from Thirty's face as the desperate wind merchant tore toward him. He panicked and swung the wrench too early.

Ras ducked, sidestepping as Thirty's balance went off-kilter from the momentum of the tool. He landed a punch to Thirty's ribs, turned on his heel and slammed his left elbow squarely into the man's throat, whose gurgle indicated a failed attempt at a cry of pain.

Thirty swung the wrench again, catching Ras in the stomach.

The pain only fueled Ras' fury as he wrapped both arms over the wrench, holding it to his body and slamming his head upward, squarely striking Thirty's nose, disorienting the minion enough to rip away the makeshift weapon.

Ras delivered a kick to the knee of Thirty, interrupting the minion's grab for the knife in the man's boot. He tightened his grip on the large wrench and swung with both arms, connecting with Thirty's temple and laying the man out flat.

Number Four looked over to see both his partner incapacitated and a fire-eyed Ras turning towards him. Four drew his musket and lined up a shot at the young man moving up the gangplank but stayed his hand, as Ras clearly intended to present him with a closer target.

Ras arrived on the deck with a wrench in his hand and malice in his heart. Four leaned casually on the railing, steadying his aim. "Funny how every single ship out here is picked clean."

"We had a deal," Ras said, seething.

"What, the one where we tell The Collective we have you and they come running? You do realize we don't actually have to have you for that to work, don't you?" asked Four. He motioned with his pistol for Ras to drop the wrench over the side of *The Brass Fox*.

Ras held his arm over the railing, but retained a firm grasp. "You see that ship over there?" he said, pointing with the wrench.

"Yeah, it was one of our first."

"That's my father's ship," said Ras. A bit of motion beyond Four caught his attention.

"Family reunion, how sweet," Four said, "Toss it."

Ras took a deep breath and threw the wrench high over his head. A familiar bang and hiss of uncoiling cable filled the air as a magnetic grapple tore the musket from Four's hands and continued onward to strike the airborne tool. The wrench/musket hybrid fell straight back into Ras' outstretched hand.

Four looked behind him. Callie leaned out of the Captain's quarters' porthole with the grapple gun engulfing her left arm. The cable connected her directly to Ras, who busied himself with prying the musket from the magnet with little success.

Giving up on freeing the musket, Ras aimed the wrench/musket hybrid at Four. "You're leaving my ship or this world."

The grizzled man raised his hands slowly, palms open.

The moonlit sky grew dark as a labored screech filled the bone-yard, distracting everyone onboard *The Brass Fox*. In the dense fog, a hulking black figure eclipsed the moon, arriving from the direction of *Solaria* and rapidly increasing in size.

It appeared Dr. O would indeed snag his dreadnaught.

Four used his opportunity to seize the taut cable next to him, jerking Ras off balance.

All squabbles about who possessed the gun on the ship became moot when it became apparent that the dreadnaught was on a collision course to crush *The Brass Fox* and every other airship surrounding it.

Ras tossed the musket/wrench overboard through the rope netting and made taking off his highest priority.

"Callie! Cut the cable!" Ras shouted as he began ascending the stairs toward the bridge.

"How?" she asked, looking the device over.

After failing to reel in the musket, Four began running toward Ras, throwing an easily dodged punch.

Using Four's momentum against him, Ras hooked Four's leg with his own, causing the minion to tumble down the stairs to the deck as Ras arrived on the bridge and worked the controls at the console to start up his one engine.

The groan of the behemoth grew deafening as *The Brass Fox* began its ascent. Behind them, a concussive shockwave caught up with the ship as the tail of the dreadnaught's body collided with the ground, and *The Brass Fox*'s single engine revved as hard as it could with little effect.

Four finally worked free the musket/wrench and aimed it at Ras.

"Do you honestly think shooting the pilot is a great idea right now?" Ras looked up to gauge how many moments remained before the front half of the dreadnaught crushed them.

Too few.

He spun the wheel hard to port as *The Brass Fox* limped off perpendicular to the collapsing warship.

"C'mon!" Ras yelled at the console, smacking it. The ship lurched forward, spurred on as the dreadnaught's front came crashing down, crushing half of the boneyard under its mass and narrowly missing *The Brass Fox*.

The impact shot out smoke and debris in a gust that sent *The Brass Fox* swinging violently side to side underneath its balloon.

A scream from Callie and the absence of Four alerted Ras to a severe problem. He set the ship's controls to continually gain altitude and dashed down the steps to enter the Captain's quarters, but ran into a locked and jammed door. He threw his shoulder into it repeatedly until it finally gave.

Inside, he found Callie half hanging out of the porthole.

"How do I detach this?" she screamed.

Ras ran up and hugged her around her waist, catching a glimpse of Four dangling below from the wrench on the other end of the cable. He braced a leg against the wall and pulled her fully back into the room. "Middle button! Reel him in!"

Callie pressed the button to start spooling in the cable as Ras grabbed it and began to pull hand over fist.

"Help me pull!" Ras said with a grunt.

Callie heaved back on the cable with Ras until Four's arm swung into the frame of the porthole.

Ras grabbed the arm and stuck his head outside to see the ground disappearing beneath them into fog. He reached down and pulled something tucked inside Four's belt.

"What are you doing?" Four demanded.

Ras examined Dr. O's engine disabler, ignoring the question. He turned to Callie, grabbed her wrist, and worked the mechanism to cut the cable. "That is how you release the cable." He looked coldly at Four. "And this is how you release the man that killed your father."

Before Ras could act, the ship shook violently, causing Four to lose his grip on the porthole, and he disappeared with a scream and a whipping trail of cable.

Ras and Callie ran back to the deck and surveyed the night sky. They cleared the cloud level to find half a dozen Collective ships in hot pursuit.

"We're so close!" Callie said.

"Close to what?"

Callie pointed to a set of cliff faces off in the distance. "The Wild."

Another cannon salvo rocketed past the ship from behind. The explosion in front of them gave the full picture as three silver ships without balloons or biplane wings flew toward them. Their shiny metal hulls gleamed in the night's light as they returned fire with a series of rat-tat-tat blasts. Dozens of small cannon balls whizzed past *The Brass Fox*, and many collided with the pursuing Collective vessels, sinking one of them.

"You don't think…" Ras said.

"Elders," Callie said.

The Collective ships overtook *The Brass Fox*, engaging in a clumsy dance with the nimble silver fighters.

The smaller ships darted about with pinpoint proficiency, firing their small repeater cannons at the medium-sized Collective ships. Thankfully they didn't appear to have taken much note of the wind merchant vessel as a target yet.

Ras pushed down on the wheel, dropping altitude until they once again fell beneath the cloud level and out of the battle.

A loud series of booms erupted behind them. The Collective dreadnaught lost her engines, but still had her teeth and her mission.

Spinning the wheel starboard, Ras drove the ship into what evasive maneuvers she could muster. "We're going to have to go back up!" Ras said, hefting back on the wheel.

"It's worse up there!" Callie said.

"I've only got one engine down here. Up there I can kick on the Helios engine."

Dixie began to stir, and Callie moved over to check on her.

"Callie, I really don't know where I'm going without you right now," Ras said. "There's not much we can do for her."

The Brass Fox once again lifted above the clouds and into the clear sky, rejoining the fray. Several blind shots from the downed dreadnaught ripped through the clouds far to port.

Ras focused his attention on the newest part of his dashboard. He flipped three switches to prime the Helios engine and pulled back on a knob to start it. A whining noise hummed to life below deck for a moment and then died.

Another two Collective ships, larger than their mini-cannonball riddled predecessors, joined the battle.

"Ras?" Callie pointed to the Elder ship diverting its attention from its battle with the Collective to *The Brass Fox*.

Ras whipped his head over, seeing the vessel while he furiously flipped the three priming switches once more. Again the Helios engine purred and died.

"Why?" Ras shouted, slamming the dash. The Elder's mini-cannon roared to life behind them as Ras began evasive maneuvers. Several shots ripped through the hull behind them, forcing them to dive as chunks of wood and splinters flew through the air.

Ras helped Callie stand and once again hefted on the wheel. "Work!" he ordered, cycling the truant engine once more. The whole ship hummed, vibrated, and then roared ahead with a new vitality.

"Good girl!" Ras laughed. He pulled the wheel to port to avoid the next salvo from the Elder fighter and to assess the battle.

The two larger Collective frigates brought their full arsenal to bear, firing and connecting their deadly green beams with an Elder fighter. The vessel was incinerated, sending the rest of the squadron into evasive maneuvers.

A well-aimed shot from the other frigate clipped the Elder fighter trailing *The Brass Fox*, sending the remaining half of the small ship plummeting.

Ras surveyed the area, trying to regain his bearings. He felt a hand on his shoulder and saw Callie pointing to a specific point along the cliff wall. Ras nodded and jammed the throttle full ahead, leaving the heat of the battle, but not unnoticed.

Two of the Collective ships comparable in size to *The Brass Fox* broke off as the frigates concentrated on the last Elder fighter.

"Hal said the path is a maze. If we can lose them they won't know where to go," said Callie.

Ahead, the cliffs loomed and Ras saw dozens of canyon entrances of various sizes. "Which one?"

Callie stepped away from him, moving with a graceful, ethereal quality. Her blue eyes took on a slightly purple hue as she surveyed the different entrances. She pointed slightly starboard as she continued down the steps to the deck, walking toward the bow of the ship.

Ras corrected his course until her arm pointed directly in front of her. *The Brass Fox* entered the canyon Callie had selected, and moments later The Collective ships followed in its wake. Framer's Valley came to mind, but Ras shunted the lingering memory as far away as possible.

The walls of the canyon started out wide enough for one of The Collective ships to pull alongside Ras' starboard. It slammed against *The Brass Fox*, almost crashing it into the opposite wall.

"Ras!" Callie shouted. Up ahead the canyon split and Callie pointed to port.

Ras pushed against The Collective ship as they approached the fork in the path. Wood creaked and splintered as the vessels collided again.

The positioning plan worked, as *The Brass Fox* and The Collective ship separated to avoid smashing into the stone fork.

One ship was off course, but the other Collective ship, which had hung behind, still followed *The Brass Fox* as the path curved and twisted.

Ras shoved the wheel forward to dip below a rock bridge connecting the canyon walls. The Collective ship careened into it, but even this did little to deter it aside from creating a more generous gap between the vessels.

Callie pointed starboard as another fork approached, then port.

Port.

Starboard.

Port.

Port.

The intricacy of the canyon's splintering architecture path amazed Ras. He looked behind him for a moment to see if his pursuers had lost their way.

They hadn't.

"Port!" Callie shouted, bringing Ras' attention back again to piloting just in time for him to see the rapidly approaching fork. The curve ended with a straightaway that led to the end of the canyon.

"Dive!" She pointed to a cave entrance along the floor of the canyon.

"But we're—"

"Dive! Now!" she shouted.

Ras shoved the wheel, descending sharply into the maw of the cave. The Collective ship continued straight and Ras heard a horrific crunch and series of explosions echo through the cave as pieces of a crumpled Collective ship rained down behind them.

Blind, Ras throttled back to a stop. "What was that?"

"Painted wall. Time is streaming out from this cave," Callie said as she approached the bridge.

Ras grabbed the KnackVisions to see if they would provide any clarity. The Energy level in the cave was nearly nonexistent. He swapped them out for the green minion goggles and the vast expanse of the cave nearly took his breath away. "Callie, come look." He then thought better of it as he propped the wheel and began walking over to her to prevent her from stumbling around the deck.

She walked slowly, gracefully. "I can see, Ras. Time is thick here." She spoke at a slower rate that caught Ras off guard.

"Like KnackVision?"

"Yeah, purple KnackVision, but with headaches," she said.

Ras moved quickly to her. "Better?"

"Yeah, my head isn't throbbing now, but I can't see anything," she said with her usual cadence. She squinted and held up a hand to keep the green glow of Ras' goggles from bothering her. "A worthwhile tradeoff."

Ras led her by the hand back up to the bridge. A funny noise came from the one working Windstrider engine.

"What is that?" Callie asked.

"Energy is so thin down here, it must not have enough to scoop."

"I guess The Wild has been blocked off for so long, not much Energy could make it in," Callie said.

"Callie?"

"Yeah."

"You led us into The Wild."

"You *flew* us into The Wild," she said, embracing him. "I knew you could do it."

"Oh, you two are so cute it's enough to make a girl barf," Dixie said, sitting up.

"You all right?" Ras asked.

"All that flying made it hard to sleep. What happened to whats-his-number?" she asked.

"Not onboard, and that's all that matters." Ras took a moment to study an almost endless flat cavern, then removed the green goggles and handed them to Callie. "Make sure she's all right, okay?"

Callie donned them and made her way over to Dixie. "I'll let you know if anything comes up, like a cave wall or giant monster."

"That's a fun thought," Ras said.

Callie knelt down by Dixie, who stuffed something small into her pocket. "You okay? Is there anything I can get you?"

Dixie held her head, touching the sticky matted hair by her temple. "There's something in my bag down in the hold that I could use."

"Sure, what is it?"

"If you could just bring the whole bag, I'll find it," Dixie said.

Ras watched Callie's bobbing green goggles disappear into the hold. He pulled on the KnackVisions to have some semblance of sight.

"So, looks like you made it to The Wild after all," said Ras. "I bet all of your friends will be jealous."

"Yeah…why are you talking so fast?" Dixie asked, her speech slurred.

"I'm not. You're talking slow."

"That's the first time anyone's accused me of that," she drawled.

"Must be the Time in here," Ras said. "Doesn't affect me."

"Lucky," she said. "Hey…I'm sorry about what happened back there."

The thrill of the escape had all but erased the time in the bone-yard from his mind, and he felt ashamed for letting something that important lapse. "You shouldn't feel responsible for fake family members, right?"

"I guess," Dixie said with a shrug. She tried to stand but failed.

"I just can't believe how close my dad got. I mean, the cliffs couldn't have been more than ten miles from the boneyard. I have no idea how he would have made it through the maze, though… Maybe he had a map or something." He looked over at Dixie, who stared blankly into the darkness, evidently finished with the conversation.

Callie climbed back up from the hold with a bag and returned to the bridge, depositing the duffle next to Dixie. She removed the goggles and handed them to Ras, then wrapped her arms around his left arm and leaned against him. "Headache."

He extracted his arm from between hers and placed it around her shoulders. Her head nestled against his chest and he feared for a moment she would notice his heart pounding.

The smallest hint of morning light peeked through the mouth of the cave, spilling in to fill the cavern. Ras noted they weren't moving nearly as fast as his instruments indicated, and he tapped them a couple times in an attempt to jar the needles into the correct positions. They stayed.

"Why are we moving so slow?" he asked himself.

"Hold on," Callie said as she took a step away from Ras, noting her surroundings, then laughed.

"What?"

"The ship sped up," she said with a slowed voice. "No, wait, I slowed down." She lifted her eyebrows as she turned to Ras.

"That part I get."

Callie returned to him. "And now we're back to crawling. You must have some sort of equilibrium around you." She hugged him tight once more. "It's just more noticeable now that the Time is thick."

"Oh. If you want to take a step away so the trip doesn't take as long, I won't be offended," Ras said.

"I'm good." She pointed to his watch, then the clock on the dash. They were already a few minutes off from one another. "Think of it as a super power."

"One I can't tell I have."

"You'll be faster than everyone else in The Wild," she said.

"I'd be perfectly content not to see that in action," Ras said. Something glinted along the floor of the cave near the entrance. As the sun crept higher, the glint became two illuminated lines. "What is that?"

"What is what?" Callie asked.

"There." Ras pointed to the lines and Callie pulled Ras over to the edge of the bridge to investigate.

"It looks like train tracks," she said casually, then paused. Her eyes widened. "Ras, it looks like train tracks!" Her eyes hungrily searched the floor of the cave far beneath them for more information. She looked over at Ras, then at the green goggles dangling around his neck. She nearly ripped the strap off as she pulled them up over his head.

"Hey!" Ras said, rubbing a maligned ear.

Without bothering to strap the goggles on, Callie placed the green circles over her eyes. "Put the ship down! Put the ship down!" she shouted, then whipped around, still mad-eyed with goggles.

"Hang on, what did you see?" Ras asked.

"A white train."

CHAPTER SEVENTEEN
The White Train

THE SMOOTH METAL GAVE THE LARGE LOCOMOTIVE A SLEEK LOOK, soaking up and reflecting the little bit of light filtering into the cavern. Callie stood directly in front of the lifeless machine on the cave floor, staring it down as she squeezed Ras' hand tightly.

"Have you ever seen one of these outside of your dreams?" Ras asked, "Like in a book or something?"

"Hal had a model of it on his desk," Callie said, bathing Ras with the glow of her goggles.

Ras paused. "So, this is mind-boggling and everything, but what are we doing besides looking at it?"

"I don't know if I can make myself go in," Callie said, stepping to the side of the tracks to inspect the multi-car train.

"I hate to rush you, but I also hate *The Fox* sitting there when Elders might be just outside the cave," Ras said quietly.

"We'd run into them eventually, right?"

"I'm glad we're being optimistic…"

Callie stepped purposefully toward the second car, pulling Ras along. The train looked fresh off the assembly line, free of rust or wear. She took a hesitant step up to the doorway.

"I don't like this," Ras said. "What if there are Elders, just waiting to activate when someone comes onboard? I mean, who else would ride this from The Wild?"

"I don't know, but there has to be a reason I keep dreaming about this," she said. She tugged on Ras' hand and pulled herself up into the entrance of the passenger car.

"May I remind you I promised to keep you safe?"

"You are, aren't you?"

"Yes," Ras said, stepping up into the train. His KnackVisions did next to nothing to pierce the darkness. "But part of protecting you means not letting you walk into dangerous situations."

"It's empty, Ras," Callie said. "There's nothing in here but seats."

Ras stepped in and steadied himself by clamping his free hand on the fine leather back of one of the padded benches. He wondered when machines had begun appreciating the finer comforts. "All right, so why would someone abandon a train in a cave?"

"They built a railroad through here, so they obviously meant to use it," Callie said.

"Do you think it ran to Bogues?"

"Maybe it shuttled supplies during the war," Callie said, continuing her slow walk and inspecting each seat.

"Airships would have been more effective," Ras said. "People? How big are the seats?"

"I guess Elder sized," she said. She hoisted herself up to sit on one of the seats. "It's bigger in my dreams though."

"Mind if I borrow your eyes?" Ras asked.

Callie removed her goggles and offered them to Ras.

The interior of the train came into view. He saw Callie sitting, nervously swinging her legs off the edge of the seat. The floor and ceiling held ornate matching patterns. Still gripping Callie's hand, he knelt, inspecting the space underneath the benches.

Four seats down lie an abandoned box.

"Found something," Ras said, pulling Callie from her seat and guiding her further down the train.

"What?" Callie asked excitedly, almost tripping in the darkness.

Ras leaned underneath the bench and hefted the two-foot wide box by its handle, then placed it on the seat in front of him. He extracted the goggles from his head, held the left half to his right eye, and pulled Callie in close until the sides of their heads leaned against one another. He placed one lens over her left eye.

"It's a suitcase!" Callie said, her words reverberating through Ras' head. She eagerly reached her free hand to work the latches. With two clicks, the restraints snapped open, revealing a small treasure trove of information.

Before them lie baby clothes, photos of a man and woman holding a child, papers, and several small plush toys.

"They were taking children from Bogues?" Ras asked.

"No, look at these papers," she said, "I recognize this writing."

Ras picked up one of the pieces of paper, inspecting the funny looking scrawling. "Hal?"

"Hal."

"I'm going to have a lot of questions for that man when we get back," Ras said. He pulled away from the lens and noted a little more daylight spilling into the cabin through the window curtains. Something caught his eye and he brushed open the thick material, revealing three metal figures standing along the cave wall.

Elders.

"Callie?"

"Yes?" she asked, lost in the pictures.

"I think we should go."

"Can't we see what else is in here?" Callie asked while closely inspecting the contents of the case.

Ras tapped her on the shoulder. She turned her attention to the window, then gasped.

"Why aren't they moving?"

"I don't know, but that seems like the kind of question you ask in a story and then they start moving," Ras said.

A pause. "But we can't leave yet," she said. "Not when I still have no idea why I've dreamed about this place."

"Maybe you saw pictures of trains when you were little."

"No, the details are exactly the same." She ran her hand over the paneling around the window, taking a fistful of curtains.

"What sort of answers could there be? There are Elders out there and there's confusion in here," Ras said, pointing to the contents of the case. "I'd feel a lot better mulling over our clues with a tankful of Wild air."

"But then we can come here on our way out?" Callie asked.

"You're the only one who knows how to get here, so I think it's safe to say this all will be here any time we want to visit." Ras gave one last look to the Elders, wondering if he was just imagining the machines having stepped closer. He moved away from the window, gently bringing Callie with him.

"Ras, what am I?" Callie asked, resisting his pull.

"You're a beautiful girl who is reading way too much into a train."

Callie stared at Ras blankly. "You think I'm beautiful?"

Ras' expression softened and he gave a faint laugh. "Have you ever looked in a mirror?" He took a deep breath. "All of this we can talk about while moving."

She nodded, not meeting Ras' eye, then shut the case with her free hand, allowing Ras to guide her away from her dream train.

As they exited the passenger car, the metal men still stood fifty yards away, stationary. Regardless, Ras started into a jog toward the gangplank of *The Brass Fox* and quickly boarded.

Dixie sat slumped against the bridge's railing, head cradled in her hands. "Find anything?"

Callie held up the suitcase with a melancholic look on her face. "More questions."

"Well, life's no fun when you run out of those," Dixie said. Her eyes narrowed at the pair and a sad grin grew. "Aww, you're holding hands now."

"Medicinal purposes," Ras said. "Right?" He looked to Callie, who nodded.

Moments later, Ras pulled *The Brass Fox* back into the sky and headed for daylight. Ras worked the controls one-handed while Callie silently studied the photos in the suitcase.

As they glided through the mouth of the cavern, The Wild met them in all its barren, craggy glory. The parched ground extended beyond the cliffs to a horizon scattered with mesas and jagged mountains. Ras wondered if it had always been so bleak or if being cut off from Energy had killed the vegetation.

"No wonder The Elders wanted to escape," said Callie.

"Seems fine for automatons. Sparse on amenities…but I guess all you'd need is an oil can," Ras said.

Dixie furtively fished something out of her pocked and rolled a piece of paper into it. She then pulled a pistol from her bag.

"Ah, Dixie? Where'd you get that?" Ras asked.

She loaded the gun with something that looked like a tube. Conflict played across her face as she pulled back the hammer. "I am so, so sorry." She lifted her arm to the sky.

"No!" Ras dove for the pistol, but even in his slightly faster state he couldn't reach her in time. She pulled the trigger and two things fired out of the barrels. One of them Ras couldn't see, but the other was a flare.

"You really shouldn't have come back for me," said Dixie.

Ras clenched his jaw, backpedaling. "Who did you send that to?"

"What's going on?" Callie asked.

"That gun fires off a flare and a tube with a message that will travel to a predetermined place if it's within range. Smart," said Ras. "The Collective wanted to get into The Wild, and I'm guessing we just brought one of their couriers."

"What?" Callie asked.

"The fight in the alley, I bet that was staged," Ras said, "Two co-workers drew the short straw so you could play up the sympathy and owe me a favor."

"If it's any consolation, I wasn't lying about that," Dixie said. "They were sky pirates, but I did pick the fight."

Callie looked stunned. "Why would you do this? Entire cities are falling out of the sky because The Collective controls Energy. What do you think will happen when they can regulate Time too?"

"Hunt down and kill sky pirates. How many people don't have to die if one side is frozen?"

Ras's backtracking finally landed him at the console. He jammed the throttle forward and dashed down to the deck, disappearing into the Captain's quarters to retrieve his grapple gun. He returned to see Dixie pointing a flintlock at him but he continued to lace up the straps.

"Stop the ship, Ras," Dixie ordered.

Ras returned to the controls, ignoring the threat. "Have you ever been to *Verdant*, Dixie?"

"Oh, don't start that," she said. "*Verdant* sank before you left me at *Derailleur*. If I'd told you then you wouldn't have kept going to The Wild."

"You're lying," Callie said, turning to Ras. "She's lying, right?"

"She had better be, because she's trying to take away the last thing between me and desperation, and none of us wants to see what that looks like again."

Callie stepped between Ras and the pistol. "If *Verdant* is gone, then he's all I have left, and you're not taking that from me."

Ras looked up and sighed. "She can't shoot you. You're too valuable to The Collective."

"Not anymore," Dixie said. "They needed her to get into the Wild. It's you they want now." She kept the gun trained on Callie.

"Why would anyone want me?" Ras asked.

"You're an anomaly. In a world where Time can be stopped, how much do you think people would pay to opt out of that system?" Dixie asked. "Stop the ship." She gestured the gun at Ras, then returned her aim to Callie.

Ras angrily jerked the throttle back. "So what did you get for leading The Collective here?"

"Satisfaction."

"Mmm…I would have bargained to get *Solaria* off the ground for something as impossible as breaching The Wild."

Dixie stood silent.

"So you are Dr. O's granddaughter," Ras said, "and you're doing what you had to do to save your city—"

"If I don't get you back to *Derailleur*, Foster's deal is off," Dixie said.

"You accomplish your job and he makes his promises conditional on future tasks?" Callie asked.

"What?" Dixie asked.

"I'm just wondering how many things he'll get you to do before he sends you on a suicide mission," Callie said, "or just kills you when you decide you've had enough—"

"Shut up, both of you," Dixie said. "We're done talking."

HOURS PASSED BEFORE A VOICE BOOMED over distorted loudspeakers, "Surrender all arms peaceably and prepare for boarding. This is your only warning."

A Collective ship exited the cave and glided to a stop alongside *The Brass Fox*, then extended its plank to bridge the gap for a dozen armed men. An officer from the other ship spoke in legalities that Ras summarily ignored as he watched Callie be restrained and dragged off his ship. Cuffs ratcheted too tightly around his wrists.

A slap to the face by the gaunt officer brought Ras' attention upon him. "I said, are you ignoring me?"

"Yes. Yes, I am," Ras said.

The officer motioned to one of his men, who stepped up and buried his fist deep into Ras' stomach, forcing the wind merchant to suck for air and drop to his knees.

"Your ship is hereby property of The Collective, as it was discovered unmanned upon our arrival," the officer said. "Correct, Higgins?"

The soldier chuckled darkly as he picked Ras up and manhandled him down to the deck and over the broad plank onto The Collective's ship.

Callie stood guarded by two men on the far end of the deck. She looked pale, and any motion Ras made toward her was met with force.

"You're killing her!" Ras shouted. "She can't be away from me out here."

She screamed in pain, closing her eyes.

"A rather romantic notion," the officer said.

"He's not lying," Dixie said. "You should probably keep them together or—"

"I did not ask for your opinion, whelp."

"Captain! Bogies inbound!" a crew member shouted, pointing upward. "Descending!"

Before The Collective ship could move, a dozen silver Elder airships dropped down to match altitude. One ship pulled close enough to reach a gangplank across.

"Ready arms!" the officer commanded. "They're boarding!"

With a snap-hiss from the Elder vessel, a dozen large clockwork soldiers filed out onto The Collective ship's deck. Muskets fired, clouding the area with smoke as the eight-foot tall metal men marched forward, their thick arms swinging, knocking Collective personnel overboard. The volleys of small arms fire did little more than dent their finish.

Two of the clockwork beasts headed straight for Callie, relieving her of her guards. She opened her now-purple eyes in terror.

Ras watched the scene play out in slow motion before him. Ducking beneath his slowed escort, he snatched the keyring and freed himself from his restraints. Dashing through the chaos toward Callie, he sidestepped one Elder's lumbering swipe and ducked beneath another.

Ahead, one of the Elders near Callie sprayed her with a gas from a canister attached to its wrist.

With the cuffs now unlocked, Ras' plan was to tackle Callie over the railing and grapple back to his ship. His plan could have worked if not for the Elder next to Callie, which backhanded him mid-dive, altering both his path and his ability to remain conscious.

*   *   *

CALLIE AWOKE AT A SHARP PAIN in her arm that made her gasp. She knew the familiar stick of a needle from many doctor's visits, but her physicians had never restrained her arms and legs like this.

The Elder that had stuck her turned and stomped down a short corridor that opened up to the ship's bridge.

The inescapable gurney was placed inside a half bowl designed to latch with the domed encasement hanging above her.

"Does anyone feel like telling me what's going on?" Callie said weakly, trying not to look at the uncovered needle. None of the twenty or so machine men acknowledged her request. She felt as if an invisible hand were pushing her deeper into the gurney. They were ascending.

She wished she could be fascinated with finally seeing The Elders up close. The idea of how the automatons must have been constructed baffled her, and the best explanation she could muster resembled the stories of alchemists or magicians from her library.

The Elder at the head of the bridge spoke in flowing and elegant sounds, at least for speech piped through speakers.

Callie watched the twenty machines reach up and grab their head, pull, and dislodge the metal shell to reveal people underneath. They weren't clockwork giants, but merely men and women in large suits, albeit tall men and women in large suits.

The chief Elder turned from his position and walked down the central walkway, either side of which held a pit of crew. His buzzed hair and gaunt face gave him a very austere and martial look. Approaching Callie, he towered over her with a stern expression which softened as he took a knee and brought himself down to her level.

The commander spoke in a melodic, soothing tone, then awaited a response. His eyes held pity.

"I…ah…" Callie muttered in utter confusion until it dawned on her; they thought she was an Elder too. She attempted to parrot the last phrase issued by the commander.

His face contorted and his eyes narrowed.

She didn't know how to keep up the ruse. Her eyes darted around until she saw a familiar face in the pit. "Carter?"

The commander turned to his crew, then back to Callie. "Carter?" he asked, pointing to his man.

Callie nodded, and the commander barked an order. The tall man left his post and stood at attention upon reaching his leader.

The commander spoke to Carter, who relayed the message. "The commander wishes to know why you won't speak Illorian."

"What's happening, Carter?" Callie asked.

Carter explained something in his native tongue that sounded far lengthier than a mere translation to the commander, who interrupted, then finally spoke in words Callie understood.

"The close call must have addled your mind," the commander said in a tender tone. "We almost lost you. You weren't meant to be brought so low. Did your family not tell you that you were a Conduit?"

Callie shook her head.

"And do you know what that means in times like these?"

"What? What does that mean? Times like what?" Callie asked.

The commander turned to address her. "It means, my dear girl, that Illoria needs you more than anyone else right now. I'm so sorry."

"Sorry for what?"

The commander looked to Carter. "You have leave to send condolences to her family. The main gate will soon be breached, so move quickly. Please tell them that Illoria would be lost without her." Without addressing Callie again, the commander left to return to his station.

"Carter, tell me what's going on," Callie said.

"Where are your friends? I don't have much time," Carter said.

"I don't know. We came through the pass with the white train in it."

"The Children's Pass?" Carter asked.

"I don't know, we just flew through there," Callie said. "Why is it called The Children's Pass?"

"I don't have time to explain it—"

"Carter, please. I need to know."

Carter looked over his shoulder. "Every Illorian knows about The Children's Pass."

"I'm not Illorian!" Callie said.

"You're a Conduit, and probably the only unfrozen one left," Carter said, "You're Illorian."

"Humor me," Callie said quickly. "Why is that train in The Children's Pass? Pretend I forgot."

Carter sighed. "Fine. The short of it is that The Outsiders used a new weapon on us during the great war, so we shut ourselves in and sent children away on trains in case they bombed our cities," he said, "The Children's Pass was thick with Time and its train got stuck, so when the Elders tried to block every pass into Illoria, they couldn't bring themselves to destroy the pass with the children in it."

"And…what happened to the children?"

"I thought they were still down there," Carter said, "Whenever someone goes to check, they don't come back."

Callie lie silently, processing the information, wondering if her dreams weren't based on memories. "How old would one of those children look today if they were still alive?"

"I don't know. I guess it depends on when they left the tunnel. I really have to go, Calista," Carter said, "They're going to use you to freeze the Outsider fleet."

"What? How?"

Carter gestured to the mechanism surrounding her. "I don't know what the Outsiders call it, but they used this against us in the war. I'll try to find your friends. You don't deserve to die like this."

"Die?"

"I'll hurry," said Carter, dashing off.

The commander spoke into the loudspeaker and the top half of the sphere descended atop Callie, sealing her in with a hiss and giving her only a small porthole to see the start of the second Clockwork War.

CHAPTER EIGHTEEN
The Signal

A SLAP JERKED RAS BACK INTO CONSCIOUSNESS. FLAMES CRACKLED all around him as he lay on the deck of a sinking airship. His ringing ears permitted him to hear what sounded like dull roars and screams.

He opened his eyes to see Dixie straddling him, shaking his shoulders. He couldn't make out what she said, but it seemed urgent. Another explosion went off behind her as Ras foggily began to extricate himself from her grip.

The Elder ships were specks on the horizon, and Ras' understanding returned to him, if not his hearing. Dixie latched onto his left arm and patted the grapple gun. She pointed up, yammering a million miles an hour.

Ras struggled to sit up, and his eyes followed where she pointed. *The Brass Fox* hung, untouched. The balloon above them leaked air and the ship rocked again as another barrel of the fuel supply exploded, dislodging the back half of The Collective vessel and sending it plummeting. The front half shook and Ras scrambled to his feet.

"You want off this boat?" Ras asked. Nothing she could say would convince him to save her, but it worked to her advantage that he couldn't understand her.

All he could see was a scared girl without any other options.

Would you save the rest of The Collective too? he wondered. He had to decide soon; the ship continued to drift further away from *The Brass Fox*. *Idiot*, he chastised himself and stepped around a burning portion of the deck to get a clear line of sight on *The Brass Fox*. He aimed the grapple gun and looked back to Dixie. "This is the part where you hold on."

She rushed up and wrapped her arms tightly around his neck as he fired the device, connecting to the side of his ship. Ras and Dixie swung forward from the railing of the Collective ship as it drifted to a fiery demise in the wasteland.

Ras began retracting the cable, pulling both of them toward the ship while he tried to keep an eye on the vanishing Elder vessels. For the next three minutes he stared, determined to log their heading as soon as he reached the bridge.

The sound of the whipping wind indicated that his hearing was slowly returning.

Once over the railing of *The Brass Fox*, Ras ducked out from underneath Dixie's arms and ran up to the bridge to estimate the compass' bearing of the now vanished ships. "One-twenty-one." He then spun on his heel and strode straight past Dixie, picking up her black duffle bag and immediately tossing it overboard.

"Hey!"

Ras could mostly make out what she said if he watched her mouth, and having a good idea of how one might react to losing all of one's possessions helped.

"I don't think you're in a position to complain," Ras said. He reached under the dash, collecting Dr. O's engine disrupter. "I don't want any more surprises out of you."

"The only picture of my parents was in that bag!"

Ras looked over the side of the ship for effect. "It still *is* in that bag. You're welcome to go get it." He walked down to the deck and looked back. "Just because I didn't let you die back there doesn't mean I'm taking passengers," he said before climbing down into the hold.

Walking up to the jetcycle, he disabled its engine, assuming the idea of Dixie stealing the ride had already crossed both their minds.

The purr of the Helios engine turned to a roar as the ship accelerated and descended. "Dixie!"

Once above deck, he looked around for any other ships she might be trying to evade. There weren't any.

"The bag's that important, huh?" Ras asked, walking up to the bridge.

She didn't respond.

"Dixie, I'm sorry your city sank. I'm sorry you lost your parents, and I can't even imagine what you went through afterward."

"You're right, you can't."

"Have I done anything to hurt you?" he asked, stepping closer.

She shook her head.

"How about Callie?"

"No."

Another step. "Even if *Verdant* has sunk, which means I'm responsible for the death of my mother, I still have a chance to save someone I love, and I'd like to think that if you had that opportunity, you'd do whatever it took to save them."

Dixie landed *The Brass Fox*. Two halves of The Collective ship burned bright in the distance. "She left you something by her typewriter," Dixie said, lowering the gangplank.

Ras stared at her, and then walked down to the Captain's quarters.

Inside the cannonball-wrecked room, light shone in at odd angles. On the floor next to the lone table lie Callie's ruined typewriter. He gently lifted it, revealing a small wooden box wrapped in scraps of an old map.

Atop it read "For Erasmus" in Callie's handwriting.

Ras gingerly found the corners and unwrapped the box without tearing the paper. Lifting the lid revealed what at first looked like a jumble of replacement typewriter keys. He looked over to her typewriter and noticed about a dozen keys pried off their stalks.

He picked up one key and the rest lifted with it. Calista Tourbillon had left Ras a message.

The bracelet read: D-O-N-'-T-G-I-V-E-U-P.

He wouldn't. Not in a million years or a million miles. He would rescue Calista Tourbillon, and he pitied the man or machine that found him-or-itself between him and his mission.

Strapping the bracelet on, he strode back to the helm. Dixie was nowhere to be found. "Dixie?"

"I'm down here," she replied from outside the ship.

Ras looked over the edge to see her sitting on the ground next to her bag. "Smart move, disabling the jetcycle," she said. "I take it you found the message?"

Holding up his right wrist, the bracelet jangled. "How'd you know about this?"

"Girls talk," said Dixie. "You two idiots were made for each other."

"You just going to wait here?"

"Another wave is coming. They'll look for survivors by the distress beacon." She paused. "Ras?"

"Yeah?"

"I was lying about *Verdant*. I just needed you to stop."

Ras exclaimed in joy, "Oh you lying little…" Then he grew sober. "What are you going to tell the next wave?"

"Stick around much longer and you'll find out," she said. "Go find your girl."

"Dixie, you probably doomed us all, but thank you."

"If I had a dime…"

Ras ran back to the controls, aimed the ship at one-hundred and twenty-one degrees, and took off into the vastness of The Wild.

He half expected to catch up with The Elders, imagining Callie overloading without him nearby, especially with Time flowing so heavily in the air, but he reasoned that either whatever they sprayed her with nullified the effect, or she couldn't overload while unconscious.

In the distance a spherical cloud with a purple glow at its core hung in an otherwise cloudless sky. It reminded Ras of a purple Convergence.

"Callie?" Ras asked, wondering if she had overloaded, trapping her captors. Freeing her from an Elder ship would put them in the midst of a group of hulking Clockwork monsters as soon as he unfroze her, but he reasoned he could tether at least a few of the Elders to their ship with magnets and cables—

A slow groan interrupted his train of thought. It growled from his comm unit, unnerving him. *Is this how Elders communicate?* He smacked the unit to see if it was simply malfunctioning.

The machine stopped for a moment, then began looping the groan at an increased speed until it began sounding more and more like a voice.

"Maaaaaaydaaaaaaay," it groaned, then looped again at a faster rate.

Ras unplugged the comm unit to reset it, then plugged it back in to hear more of the message so it could speed up and loop again. Pilots never just shouted *Mayday* by itself.

The groaning continued over the comm as Ras sailed closer to the sphere of glowing cloud. Something had been caught at the center and had sent out a distress call.

Ras checked his coordinates against his memory of the ones Hal had given him. He was close to the collection spot for the *Verdant*-saving air, but he had a promise to keep to Callie.

Regardless, he decided to start the collection process just in case.

He approached the cloud at a good clip, searching for a possible break to see if it was the Elder ship that had taken Callie.

At another smack, the comm unit started looping the next part of the message that was slowly working its way out of its Time-prison. Loop after loop, the message continued to clarify in a low register: "…Mayday! This is…" Faster it ran until a man's regular speaking tone escaped.

A tone Ras remembered.

A tone Ras *knew*.

"Dad?"

The Brass Fox lurched to a complete stop after colliding with the invisible bubble, which had a larger radius than Ras guessed, not that launching through the air at the *The Brass Fox*'s former speed afforded much time for rational thought.

He smashed through the top of the steering wheel, sailing forward and leaving a trail of wooden shards freezing behind him as they lost proximity with the Lack, who now flailed wildly past the front railing of his ship. Falling into the purple sphere left a wispy trail of cloud behind Ras as he shot inside.

In the murky fog, he rocketed toward the obfuscated source of the purple glow: a frozen wind merchant vessel hanging in the midst of a forty-five degree descent, halted explosions billowing out from its underbelly.

Ras careened into the back of the mercifully forgiving balloon, but bounced downward and landed hard on the bridge of the forward slanting ship. He struck the railing, vaulting him head over heels and flipping down onto the deck. Cracking pain filled his head as he continued his slide down the angled deck before spinning around and instinctively squeezing the trigger of his grapple gun to hit something. Anything.

As soon as the magnet shot forward and left his personal space, it froze, leaving a tangle of cable suspended in front of him. Gravity dictated his descent continue, but the spooling cable now anchored him to the sky.

The front railing stopped his descent with a hearty crack, completing the wind merchant's haphazard transfer from one ship to another.

Ras afforded himself a moment to take in his surroundings. He couldn't even begin to process the mechanics of his fall. Beyond the suspended cabling he spotted a man on the bridge with glowing purple eyes, his mouth contorted into a scream. He held his stomach for reasons Ras couldn't discern due to distance, but this was his world. His bubble.

Elias Veir was nowhere to be found.

Ras felt stupid for letting himself get his hopes up. He wondered if he had misheard the voice or just wished so badly to be wrong about the boneyard that he had reopened the wound in order to properly mourn.

He stood, pain shooting through his battered body. Amidst the debris piled against the front railing, a small comm transmitter with a ripped out wire lay at his feet.

What are you doing so far from the bridge? He bent down to inspect it. *Can't exactly hail a mayday without this.*

Leaning over the railing, Ras peered down into the foggy cloud. A man in stunted free fall hung not twenty feet below the doomed ship. His features were difficult to make out in the haze, but Ras knew whom he saw.

"Dad!" Ras shouted. He felt stupid for the tears shed in the boneyard, yet relief washed over him in the knowledge that he wasn't alone in The Wild. With heart racing, he almost called out again, but knew deep down that his father couldn't hear him. But, with any luck, the next thing Elias would know, he'd be on *The Brass Fox*. The details of how Ras would make it back onboard his ship felt trivial at the moment.

The cable anchored in Time supported his weight, but he had difficulty trusting the concept. With a smile he couldn't lose if he tried, Ras spooled out cable and lowered himself over the edge of the ship.

As he neared his father, Ras realized he was looking at a slightly older doppelganger of himself with shorter hair and the same build.

His father hadn't aged in ten years.

Elias' back was to the ground and his face held a sadness Ras had never glimpsed as a child. The look of fear mixed with a lack of acceptance of the terms of his fate made Ras realize even his father was human after all.

After a moment more of lowering, the two men were level with each other. Ras inspected the long lost man. Elias sported the short beard that Emma had always ordered him to shave after returning from trips.

Although only in his mid-thirties, Elias' face was tanned and well worn from his time out with the wind. Wrinkles lined the creases around his eyes and mouth, reminding Ras of his father's ease with a smile.

Ras wrapped his arm around his father's waist.

ELIAS VEIR SNAPPED INTO A WORLD foreign to him. The airship that had catapulted him to his death not moments ago now hung motionless, no longer careening forward in a blaze.

His extremities fell back as some new harness wrapped around his midsection. Pain shot through his back as he recoiled, and the sound of straining cable filled his ears.

Pulling his head up, he could see a grapple gun cable running over the railing of his ship, then realized his so-called harness was actually another man.

"What's going on?" Elias asked carefully. He turned his gaze from the man holding him to the ground far beneath him. Grasping tightly onto the belt of his unnamed savior, he positioned himself across the man's back.

"You're okay, we're okay," the man said, "Just stay close." He pressed a button on his grapple gun and the two of them ascended until they climbed over the edge of the ship's railing and back onto the deck.

Elias wrested himself free from the man's shoulder and took a step backward, still in shock over the fall.

Suddenly, the man in front of him reappeared, once more hoisting Elias over his shoulder.

Elias once again freed himself, only to instantly find himself returned to the same position.

"How are you doing that?" Elias asked to the back of the man's head.

"You're trapped in a…Time…bubble…thing. I'm not. Long story."

"Who are you?" Elias asked.

"That's a shorter story, but one I should probably tell back on my ship," he said, "You can stand if you stay close, I think."

"Oh," Elias said as he let himself down from the man's back, keeping his hand on the man's shoulder. Pain pulsed in his leg as he noted the bit of wood paneling still lodged in his thigh. He gritted his teeth, pulled it out, and tossed it to the side. "You know, I'm still not entirely over the fact that I'm not falling."

"Who is your friend?" the man asked, indicating the Time Knack.

"Oh, poor soul. That's Morris." Elias stepped forward and instantly the man popped into Elias' direct field of view. The two stood face to face for the first time.

"Remember, I need you to stick close," the man said before spinning on his heel to hide his face. There was something familiar about him.

"Sorry about that," Elias said.

"Morris, you said? Where's he from?" The man asked, avoiding the line of discussion. He led Elias up the stairs to the bridge.

"Here," Elias said. "He's Illorian. He's...*was*...my guide."

The man turned to look at Elias. "Wait, I thought there weren't any people here. It's called Illoria?"

"The man outside the bubble is surprised by what happens here? Interesting," Elias said, arching an eyebrow. "Hold on, I know who you remind me of. My wife. Around the eyes, mostly." He let out a deep breath. "Sorry, that was going to drive me crazy."

"Huh," the man said, leading Elias to the edge of the bridge. "See that dark spot in the clouds? I'm going to need you to stand here and fire the shot." The man unstrapped the grapple gun from himself and handed it to Elias. "It'll freeze as soon as it gets away from me, but once I unfreeze Morris—"

"Where..." Elias inspected the grapple gun. *His* grapple gun.

"I'll explain as soon as we're back on my ship," the man said, still offering the device.

"What's your name?" Elias asked, accepting it.

"On the ship, please," the man said. "Now, after you shoot, I'll unfreeze Morris, which will take this ship back into free fall and my ship back to full speed. I need you to account for those factors."

"Yeah, got it," Elias said. "What happens to Morris?"

"He'll fall a bit and then probably overload again, freezing the ship without us on it," the man said, "Who is he?"

"The grandson of someone very important," Elias said. "I can't leave him."

"We're going to have to," the man said, "But hey, he's survived ten years like this, who's to say—"

"Ten years?" Elias exclaimed. His mind spun. "Are you saying I've been frozen for ten years?"

The man sighed. "I just need you to make that shot."

Elias took a moment to process. He looked at the man's jacket, grapple gun, and face. His eyes narrowed. "No." A long pause. "Ras?"

"Yeah, dad."

Elias threw his arms around his son, catching Ras off-guard. "Oh...my boy...you got big." He heaved a huge sigh, thankful that his son evidently hadn't read his letter of warning not to take to the skies. But, ten years. Gone. *What about Emma?* His mind flooded with questions.

Ras enthusiastically wrapped his arms around his father, reaching all the way around for the first time. "I found your ship, I thought..."

"Hijacked. Sky pirates," Elias said. "Morris and I had to find this tub to continue." He released his son, holding him at arm's length to take a good look at his boy. "Where did you find it?"

"Outside *Solaria*—"

Elias laughed. "They flew it into the boneyard?"

"You knew about that place?"

"I guess it's not bedtime story material," Elias said. "How in Atmo did you find me?"

"Hal gave me coordinates, but he didn't tell me you were going to be here," Ras said dismissively, "Look dad, I hate to rush this but we really need to get back on my ship."

"One more question, just in case we don't make it," Elias said, finishing strapping on his grapple gun. "How's your mother?"

"Still waiting for you to come home, but if we don't hurry there's not going to be a home to get back to."

"Fair enough," Elias said, beaming at his grown boy. He took aim, adjusted up and slightly to the front of the ship. "That's probably enough lead..." He squeezed the palm trigger.

* * *

RAS STEPPED BACK, stopping his father once more. The fact that Elias so casually accepted the idea of *Verdant* not being around when they made it home gave him pause. He walked over to Morris. "Hopefully this will just be another moment and then someone will be here to help you," said Ras, before placing his hand on the wounded man's shoulder.

The ship lurched, sending Ras off his feet and flying upward as the ship continued its doomed course. Panic shot through Ras. While he had acclimated to falling, he missed the grapple gun.

A hand clasped tightly around Ras' forearm. "I got you." Elias pulled him in close as the cable continued to spool out.

"Did we miss the—" Ras body jerked under Elias' grasp and the two Veirs soared away, trailing behind *The Brass Fox*. The doomed vessel disappeared below the cloud bubble before freezing again in a new position.

The view in front of them caused Ras' heart to sink. In the distance, cliffs loomed, ready to smash *The Brass Fox* if it didn't gain altitude soon.

The two men neared the underbelly of the ship and were sucked into the collection tube, banging around until they landed inside the glass tank in the ship's hold.

"You were pulling a collection?" Elias asked over the loud vacuum.

Ras released his death grip on his father. "Hal told me he needed air from these coordinates."

Elias chuckled. "I'm glad the message tube made it to him."

"How do we get out of here?" He didn't know how long they'd have before they struck the cliffs, and every second could be the one that killed them both.

"Gonna have to break the glass. Shame." He reared back to strike the glass with the grapple gun.

"You can't!"

"Why not?"

"Because Hal needs air from here for his ship and if I can't collect it, then I've sunk *Verdant*."

"How could you possibly have sunk *Verdant*?" Elias asked.

"Because I destroyed the last Convergence and if I bring Hal air he'll pay to replace *Verdant*'s engines with Helios ones and pay for fuel and—" he rambled on as fast as he possibly could.

"Ras, Ras, it's okay," Elias said.

"How?"

"Trust me." Elias swung his left arm back into the glass, shattering the containment tank around them.

Glass showered down while Ras scrambled across the hold and ascended the ladder up to the deck. Above, he saw the cliffs growing closer. Too close for him to make it to the bridge in time. Too close for him to save Callie or *Verdant*.

He had rescued his father just in time to ram them both into a cliff.

The slim likelihood of success didn't stop him from trying. He dashed toward the stairs up to the bridge. As he ascended, the ship shifted, causing his footing to slip. Gravity slung him back down the stairs. The ship turned hard to port and while it still neared the cliffs, it now did so at an angle, striking them with a glancing blow, which earned it yet another battle scar and sent it back out into the open skies.

Ras picked himself back up and shouted down to his father. "What did you do?"

Elias poked his head up from the hold. "More than one place on a ship you can steer her. We lose anything important?"

Ras dumbly shook his head. "I don't think so. Just another step toward winning Atmo's ugliest wind merchant vessel…which I guess isn't technically even a collection ship anymore." He stared off to the horizon, lost in thought.

"Never insult your girl, Ras," Elias said. "What's her name?"

"*The Brass Fox* or Callie?"

Elias lifted an eyebrow. "The neighbor girl? You two together?"

"No, and that's the problem," Ras said. "Well, one of many."

Elias nodded thoughtfully and walked up to the bridge.

"Dad, how am I supposed to save *Verdant* now?"

"You never were, so don't worry about it," Elias said, studying the controls. "I like the layout. You build this?"

"Yeah…wait, you mean Hal wasn't going to replace the engines?"

"Maybe, maybe not," Elias said, then slapped his son on his arm and gave his winning smile. "So, Callie Tourbillon. I always figured you had a thing for her." Elias monitored the control panel, striking out on a new heading.

"Dad! Where are you going? I have to save Callie."

"And the rest of *Verdant*, I get that—"

"No, the Elders have her. We came to The Wild—I mean Illoria—together and I was just on my way to get her back when I ran into you."

A screech resounded far and wide across the barren plains of Illoria.

"What's that?" Ras asked.

Elias' eyes widened. "The main gate. Someone did my job."

CHAPTER NINETEEN
The Reclaimer

ELIAS PILOTED *THE BRASS FOX* ALONG THE CLIFF FACE THEY HAD brushed earlier in a weak attempt to hide in the cloudless sky. "Did anyone follow you through Hal's pass?"

"A Collective ship followed us," Ras said. "I'm sorry."

"No, you're fine. Great even," Elias said. "I never thought I'd be thanking The Collective."

"Why did Hal want the gate opened?" Ras asked.

"Venting Atmo of excess Energy. Levels would get so low that they'd have to pull *The Winnower* off the Origin so cities wouldn't fall."

"No offense, but I think you're giving The Collective too much credit," Ras said. "They pulled out from The Bowl when I lost us our last Convergence."

Elias grimaced. "Well, if they're going to control Time, they're going to need to release their grip on Energy, and the Elders aren't giving that up without a fight."

"Wait, wouldn't opening the gate flood Atmo with Elders?"

"We had the Great Overload, they had the Great…well, I don't know what they called it, but instead of Energy Knacks blowing up into Convergences, Time Knacks froze cities. Most of the Illorians became stuck in Time after the main gate was built, so they shouldn't have the forces to subjugate Atmo anymore. The only 'Elders' left are the ones in the ships that were flying high enough to miss out on the freezings. Their third-generation military is basically all that's left, but they should be able to keep The Collective away from controlling the Time Origin."

"Dad, things have changed since you've been gone. The Collective developed some sort of Energy weapon."

"Sounds like they're asking for another Great Overload. Is it like an Energy filled cannon ball or something?" Elias asked.

"It's a beam of some sort. Disintegrates ships. They're going to rip through what's left of Illoria, and the Elders have Callie," Ras said, running his hands through his hair until his fingers became tangled in the knots. "Even if The Collective winds up controlling Time, I can't let them go through Callie to do it, and I have no clue where she is."

Elias looked at his son. "I guess the old plan ain't what it used to be."

"If you want to find a way back to see mom again, I understand," Ras said. "*Verdant's* sunk no matter what; I'm sure she could use some help."

His father leaned against the dash, deep in thought for longer than Ras expected. He had always imagined his father to be quick with a plan and bold in its execution, and Ras worked hard not to feel disappointed as he waited.

"Why didn't you tell me I was a Lack?" Ras said, breaking the silence.

"Ras, don't call yourself that," Elias said.

"How hard would it have been to tell me?" Ras asked. "Maybe you could have had mom do it if you didn't want to."

"She didn't know what you...or she could do to someone," Elias said. "I never told her."

"Well, she certainly seemed to have a good idea," Ras said. "Did you know that mom was a La...could stop you from overloading?"

Elias nodded. "Just about anyone from below the clouds can."

Ras opened his mouth to speak, but no words came to him.

"There's a reason your mother never talked much about her family."

"You're telling me mom is a Remnant?"

Elias sighed, wiping his hands across his tired face. "Please tell me you never used that word around your mother. I never let you say it before."

Ras had forgotten how sternly his father used to reprimand him as a child when he repeated that word after hearing it from schoolmates. "But you're saying mom's from below the clouds."

"I am."

Ras laughed.

"What's so funny?"

"Nothing, it's just all those times I've been called a '*son of a Rem-*'" he cut himself off. "Why didn't you tell me?"

"The way people in Atmo treated those that were forced to stay behind like they were better than them," Elias said. "The Atmo Project could only bring on so many, and the more people they brought, the shorter the amount of time before the floating cities became overpopulated. It's a different world down there."

"How did they survive?"

"Well, one of the criteria for being moved to the Atmo Project was Energy sensitivity, so the ones left behind were obviously less at risk to blow up. After a few generations, the ones that had low sensitivity survived, had children, and I guess living so closely to Convergences eventually built up their immunity."

"And The Collective has avoided them...I'm probably the first one they studied," Ras said

"Probably," said Elias, "Some day I'll have to tell you how your mother and I actually met."

Off in the distance a ragtag fleet filtered into The Wild through the main pass, well beneath the Illorian fleet, maintaining a healthy gap. Mixed in with airships bearing The Collective's insignia were maroon and black painted vessels, making the fleet look about as far from uniform as one could expect of the biggest force in Atmo.

The Dauntless brought up the rear, dwarfing the rest of the vessels.

"What is Bravo Company doing here?" Elias asked.

"Hal thinks they're just another arm of The Collective," Ras said, "and right now I'm not inclined to disagree."

"I guess they didn't want to risk *The Halifax*."

"They don't have *The Halifax* to risk. Callie sank it. Sort of," Ras said with a shrug.

"You're going to have to tell me about that one later," Elias said. "Looks like the war's about to start." He brought *The Brass Fox* to an idle and tapped the fuel gauge. "We can't afford to fly blindly," he said. "They probably took Callie higher than we can climb."

Ras left the bridge and began descending the stairs to the deck.

"Where are you going?" Elias asked.

"Well, I promised her I would keep her safe, so I'm staying here to find Callie so you can get back home and I won't waste fuel."

"How?"

"I'm taking the jetcycle," Ras said.

"Mom let you buy a jetcycle?" Elias asked before receiving a look from his grown son.

Ras began climbing down into the hold, but stopped before disappearing entirely from Elias' view. "You accomplished your mission. Maybe Hal will pay for *Verdant*'s engines for that."

"Erasmus Veir," Elias said, making Ras feel ten again. "Not fifteen minutes ago I was reconciling myself to the idea of never seeing you or your mother again. What would I say if I came back without you?"

Ras returned to the deck, standing tall. "Mom needed you, not me. *Verdant* needs you, not me. All of Atmo, for that matter," he said, sweeping his arm around. "If I hadn't led The Collective here, this war wouldn't be happening, and I think we can all agree that either side winning that war means Atmo loses. I have one chance, however small, to make a difference to *one* person—who wouldn't even be here if it wasn't for me—and whether The Collective freezes us all or The Elders rip apart Atmo, I owe it to her to try."

The two men stared at each other for a long moment.

"Tell mom I love her," said Ras, turning to climb down to the hold.

"Ras."

"What?"

"I'm proud of you," Elias said, tossing his son the grapple gun.

"Dad?"

"Yes?"

"Incoming!" Ras pointed to two Collective gunships in the distance as they opened fire.

"Hang on to something!" Elias brought the ship into a dive along the cliff wall. Shots blasted into the rock face, raining debris down onto *The Brass Fox*'s balloon and deck.

The Brass Fox had already sustained enough damage that it didn't respond as quickly as it used to, and Ras felt like apologizing for each sluggish response to his father's commands. *The Silver Fox* it was not, but Elias made no comment and focused on the task at hand.

One of the larger gunships dropped low to engage the wind merchants, lining up to release a salvo.

"No gun on this thing, huh?" Elias asked.

"Mom wouldn't even let you have one."

"I thought I'd ask," Elias said, "I need you to man the anchor!"

The shots rang out from the gunship as Elias pulled back on the throttle. One of the shots clipped the nose of *The Brass Fox*.

"You need me alive, remember?" Ras shouted at the gunship as he ran over to the anchor crank.

"When I say, release it!" Elias shouted, pulling back hard on the fragmented wheel. *The Brass Fox* rose above the larger gunship, overtaking its sluggish opponent. "Now!"

Ras threw the lever, dropping the anchor onto the front of the balloon. With a shudder, *The Brass Fox* pulled back as its anchor raked across the canvas from bow to aft, forcing the gunship to dive under its own weight.

The gunship's engines attempted to overcompensate for the lack of lift, only slamming the ship harder into the ground. The impact ripped up the cracked soil, leaving a scar in its wake. The anchor caught on the metal frame of the gunship, and jerked *The Brass Fox* down until the chain snapped.

"Where'd you learn that?" Ras called back.

"Just made it up!" Elias laughed manically, then noticed the second gunship taking a ranged approach. "Got any other tricks?"

"Get above that one!" Ras shouted as he ran down to the hold entrance. The dark room chimed with every twist and turn as the shattered glass sloshed around the belly of the airship. He descended the ladder and carefully gained a foothold amidst the shards. Tiptoeing and nearly falling with each evasive dip, dodge, and juke of his ship, he managed to extract a large wrench that clung to the magnetized tool bench.

He heard his father call from above. "Better hurry! We're above 'em, but not for long!"

Ras hauled himself back up to the deck and loaded a spike into the grapple gun. Motioning with the wrench, he said, "After I rip the balloon, buzz back and I'll grapple back!" In a fluid motion, he attempted to swing the wrench into his holster, but missed. The heroic moment evaporated, and Ras appreciated his father's missing of the botched attempt. He slid the wrench into the holster with a bit more care.

Elias smiled. "Good idea." It was a relatively safe plan, which was what Ras assumed his father particularly liked about it. It kept Ras out of the line of fire and even if it didn't succeed in ripping the gunship's balloon, he had an exit strategy.

The Brass Fox slipped into a hard turn to port, and Ras held himself upright by the rope rigging, looking down at the gunship. He lined up a shot and ripped through the airship's generous balloon to connect, but a quick bump in *The Brass Fox*'s altitude yanked Ras overboard.

The fall wasn't far, but Ras wasn't entirely certain he wouldn't have passed out from the height in his *Verdant* days. He plummeted, reeling in cabling so he couldn't fall beneath the body of the gunship after sliding from the envelope.

He hit the canvas atop the airship, bouncing a bit before pulling himself back to the puncture point by the cable. Unholstering the wrench with his right hand, he swung down to rip at the canvas below, opening up a big enough hole in the envelope to see inside.

He loaded up another charge and fired off the spike grapple again, targeting the forward ballonet. The spike pierced the bladder, then continued onward to strike the deck below. "Let's see you climb without that," Ras said, chuckling at his clever little plan.

Shouts of Collective crew erupted, and before Ras could cut his cable and his losses, he was pulled arm first into the balloon. Bouncing off the bladder of the faltering forward ballonet, he threaded through the puncture like a large needle.

Falling inside the Energy-filled ballonet was an easy way for a Knack to die, and Ras always wondered what its innards looked like. The bland interior left his childhood curiosity sated yet disappointed as he fumbled for the cable disengaging mechanism. Another heave from below caused him to once again follow his arm through the puncture to the deck.

What concerned Ras more than nearly falling onto his own spike were the half dozen Collective midshipmen he fell onto before landing awkwardly onto the deck. They grinned over their prize of a saboteur.

"Hi," Ras said in a groan from the fall. For a moment he wished he had prepared something witty, but in hindsight he appreciated that the swift kick to his midsection he promptly received would probably have been far worse if he had done something along the lines of insulting one of their mothers.

"It's the Lack!" one of the men called up to the officer on deck. "

The idiot came to us!"

"Then who is flying his ship?" another man asked.

"Doesn't matter! His ship don't have guns, right?"

A rat-tat-tat issued from above, lending uncertainty to that assumption. Small cannonballs ripped through the gunship's balloon, impacting onto the deck and sending the crew running for anywhere they assumed wasn't about to receive a projectile.

Ras balled himself up to lower his profile and reeled in the cabling as quickly as possible while loading up one of the magnetic charges. He knew the sound of an Elder fighter's weaponry, and it sounded like his ticket to the Elder fleet.

He scrambled over to the railing and scanned the skies for the fighter when he heard a click of a musket hammer being pulled back behind him. "If we're going down you're going down with us."

Ras slowly lifted his arms to the sky and turned around to see two men with their rifles mounted. "What?" he asked. "It's not like I've got anywhere to go."

"We know how that grappler works. We ain't dumb," said one of the crew members, oblivious to the Elder fighter lining up a strafing run far behind them.

"I'm not saying you aren't, but if there's one thing you're *ain't*, it's perceptive," Ras said, nodding to the rapidly approaching bogey.

The gunship blared its cannons and the Elder ship spun in a corkscrew maneuver, lithely dodging the incoming fire. Ras mouthed a countdown as the fighter approached a grapple-able range with its cannons blazing.

Four, three, two—It buzzed over the top of the balloon and Ras adjusted his already raised left arm, firing into the air where he expected the Elder ship to pop out on the opposite side.

Connection.

Ras jerked away from the deck, his grunt alerting his former captors. They spun back around and fired inaccurately at the now moving target.

As Ras watched the Collective gunship sink, *The Brass Fox* chased after the Elder ship but was absolutely outclassed.

The nosedive of the fighter cut short any of Ras' mental celebrations for being on the path to find Callie. "No! What are you doing?" Ras shouted into the howling wind. "No! Up! Up!"

Deaf to Ras' instructions, the pilot continued his descent, slowing his ship's speed. Ras found a small amount of solace in the idea that *The Brass Fox* now stood a chance to catch up and that if he had to face an Elder, he wouldn't have to do so alone.

Ras touched the ground first and he quickly cut the cable before the ship could drag him along. He loaded up a magnet grapple charge as the fighter landed and wheeled around in a semicircle to face him.

The cockpit hatch popped open and a large machine man exited. He stood at least seven feet tall and kept a constant gait toward Ras, who aimed his grapple gun as menacingly as possible.

"Drop your weapon," the machine commanded in a low tone.

"So you can beat me to death?" Ras asked, letting the machine get a bit closer so he wouldn't need to aim quite as much. He glanced, *The Brass Fox* flew toward him, but it looked like the Elder would reach him before Elias. "I'm...I'm warning you! This thing is electrified! And you...really...don't want that," he said.

Without giving the machine a chance to respond, Ras squeezed the hand trigger and the magnet flew at its intended target, clipping the top of the Elder's head, but the metal hunk stuck. In an attempt to throw his opponent off-balance, Ras flung himself backward with the taut cable.

Ras expected to feel a tug instead of falling straight to the cracked ground with a cloud of dust.

"What have you done?" a man's voice called out in a decidedly non-robotic tone. The "head" lay on the ground between Ras and the Elder, revealing a familiar face.

"Carter?" Ras asked, "What are you—"

"Stand back! Illorians can't be this low—AAARGH!" he screamed, falling to his knees. His eyes glowed purple before he froze into place.

The Brass Fox finally caught up with gangplank already lowered.

"Hurry up, get in!" Elias said.

Ras noted that Carter's bubble didn't extend far enough to encompass *The Brass Fox* or Elias. "It's all right, I got this."

"Be careful."

"I'll be right back," Ras said. He strode up to the helmet while spooling in the cable before cutting it, leaving the magnet and small clip of cabling sitting atop the metal headpiece like a tiny hat.

Scooping it up, he placed it over his head and turned back to his father. "How do I look?"

"Like the stuff of nightmares?" Elias asked, uncertainly.

Ras walked up to Carter and placed his hand on the Illorian's neck.

After a moment, Carter's frame loosened up and he jerked to look at Ras. He grabbed the helmet from Ras' head and slid it quickly over his, sealing it in place.

"What? How did—? I thought I was gone," the mechanical voice said with more relief than Ras thought possible from a giant robot.

"I'm full of surprises," Ras said, smiling. "Well, one surprise that I keep having to use again and again."

"You reclaimed me."

"Re-what now?" asked Ras.

"You're The Reclaimer!" Carter said emphatically.

"I like the sound of that a lot better than 'The Lack.'"

Elias called out from the bow of *The Brass Fox*, "Ras, do you know an Elder?"

"I'm not a true Elder," said Carter. "My great-grandfather was. This was his suit. The Elders were only around during the war with the Outsiders…or frozen in the cities, waiting to be saved by The Reclaimer," he said. "This is perfect!"

"Hold on now, I'm just trying to find Callie—"

"Yes! Callie!" His tone turned grave. "You must come with me, now."

"You know where she is?"

"I'm afraid I do. She is being used as the last weapon against the Outsiders and it's going to kill her." Carter looked back at Elias. "Your brother is welcome to come."

INSIDE THE ENCLOSED COCKPIT, three of the four seats were occupied. Carter looked like the parent, escorting the two undersized children who filled half of their seats. Ras' eyes were fixed on the scene ahead.

Two fleets hung motionless at different altitudes. Even from here, their intentions were obvious: they were engaged in silent negotiations, each one underbidding the other in an effort not to go down in history as the instigator of the Second Clockwork War.

"I don't understand how you're flying this thing," Elias said. "There's barely any Energy out here."

Carter huffed in amusement. "Our engines don't run on Energy," he said, "The friction of Time is sufficient."

"How can she be used as a weapon? All she can do is freeze the area around her," Ras said.

"Maybe the rest of the Illorian fleet wants to be preserved to prevent a war," offered Elias.

"Hardly," Carter scoffed. "We would never let Outsiders have the Time Origin. It's an Elder's sacred duty to protect it at all costs."

"All right, but how does Callie—" Ras stopped as the two fleets off in the distance suddenly launched their opening volleys. Tiny flecks of fighters poured in from either side, and the advantage definitely went to the Elders on that front, but when it came to the capital ships, The Collective mixed with Bravo Company heavily outnumbered the last Illorian battalion.

"If Callie is the weapon that will '*save Illoria*,' why are you bringing us to her?" Ras asked.

"The Elder Council voted unanimously against using any form of Time against our adversaries in the last war, even at the cost of losing," Carter said. "The Outsiders shut us in, secluding us with Time and preserving our cities until someone like *you* could unfreeze our people."

"Is that the deal, then? You trade Callie for me unfreezing all of Illoria?" Ras asked.

"No, that is your choice and yours alone," Carter said. "However, I would mention that Fleet Commander Archer would be far more likely to offer up his only weapon in exchange for freeing his long-frozen countrymen to aid him in battle."

"But it is his choice," Elias said as though there were still an option.

"The Outsiders have finally opened the main gate, letting Time once again spill out to the rest of the world instead of bottling up here, but it will not thin the air nearly enough for the Conduits to be reclaimed."

"I reclaimed you, so are *you* a Conduit, Carter?" Ras asked.

"Every Illorian is to one degree or another when brought too close to the Time Origin, but Callie is a true Conduit...sensitive enough to be set off and power the weapon," Carter said.

Ras looked about the Elder fleet. There were no obvious leading ships. "How do we know which one she's on?"

A Collective frigate shot a green beam at one of the Elder's larger vessels, disintegrating a quarter of it, and it began to falter.

"What in Atmo?" Elias exclaimed.

"We must hurry," Carter said.

Every Elder ship simultaneously launched its volley back at The Collective's fleet. The beam-firing frigate received only one of the dozens of cannonballs. The ball impacted on the surface, then stuck.

The frigate halted immediately, along with a couple nearby biplanes.

"They're using it!" Carter said. "I don't think she'll be able to handle too many uses."

By now they had entered the radius of the battle. The initial beam strike from the frigate had been merely a warning to the Illorian fleet, but since the Elders had something that posed a true threat, The Collective's full assault began.

Beams filled the skies, decimating Elder fighters and airships alike. Several Illorian ships huddled around one ship in particular, providing cover as another set of volleys froze a cluster of smaller Collective ships.

"There! Is she on that one?" Ras asked.

"No, the cluster is a decoy," Carter said, pulling back on the fighter's controls. "Commander Archer needs a higher vantage point. She's with him." Carter pointed up at a lone ship that launched another set of shots. The resulting impact froze a pair of gunships.

It was difficult to tell whose side the tide of the battle favored. The Elder fleet swarmed to provide moving targets for their opponent's one-shot-kill weapons while much of The Collective fleet hung completely still or rocked back and forth, their weapons recharging. The only telltale sign were the frozen cannonballs and fighters stopped outside the freeze radius. Their numbers hadn't thinned visibly, but they were far from full strength.

Carter's fighter flew toward the flagship as he brought the comm unit to his mouth. He spoke in Illorian.

A female voice squawked back through the comm unit.

"They won't let us land," Carter said. "I'll tell them I have The Reclaimer onboard." He spoke once more into the transmitter. The woman's voice was joined by a gruff, curt man's voice. Carter responded adamantly. A pause.

"What is he saying?" Elias asked.

"He says that if I have The Reclaimer, then I should be flying to our capital city."

"Not without Callie," Ras said. "Can you ask about her?"

Carter spoke again, then received a response. "He says she's not doing well."

Ras slammed the dash. "Tell him I won't reclaim anything unless—"

A bright beam penetrated the flagship.

CHAPTER TWENTY
The Getaway

RAS COULDN'T PEEL HIS EYES AWAY FROM THE CARNAGE. HALF OF the command ship's engines had failed, tilting the vessel until its propulsion sent it listing wildly to the side before flipping it over entirely.

"No!" Ras shouted, then looked back to his father, who just stared agape out the front window.

Escape shuttles began breaking away, and Carter pulled on the controls to avoid colliding with one of them as the flagship dropped beneath their altitude.

More beams shot through the sky, intercepting one of the escape shuttles and forcing Carter to pull the fighter into further evasive maneuvers.

"You're sure she was in there?" Ras asked, gripping his restraints.

An Illorian voice squawked over the comm unit.

"We're retreating to the rally point," Carter said, "I'm sorry."

"What if she's still in there?" Ras shouted. "We have to at least check."

"How?" Carter asked, still pulling the ship into a climb.

"If she gets too low, she'll overload and the ship will freeze," Ras said. "Then I can get in and save her."

"But as soon as you do, you'll both fall to your deaths," Elias said.

"It doesn't matter," Carter said, "the weapon she fueled contained any overloading inside itself. We're going to have to hope they brought her to a shuttle."

THE RALLY POINT consisted of the fifteen remaining Elder vessels hanging just outside the perimeter of a city twice as large as *Derailleur*.

Most of the city lay preserved with airship traffic halted above it, awaiting their Reclaimer.

Several of the ships sitting at the edge of the bubble over the Illorian capital city hung half preserved, half aged, delineating the boundary.

The newly designated command ship looked quite similar to the one Ras had recently watched fall, and after a quick landing of Carter's fighter atop the command vessel's deck, the Veirs followed the hulking machine as he led them inside the ship and down to the bridge level. The doors whisked open, revealing two Elders standing guard.

One of the guards asked Carter something.

Carter pushed Ras forward. "He wanted to know which one of you is The Reclaimer." He turned to Elias. "You'll have to stay here."

The guard's counterpart clasped his hand on Elias' shoulder.

"I'll be fine, Ras," Elias said.

"Tell him The Reclaimer needs him," Ras said, nodding to Elias.

After a brief argument, the Elder released Elias, and the two men continued on with Carter to a circular waiting room reminiscent of Hal's study to await further instructions.

"What was this weapon they put her in?" Ras asked.

"We salvaged it from an Outsider ship during The Clockwork War," Carter said. "It siphons off the overload, filling a container within a cannon ball."

"And when the cannon ball strikes, the container breaks, releasing the weapon?" Elias asked.

"That is my understanding of it," Carter said. A small grin played across his lips as he looked at Ras.

"What could be entertaining at a time like this?" Ras asked.

"I'm sorry," Carter said, removing the smile, "It's just...you're The Reclaimer. It's been so long that people have stopped believing you exist."

An announcement blared over the loudspeakers.

"Fleet Commander Archer survived," Carter said. "His escape shuttle just arrived."

Within minutes, a full entourage of large, walking machines entered the now cramped room. They removed their helmets.

"The Reclaimer is an Outsider?" Archer said, looking down at Ras.

"Where is she?" Ras asked. "We can discuss my height later."

"She?" Archer asked, looking up to Carter.

"The Conduit, sir," Carter said, "The Reclaimer brought her into Illoria after rescuing me from a band of Outsiders."

"How did they get in?" Archer asked.

"According to the Conduit—" Carter began.

"She has a name!" Ras said. "And if you don't tell me where she is, you can forget about any help."

Archer stopped, paused to recompose himself, then turned to stare down Ras while still addressing Carter, now in Illorian.

Carter responded in kind, prompting Archer to roar in anger. "The Children's Pass? Napier is mocking us with more spies!"

"I'm not a spy," Ras said.

"Nobody in the last century has entered through The Children's Pass if they haven't been sent by Halcyon Napier," Archer said. "Don't lie to me. That turncoat sent you, didn't he?"

"Sir?" Carter asked. "In briefly speaking with the girl, it sounded like she might be one of the lost children."

Archer paused for a moment, eyeing Ras, then Elias.

"I'm just here to find Callie," Ras said. "Please tell me where she is."

"We couldn't have freed her from the weapon even if we wanted to," Archer said. "The overload would have encompassed our entire fleet, and Time would have been lost to the Outsiders."

"What stands between them and the Time Origin?" Elias asked.

"If The Reclaimer continues to be petulant, nothing," Archer said. "I must say I expected more."

Ras didn't care about Archer's expectations; he just wanted to find Callie. "That weapon caused her to overload, yes?" he asked.

Archer nodded.

"If the weapon contains the frozen time around her, then nothing could break into that, right?" Ras asked.

Elias stepped up next to his son. "She would be safe inside, even if there was a crushing force."

"Even if she is still alive, this is all pointless if the Outsiders harness Time the way Napier taught them to harness Energy," Archer said. "You must reclaim Caelum."

"Cae-what?" Ras asked.

"Our capital city," Carter said, "the one we're flying above."

"The vast majority of the Elder military is contained within its radius," Archer said. "Freeing them is the only way a proper defense can be mounted against such a force."

"What would happen if the Outsiders controlled Time?" Elias asked.

Archer scoffed. "The world would tear itself apart," he said. "Illoria has been ravaged enough by the disproportionate concentration of Time within its borders, but it doesn't take much imagination to see what would happen if half of the world moved faster than the other half." He huffed. "The vain pursuit of immortality will kill us all."

"Do I have your word that if I reclaim Caelum, your war will go no further than with these Outsiders?" Ras asked.

"That will be up to the Council," Archer said.

It would have to do. "Fine. If you want me to save the world, you're taking me to the wreckage."

Narrowing his eyes, Archer spoke in a soft but gruff voice. "You ransom the world for a girl," he said. "I hope she's worth it."

CARTER'S FIGHTER QUICKLY BROUGHT Ras and Elias back to *The Brass Fox*. Ras reasoned that an Elder fighter returning to the battle would arouse more trouble than a beaten up wind merchant vessel that could have easily passed as a recently acquired member of Bravo Company.

"If it's all the same, I'd like to come with you," Carter said, his voice tinny through his helmet as they stood next to *The Brass Fox*'s gangplank.

"What if someone spots you?" Ras asked.

"If that ship is crumpled all around her, I wouldn't mind a little extra muscle," Elias said, patting one of Carter's metal arms.

"Maybe it'd be best to ride in the hold until we get there," Ras said.

Ras lowered the bay door, and Carter's boots crunched through the thick shards of the collection tank.

With a little coaxing at Ras' hands, *The Brass Fox* took off. The fuel gauge showed they were running on fumes, so he eased on the throttle.

"Hey, son?" Elias asked, leaning against the bridge railing.

"Yeah?"

"You've got an Elder in your hold," Elias said with a tired smile. "Isn't that a children's limerick?"

"Not one I know about."

"I think I remember your grandfather singing something along those lines when he thought nobody was around," Elias said.

"What makes you bring it up?"

"I don't know," Elias said. "I just lost ten years with you. I was supposed to tell you little stories like that about my dad, I think."

Ras took a deep breath, letting the foreign wind tussle his hair and fill his lungs. "I missed you."

"I'm sorry about that," Elias said. "I know it couldn't have been easy."

"You were just trying to help."

Elias pursed his lips and gave a slow nod.

"Dad, I have a question."

"Shoot."

"Did you make a deal with Foster Helios before or after you found Hal?" Ras asked.

"Are you wondering whose side I'm on?"

"I guess it doesn't matter—"

"No, it matters, Ras. It matters very much," Elias said. His eyes hardened; the look frightened Ras. "But I guess either way, I may have made a deal with a devil."

The thin lines of smoke ahead grew in the daylight along the parched ground strewn with airship pieces, giving the air an acrid stench. Above, The Collective and Bravo Company intermingled, stranded in Time.

"I'm not seeing any movement," Elias said, holding a hand to his brow and leaning over the edge of the ship.

"Maybe they've left," Ras said, craning his neck. "I know I wouldn't want to fly around invisible traps."

They passed the first pieces of burning fuselage, broken biplane wings, and cannons embedded in the cracked dirt until they reached the Elder command ship, pancaked under its own weight.

"Carter," Ras called out, "we could use your expertise about now."

"Cartography?" he yelled up from the hold.

Ras pulled *The Brass Fox* into a lazy circle around the half-ship, then set the airship down next to the side of the command vessel that the beam had blown away. Ras hoped Callie wasn't on the half of the ship that was missing.

The bay door opened and Carter immediately got to work, harnessing the power of his mechanical suit to clear the larger pieces of debris from the flagship.

Soon the three men were walking in the dark of the belly of the upside-down vessel. Carter twisted a part of his suit's left forearm and brought a light to bear.

"Carter, you mentioned you thought Callie was one of the lost children," Ras said. "What did you mean by that?"

"She said you came through the Children's Pass," Carter said, "and she's obviously Illorian if she's a Conduit. It would also explain her not knowing our language."

"She's always dreamed about that white train," Ras said, before stopping his gait. "How old would that make her?"

The metal body's shrug looked almost comical. "It depends on how old she was when she left the train, but she'd be older than the great war. I suppose that would put her somewhere a little over a century old."

"What do you think?" Ras asked, picking back up on the pace.

"I've never seen a true Conduit before," Carter said. "It would make sense if she was from a previous generation, and even more sense that she was adopted and placed somewhere far away from the Time Origin after being stuck in dense Time for so long." Sparks flared occasionally, periodically illuminating the corridor as they approached the door at its end. "We're almost there." With a few lumbering kicks, Carter burst through to the other side, which was flooded in light. The main deck of the bridge lie ruined.

At the end of the room, a sphere hung from a collection of loose pipes and wires. A purple glow emanated from its lone porthole.

"Callie!" Ras said, pushing past Carter in a frantic dash that disregarded the mangled metal and broken glass littering the bridge's domed ceiling. He was soon wading knee-deep in a sea of sharp pain.

Carter walked forward, crushing the debris under his boots, and eventually collected Ras, carrying him to the other side of the room.

Through the porthole in the sphere, Ras could see an upside-down Callie, mid-scream. Once past the dome, Ras dashed to the sphere, feeling it over. "How do we open it?"

"I doubt any of the controls in here work," Carter said.

"I guess bashing it open is out of the question," Ras mused.

"Can you reclaim her from a distance?" Carter asked.

"I have to be right next to her," Ras said. "Hold on. I have an idea." He placed himself against the wall of the sphere and pointed to the porthole. "Punch it."

Carter reared back and threw his fist into the porthole, shattering the glass and knocking the sphere off its pipes and wires.

Before the orb could roll, Ras slid himself into the new opening and looked at the inverted Callie. He placed his weight against the wall, walking the ball around until Callie turned upright.

Although restrained, Callie arched her back away from the gurney.

Ras undid the clasps on her wrists and waist before placing his arms underneath her. "I got you, I got you," he said.

The purple glow faded from her eyes and she collapsed into Ras' arms. He carefully placed her back down on the gurney, then slid his arms out from underneath her frail body, wiping away some matted hair.

The weapon had robbed what little color she had possessed.

"Hi," Callie said, wrapping her arms around him tightly before falling back down to the gurney and closing her eyes.

"Hi," Ras said. He looked down at the woman he loved, taking in every detail from the new freckles on her face to the chipped pale blue fingernail polish on her delicate hands. "Calista Tourbillon, I love you. I've loved you since the moment I met you, and I'm a fool for not telling you sooner."

"Hmm, that's nice," Callie said as unconsciousness took her.

Ras sighed. "Nice timing, Ras," he chided. Placing his arms under her knees and back, he then carried her out of the sphere and back to *The Brass Fox*.

RAS BROUGHT CALLIE to the bed, gently placed her among the sheets, and tucked her in. Sitting on the floor next to the bed, he held her hand as he watched her sleep.

Elias was standing in the doorway; Ras wasn't sure how long he'd been there. "After all you two have been through, you're going to need as much rest as possible if you're making a run into Caelum tomorrow. I'll get the jetcycle primed."

"You'll need the gun under the console to re-engage the engine," Ras said. He watched his father leave, then looked around the wrecked room and amused himself with the idea of returning to *Verdant* and offering the ship back to Tibbs in its current state.

A world with Tibbs in it felt like a lifetime ago. Still holding Callie's hand in his, Ras rested his head against his father's balled up coat. Everything was falling apart around him, but he still held hope for a world with Callie Tourbillon in it.

Light poured through the cannonball holes in the wall, crawling across the floor and up the wall as the day ebbed into evening. Ras fought the urge to nod off. He couldn't separate himself from Callie so soon after finding her. Fear crept into his mind that he would awake with some new threat stealing her away, and he wanted to delay that possible reality for as long as he could.

He would just rest his eyes, though. Just for a moment.

RAS AWOKE TO THE SENSATION of hair being brushed out of his face. His legs were asleep, an unpleasantness which was compounded by the pins-and-needles sensation of someone sitting on them.

He opened his eyes to a view of Callie. Her face was close to his and still as beautiful as ever. Her smile was tired, but she looked as vibrant as one could after enduring her time in the weapon. "I don't think there's a better feeling than waking up without a headache after going to bed with one."

Ras smiled, using his right hand to rub his eyes, and Callie caught his wrist, inspecting the typewriter key bracelet.

"You got my gift."

"Dixie told me about it when the Elders took you," Ras said. "Why'd you do that to your typewriter?"

"After your dad's letter, I thought it was important for you to remember your best quality."

"So, 'good at falling' had duplicate letters?"

"Basically," she said, laughing like chimes long absent from Ras' ears. "Sometimes people just need a reminder that someone else sees their good qualities." She looked down, then back at Ras. "It's why I don't worry anymore when I overload. It hurts, but before I know it you're right there."

"Callie, how much do you remember before you fell asleep in the sphere?" Ras asked.

"It's all I dreamed about."

"Good, saves me time," Ras said. Before she could say anything, he had her in his arms, pulling her in close for the kiss he had waited the entirety of his life for. She reciprocated immediately, drowning out the rest of the world. The pain, past, present, and future didn't matter. This moment was theirs and was well worth everything Ras had gone through to get there, and he couldn't imagine anything that would make it not worth it.

He had a future to fight for.

The door flung open as Elias stormed in, "Rise and shine, kiddos," he said before spotting them. "Oh." He laughed awkwardly. "When you two get a minute, I'm sure the impending doom above us will still be there."

Ras and Callie looked at each other. "Well, that kind of kills the mood," Ras said. "What is it?"

Elias opened the door wide enough for them to see out to the horizon and the city-sized machine that filled it. "Good news. They brought *The Winnower*."

Callie stood and Ras attempted to do likewise but fell back onto the bed thanks to his still sleeping legs. "I was wondering how they would harvest Time," Callie said. "Why is that good news?"

Ras laughed heartily. "If we free the Illorians, they'll destroy *The Winnower*, which means The Collective won't control Time or Energy."

"Wait," Callie said, "So if *The Winnower* isn't harvesting Energy right now, the Energy Origin is flowing out to the rest of Atmo." Her eyes went wide. "Ras, you saved *Verdant*!" She leapt to hug him. "I knew you could do it!"

"Dad started it," Ras deflected, but accepted the embrace. "I didn't know what I was doing."

"You think I had any clue?" Elias asked.

Callie released. "But what happens after *The Winnower* is destroyed? What's stopping The Elders from attacking Atmo again?" she asked. "It's not like they've had any time to think about what they did."

"That Energy beam should even things out," said Elias.

"So the goal is just to hope they bloody each other to the point that neither can control Atmo, and *The Winnower* needs to fall?" asked Callie.

"That pretty much sums it up, yeah," Ras said.

"I think I miss sky pirates."

"Oh, they're up there too," said Elias.

Callie nodded, then stared ahead, lost in thought.

"You all right?" Ras asked.

"Oh, yeah. I'm just not sure I like our options."

"Can you think of any others?" Ras asked.

She looked at him. Sadness filled her eyes and she shook her head.

"I fixed up the jetter last night," Elias said. He led Ras and Callie to the cracked ground outside the open bay door. The jetcycle looked like an entirely new beast, polished and detailed.

"Can't have my boy saving the world in a dirty jetter, plus now with Energy filtering in here finally, it should run better." He beamed. "I'll stay a few miles out of the perimeter so I don't get your ship stuck."

Ras looked at *The Brass Fox*. "I'd better not see a scratch on her."

"You're going to hurt yourself squinting," Elias said.

The jetcycle beckoned. Ras threw his leg over the seat but waited for Callie to settle in before firing up the ignition and revving the engine several times.

"What'd you do to her?"

"Nothing you wouldn't have done eventually," Elias said. "You better get going. *The Winnower* has a head start." He tossed Ras the grapple gun.

"Thanks, dad."

"You better keep her safe," Elias said, nodding at Callie. "Mr. Tourbillon always scared me a little."

Callie gave Elias a look and then jabbed Ras as he laughed.

The jetcycle shot forward on its wheels, leaving behind a contrail of steam as it accrued enough speed to lift off. The handling was better than he expected.

"Can you tell which way the Time Origin is?" Ras asked.

She pointed a little to port.

"You can tell even next to me?"

"It's the only source in the world," she said. "It's like my internal compass. I've always known which way it was, even was before I knew it existed."

The Winnower grew in size as they approached it. Ras spotted Caelum in the distance, but couldn't take his eyes off the massive flying structure, now adorned with scores upon scores of balloons and propelled forward with engines similar to *Derailleur's*.

Dozens of airships escorted it, and as Callie quickly pointed out the curved contrails, Ras noticed several jetcycles had altered course to head directly for them.

"Hold on tight!" Ras said, opening up the throttle as half a dozen jetcycles fell in behind them. They had nowhere to hide above the plains. Their only hope was that Elias had eked out every last ounce of speed from the machine.

Callie looked behind them. "They're gaining!"

"I see!" Ras glanced at the side-view mirror, then saw Caelum and the Illorian fleet as they slowly grew in his sight.

"We're going to have to lose them in the city."

"But it's frozen!"

"Only half of it. Look!" She was right. The right side of Caelum had ships still in pristine condition stuck above it.

Ras dropped altitude to pick up a little speed. "Can you see the Time pockets?" he asked as they soared above a flat paved surface. Skiffs sat in scattered clusters.

Their pursuers pulled in low behind them, and the leader fired a shot from a front-mounted gun.

"Yes, pull up!"

Ras pulled back on the handlebars and they rose over a group of stopped skiffs below. The leader's jetcycle halted suddenly in the invisible bubble.

"Nice!" Ras shouted. He noticed the preserved areas of road were the ones containing the skiffs, but couldn't coax the remaining five pursuers to maintain a lower altitude to chase him.

She leaned in tight. "Get them to go through those arches!" Ahead at the borders to the city were series of five-story tall arches acting as gateways into the metropolis. "Line up with the one that still has grass on the ground and change at the last second."

Racing toward the city gates, Ras had only a moment to appreciate the old architecture and the imposing stone statues staring disapprovingly down at him from the buildings. He spotted an arch with vegetation instead of cracked dirt and accelerated toward it.

With only a moment to spare he swerved to port and two of the five followed, avoiding the trap that snared three of their comrades.

Small arms fire ricocheted off of the back of Ras' jetcycle, prompting Callie to shout. "I don't see any more bubbles!"

Ras turned a corner and entered a pathway between two large sets of golden buildings. The Collective fleet and Bravo Company hung above, awaiting the approach of *The Winnower*.

"If we just go into the big bubble, they'll get stuck!" Ras said.

"We'll get thrown off at this speed," Callie said.

He looked behind him and loaded up a magnet-to-spike grapple as they roared down a straightaway, two jetters still in pursuit.

Leaning back over Callie, Ras lined up a shot that struck the jetcycle behind the leader, then fired the spike into the building on the opposite side of the path. The cabling clotheslined the leader, unseating him and ripping the second jetcycle from its course, slamming it and its rider against a wall.

"Yes!" Ras cried out. "Now, where's the biggest bubble? I don't want to run into it. If you stay close you won't overload."

"It's further down this path," she said, and Ras felt dumb for asking the question, as up ahead there stood a public square with a fountain in the middle, half stuck in mid-flow and half parched.

Ras slowed the vehicle down and brought it to the ground just up alongside the unfrozen half of the fountain.

Callie hugged him tightly for a long moment, then released. "I think there's another option to save the world," she said.

Ras dismounted from the bike and looked back at her, offering his hand to help her down. "What's that?"

"I always wanted to see the world, and you gave me that," she said.

"What are you talking about?"

"I can't bear to let everything I've seen get destroyed by one side or another."

"There's always going to be some sort of evil in the world," Ras said.

"Yeah, but the world can wait to see them again," Callie said, quickly shifting forward to the driver's seat of the jetcycle. She kicked it on, peeling away from Ras.

"Callie! What are you doing?"

The bike shot forward down the road before lifting off. "Buying the world some time," she shouted as she rocketed toward *The Winnower*.

Ras watched the jetcycle stop abruptly in the midst of The Collective Fleet. They wouldn't make it to the Time Origin for millennia if not longer.

Callie Tourbillon had saved the world.

Chapter Twenty-One
The Winnower

RAS STROLLED THROUGH THE CITY OF CAELUM, A GHOST AMONG A population that would never notice his visit. Children played in the streets, men and women dined in restaurants, not knowing the next time they would find themselves living in equilibrium with the rest of the world.

Everyone in the city craned their necks, looking up to the sky as they had for the past century, probably wondering why the alteration of day and night was flashing about them in a strobe pattern. Ras assumed it was the only hint to them that something was amiss.

Does she even want me to save her? She placed herself in a situation where he couldn't grapple up to her or fly *The Brass Fox* high enough to jump down to her.

He didn't want anyone else unfreezing Callie hundreds of years from now, if not thousands. It was his job, and so far he had been able to fulfill his duties.

Imagining not figuring out a solution until he was a geriatric scared him, and an eighty-year old Ras popping in behind her on the jetcycle probably wasn't what she had envisioned.

Ras knew if he didn't have a plan that would end the war with Atmo intact, she would just find another way to refreeze herself, this time with resentment.

He couldn't free the Elders with Callie's power in effect, but he probably *could* do some damage to *The Winnower*, which might be enough to convince Callie not to insist on being the lone wrench in The Collective's gearwork. Ras just needed another wrench.

Or a gun. *Dr. O's gun.*

The technology had brought down a dreadnaught, and *The Winnower* couldn't be so much different.

Ras sprinted back in the general direction of *The Brass Fox*, exiting the metropolis of Caelum.

Miles later he arrived at his ship, hopelessly out of breath.

A clanking sound repeated in the hold.

"Dad?"

The clanking stopped and Elias walked out, sweaty and covered with grease. "Sorry, I was just fixing the Windstrider, I didn't hear the jetcycle pull up..." he said, trailing off. "What happened?"

"She picked the third option," Ras said. "She stopped them. All of them."

Elias stepped out of the hold, looking back toward the fleet. "That wasn't the plan..."

"I'm getting her back."

"You're going to unfreeze The Collective?" Elias asked.

"I'm going to save Callie. Where's Carter?"

"He went back to his ship," Elias said, "How exactly are you going to rescue her?"

"I'm going to need an Elder," Ras said, walking past his father and up to the helm. The gauges on the engines read that enough Energy had finally filtered through the air to make the Windstrider scoops usable once again. "Let's see if we can't reach a willing party," Ras said, lifting the comm unit. "Attention any Illorian craft on this frequency, this is The Reclaimer. I need a lift. Over."

The comm crackled back, "Reclaimer? That's a myth. Who is this?" The voice had a familiarity to it but wasn't Carter. He couldn't pin it.

"Erasmus Veir, who is this? Over."

The voice changed to another familiar tone. "Ras! You made it!"

"Hal!"

"Send me your coordinates, I'll be right down!" A youthful laughter erupted, then looped and sped up until Ras smacked the machine. Elias ascended the steps up to the bridge.

Ras read from his instrument panel and received confirmation from Hal.

"So why do you need an Elder ship?" Elias asked.

"Tropo-capable flight. He can probably get me higher than Callie's bubble and drop me down." Ras smiled, then ran to the quarters and returned with Dr. O's gun, tucking it into his waistband.

The Kingfisher descended from high above, settling easily next to *The Brass Fox*. Its ramp extended, and the procession of the crew covered in Elder attire was led by a clockwork giant who Ras assumed to be Hal. He stopped, halting everyone on the ramp. "It's good to be home!" he said. "Used to be greener."

The Veirs disembarked, meeting Hal's entourage between the two vessels. At the sight of Elias, Hal exclaimed and threw his arms wide. "It worked!"

Elias nodded. "Sorry it took so long."

"For as long as I've been trying, a decade is a trifle. Where's my grandson?" Hal asked.

"Grandson?" Ras repeated.

"Morris is hurt badly," Elias said. "He'll need attention immediately after unfreezing."

"Hmm. Where is Callie?" Hal asked.

"She stopped the war," Ras said.

Hal looked back at The Collective fleet hovering over Caelum.

"You left her alone this close to The Time Origin?" Hal's rage flared through the speakers on his suit.

"She left me, sir, and I need your help getting her back."

"You'd save her and restore your greatest enemy?" Hal asked.

"I would," Ras said.

"Excellent. Best deal with them now rather than later."

"Callie won't let me unfreeze Caelum."

"I'd rather you not, actually. Not yet. The Council is likely still set on ravaging the rest of the world. Gives me a chance to talk to what's left of the Illorian nation. I'd wager their blood has cooled since The Clockwork War."

"If I can reclaim Callie, I can disrupt *The Winnower*'s Energy intake and damage its engines. It should slowly sink after that."

"Not if I can convince the rest of the Elders to see past our differences and move to sever its balloons," Hal said. "A fall like that should be sufficient to render it irreparable."

"You can get them to do that?" Elias asked.

"I've had a speech prepared for a long, long while, and I can be quite persuasive," Hal said, "Plus, I'm the only member of the Council left unfrozen. That should help."

ONCE AGAIN ABOARD *THE KINGFISHER*, Ras watched the ground and *The Brass Fox* shrink beneath him.

"Why didn't you tell Callie she was Illorian?" Ras asked Hal, who took off his helmet and looked back plainly at him.

"I told her she was a Time Knack," Hal said. "I assumed she would discover the rest when she saw the train."

"So you basically didn't want to tell her she was over a century old?"

"A woman's age is a sensitive subject, is it not?" Hal asked, then chuckled. "Every Illorian knows about The Children's Pass, so I sent wind merchants in to collect air, keeping me alive and thinning out the cave—"

"Until one day the train made it through to the other side?"

"Exactly. Dayus took it upon himself to find homes for each child among Atmo parents," Hal said. "Little did we know being frozen for such a long time had its side effects on young children."

"The headaches?" Ras asked.

Hal nodded.

"Is that why she was moved to *Verdant*?"

"Dayus thought it wise to keep her as far away from the Time Origin as possible," Hal said. "It was a fortunate thing that she lived so close to The Reclaimer."

"*A* Reclaimer," Ras said. "But go on."

"The rest of the children weren't so lucky," Hal said gravely.

"Did you know my father survived?"

"A decade ago I received his coordinates," Hal said. "At best, I felt it would bring you closure if he had passed. At worst, I would have received my tank of air and maybe lived long enough to see the world put right." A slight smile played across his lips. "You've gone above and beyond, Erasmus. Above and beyond, indeed."

The Kingfisher ascended higher than *The Winnower*, higher than The Collective fleet, to a dizzying altitude, and Ras fought his old foe as waves of nausea lapped up to the shores of his mind to remind him he wasn't completely cured.

Dayus returned to the room carrying bundles of ropes and a pair of thick leather gloves and handed them to Ras.

"And how will ropes keep you safe?" Hal asked.

"As long as I can feed it out of my bubble, it anchors in Time and I can lower myself down to her," Ras said. "After I fall a bit."

"I don't envy your trip."

Ras stepped out of the bay, his shoulders swaddled in rope. He removed one coil and readied it.

A voice over the intercom spoke. "Sir, we are in position."

Ras donned his goggles and gave a thumbs up. The bay opened and the wind wailed in. "Next time," Ras shouted, "just tell me my dad is alive."

"Next time!" Hal said.

Ras shut his eyes and gave in to gravity. The Collective fleet looked like miniatures from this height. Although he saw thin strips of contrails criss-crossing the sky beneath him, he had no way of telling which one was his jetcycle from this altitude.

He knew he had entered Callie's bubble when the wind no longer moved to meet him. As he flew through trapped sound, it sped up before him and slowed down behind him, coming alive, briefly greeting him upon his arrival, and dying with his departure.

He readied the first coil of rope as he slipped past the highest ships of The Collective fleet. *There.* Only one contrail angled toward the fleet from Caelum. He thought he could almost spot the red speck of Callie's hair.

Ras let the end of the rope feed out above him by just a little. The top caught the edge of his bubble, jerking him from his fall until it promptly snapped, not capable of supporting his weight at such a speed.

He dove past another set of fighters amidst a few green frozen beams aimed at the remainder of the Illorian fleet.

Ras uncoiled more rope, which froze above him and his gloves slid along its surface, heating his hands until he reached the end and the rope slipped from his grasp.

He re-entered free fall; he was approaching Callie far too quickly. The rope trick wasn't panning out as he had imagined. His fall slowed slightly, but if he didn't think of something, he would soon reach terminal velocity. He needed something more substantial.

Elias' jacket.

Ras spun as he tussled with his father's coat, freeing all but his right arm. He let the long and heavy tail of the coat catch the wind and create drag as it tattered against the fringe of his bubble. The coat began shredding but slowed his descent and even afforded him a stop about fifty feet above her.

He fired his grapple gun into the sky directly above him, anchoring the cable into Time. He released his right arm from the coat, letting the tattered fabric hang above him. Spooling cable out, he lowered himself.

On approach he could see what under normal circumstances would have been the blue of Callie's eyes. His calculation had been slightly off, and he found himself five feet to her left. He swung himself back and forth until he snapped the cable and landed on the back of the jetcycle.

Wrapping his arms around her, he immediately tightened his grasp around her midsection as the world rocketed back to life and the jetcycle shot forward.

"I've been meaning to ask what it's like to keep getting younger than me," Ras said.

She started. "What are you doing?"

"Despite your best efforts, I'm keeping a promise." He reached up, placing his hands over hers on the handlebars.

"You just saved The Collective!" she said.

Ras had the brief thought of Callie throwing herself off of the jetcycle and tightened his grip on the controls. "Short term side effect," he said. "You remember Dr. O's gun? We're going to disable *The Winnower.*"

"If I keep doing this," Callie said, using her newly freed hands to cradle her head, "It's going to kill me."

"I won't let that happen," Ras said, turning the jetcycle around and staying well above Caelum.

From behind, *The Brass Fox* zoomed toward them with Elias at the helm. The vessel dodged fire from the capital ships, pulling up parallel with the jetcycle. Ras slid the vehicle into the open bay door of the moving target and cut the engines as the hold swallowed them.

Ras disengaged the jetcycle's engine. The machine fell to the floor of the hold before sliding into the back wall next to the repaired

Windstrider engines. Ras and Callie left the bay and made their way up to the bridge.

Elias flew like a madman, chasing down *The Winnower*. "Glad you both could join us!" Elias said, bobbing and weaving, the ship fully under his command.

The Brass Fox passed the last of The Collective's vessels and Ras realized their Helios engines were stunted by the addition of Energy on the wind. Without a cloud layer to keep the element down, the fleet had become reliant on their underpowered backup scoops.

The Winnower approached the Time Origin, which tinted the sky purple. The crystal structure jutted out from the ground, humming in a low frequency throb.

Ras watched the surrounding ships creep along through the sky. He leaned in to Callie and asked, "Is it just me or are things slowing down even more?"

"You might want to share that with your dad," Callie said before leading Ras by the hand up to Elias.

After they approached the bridge, Elias stared in surprise. "How did you just run like that?"

Ras placed his hand on his father's shoulder, bringing Elias into his sphere. "Being a Lack has its privileges."

The weapons on *The Winnower* roared to life, firing shots at *The Kingfisher* and the last survivors of the Illorian fleet as they swarmed around the station's many balloons. When it became apparent that firing at the close quarters combatants would more likely do the Illorians' work of puncturing its balloon systems, it focused on the one long-distance target, *The Brass Fox*.

With Elias' heightened reaction time, cannonball trajectories were easy to predict and avoid, but the Energy beams tested Elias' piloting abilities as the airship closed the gap, moments away from being able to land on *The Winnower*'s surface.

A sickening green light flashed where the front of *The Brass Fox* used to be. The foredeck vaporized as the momentum of the aft carried the remainder on a collision course with the side of *The Winnower*. Elias did all he could to steer half of his son's ship to no avail.

Ras held tight to Callie and shouted at his father to hold onto him. He fired off the grapple spike into the nearest balloon of *The Winnower* as *The Brass Fox* fell away underneath them, smashing hard into the side of the floating city before falling to the deep below.

The crash resonated deep within Ras as he swung forward. All of the time and love spent on his ship, and she was gone in an instant. He wished he had time to mourn her, but they passed over the main deck of *The Winnower* and struck the large glass dome covering most of the city's top. He released the cable and the trio slid down the dome's side until they bowled into the first line of an armed troop of awaiting guards.

The trio spun and Elias fell away from Ras, then Callie. The wind merchant collapsed to the ground, rolling a few times before fully stopping.

"Callie!" Ras called out, but the name hung hollow as all sound once more deadened around him. He looked up to spot Callie, stuck mid-roll and overloaded.

Ras took his cue to begin the process of single-handedly disarming fifty men, one at a time. It took nearly ten minutes to rip away all of the weapons and toss them over the side of the station, where they hung in the air. He then secured half a dozen pistols for Elias and himself.

He returned to Callie and knelt beside her fallen form. He reached out his hand, but stopped just before touching her. This was the calm before the storm. As soon as he broke the spell, they would have to keep moving and he didn't know if they would ever stop again.

This needed to be her last overload.

With a musket in his right hand, he cradled her head with his left. The sound of the wind returned, and carried on it were the grunts and shouts of confusion from the guards.

Ras waved his pistol at the unarmed men. "Back off!" With a sufficient radius cleared, he looked down to Callie. "You all right?"

"No," she said and pulled herself to her feet. "We're so close to the Origin, I can barely think straight." She tightened her grip on his hand, standing as close as possible to his island of stability.

"Dad?" Ras asked, pulling Callie over and joining the man wielding a pair of pistols with more tucked into his belt. "Put your hand on my shoulder."

Elias obliged and stared at the field of sluggish guards. "I still don't get this."

Ras moved toward a set of stairs that ten more guards were ascending. Armed. He pulled the wrench from his holster. "Follow me as best you can, dad. I'll be right back."

With Callie in tow, Ras strode forward with wrench at the ready to confront the new threat. The first guard's rifle emitted a spark and smoke, alerting Ras to sidestep the musket ball's trajectory before it entered his bubble.

A swift upswing of the wrench dislodged the rifle from the lead guard's grasp, bending the barrel. Ras connected the wrench to the man's side, swatting him out of the way, then dealt with the next guard, who was just reaching the top of the stairs.

Ras threw the wrench, letting it slowly sail away to strike the next man squarely in the sternum. The guard was sent drifting backwards into the eight following men with little to stop their glide until they hit the bottom stair.

Slipping on the KnackVisions, Ras surveyed the glowing engines among the teeming network of pipes and devices vying for his attention.

"Eight engines. Each probably has its own intake," Ras said. He pulled up the goggles and saw his father aiming both pistols back at the dozens of guards ready to charge.

In a few short strides, Ras once more introduced Elias to equilibrium.

The trio headed back toward the stairs, careful not to entangle themselves with the men still tumbling backwards. Ras reached over to collect the wrench still hanging in the air and holstered it.

Once inside *The Winnower*, Ras increased his pace. The faster he moved, the more of a blur he was to the men in dark blue uniforms.

"I hate to be the spoilsport, but what's our escape plan?" Elias asked, struggling to keep a hand on his son.

"We could just ride this thing to the ground," Callie said. "For as much as the Origin slows everyone down here, I can't imagine the fall would be too bad."

Ras stopped at an intersection, spotting men in uniform alert to their presence and giving chase as best they could. "We'd starve before it touches ground." He searched the area. "Anyone let me know if you spot a stairwell."

"Don't feel like riding the elevator from now until eternity?" Elias asked.

"Do you?"

"Not particularly."

They continued forward and Ras traced the courses of Energy with the KnackVisions to a reinforced door with what looked like a dead area behind it. *Stairs?*

Ras tugged on the door's handle. It budged slightly, not fully under his influence. The hinges protested and the guards were closing in.

"Callie, hold on," Ras said, putting her hand on his neck before he flattened himself against the door. He placed his right hand and foot near the hinges while working the handle with his left hand, then awkwardly pushed off with the remaining foot. The door gave way quickly, swinging open.

"If we make it out of this, can we make sure that part is omitted from the story?" Ras asked.

"I think everyone will love the door hugging part," Callie said.

Ras made a face, but was thankful she seemed more herself. Taking her hand once more, he took two steps forward into a dimly lit room and almost doubled over the railing of a spiral staircase before Elias' grip on his shoulder kept him from falling.

"Easy now," Elias said, "I know it's a lot of stairs, but you don't get to take the shortcut."

"Thanks."

The goggles confirmed they had many flights to go before reaching the engines. The trek back up didn't excite him. After half a dozen floors passed, something caught the corner of Ras' eye.

Movement.

A man in a white lab coat stood on the stairs above them on the other side of the shaft, staring at Ras.

"Anyone else remember passing him?" Ras asked.

"So this is your world?" The scientist asked in a voice just slightly slower than normal. "Marvelous."

"What do you mean, my world?" Ras asked.

"Ras, we should go," Elias said, encouraging his son forward with a gentle push.

"This equilibrium. It took us a while to unlock its potential, but here we are." He bowed slightly. "I thank you."

Ras quickened his pace. Whatever The Collective had taken from him wouldn't benefit them if they couldn't control Time.

With nobody else in the stairwell to oppose them for the next thirty floors, they exited through a door already being held open by an engineer.

Ras shoved the unsuspecting engineer back as they passed through the threshold. The corridor was full of men in jumpsuits, gathered at portholes and staring out at the Time Origin.

Giving everyone in the hallway a wide berth, Ras walked until he spotted the first engine.

The system looked nothing like he expected.

The Helios engine on *The Brass Fox*—what remained of her—was a cheap looking replica of the older Windstrider model, but what he saw looked more like a giant metal sphere with glowing portholes large enough to walk through.

"Is that…?" Callie asked.

The device was three times larger than the one the Elders had placed Callie in.

Something didn't add up. The KnackVisions told him the sphere fed directly to the encased Helios engine, but nothing fed into the sphere. Ras placed his face up against the porthole to see why.

A Convergence floated inside.

"The gun is useless," Ras said, pulling Dr. O's pistol out from his waistband.

"But you're not," Elias said. "You can dissipate it." He looked around at the engineers, who were slowly turning their heads toward the fast-talking trio, and pointed a pistol at them as a warning. "You can't destroy a convergence with a collection system."

"What are you talking about?" Callie asked.

"I fed off a Convergence for a while before you were born—"

"Mom told me," Ras said.

"But what I didn't tell her was that it didn't fall apart until I brought her too close to it. Did you get close to the Convergence you destroyed?"

Ras remembered the Convergence in Framer's, then the one that he and Callie had swung through before it brought down The Halifax. It didn't matter that he'd tried to collect the Convergence at Framer's. Just being close enough to it did the trick. "I'm the gun."

Elias nodded.

Ras flipped Dr. O's gun around and struck the porthole with the handle, cracking the glass.

"Wait!" Elias said. "I can't be this close to an open Convergence without you by me. Don't move too quickly."

"Got it." Ras swung again, smashing the large pane of glass.

With Callie and Elias clinging tight, Ras entered the sphere to the sound of a screaming choir.

"It's horrible!" Callie said, burying her head in Ras' chest.

The green sphere fluctuated, then with a gust, evaporated into invisible Energy. What remained was a man burned head to toe laying strapped to a gurney with wires and tubes feeding out of him. His eyes glowed a radiant green.

"H-h-help me," the man said, choking. "Let me die, please. They won't let me."

"Who?" Callie asked, barely able to look at the marred visage.

"Th-they said I would save Atmo," he said before beginning to convulse. "Not like this." His convulsions stopped and klaxons began blaring out in the corridor.

"So this is how they make fuel," Elias said, pointing to the dead man's tubes. "They siphon off Knack overload before it can join a Convergence."

"Helios engines run on pain," Ras said. He wondered how often The Collective needed to replace Knacks. "How many people do you think know about this?"

"Not enough," Elias said.

Ras led Callie and Elias out from the sphere. He stared at the engineers in disgust as they began crowding around the formerly operational fuel-making device.

The ship shuddered as one of the engines beneath them ground to a halt.

Seven more.

"ANOTHER ENGINE'S DOWN!" a helmsman shouted to Foster Helios III. "We're losing our fuel supply!"

Foster kept his gaze out *The Winnower*'s command center window, watching the Illorian ships take diving swipes at the balloons. "Then send a fresh set of Knacks for it," Foster said, "I won't have this mission failing because we forgot to swap our batteries."

"No, sir," the helmsman said, "We're losing the Knacks because the Convergences are destabilizing—"

"Convergences don't destabilize," Foster said, turning to glare at the officer. It was common knowledge. Of the hundreds of Convergences the diver team had collected from the world below, they had never lost a single one. He walked over to the station showing eight lights with readouts next to each. Six green, two red. "Son of a Remnant."

"Orders, sir?" A third light on the console flipped from green to red and *The Winnower* began to tilt.

"Release the Lack Squad."

CHAPTER TWENTY-TWO
The Fall

DESTROYING THEIR THIRD CONVERGENCE GAVE RAS HOPE FOR THE mission. While seeing the aftermath of a Knack perpetually in overload turned his stomach, it gave him new vigor to fight The Collective.

He just wished Callie didn't need to repeatedly see it.

Ras stepped out of the sphere's porthole and turned to face the fourth engine on their checklist. The tilting vessel was a good sign their plan was working.

"How many of these do we need to take out before this thing starts falling?" Callie asked.

"This next one might do it," Elias said. "Losing half your engines is one thing; losing all of them from the same side makes it unstable."

"Then let's hope Hal's doing his part," Ras said.

A five minute rush got them to the next engine, and *The Winnower*'s staff moved so slowly that Ras assumed they must be directly over the Time Origin by now.

It might take years for *The Winnower* to complete its mission in the eyes of Atmo, even if it was only months to the crew. The absence of *The Winnower* from the Origin of All Energy would likely throw Atmo into chaos. Unless The Collective had a backup plan, fuel reserves would be depleted and sky pirates would be emboldened.

All lovely things for Foster to duck out from.

All lovelier things to save Atmo from upon the triumphant return of Foster Helios III, banisher of Elder and sky pirate alike. They might even make him King of Atmo if such a thing were to exist.

Ras wouldn't let it.

"Do you hear something?" Elias asked.

As they neared the next engine, Ras heard a fourth set of foot-falls rapidly approaching from behind and saw the blur just before it collided with him, flinging him forward and ripping his hand away from Callie's.

With the wind knocked from his lungs, Ras flailed madly before colliding with the sphere and crumpling to the base of it. His head swam and he sucked for air.

Moments later, Callie overloaded.

One of the half dozen newly materialized soldiers walked up to him at a leisurely pace. Older. Gray hair and wrinkles adorned his crazed face. He grabbed Ras by the throat and lifted.

"Thought you could sink us, huh, Lack?" the soldier said, his black eyes looking manic. He slammed Ras against the sphere, retaining his vise-like grip around Ras' neck.

With a clamped throat and burning lungs, Ras fought the pain and the blackness that haunted the corners of his vision. He kicked at the soldier to little effect.

"Do you realize how long I've been waiting for this moment?" he asked. "Me and my men have had to watch the world inch by just in case you and your girl arrived." He shook Ras violently. "Look at what your Lack serum did to me! I was twenty-three when we came here!"

From what little Ras' clouded mind could guess, the squad's job was to clear out anything that hindered The Collective's path to the Time Origin. Which meant they would likely kill Callie next.

Ras threw a right hook, which the soldier promptly caught and pinned. Ras would have cried out in pain if he could, but the soldier took the feint, locking up both arms. Ras then swung his left arm with the grapple gun against the porthole glass, cracking it.

Again, again. Ras could feel the life being choked out of him.

One last blow smashed the glass and The Convergence's Energy seeped out into the corridor. The soldier lost his grasp and Ras' oxygen deprived body fell limp.

The soldier screamed, waving the Energy-thick air away, but he had already taken several deep breaths. He clutched his head as the Lack injection did its job, fighting to reject the intruder, immunizing itself and pulling double duty against Energy and Time, wreaking further havoc on his body.

Ras gulped for air, finally filling his lungs with relief just in time to scream in surprise as an aged corpse collapsed next to him. The black in his eyes returned to a pale green, and the frail body of a man well past a century of life stared at Ras from the floor.

Scrambling up against the engine, Ras watched the other five soldiers, all staring wide-eyed at their fallen leader. None dared to step forward to challenge Ras in his fog of death.

Ras stood, his chest flooding with pain as he learned what a broken rib felt like. "Run," he coughed as he walked toward them, his bubble pushing Energy away. He unholstered his wrench and strode toward his opponents.

The soldiers backpedaled down the corridor, and Ras gave chase until they disappeared around the corner.

Turning on his heel, Ras still struggled to catch his breath when the usual operational sounds of a flying city returned to his ears. "Callie?" He jogged past the damaged Engine and spotted his father with his hands held high at the prompting of a handful of armed men.

A few feet in front of Elias, the scientist from the stairwell cradled Callie in his arms as he finished depressing the plunger on the syringe into her neck. He clicked his tongue at Ras in disappointment. "You really shouldn't leave this one alone." He spoke in a normal tone while the guards by Elias still moved at a slowed pace.

"Ras, how are you over there?" Callie asked, then reached up to feel the needle in her neck.

The scientist shushed her like a young daughter. "Now, now, you mustn't get worked up. I just saved your life."

"What did you do to her?" Ras walked toward the scientist with wrench at the ready. The guards moved their guns from Elias to Ras, stopping him.

The scientist released her and she struggled to find her footing as she ran to Ras, burying herself in his embrace. "I don't want either one of you to get damaged," he said. "You both have years and years of valuable research left in you."

"I feel funny," Callie said, "like I brushed my teeth for too long, but all over." She looked over Ras' shoulder at another set of guards joining the standoff. "What did they do to me?"

"I think they stopped you from being a Knack," Ras said, holding her.

"Very perceptive, Mr. Veir," the scientist said, offering a polite clap. "We're branding it as 'Void,' but yes, this newest batch has proven most effective. Your weapons, please." The scientist motioned for several of the guards to relieve Ras of his wrench, pistols, and grapple gun. "Mr. Helios has a very strict no weapons policy in his lab."

"The soldiers," Ras nodded to the corpse on the floor. "Did they get the same injection?"

"Them?" the scientist asked. "Oh no, no. We hadn't perfected the serum yet." He smiled. "We shall be spending quite a bit of time together in the future, Mr. Veir. My name is Dr. Lupava."

Elias was corralled in with Ras and Callie. His hands shook and his breathing was labored as the three were bound with handcuffs.

"You all right, dad?"

"Just a lot of Energy in here," he said, strained. "I'm fine near you."

Half a dozen men in engineer garb approached the engine sphere, wheeling in a sedated man on a gurney and lifting him in through the open porthole. The tubes and wires from the dead Knack were transferred to the new recruit.

A second team of engineers arrived, quickly replacing the broken porthole glass and sealing the first team in. A hissing noise preceded one of the engineers' overloading and taking the rest of the men up in a blaze, birthing a new mini-Convergence.

Beneath, one of *The Winnower*'s engines roared back to life.

"There we are, good as new," Lupava said. "Shall we to the elevators, then?" He offered a sweeping gesture.

"How many times does that trick work?" Elias asked.

"We get plenty of headstrong new recruits all the time," said Lupava. "But to think, they would still be alive if you hadn't destroyed our Convergences in the first place. Pity."

The group began their walk to the elevators. The soldiers jogged in order to keep up with Lupava, Ras, Elias, and Callie until the group reached the wide double doors.

"I know this will be a terribly long ride for us," Lupava said as he pressed the button to go up, "but please, do try to have some patience."

The doors slowly opened, revealing a large, circular transport with a single person standing in the middle.

Dixie Piper.

"Ah, glad I caught you before you made it to the lab," Dixie said slowly. "Foster wants to see the prisoners before you begin your experiments." She had a black left eye and scrapes on her right arm where her jacket sleeve had been ripped away.

"I was informed of no such thing," Lupava said, stepping into the elevator with a few guards. "He can see them in the lab."

Dixie raised an eyebrow. "You feel like telling him that in person?"

"What are your credentials? I am not familiar with you," Lupava said, looking her over.

"I led you into The Wild," she said, pressing the elevator button for the bridge. "What floor should I drop you off on?"

Dr. Lupava pressed another button as the elevator doors closed. "A little caution goes a long way, young miss."

"Dixie, never thought I'd—" Ras began.

"Shut up." Dixie looked over to Ras. Her eyes didn't hold hatred, but instead a melancholic resolve. "You know, only an idiot would try to pull eight plugs, one at a time," she said. "I can see you trying to take down three at once, especially with a speed advantage." Her eyes flitted to one of the guards, then narrowed. "But even then you have a small window of opportunity." She lifted a small pistol and fired, dropping Dr. Lupava and throwing the elevator into chaos.

Ras flung himself at one of the guards before the man could raise his rifle. Connecting his elbow to the guard's temple, Ras shouted to distract the other two armed men.

Dixie sprang into action, dipping and sweeping the legs out from a second guard, then wrested the rifle away and slammed it against the man's forehead, silencing his surprised cry.

A shot rang out toward Ras before Elias could throw his shoulder into the third guard, slamming him against the elevator wall. The musket ball moved slowly enough for Ras to spin his guard into its path, then ripped into the man's back as it entered Ras' sphere of influence.

The guard in Ras' grasp collapsed to the floor as Dixie ran over, silencing the pinned guard with a twist of the neck before he could get a call out.

Dixie threw her arms around a motionless Callie. "I thought I lost you guys."

"I'm sorry, I'm confused. What changed?" Callie asked.

"India Bravo flying into battle with The Collective, that's what changed," Dixie said as she pulled herself back to face Callie. "The next ship coming through the pass was crewed by a mix of sky pirates and men in Collective uniforms. We had a bit of a disagreement," she said, pointing to her black eye. "I've been going after the wrong target. Well, not the wrong target, but my scope has been too limited."

"What are you saying?" Ras asked.

"I'm saying Foster Helios has to die, and you all are my ticket to the bridge," Dixie said. "Oh, and I'm sorry about the whole betrayal thing. I'll make it up to you somehow."

"Hold on, killing Foster won't take down *The Winnower*," Ras said.

"No, but there are plenty of lovely controls on the bridge that we can smash to make that happen after Foster is dead," Dixie said with a smile.

Ras offered his cuffed wrists, but Dixie pushed them away. "No, you have to stay like that. Foster will think something's wrong if you're not cuffed." She stepped over to the body of one of the guards, dragging him into the side of the circular elevator. "Are you just going to watch me work?"

Ras stepped over and helped her drag the second guard.

The elevator chimed. Dixie picked up a musket before stepping behind the trio and aiming it at Ras' back. "Just play along."

The doors swept open, revealing a far more ornately decorated part of the ship and a path opening up to the command center of *The Winnower*. Dozens of crew sat at their positions around the large room, monitoring their stations. Nobody looked up to address the newcomers.

On the other side of the room stood a figure swathed in a tailored, gray uniform, staring out the massive window, with his hands clasped behind his back.

"Sir?" one of the officers said.

Foster turned, spotting Ras, Callie, and Elias walking forward, cuffed.

"Guards!"

"Got it covered!" said Dixie, stepping out from behind Ras, showing her rifle was aimed at the wind merchant.

Foster flattened his hand, motioning for the guards to hold. He stepped down from his platform to the main level of the room. "I see you've finally reeled in the Knack and the Lack. And who might I ask is the bonus piece? Are we working for extra credit to return to my good graces?"

"His father," Dixie said.

Foster took a couple of cautious steps forward to inspect Elias from a distance. "Very interesting."

"He spent a while in a Time bubble," said Dixie. "Might be worth studying the long term effects of being frozen."

Waving a hand dismissively to Dixie, Foster addressed Elias. "Someone's been well preserved, hasn't he? You spoke with my father, if I recall."

Elias nodded.

"He was a difficult man with which to obtain an audience, let alone strike a bargain," Foster said. "What did he offer you?"

"Does it matter?" Elias asked. "I'm not expecting you to fulfill his obligation."

"Obligation? Oh, yes. You were supposed to give us the location of the Origin." Foster looked back out the window at the purple hued sky. "Looks like we did quite all right on our own."

"You wouldn't have found it if I didn't make it here first," Elias said.

"Appealing to my sense of honor now?" Foster asked.

"Just stating a fact."

"Tell me what he offered, and don't be difficult," Foster said, sliding his hand down to an ornately designed silver pistol hanging at his side.

"He promised to stop harvesting the Convergences around *Verdant*."

Foster laughed. "Now that's a promise I can most certainly keep. Isn't that right, Ras?"

Ras' eyes flitted about, trying not to focus on Dixie moving to casually flank Foster. "You run this place with Knacks," Ras said in an attempt to get Foster to focus on him.

"Given yourself the tour, it seems," said Foster. "Very impolite."

"I can see why you wouldn't allow people to know how you make fuel," Ras said.

"There is a penalty for trespassing, you know," Foster said, pulling the pistol from his holster and remorselessly aiming it at Callie. "And you, you should be grateful."

Callie glared at him. "Why?"

"I cut your tether to your idiot Lack," Foster said. "You don't have to stand two inches away from him. Then again, the serum essentially made you a Lack yourself, so I'm not sure which is worse." After a moment, he dropped it to his side. "Oh, Lupava would go on and on if I shot you," Foster said, then turned to Ras. "You're annoyingly difficult to dispatch, did you know that?"

Foster leveled the pistol at Ras and squeezed the trigger. The end of the barrel glowed green, and Ras felt a sharp shift in momentum throwing him to his right.

Callie had shoved him out of the way.

The beam emitted from the barrel struck her midsection, throwing her back as she cried out in pain. She struggled to put out a small fire from her shirt, but her hands came up covered with blood in the attempt.

"No!" Ras shouted, scrambling to pick himself up. He lunged at Foster, who easily shifted targets to Ras' chest. The beam stopped just before striking him. However, the force from the blast knocked him backwards. He slid on the polished metal floor until he stopped next to Callie.

"See? Not perfect, but better than our first test subjects," Foster said, inspecting his toy. "That should have put a hole straight through both of you."

Ras inched over to Callie. "Callie! Are you all right?" He looked at the pain in her eyes, then down at the blood escaping to the floor from her hands clenching her stomach.

"Any other volunteers?" Foster asked, pointing the gun at Elias.

"I'll have a go," Dixie said.

Foster turned and saw the musket pointed at him. Dixie fired and his uniform blew open over his heart. He crumpled to the floor.

In moments, bodyguards moved to tackle Dixie and knock loose the rifle.

"Do you have any idea how long it'll take to get a replacement suit sent from *Derailleur*, especially out here?" Foster asked, pained. He stuck two fingers in the hole in his gray uniform, ripping at it and revealing a black mesh layer of clothing. "I'll have to thank Lupava." Foster righted himself and aimed the gun at Dixie. "You mentioned wanting a turn."

Elias launched himself at Foster's back, getting his cuffed arms around Foster's neck as guards rushed to stop the loose prisoner.

Foster's gun fired.

The struggle stopped.

"Dad!"

Foster ducked out of the other man's embrace and Elias fell to the ground, reaching for his absent leg, eyes glowing green.

"He's a Knack!" Foster shouted, then looked at Ras. "Stop this!" He dashed out of the room as crew members ran away from their stations in a panic. Lights fluctuated and screens flickered. Winds howled as Energy began pooling in from everywhere to join Elias.

Even if the explosion of an overload wouldn't destroy *The Winnower*'s bridge, having the loose mini-Convergence of his father bouncing around the control center would surely do it.

Ras couldn't watch his father die. He scrambled to be alongside Elias, sliding in next to him. "Dad!"

"Let me go!" Elias said, pained.

"I can't!" Ras placed his hands on his father, watching for the green glow of his eyes to subside. It didn't. "Why isn't this working?" He shouted, fearing his father was at the point of no return.

"Callie! Help me!"

She looked at Ras, then back to the pool of blood. She mouthed something Ras couldn't make out. He needed another Lack strong enough to repel his father's overload, but she wasn't moving.

Ras began dragging his father's body over to her. The room rattled violently. Ras had never seen the formation of a Convergence and he was determined not to find out how the process went quite yet. Callie gasped as Ras slid Elias next to her and her blue eyes turned black. Ras placed a hand on Callie, the other on Elias.

"You are not leaving me!" Ras shouted. "I won't let you!"

The beginnings of a Convergence glowed about Elias, dancing along his skin, emanating from where his leg used to be.

Dixie crawled away from the epicenter of Elias, backing up against the wall.

The Energy danced over to Callie, swirling around her. She screamed, throwing the Energy away in a one-foot radius from her body, then further, scrubbing away the Energy that had pooled into Elias' skin.

Sparks showered throughout the bridge. The room filled with a vortex as the Void fought the Energy. With one more scream, the Energy blasted away to the far corners of the bridge, shattering every window.

Elias exhaled sharply as his eyes returned to their hazel hue.

Callie's blue eyes remained black as *The Winnower* lurched and canted slightly at an angle. They were dropping. Warning klaxons went wild inside the nearly empty command center and green lights flipped to red all over the room.

"The Convergences!" Ras said. "I think you just took down eight Convergences at once!"

"What just happened?" Dixie asked, trying to find her footing.

"*The Winnower* ran out of fuel," Ras said.

Shouts erupted from the corridors outside the bridge as loud crashing noises filled the room.

Callie's eyes returned to blue, looking down at her bloody stomach.

"You're going to be all right," Ras said. He gently lifted her and looked up to see three mechanical giants clomp into the room.

"Ras!" said the Elder leader. Through the filter Ras was fairly certain it was Carter. "Napier is about to sever the last balloon."

One Elder scooped up Elias while another reached out to take Callie. Ras shook his head. He had promised to protect her, broken ribs or not.

"She with us?" one of the Elders asked, pointing at Dixie.

"They talk?" Dixie asked.

"Don't let her fall behind," Ras said.

The group left the bridge and joined the flow of men and women in Collective uniforms through the corridors. Carter and the other unencumbered Elder cleared a swath through the hallway with their swinging metal arms until they found the stairs.

Carter turned to Ras. "Hand me Callie, or I'm picking you both up."

Ras obliged and was hefted by the third Elder along with Dixie. The mechanical legs pumped their way up the spiral stairs faster than Ras could have ever managed on a good day.

Before he knew it, daylight shone in his face as they returned to the top of *The Winnower*. *The Kingfisher* hovered nearby, and down twenty yards along the deck a Collective shuttle was loading up with scientists and Foster Helios III.

Foster finished securing his grapple gun and looked up at Ras' party. He pulled out his Energy pistol and lined up a shot when *The Winnower* rocked. The beam went wide, missing everyone. On the opposite side of *The Winnower*'s balloon rig, Illorian ships were severing the last cables, leaving only the ones by *The Kingfisher*.

The structure pivoted into a swinging fall. The Collective shuttle sitting on top suddenly began sliding and plummeting, taking the scientists with it. Foster fired his grapple gun, connecting with the edge of the deck as up became sideways.

The Elders climbed up the side of *The Winnower*'s newly oriented top to the hovering Kingfisher. Once over the edge, Carter walked Callie inside the ship. The Elder carrying Ras and Dixie dropped them just before being obliterated by a green blast.

Foster finished clambering his way up to the top of the sideways Winnower. The only option for his survival was *The Kingfisher*, and he held the means to force his way aboard.

"No!" Ras shouted as he ran toward Foster to close the gap. It would be too easy for Foster to shoot down *The Kingfisher* if Ras climbed aboard to escape.

Foster fired another shot, striking Ras' outstretched hands. The force snapped his cuffs apart, and he barely held his footing. The fact that the Energy dissipated didn't erase the sting from the blast, but he kept moving forward. Foster fired once more, this time toward Elias and Carter, but the shot went wide.

Foster would have to go through Ras.

Meeting up with Foster, Ras leapt for the gun, but found a grapple-gun-fortified left arm plant firmly into his stomach.

Ras threw his head forward, smashing Foster squarely in the nose as both of Ras' arms focused on wresting the gun away. It pointed up, firing into the last set of balloons, starting *The Winnower*'s final plummet toward the Time Origin. Ras dove into Foster in a flying tackle as the two men lost their footing and began sliding over the edge.

"No!" Callie's faint cry barely made it to Ras' ears as he fell over the edge with Foster.

Foster fired the grapple gun toward the side of *The Winnower*, anchoring himself as the pair swung over the cusp and slammed into the side of the city.

Ras had a good grasp on one of Foster's legs, but received multiple kicks from the other. Ras reached up to Foster's belt, pulling himself up as Foster began retracting the cable.

Looking up, Ras saw that *The Kingfisher* still hung in the air. Dixie, Carter and Elias had made it aboard. The fact comforted Ras as he clung to Foster and the grapple gun brought them back to the edge of the doomed vessel.

Hauling himself up, Ras landed a punch squarely into Foster's stomach, then was instantly reminded of the armor that had saved Foster's life earlier as a throb of pain echoed from his hand to the rest of his arm.

Foster fired another Energy shot into Ras, failing to notice Ras working the cable release on the grapple gun. The snap of their lifeline immediately sent them both into free fall.

The Winnower's descent was nothing compared to their Lack-aided fall, and soon the men careened toward the sideways glass dome covering the middle of the city.

Spinning Foster around to take the brunt of the collision, Ras pulled himself tightly into a ball as they smashed through the glass dome. Their descent slowed as shards rained down around them.

Now on the underside of the dome's curve, they rolled down until Ras lost his grasp on Foster. He continued his slide down the glass as Foster joined *The Winnower* in its slowed fight against the friction of Time. With nothing to hold onto, Ras did his best to slow himself with his palms and boot soles, but continued to slide faster than Foster.

The end slope of the glass dome led to the interior ring of *The Winnower*, and while it was full of pipes and sharp bits of machinery that Ras bounced into, he was thankful it didn't lead to more open sky. Rolling to a stop, Ras looked up, spotting Foster in his own floating tumble along the dome. It would be a minute until he would reach Ras.

Time for a breather. Ras closed his eyes for a moment and took a deep, pained breath. He needed to get the grapple gun from Foster. Without something to anchor him, he'd fall to his death or die of dehydration on *The Winnower*.

Foster still slid as he loaded up another grapple charge. To Foster, *The Winnower* was crashing with him, which didn't afford a man much time to think, let alone plan.

Ras willed himself to stand. He had to use his relative speed to his advantage to get the grappler from Foster.

"You can do this," Ras said to himself, then began running up the glass slope, his boots gaining enough traction to reach Foster.

For a moment, Foster entered Ras' equilibrium, falling faster before he swept Ras' legs and sent both men back into a slide.

Ras used Foster's disorientation to undo the gun's body harness strap before receiving a punch to his temple, knocking him aside and slowing Foster once more as Ras tumbled back down to the dome's edge. He stood and prepared for his second run up the glass.

Foster turned and trained his silver pistol on Ras.

"How many times do you have to shoot me before you realize that doesn't kill me?" Ras asked, fully knowing how silly it would sound in a sped up voice to Foster.

Foster dropped his aim from Ras to the glass just beneath the wind merchant before firing. The beam melted a hole underneath Ras, who suddenly realized suggesting other targets hadn't been the best idea.

Ras dropped, only to save himself by a tenuous grasp of thick, jagged glass.

Staring down at the Time Origin brought back Ras' vertigo, shaking his existence. His arms trembled as he tried to pull himself up to no avail. The curved glass distorted his view of Foster as the man slid closer to Ras, but he could make out the man in gray's rolling to avoid falling into the hole.

Finally sliding to the edge of the glass, Foster stood and sauntered over to the edge. His slow speech gave his voice a more authoritative sound. "I suppose at this point I'll have to take pleasure in the small victories." He lifted a leg to stomp on Ras' bleeding fingers.

"You kill me, you lose your ticket home!" Ras shouted.

Foster lowered his leg. "Go on."

"You drop with me, I can get us safely to the ground and walk you out," Ras said, struggling to retain his grasp. "You stay here, you'll be stuck in Time forever."

Foster laughed a deep, booming laugh. "If I keep riding this, the next thing I know my Lack squad will be picking me up."

"Wait, wait, wait!" Ras said. "But how many years will pass before that happens? What will happen to Atmo during that time? I can get you out now."

"No, thank you," Foster said in mock appreciation, then raised his leg to stomp.

The boot came down, crunching Ras' left hand against the sharp glass. With a cry of pain, Ras released the glass and grasped Foster's stomping foot, then he allowed the weight of his body to pull Foster through the hole with him, and both men continued their rapid descent.

"No!" Foster cried out as he struggled to bring his left arm about to grapple *The Winnower*, but Ras worked to pin the arm down.

Ras threw a right hook into Foster's jaw, then worked to undo the grapple gun strap by Foster's elbow, struggling to overcome the slippery addition of blood into an already difficult process. He received a knee to his stomach.

"Why. Won't. You. Die!" Foster wriggled his left arm free as they passed by the last of *The Winnower's* surface and swung around to aim at the gigantic structure.

The grapple charge fired, but the cabling tangled in Ras' sphere and didn't shoot forward to meet *The Winnower*. Instead, it launched into a haphazard coil that only began to straighten itself out as the weight of the two men pulled down on it, slowing their fall with its drag.

All around them floated flaming debris with bits of cloth, metal, and smoldering wood. Ras looked down to see the back half of *The Brass Fox* thirty feet beneath them, facing forward to reveal the Windstrider engines and the open door to the Captain's quarters. Its balloon dragged above it.

Ras swung his weight to line them up with his ship and clung to Foster's left arm, then worked the cable release.

The snap returned the two men to free fall. Foster wrested Ras away with a stern kick that sent Ras into the embrace of the collapsed balloon, breaking his fall as Foster's stunted trajectory led him to the hold.

Caught in the patched up balloon, Ras thanked his ship for once more taking care of him. Gravity pulled him out of the canvas envelope and through the open door leading to the Captain's quarters.

The cannonball-riddled wood on the back wall protested at their collision, but didn't give. He looked around the sideways room at the chairs and broken dishes collected on the back wall with him. The side walls illuminated the room with their near-frozen flames, giving off a nearly unbearable heat.

"Thanks, girl," Ras said, patting the wall he lay on. "I'm sorry about all this." His hand grazed something metallic. Callie's typewriter.

He wondered if Hal had the necessary accouterments to care for her wound aboard *The Kingfisher* as he cautiously made it to his feet. Bending over, he collected the small typewriter, then dug around until he discovered the bag of stolen artifacts from Foster's office.

Dumping the contents of the bag onto his upended bed, he surveyed his resources. The dueling pistol looked to be the only thing he could use against Foster, so he tucked it into his belt.

Ras hefted the typewriter into the old leather bag and slung it over his shoulder. He slid his bed frame on its end, then climbed up until he could reach the bolted-down table in the middle of the room. After a precarious balancing act, he stood on the metal base of the table, giving him enough of a reach to grasp the door handle. Using the leather bag to catch the edge of the frame, Ras hauled himself out of the room.

Standing on the wall next to the door, Ras saw Foster glide down into the hold. Ras held out the dueling pistol, but pulled back. The shot needed to be fired in close quarters to not waste his one opportunity.

The formerly patched hole in the deck created at Framer's Valley acted as Ras' vertical entryway into the hold. Foster came crashing down into a pile of broken container glass next to one of the Windstrider engines.

The Brass Fox knew how to accept intruders.

Ras slid over among the glass shards and pinned Foster to the makeshift ground with his knee. He aimed the pistol at Foster's forehead. "Welcome to my ship," Ras said. "Now give me the grapple gun."

As Ras focused on working the final strap of the device loose, Foster took a shard of glass and slashed Ras' chest before kicking the younger man away.

The dueling pistol clattered to the ground and Foster rolled over to grab the gun. He slowly stood, shaky from his thirty foot fall, and aimed the gun at Ras.

"Was I not good enough?" Foster asked. "Did I not try hard enough for you?"

"What?" Ras asked, quickly inspecting his new wound.

Foster stumbled, leaning against the sideways Windstrider mounted to the floor. "I did everything you wanted. Every single thing you said."

Ras noticed the pool of blood in the shards of glass where Foster had landed. As Foster shambled forward, bits of glass fell from him. "Hey, it's okay," Ras said in an attempt to defuse the situation.

"Is it, dad? Why is it okay?" Foster asked, jutting the gun forward.

"Because you did the best you knew how."

"You said that wasn't good enough."

"I was wrong."

"That's a first," Foster said, faltering. Tears formed. "I'm sorry."

"It's all right," Ras said, taking a step forward with his hand outstretched to grab the pistol.

"I tried," Foster said. He jerked his arm, pulling the trigger. The bullet lodged itself in Ras' right shoulder.

The jolt of pain sent Ras stumbling backwards, leaving Foster to gracefully collapse face down. In a brief moment of clarity, Ras realized what brought Foster to delirium: spikes of glass stuck out of the back of his head and neck.

Ras breathed heavily, nursing his right arm. He leaned in next to Foster's body and rolled him over. Arguably the most powerful man in Atmo lay in the hold of his ship, and all Ras could think about was unlatching the last strap to the grapple gun, which he did.

Sliding his arm into the hard won device, he rested his hand on the Windstrider engine.

He walked to the edge of the ship, leaned over, and saw a long drop still ahead of him. The grapple gun didn't have much cabling left on the spool. In order to not fall too far he'd have to be precise about when he fired the last charge to anchor the cable into Time.

Ras looked back over the remaining half of his burning ship. He opened his mouth to speak, but instead nodded and patted the wall before hoisting himself up to the ledge where the bay door formerly resided.

Dangling his legs over the side, he tugged one last time at all of the grapple gun's restraints before looking back at Foster's body.

With little inspiration or desire for any ceremonial words, Ras hopped off the edge before his vertigo could suggest he take more caution.

The Time Origin grew larger as gravity pulled. He needed to wait a bit longer lest the last of his cable leave him hanging way too high. *Five...four...three...two...*

Ras squeezed the grapple trigger and cable spooled out frantically, its friction slowing Ras as the ground rushed up. He held on dearly with both arms. Yards and yards spun out, slowing him as he passed alongside the tip of the crystalline spire.

A loud thwack resounded as the last of the cable snapped free from the device, leaving Ras to fall the remaining twenty feet.

With no cloth balloon to comfort his fall this time, Ras collided with the ground and collapsed with a sick crack in his leg.

Sprained, or worse.

As he looked up at the sky from the ground, he saw his ship and, far above that, *The Winnower* on its inevitable path directly toward him. The Collective was ruined. Foster was gone. He was alive, and his wrecked body wouldn't let him forget it.

A laugh escaped his lips, surprising him.

He attempted to stand on his good leg, but the unbearable pain brought him back to the ground. Taking a deep breath, he tried to push himself along with his working leg. The pain shooting throughout his body overwhelmed him, causing waves of nausea and the horizon to curve in ways it shouldn't. In an attempt to return equilibrium, he squeezed his eyes shut. Unconsciousness beckoned. Now was not a time for rest.

Opening his eyes, he surveyed the Time Origin. *This is it*, Ras thought. *I die in the shadow of the fountain of youth.*

His breathing became ragged and he fought the urge to fall asleep. This couldn't happen yet. *Callie needs her typewriter.* Ras shook his head clear, then glanced down at his right arm clutched to the gash across his chest. The bracelet almost mocked him.

Don't give up. He would just close his eyes and think of Callie.

No! Ras opened his eyes. *Don't give up...*

Don't give... up...

Don't...

CHAPTER TWENTY-THREE
The Reclaimers

"PUT THIS SHIP DOWN, NOW!" CALLIE SHOUTED. THE FRESH BANDAGES Dayus had applied to her midsection were already blotching red in a few places. She steadied herself against the bookshelf next to the fainting couch Elias lay on in Hal's parlor. The ship rocked from side to side, and Dixie steadied the one-legged man.

"Miss Calista," Dayus said, holding his hands out, "I have been instructed to not let you leave this room."

"Then you're killing him!"

The Kingfisher bounced again, throwing them both off-balance. "May I remind you that there is a battle still going on outside?"

"Then why are we...why are we still in it?" Callie asked, pulling herself along the bookshelf toward the exit. "I can keep us from freezing if we head toward the Origin. Nobody will be able to follow us." She blinked hard, focusing on staying conscious.

Dayus cut her path off. "By the time this ship reaches Erasmus, countless years will have passed for him and the rest of the world," he said. "Atmo will be thrown into chaos, and they're going to need someone to guide them. The Illorians will lose patience waiting for Halcyon. They'll invade Atmo in retaliation for The Collective's actions."

Callie thought for a moment. "Dayus, please. I can keep the ship from getting stuck." Her stomach shot a new wave of pain through her, causing her to cringe.

"Are you so certain of that as to risk the world?" Dayus asked.

She wasn't. For all she knew, the serum Lupava had given her might have been temporary.

Dayus sighed. "Calista, I need you to understand something. You are the last surviving child from the train. I found your adoptive parents and only released you upon the condition that they take you as far away from the Time Origin as possible," he said. "I can't let you do the exact opposite of that."

"The last?" Callie asked. To hear someone finally confirm her suspicions gave her an odd relief in the wake of learning that everything about her past was a lie. But, such truths would have be examined later. *If there was a later.*

"Yes, and it has pained me to watch each child die off," Dayus said, compassion filling his eyes. "Something happened to them all after their time in that tunnel. Please don't let me fail my mission."

"Ras kept me alive," Callie said, half to herself. "Time is everywhere, Dayus. Maybe being in *Verdant* helped, but the only thing that stopped my pain was Ras." She swayed, and Dixie stood to support her. "And I'm not about to let him die when he's spent most of his life keeping me alive. Let me take a shuttle."

"You're in no state to go—"

"I'll fly her down there," Dixie said, getting a better grip on Callie. "If we get stuck in Time, we get stuck in Time. I'm all right with a fresh start." She smiled faintly. "Don't worry, Stretch. At least if we freeze, you'll die knowing she outlived you."

Dayus eyed Dixie, then Callie. He stooped and collected a fresh wrap of bandages from beside the couch. "She's going to need these."

CALLIE WATCHED DIXIE work the controls of the shuttle as the door to *The Kingfisher* sealed, separating them from Dayus.

"Do you know how to fly this thing?" Callie asked from the bench, carefully buckling herself into her restraints.

Dixie studied the controls. "Nobody told me everything would be labeled with gibberish." She turned back to Callie. "Hold tight, this might get interesting."

"Define—"

The third lever Dixie pulled ejected the shuttle mid-flight. The wings telescoped out, and the one to port struck *The Kingfisher* as it continued to fly forward, sending the shuttle into a spin.

Callie felt her stomach painfully lift as she clutched her restraints, waiting for the engines to engage. Moments passed and they continued to fall. "What are you doing?"

"Making us a harder target," Dixie shouted back, flipping switches, pulling levers, and mashing buttons at random. They plummeted past Illorian, Collective, and sky pirate ships alike.

"Intentionally?"

A blast from the engine shot them forward, upside down. The restraints dug into Callie's shoulders. Dixie pointed to the spire of the Time Origin in the distance. "Is that little black spot him?" Her speech showed signs of slowing as she rolled the shuttle to the correct orientation.

"Dixie?" Callie asked.

"What?"

"Say something."

"Like?"

"Just talk about anything. Be yourself," Callie said.

Dixie looked back, furrowed her brow, then shrugged. "When I was six we had a cat named Bootsie, not because of her white paws but because she liked to hide in my dad's boot—"

"Land the shuttle!" Callie commanded.

"Hold on, why?" Dixie's speech was continuing to slow. The new-found Lack ability wasn't holding up well against such a close proximity to the Time Origin. Before long, her sphere of influence might shrink to the degree that she would find herself trapped inside the shuttle without an escape.

"Please," Callie said, "just land."

They were nearly a mile away from the towering structure that bathed the world around it in purple.

Dixie pushed down on the controls. "Let's hope one of these puts down wheels." She played with the controls: console lights flicked off, windshield wipers swiped, and a bout of static hissed across the speakers. Finally the ship lurched slightly. "I think that might have done it."

"Might?"

"We're landing one way or another," Dixie said. "What's the rush?"

"Dayus was right. I would have gotten *The Kingfisher* stuck."

Dixie evened up the shuttle, then descended until they skimmed along the ground. "What are the chances he's alive?" she asked.

"I don't know."

The shuttle dropped, bouncing on the craggy ground. Dixie pushed the controls back down, forcing the ship into a rough landing and an eventual halt.

Callie undid her restraints. "Hopefully I'll be back before you know it." She stood, felt a dizzy spell wash over her from the pain, then closed her eyes to steady herself. Working the shuttle door's release, Callie pushed her weight against the exit until it cracked open enough for her to slip out.

An oppressive, dry heat assailed her as soon as she made it outside the shuttle. The ground ahead looked distorted; the heat waves were caught in a Time thicker than she experienced.

Clutching her stomach, she picked up into a jog. Every footfall sent a shock through her body, and the distortion made it nearly impossible to tell how much further she had to go.

After five minutes of jogging, she noticed the white wrap had turned almost completely red, and the sight of blood shocked her into a walk.

Not much longer, she thought, unsure of whether she meant how far she had to go or how far she could go. The crystal spire seemed to grow in front of her, forcing her to constantly reestimate how high the structure actually stood.

Above the peak of the Origin hung the wreckage of *The Brass Fox*, and for a moment Callie worried that Ras was in the impossible-to-reach ship, but a dark blur ahead gave her hope.

She picked up into a shambling jog again. Something felt wrong in her midsection, but it was too late to turn around and have Dixie fly her away. "Ras!" she shouted, but the name rang hollow in her head.

The dark form became less blurred by the heat waves as she neared. It was Ras, but he wasn't standing. His prone form lay stretched on the ground, ten feet away from the Time Origin's base. She picked up speed as fast as her body would allow, until she slid in beside him, kicking up dust that froze once it left her receding radius.

"Ras," she said, "wake up." Kneeling, she brushed his hair off his forehead. *That usually does the trick.* Looking down, she noticed just how much blood soaked his shirt and shoulder, the excess of it dripping to the parched ground beneath him.

Without thinking, she put her ear to his chest. She couldn't tell if she felt anything over her own racing heart. Lifting her newly sticky cheek from his torso, she saw his bracelet clutched in his hand. "You listen to me, Erasmus Veir." Tears began forming. "You don't know how to quit, you understand? You've never given up on me before, so you can't start now." She dropped to her side, wishing she could have done more. Placing her hands on his left arm, she shook him violently until the pain knotted to an unbearable level. "I was supposed to stop them, not you. You were supposed to go home and have a family again." The deep pulse of the Time Origin seemed to grow louder as if welcoming her toward sleep.

The sound of the wind came to her ears, joined by the crackle of fire rushing toward them. Above, *The Brass Fox* had dislodged itself from its moment in Time and raced toward the ground. It crashed down ten feet beside them, sending debris flying. Callie instinctively shielded Ras from the scraps of glass and flaming wood. She then looked back to Ras' bloodied face as the calm returned.

She wiped away a tear. "I'm your navi...you're not supposed to go anywhere unless...unless I tell you..." The pain forced her to lay down next to him. Struggling to shift his left arm out, she rested her head on the crook of his shoulder. There was comfort there, like the side of her head was made for it.

"I love you," she said softly, closing her eyes. "I always have."

Epilogue

EMMA VEIR STOOD ON THE END OF THE PIER NEXT TO HER FAMILY'S empty slip the same way she had for the past two weeks. The sunset filled the skies with a brilliant red.

Her family. It was one thing to live in denial that Elias would one day arrive unannounced, but without her son by her side, she could only stand alone for so long before hope slipped away.

Looking over the edge at the clouds below was a dangerous pastime. A waver in balance, and she'd make a hasty return to the surface. She shut her mind to the idea, but knew the thought would rear its ugly head again.

"You'd see them just as soon if you took a couple steps back," Old Harley said. This was his third and final round of the day that ended with him checking on her. "I know I'd feel a lot better."

Emma appreciated that someone still cared. The tapping of Old Harley's cane grew closer.

"The boys made a few extra windcakes," Old Harley said, stopping a few feet short of her. She turned and saw him extending his old lunch pail. Emma faintly smiled and shook her head. "At least the Energy levels are at their highest in over a decade," he offered.

"What does that mean?" Emma asked.

"Nobody from The Collective will confirm it, but the city council thinks *The Winnower* is broken," Old Harley said. "And nobody's seen hide nor hair of Bravo Company ever since they left. I don't know what your boy did, but it's a step in the right direction."

"It's not enough, Harley."

"I know," he said. "But maybe he's not done walking."

"I don't know how many more sunsets I have left in me," Emma said.

"The thing about sunsets is, if you wait long enough, it's a new day," Old Harley said, stepping up alongside Emma. "The world keeps turning, and we keep on riding."

Emma eyed the horizon. More wind merchant vessels had been collecting in The Bowl lately, and a few of them looked cruelly similar to *The Brass Fox*.

"I know the clean-up crew is still taking volunteers. If you could use a distraction, I'm sure they—"

"I couldn't focus when I volunteered. They don't want me back."

Old Harley sighed. "I am sorry, Emma. I truly am," he said. "Ras turned out to be a fine man, and I count you responsible for that."

"At what point do you let go?" Emma asked, looking over at Old Harley, eyes searching him for an answer. "When is it enough?"

"Maybe you'll see them again," Old Harley said. "Before the winds took my Lana from me, she told me that goodbye was for just a little while. I'm holding her to it."

Emma turned, placing a hand lightly on Old Harley's shoulder. "Thank you. I think I needed to hear that." She began walking down the pier, leaving Old Harley by himself with pail in hand.

"Emma?" Old Harley asked, his voice quietly urgent.

"What?" She looked back at Old Harley, then followed the line of his outstretched hand to where it pointed. In the far distance, a white airship descended from high above. A light flicked on and off, repeating a pattern. "Is that..."

"*The Kingfisher*," Old Harley said reverently. Other airships diverted their flight paths to watch it, and the dockhands began gathering to gawk at the white vessel.

"What's the message?" Emma asked. The ship was coming straight for them.

"It keeps repeating: I'm home, baby, I'm home."

"Eli?" Emma ran back to the edge of the pier, clutching the loose material of her dress as she waited for the white ship to complete its voyage.

"Over here!" Old Harley shouted, waving an arm and leaning on his cane. "I think word is spreading." He tapped Emma, prompting her to look over her shoulder. A small crowd was amassing behind them.

She didn't care as long as they didn't get in her way once the ship landed. The last few minutes before the ship docked felt like an eternity.

Old Harley scurried to his usual position to await a rope with which to tie the ship down as the vessel glided into the Veir family slip. Before *The Kingfisher* came to a complete stop, the main hatch hissed open with a wash of steam.

"Emma!" an almost forgotten voice shouted out from the haze, and a figure leapt out from its midst, landing with a falter next to Emma.

She instinctively reached for the man, keeping him upright until her hope became reality. She flung her arms around Elias. "I thought I lost you."

Elias embraced her tightly, swaying her back and forth. "I'm here, baby, I'm here." He bobbled, but caught his balance. "Well, most of me."

Emma looked down. One of Elias' pant legs was empty.

"Long story."

She looked deep into his eyes. He looked worse for wear, but otherwise just how she last remembered him. "How are you…" She ran a hand over his cheek.

"The Wild's a funny place," he said, then pulled her in for a long, passionate kiss before releasing.

Old Harley received a rope from the man wearing a hat, who touched the wide brim in a note of respect toward Emma.

She looked back at her husband. "Where's Ras?"

He looked to the horizon. "I don't know where he is, exactly."

Emma threw her arms around him. She felt numb, and hated that she believed such news seemed inevitable as soon as she watched her boy leave the docks. The weight of it was too much.

"It's all right, baby. I'm sure he's fine," Elias said softly, his breath tickling her ear. "I think it's time you spent some time with your family."

She pulled away, looking deep into his eyes. "What about you?"

"Don't worry, I'm coming."

"But you'll overload," she said.

"Not with you."

Old Harley secured the rope, then stepped toward them. "Sir, are you leaving us again?"

"I'm afraid so, Harley," Elias said with a sad smile.

"Oh," Old Harley said. "If it's not too much to ask, I've always... oh, never mind."

"What is it?"

"Well, it's just that that's *The Kingfisher*," Old Harley said, gesturing to the ship. "And I've always wanted to meet the captain."

"He's not onboard, but if you'd like to come with us, we're about to go meet up with him."

The Kingfisher's landing gear extended, settling down on a patch of soft grass alongside a lazy river. The soft roar of a waterfall played in the distance, mixing with the sound of the ship's ramp lowering.

Emma stepped out first, followed by Elias, who appeared to be still familiarizing himself with his set of crutches. Old Harley took a bit of convincing from Elias to step out onto the grass. He nervously surveyed his new surroundings.

"So much for a nap," Dixie mused, pulling her feet off the console of the shuttle. She drowsily pulled a lever, opening the smaller vessel's hatch. "Hey! Over here!" she called out.

Emma peered over at the shuttle, then broke into a run at the sight of the two figures carefully exiting the vessel.

Even with most of his body swathed in thick bandages, Ras was able to lift his left arm to accept his mother's embrace.

"Hey mom," Ras said, his right hand still laced with Callie's.

"What happened?" Emma asked, taking in the sight of her boy. She leaned over to hug Callie next.

Ras looked down at his battered body. "Just about everything."

"Do I get a hug?" Dixie asked. "I did kind of save them both."

Emma smiled. "I don't know who you are, but—"

"Dixie Piper," she said proudly. "People call me Dix, Dixie, Pip—"

"Just call her Dixie," Ras said, giving her a lopsided grin.

"You only get to make a first impression once, Ras."

"She pulled us away from the Time Origin," Callie said. "I think you two will get along just fine."

"Yeah," Dixie said, then shot a look at Ras. "You're heavy."

Elias hobbled forward with Old Harley and Dayus. Emma slapped his arm. "Why didn't you tell me you knew he was alive?" she shouted.

"You didn't ask if he was alive. You asked where he was," Elias said, fighting a smile that Ras presumed would earn him another slap. "This place doesn't have a name as far as I know."

"I was crying!" she said.

"I thought you were happy to see me—"

"Mom! Dad!" Ras said, raising his voice and stopping their argument. "It's all right, we're here. We're fine."

"Why didn't you come back to *Verdant*?" Emma asked.

"We can't," Ras said, looking over to Callie. "At least not together. As best we can figure out, if Callie and I get close enough, we overload, which I guess for someone with Void means destabilizing a Convergence or knocking away concentrated Energy."

"Or normalizing Time," Callie said.

"Right, or that," Ras said. "We didn't want to save *Verdant* just to accidentally knock out her Energy reserves as soon as we bumped into each other."

"And I'd prefer to heal a little before I convince Daddy that our trip was a good idea," Callie said, prompting a sage-like nod from Elias to Ras.

"Or tell them that you are over one-hundred years old," Ras said.

She pursed her lips. "For the last time, I'm not one-hundred and three years old, I'm nineteen…I was just born one-hundred and three years ago."

A confused look played across Old Harley's face. "I'm going to need a primer on all this Void-talk," he said. "So where's Hal?"

"Back in Illor—back in The Wild," Dayus said. "He has work to do."

"Harley, I thought you said you wanted to meet the captain," Elias said.

"I do."

"Well, he's right here," Elias said, gesturing to his son.

Ras gave a slightly embarrassed grin. "Hal thought of it as a prison after all those years," he said. "It's mine as long as I don't rename it *The Platinum Fox*, or some other *Fox*. I'm going to need a crew, though."

"It doesn't look like a wind merchant ship," Emma said.

"It's not. I don't think I'm a wind merchant anymore," Ras said. "*The Winnower* is gone, and as soon as the rest of Atmo finds out that The Collective has been using Knacks to make their fuel, there's going to be an uprising. Callie and I are going to have to clear the ground of Convergences before the cities can land safely once they run out of fuel."

"The Collective has been doing what now?" Old Harley exclaimed.

"We're going to need someone who knows the surface," Elias said, wrapping his arm around his shocked wife, "and I can only think of one person I want to guide us."

"How many crew members are you going to need?" Old Harley asked, raising his eyebrows hopefully.

"I'm still trying to figure that out," Ras said. "Can you think of any candidates?"

"A few," Old Harley said. "Not everyone has someone waiting for them back on *Verdant*, and some of us might jump at a chance to save the world."

Save the world, Ras thought. *That's a far cry from trolling for Twos.*

Elias put a hand on Ras' shoulder. "I'll take Harley and your mother back to *Verdant* to see who we can find. You kids are going to need your rest…it won't be long before we hit more turbulence."

Ras looked back at Callie, who squeezed his hand, prompting a reflexive smile. The girl who dreamed of seeing the world now had to do just that in order to save it, and he would fly her anywhere.

"I'm ready."

CPSIA information can be obtained at www.ICGtesting.com
Printed in the USA
LVOW041401300812

296703LV00002B/4/P